ARYA WINTERS AND THE TIRAMISU OF DEATH

ARYA WINTERS AND THE TIRAMISU OF DEATH

Amita Murray

The following is a work of fiction. Names, characters, places, events and incidents are either the product of the author's imagination or used in an entirely fictitious manner. Any resemblance to actual persons, living or dead, is entirely coincidental.

Cover and jacket design by Mimi Bark

ISBN 978-1-951709-47-1
eISBN: 978-1-951709-81-5

Library of Congress Control Number: available upon request

First trade paperback edition October 2021 by Agora Books
An imprint of Polis Books, LLC
44 Brookview Lane
Aberdeen, NJ 07747
PolisBooks.com

Chapter One

Loneliness killed my Auntie Meera.

It wasn't a stranger that she inadvertently let into her house, it wasn't a burglar or an unknown lover. None of these possibilities point to the true reason that she died a few months ago at the age of sixty-one, murdered in her own home, left naked and splayed on her kitchen floor, on a January morning when snowflakes sang arias outside her window and robins hopped on frosted branches of holly. It was loneliness.

People think it's only unfriendly people who are lonely. The ones who are rude and obnoxious, the ones who push others away. But that isn't true. Nice people are often the loneliest. People who do and say nice things, who step aside to let others pass, the ones who open doors and thank people, who smile and act as if everything is fine. Whose smiles hide the fact that they believe, deep down inside, that no one will catch them if they fall. That no one will love them if they let their true selves out. Those people, I think, the ones who are unfailingly nice, those are the ones that are most in danger of ending up like Auntie Meera.

The ones who dare not let other people in. The ones who are afraid to be seen.

Unlike my Auntie Meera, I try never to be nice. I'm telling you this right now because people don't like women who aren't nice. *She's rude*, they say. *She's so selfish and vain*. Well, that's okay with me. Because the thing is, I'm not rude, I'm honest. I'm now, at the age of twenty-seven, the person I've wanted to be since I was eight and left to live with my Auntie Meera, dropped off by my parents like a limp quiche that no one wanted to buy at the church bake sale, discarded like a wet nappy.

On that very day, when I saw Auntie Meera give her last remaining Twix to a homeless person and that homeless person threw it back in her face, I knew. I knew I wasn't going to be like her. Even before then, I'd already known I wasn't going to be like my parents. I wasn't going to pretend to care about things and people that I didn't really care about, say things I didn't mean, make promises I couldn't uphold, and more than anything, I would either love something with all my heart or not bother. No half-hearted watered-down-soup kind of love for me.

At the age of eight, you could say I didn't know who I wanted to be, but I definitely knew who I didn't want to be. And so, when my parents paid me a flying visit two months later, when they stopped by to check on my "progress," as my dad called it, and asked, *Do you like living with Auntie Meera?* I truthfully answered, *Yes*. (I mean, who wouldn't? She was a witch – or a "pagan herbalist," as she called herself. An unfailingly polite one, but still.) *Do you miss us, darling?* asked my mum. And I said, *No, I hate you*.

So, there we go. I started as I meant to go on.

My mum Surya broke into tears and said, *That's terribly rude* (she always sounded more British when she was telling you how you had hurt her feelings). And I said, *It's rude to leave your daughter so you can go travelling*. To which Auntie Meera said, *Hush, Arya*.

By this point my eyes were burning and my throat dry. I kept needing to click my tongue, something, anything to deal with the awful feeling in the pit of my stomach that I was going to explode, that I was the wrong person stuck in the wrong body at the wrong time. I needed to hit something, to scream and keep on screaming; tell-tale signs that I was deeply familiar with by age eight and already trying desperately to hide from others. (*Think of it as a nervous tic*, doctors had said sympathetically to my parents. *Just something the body does to cope with severe anxiety or excess energy, though it may look odd or unpleasant.*) To suppress the need to clear my throat, or worse, grunt – something I knew irritated my dad – I blew a Hubba Bubba bubble in the general direction of my parents, and let it pop, before I turned on my heel and ran off to do better things with my time. I told them that's what I was going to do before I did it. Only when I was well outside earshot did I allow myself some relief. I banged my fists hard on the rough bark of a tree until they cracked and bled. Still, I told myself, it wasn't the first time I'd had bleeding wrists, and at least this time it was me that had made them bleed.

Most people don't like me, it's true, and so you might not either. That's fine. I'm used to my own company. There are a lot of things someone creative can do on their own. Lace knitting. Reading regency romances that always end happily. Creating macabre cakes (which I do for a living). Watching back-to-back episodes of *Killing Eve*. Taking endless woodsy walks. Baking cakes and tarts, eating them by myself while doing some of the above-mentioned things, and then going on my exercise bike to lessen the howling guilt. Observing the new life of my former boyfriend, Craig, from his garden with a fine pair of bird-watching binoculars. Oh, and I didn't mention it, but I also have a close bond with my vibrator D'Artagnan.

Am I lonely, you want to know, like my Auntie Meera? (Though you're too polite to ask.) Kind of, but I don't mind. I really don't. People put up with a lot of bullshit to avoid loneliness, especially women. Mediocre sex. Boring boyfriends. Making friends with people who barely like you, much less care about you. I'd say it's much better to be alone than be with people and still feel lonely.

I live in Trucklewood, a village (some people call it a small town) outside South Croydon, far enough outside so that it can be thought of as the countryside, but near enough that it can still, by a stretch, be seen as part of Greater London. It's built around a hill and is surrounded by hills. Its main street is cut on top of the hill, where there is a Waitrose, a few charity shops, a frozen custard shop, a hairdressers, a florist, a post office, a tea room, and a dodgy art shop that no one ever seems to go in or out of. Trucklewood residents generally have surgically tended houses and gardens. They employ cleaners and gardeners because they can afford to, but because they're artists and hippie types, they don't want anyone else to know that they employ cleaners and gardeners, or that they get manicures or pay taxes, and so everyone acts like they're slightly impoverished.

Being an arty sort, my aunt had moved to Trucklewood a year ago, hoping to fit smoothly into the self-proclaimed bohemian community, supposedly made up of artists, young families and aging couples that were always away on cruises. Auntie Meera was killed six months after moving to Trucklewood, so she didn't get the time to fit in, smoothly or not.

Now I've let go of my flat in Bethnal Green and moved into her house – yes, the very one she was murdered in. It has many advantages, this house. It's tucked away near the woods, away from other houses. Auntie Meera was a successful herbalist. I called her a witch, but she never called herself that. "Herbalist" was as far as she was prepared to go. She had a successful home-run business in potpourri, tinctures, chants and love spells. She put some of her earnings into her house, making it airy and modern on the inside, with granite counters in the kitchen and slouchy furniture in the living areas, but she also had a lot of wild garden space. So, yes, it's isolated and very comfortable. But still not much more than a thirty-minute walk to the high street and less than that to the train station. The other advantages are that unlike my London flat where I had a bedroom that was also the living area, and the kitchen/dining room was my workshop, here I can pretty much use three bedrooms and the grounds as my work space and no one would care. I have all the room I want and I don't have to see anyone for days if I don't want to. Which I generally don't.

If I keep expecting Auntie Meera to walk into a room, if I keep hearing her footsteps creaking on the floorboards, if I can smell her herbs almost as if they're embedded in the furniture, if I wake up suddenly in the middle of the night because I think I've heard her calling my name, then I tell myself that it'll get easier with time to live with those things. That I'll get used to the cloying ache that she's left behind, the clingy feeling that the only person in the world who could put up with me is gone forever.

I moved to the cottage after my aunt died, so about five months ago, and met Craig Yards almost right away. This is the problem with loneliness, these short intense relationships that I get into—not often, just now and again, usually after a big move of some kind, or a change, when I'm still in that exciting phase where I imagine I've become a different person. Where I think I've left behind all the things that I can't stand about myself, and turned into someone else.

It's a dangerous phase, that.

And the relationships I get into in these phases are with the most excruciatingly average men. Craig is one of them: works in the city, in finance, goes to the pub every evening after work and on holiday once a year, has Netflix subscriptions, is never late paying his bills, gets his annual health check-up done on time, complains about Brexit, the changeable weather and how he doesn't work out enough, and jokes that train delays make us, Britain, no better than a *third world* country. Like everyone else who says things like that, Craig has never been to a developing country in his life. His dream is to retire early. Really, that's the extent of his dream. To live his life doing something that bores him to death, just so he can stop doing it before he's sixty.

At this point, you might think of asking: if that's who Craig is, why was I going out with him in the first place, and what am I doing now, sitting outside his house looking at him flapping about his kitchen? Well, the thing is, I was with him because loneliness does get to me sometimes, and when all is said and done, D'Artagnan is not as good as the real thing, even when the real thing is somewhat average, which, to be clear, it was with Craig.

As for why I'm sitting here now, I guess because I thought I'd be the one to break up with Craig. I figured that's what would happen once the relationship ran its course and I realised that I was the same person I'd always been, that I hadn't transformed into a more fun and lovable version of myself. Once I figured out that no matter how fast you run, you can never outrun yourself.

But instead, after two months of going out, he was the one to call it off. I'm not vain, I'm not. I'm okay-looking. I've my dad Brendan Winters's wide mouth, and my mum Surya Patel's large, unblinking almost-black eyes, bushy curls and large boobs. I'm not naturally thin, and I like food, so I have to work at being fit, but that's okay because my one saving grace is that exercise is one of the few ways I can calm myself when I'm feeling anxious. That, and making cakes – and sex, definitely sex.

So I'm not bad looking, nor am I the front page of *Marie Claire*, but I'm not average like Craig, I'm more interesting than that, so it did knock me for a loop when he broke up with me, saying that I was cold (except in bed, in which, he said, I could be a tad less slutty, if he were honest), I was mean, and I had no interest in him or his job or his many feelings, or in the future. He was right about all of that, I had little interest in him, less so in his job, and no, I don't think too much about the future if I can help it, I have too much gnawing away at me in the present, but still, it stung that someone as average as Craig broke up with me, instead of the other way around, which is what would have happened if he had allowed nature to take its course.

So I'm sitting here watching him on a balmy June evening with a pair of binoculars because I want to know what she's like, the woman called Tarina, who he's with now, who's a florist, and who he's got engaged to after dating for only two months. I'm merely curious, nothing else. And also, I was bored sitting in my cottage. I don't know if you've noticed how the walls of your house start creeping closer together as night approaches, the silence weighs deeper, and your heartbeat is suddenly the loudest sound in the world. I've often noticed it. But being proactive, I decided to do something about it. And so here I am.

Tarina is blonde, buxom, and has a soft, big smile. She makes creamy Polish cakes for the annual Easter fair. She's walking around Craig's kitchen right now in a bright pink dress and kitten heels, cleaning and dusting, and rolling pastry for a pie. I shake my head. She's Craig's dream come true, a housekeeper who looks like a Rubens. (Though, hopefully, she holds back in bed, plays hard to get and keeps her legs demurely crossed so she doesn't come across as too eager. So that Craig can feel good about himself.)

She stays for an hour or so, while Craig sits in the living room that I can see just beyond the kitchen, eating sausages cooked by Tarina and watching football. At the end of the hour, she gives Craig's sandy brown hair a kiss, they do some slobbery kissing that makes me queasy, she comes out of the house, gets into her car and drives off. I wait another hour – until about ten – and then I sneak out from under the bush that I've been inhabiting quite happily for some time, and saunter back toward my cottage.

All in all, a pleasant evening.

Chapter Two

Four days later, I'm standing in my open plan kitchen, putting finishing touches to a chocolate fudge cake.

Most people use just butter to make their icing for a chocolate cake, but I use cream *and* butter, the combination heated in a saucepan on medium heat and with dark chocolate broken into it. And my icing is almost as high as the cake itself—about an inch high. I've done the icing for this order and I'm putting finishing touches on the blood trickling down the edge and onto the platter, and the sugar dagger that plunges straight into the heart of the cake. I specialise in cakes, but people also ask me for cookies and granola. Any desserts really, as long as they come with a Tim Burton twist. I'm trying to decide if I can make the blood look bubbly (not made with artificial color, but with beetroot and maple syrup), when the doorbell rings.

I frown. My impulse is to ignore it. Besides my general anti-social inclinations, I also have a lot of baking to do. After the Dagger Chocolate Fudge, I have to complete an order for fifty cupcakes, each with one jelly eye staring from its centre, and I have a batch of my Black Widow Granola to do too. But it could be the postman delivering some cupcake stands I've ordered, so I reluctantly make my way to my door. I'm in my work gear: trainers, leggings and tank top, with a floral skort on top of the leggings today, and my curls are escaping my hairpins.

"Arya Winters?"

I raise my eyebrows. This is not the postman, or anyone I've seen in Trucklewood before. The woman – late-thirties, dark brown hair cut in sensible waves down to the shoulder, a bow-shaped plum-colored mouth, serious brown eyes – flashes a badge. She's looking me up and down, with an alarmingly appreciative light in her eyes. "As you might have heard, we're in the area looking into the murder of Mr. Yards."

I start. "Craig is dead?"

She widens her eyes. "You must be the only one in Trucklewood not to know about the murder. Do you not leave your house? Not Craig Yards, the nephew, but Tobias Yards, the uncle."

"Oh!" I feel a prick of something behind my eyes and a sudden sharp pain in my chest. "Uncle Tobias is dead?" I ask, in an uncharacteristically small voice.

The woman looks surprised. "He was your uncle too?"

I shake myself. I swallow painfully. Tobias. Not Tobias. Why can't it be someone else? I suddenly feel shaky, like I've lost something that I didn't even know I had. "No, no of course not. I only met him when I was—" My brows knit. "Do I need a lawyer to be present? Why are you here?"

She looks bored. "Why does everyone we talk to automatically start feeling guilty? Four nights ago, about quarter past ten-ish, you were seen walking past the vic's house."

"Who's Vic?" I ask suspiciously.

"The victim."

My brow clears. "Oh."

"You were walking past his house. You passed by Mrs. Sharma, the ceramic artist, who was walking her dog. Mrs. Sharma said you didn't stop to say hello."

She says it accusingly.

"So?"

"So, I'd like to ask you a few questions."

"Just because I didn't stop to make chitchat with Mrs. Sharma, doesn't mean that I killed Uncle – I mean Tobias." I can't get my head around how Tobias could be dead. The sudden, sharp pain of it. Suddenly, the world feels emptier.

She shakes her head in exasperation. "We don't think you did it. Or at least, we didn't until now." She looks severely at me. "But I want to ask you if you saw anyone around. Do you have any objection to that?"

I could have said that I had an important commission, which I did, and my sugar dagger wasn't going to sharpen itself, which it wasn't, but the truth is, I'd liked Uncle Tobias. He was Craig's uncle, but I'd got on with him the few times we'd seen each other and I don't get on with most people. "Are you sure he's dead?" I ask blankly.

She looks sympathetically at me. "A shock, is it? I'm sorry, maybe I should have broken it better. But I figured you'd know, everyone else does. And that you were just a neighbour, nothing more."

"I was. I'm sure he didn't see me as anything else. It's just—" My shoulder twitches suddenly and I grasp it. But it twitches again. I shake myself. I'm letting myself crumble in front of a complete stranger, and I never do that. I reluctantly stand aside to let her pass.

The woman is wearing a white shirt and black trousers, and carrying a trench coat. Either this is what coppers actually wear, or she's watching too many crime dramas on the BBC. We walk into my living room – a large room with lots of natural light, with a small den at one end. It's across the landing from the kitchen, the large, airy kitchen that I use exclusively for my work. My own tiny kitchen is tucked away at the end, near the garden door.

She looks at me with interest. "You're like me, aren't you?" she asks, smiling.

I look at her in confusion.

"Half and half," she says chummily. "You've got the half-white half-Asian thing *down*."

I hold my hands up. "Uh, no. I don't do that."

She waves a hand. "Oh, I know what you mean. I don't like it either, when people think they have something in common with you just because of your skin color. Boring!" In front of my astonished eyes, she's twirling her hair on one finger.

"No, I mean I don't do bonding."

She raises her eyebrows in mock horror. "Oh, right." Then she laughs uncertainly, in case I meant it as a joke. She clears her throat. I look down at her name tag. Shona Klues.

A detective sergeant with the name *Klues*? Really?

"Yeah, funny, no?" she says, smiling again. "What are the odds?" She pulls her hand through the back of her hair. "Barely had time to dry it this morning. Do you like it?"

I stare at her. What about me makes her think I do *this*?

"Your *hair*?" I couldn't sound more incredulous if it were her pubic hair she was asking my opinion about. "I don't – care," I say as clearly as I can.

"Oh," she says, not at all put out, "I guess you don't do this either." She's looking down at her notepad, laughing like I'm very funny. "So, what were you doing that evening, prior to bumping into Mrs. Sharma?"

I wince. The woman with her questions about my mixed ethnicity and the highlights at the back of her hair has thrown me, and I haven't had time to think of what to say to this – her real question. I could say that I was snooping on Craig, but I have a feeling that won't look so good to a Detective Sergeant. Plus, it could be illegal to skulk in your ex's garden and spy on him snogging his girlfriend. I bite my tongue. Shona Klues is looking patiently at me. I'm clutching my burning shoulder.

"I was taking a walk."

She nods slowly. "Long walk?"

My mind races as I try to remember if anyone saw me, other than Mrs. Sharma. Anyone who could pinpoint the exact times and locations.

Shona looks at me, with a kindly smile on her face. "Talking to the police makes people think they have something to hide. I'd say stick to the truth. Saves a lot of bother in the long run."

I frown. "I have nothing to hide. I left my cottage at about six... half past six. I walked all the way down my road, at a slow-ish pace, I took a few turns – I don't remember precisely which. I crossed the high street at one point, and walked all the way to the other end of the village. I meandered for some time."

"A lot of meandering. It was after ten when Mrs. Sharma saw you."

"Yes." I blink. "I like to meander."

She looks at me. Then writes something in her notebook. I peer over and see she's written *Likes to meander, she says...???* I frown again.

"Did you see anyone else all that evening, other than Mrs. Sharma?"

I shrug. "I passed some people. I don't remember."

"Did you stop to chat with anyone?" She pauses and looks up at me. "Or don't you do that?" She laughs at her own joke.

"Has anyone ever told you, you have a very irritating laugh?"

I expect her smile to vanish. That's how most people react to the things I say, but instead she tucks her hair behind her ear.

"Why don't you have a think about your walk and if you come up with anything, if you saw anyone, if you spoke to anyone, give me a ring."

She hands me her card. She takes it back, crosses something out with a ballpoint that materialises out of nowhere, writes something else and then hands the card back to me. I notice that she's written down a mobile number, presumably hers. She's about to leave.

"How did he die?" I ask her, something sticky in my throat. I don't want to know, yet I can't bear not knowing either. Not having some last image – however horrible – of Tobias's, nothing but a blank, somehow I can't bear the idea.

She turns around and looks at me. "Poison. We don't always like to mention the details. But his neighbour Veronica Chives found him and she's told everyone."

My eyes narrow. "How did she know it was poison? Frothing at the mouth, vomit, and so on?"

She shrugs. "No. It was very neat and clean. You could tell the man was dead, but that was it, no clue as to why."

"Then how did she know?"

"She was still there when the paramedics arrived, after she rang them, and she overheard their speculations." She looks disgusted. "Don't know what the police force is coming to, you know, Arya, I just don't."

Not Ms. Winters, Arya. Oof.

"How was the poison administered?"

She smiles widely at me with her picture-perfect white teeth. "Not just a pretty face."

I stare at her. "Are you flirting with me?" I ask sternly.

"Now that wouldn't be allowed," she says coyly. "So I couldn't possibly be." She inclines her head like a sparrow. "We're not allowed to give details, like I said. But Veronica Chives has let this one out of the bag too. In fact, you seem to be the only one in Trucklewood who doesn't know any of this. The last thing the vic ate was a slice of tiramisu. The cake was laced with poison."

I'm about to blurt out *But I made Tobias the tiramisu.* I stop myself just in time. Though I don't know why I bother. It can't be long before they find out. My heart is hammering. Why was there poison in my tiramisu, and who put it there? More importantly, wouldn't the police assume it was me that did it? After all, I'd made the damn thing, and left it outside Tobias's doorstep earlier that afternoon.

My throat is suddenly dry as the desert. I swallow painfully. Murdered on his birthday. Tobias did have the shittiest luck. And with *my* tiramisu. I'd thought about knocking, about saying happy birthday. If I had done that, I would have seen him one last time. He wouldn't have disappeared from my life, gone before I had the chance to say goodbye, just like my Auntie Meera. Before I had the chance to say that he'd touched my life. Isn't that what everyone wants? To feel like they've touched someone's life, that they've made a difference? I had never said such a thing to Tobias. It had never occurred to me. And I had never said something like that to my aunt either. And now I would never get to.

Shona Klues smiles at me again. "Call me," she says, as she leaves.

Chapter Three

I head out in the direction of Uncle Tobias's house, which is about a fifteen-minute walk from my cottage. I'd met Tobias for the first time some months ago, soon after I started going out with Craig. Maybe a couple of weeks after. Actually, come to think of it, I'd already started feeling a little bored with Craig. It wasn't so much that he didn't have anything interesting to say. I don't mind silence. In fact, I like it, it's soothing. It was more that the things he seemed to think about were so mundane. His finance job, football, the piece of skin hanging loose on the ball of his foot.

I didn't like the way he patted my bottom or called other people's wives The Missus, like they didn't have a name or any other role in life. The way he casually checked out other women when we went out to eat. How he said he wasn't religious but then kept saying that god would look after him if he looked after Number One.

I'm wondering now if it was meeting Tobias that made me stay with Craig longer than I might have done. A couple of weeks after we started going out, Craig and I stopped at Tobias's to drop off some heart medication. I would have expected Tobias to be an older version of Craig, if I had thought about it at all, which I hadn't. But he turned out to be quite different. We had stopped at his large detached Victorian house, not that different-looking from Auntie Meera's. Craig had stooped, wedged his podgy hand inside an urn that stood outside the front door, and let us in. Craig had rung some sort of dingle-dangle bell that stood on the side table, called out for his uncle, and then we'd waited inside the front door for Tobias to find us. I had spent the next five minutes studying the teal-blue walls of the hallway, every inch covered in paintings. Nothing modern, no photographs, no pencil or charcoal sketches. All impressionist prints that looked quite expensive, framed in frames that looked pretty pricey too.

"Arya," Tobias said, when he made his way out of his living room. He gave me a large, cool hand to shake. His jowls were enormous, his eyelashes black as a raven, his eyes could hardly be seen. He was a big man, who looked like he liked his food and drink. He was wearing suspenders, of all things. Craig looked even more average standing next to him.

"Tobias," I responded. I wasn't at my best when meeting new people, and I could feel the familiar tightness in my chest. My mouth was dry too and I was clutching my denim jacket so I wouldn't start clicking my tongue. There was already an ominous ticking in my shoulder.

He was wearing a chequered pair of trousers and waistcoat to boot. He had a stern, frowning face. And the darkest, bushiest pair of eyebrows I'd ever seen. *You're fat*, I wanted to say. In fact, I wanted to say it so badly I was finding it hard to breathe. The words were hovering at the tip of my tongue, desperately needing to be uttered. I was holding my breath, trying not to say it. Please, I was thinking, please don't let me say it. Please, let me turn into someone completely different this once.

But Tobias surprised me.

"I can't imagine why any woman would want to go out with a loser like my nephew. He's the most boring old sod there ever was."

Instantly my shoulders relaxed. The anxiety I had been holding tightly in my body, the anxiety of meeting someone new, of dreading that I would say things that would make them hate me, or make noises that I couldn't help, the memory of which I would hold on to for weeks, sometimes years, that anxiety left me in a whoosh.

"The sex is good," I said, as straight-faced as I could. Then I conscientiously amended my statement. "Or at least, it *is* sex."

He made a *humph* sound, but there was a lightening around the eyes.

Don't get me wrong, I never actually saw Tobias smile or lose his heavy frown the entire time I knew him, but when he was amused or when someone had sparked his interest, something relaxed around his eyes. I'm good at catching little signs like that in people, signs that they're relaxing or, conversely, signs that they're about to fly into a rage. I learnt that pretty early on in life. And I'm good at it. And I was pleased to see Tobias's face relax at my words.

"You're not his usual type," he said.

"Thank fuck for that."

And there was that thing around the eyes again, that lightening.

Craig looked bored throughout this exchange.

I can't say that I gave that much thought to Tobias after our first meeting. I didn't. But now and again you have an inkling, you meet someone and you think, hang on, here's someone like me. You think it, and the thought eases some part of your heart, the part that deep down is terrified that no one is like you, that you're so different that no heart will ever connect with yours. No one will nod in understanding at the strange things you say. There will never be a moment when someone sees themselves in you, mirrored, just for a second. In any case, I'd had that tiny glimmer of an inkling of kinship when I met Tobias.

I saw Tobias a few more times after that, once or twice when I was still with Craig, when after dinner Tobias and I drank scotch and played Monopoly, and Craig watched football or reruns of *Top Gear*, and later, when Craig and I had broken up, I bumped into Tobias a few times on the high street or at the Easter fair.

At the Easter fair, he said to me, "Escaped him, did you?"

I didn't have to ask him whom he meant.

"He broke up with me," I told him.

"Sometimes you have to do something before it's done to you."

This aspect of the situation hadn't struck me before. In fact, like I've said, I'd been a bit cut up about the whole Craig thing. I gave Tobias a rueful smile.

"Steer clear of the jelly," he warned me, before waddling off toward the wine stall.

I would have seen more of him, but I don't like asking people to do things with me in case they say no. In case I take up more space in someone's life than they are happy with. He seemed happy with his own company, and I didn't want to come across as needy in the weeks and months after Auntie Meera died. Actually, I did ask him once if he wanted company to go to the Apollo to watch some comedy, because I knew he liked to go, and he said he'd be in touch about it, and then he didn't get in touch, so I assumed he didn't want to go out of his way to spend time with me. I didn't try again.

On the way to Tobias's house now, on an impulse, I walk up Mrs. Sharma's driveway and knock on her door. Mrs. Sharma lives next door to me. She opens the door and does a double-take when she sees me. Mrs. Sharma is small, does her hair in a tight bun (it's about the size of a ping-pong ball, if you're interested) right on top of her head, and wears floral smocks and Cath Kidson aprons spattered with clay. She can often be seen trying to chat with people on the high street, generally with a smile on her face. In fact, it would be safe to say that she always has a smile on her face, a somewhat needy one, I've always thought. Except today. Looking at me, she is decidedly frowning.

"What can I do for you?"

The tone is cold, but still a polite question. This is what I don't get about people. I've hardly ever been civil to this woman. There's no way she can like me. Or even be interested in me. But she still feels like she needs to be polite.

"I passed by you four evenings ago when you were walking your dog."

"Trev."

I look blankly at her.

"The dog's name," she says patiently, "is Trevor."

I blink at her. "I have no idea why you're telling me that."

"Why are you here? I'm busy." A hint of annoyance now. "You've never spoken to me in all the time you've lived here," she elaborates, though I haven't asked her anything. "You hardly acknowledge me." She purses her lips. "At the Easter fair, when I asked you what you thought of my prize-winning prune jelly that has a hint of cumin in it, you said if someone asked you what you cared about least in the world at that precise moment, you'd say prune jelly."

"Well, it was the truth. You think all the other people complimenting you on it really cared?"

"They cared enough to pretend," she says, crossing her arms and sniffing.

"I care enough to tell you the truth."

She raises her eyebrows. "You *don't* care."

I click my tongue. Twice. The sound takes me by surprise in the still air. I swallow convulsively so I don't do it again. "I just want to know if you passed anyone else on that evening that I bumped into you. Once you tell me, I'll get out of your hair."

She leans back. "What do you care?"

"Uncle – Tobias Yards was killed that evening. Since the police are interested in the time I bumped into you, it must have been some time around then." My shoulder twitches. I clutch it. I cluck again. Twice. Damn! I clutch my cheek. "Did you or did you not see anyone other than me on the walk?"

"What are you, a private detective now?"

I growl deep in my throat. "Mrs. Sharma, is it a secret?"

She stares at her fingernails. "Why do you care, is what I want to know."

"I liked Tobias, if you must know."

A bark – something resembling laughter – escapes her. "You don't like anyone!"

"Well," I say stubbornly, "I liked him."

"Why?"

I don't have an answer. Why do any of us like people? People have explanations for this. That we knew them in a past life, that our neurosis bonds with theirs, that we instinctively recognise a kindred spirit, but who knows? Maybe it was none of those things with Tobias. Maybe I just liked that he liked who I was. He liked that I was direct and said what I meant. He didn't judge me for it, didn't make me feel like years ago I'd made the wrong choice about who I wanted to be, that that choice had left me all alone and unable to be with anyone else, but that it was too late to turn back now. He didn't make me feel like that. Maybe it was just that.

"He was as rude as you are," Mrs. Sharma says. "Didn't have a minute to spare for his neighbours."

My brow clears. "Yes, that sounds about right." That is probably why I liked him.

She purses her mouth. "You never speak to any of us, you don't come to social events, in fact, you don't even acknowledge invitations. You barely know our names. When we ask you to sign petitions for the upkeep of the local area, you don't acknowledge those either. You don't contribute to the community. Why, may I ask, this sudden interest in a local resident? Anyway, if you must know, the only one I bumped into other than you was that new man, the dishy one, the writer."

"I have no idea who you mean."

She rolls her eyes. "He's bought a place two houses down from you. But why doesn't it surprise me that you don't know the bloke? Anyway, I have things to do and places to be. So—" She looks significantly at me.

I chew on my thumb and turn around.

Behind me, she calls. "You're welcome!"

I absently turn toward her. "I didn't thank you," I point out.

She rolls her eyes and bangs the door behind me. Then the door opens again. She calls out to me. "Don't suppose you want to come in for a cuppa?" Her eyes look defensive and hopeful at the same time.

I stare at her. "Needy," I blurt out. I clamp a hand on my mouth.

A hurt look crosses her eyes.

There's no point saying I didn't mean to say that. Plus, didn't I?

I rub my forehead. It's fine, it's fine, just stop now, I tell myself. Don't say anything more. But the pressure is building again. I can feel it, moving up my spine, curling around to my stomach. I clutch my throat. I have to get out of here before I say something else. I don't even know what it'll be. These things catch me by surprise, as much as anyone else, let me tell you. I glance at Mrs. Sharma's face.

She bangs the door in my face. Again.

Chapter Four

I walk away, frowning, and don't pay attention to what I'm doing until I walk splat into a really hard object.

"Ow! Can't you look where you're going?" I say, unreasonably. Some might say that it was me that hadn't been looking where I was going.

When I stop rubbing my arm, I notice that I'm face-to-face with a stranger. Medium height, dark hair cut close to the scalp, and a pair of blue eyes that seem to be trying to drill a hole into my skull. The man is probably around my age, wearing a white t-shirt and some loose trousers, and he has an unnecessarily muscly pair of arms.

"I don't think we've met," he says. He smiles, and the skin around his eyes crinkles. He has unnaturally pink lips. I quickly look away. "I'm Branwell."

"*Branwell*?"

He grimaces. "It could've been worse."

"How?" I demand.

"It could have been Heathcliff. Though people call me Bran now, which makes me feel very virtuously fibrous."

I start to smile but think better of it. I don't need muscly men in my life. I try to peel my eyes away from his shoulders. They look hard and muscly too. I start to walk away.

"You know, it's your turn to tell me your name."

I turn around again. "Just ask people about me. I don't do – uh…" I wave a hand about.

"What?"

"You know, friends and stuff."

"Who said I want to be friends with you?"

My eyes snap to his. This is a mistake, since his are still boring into mine. In a smiling, crinkly sort of way. Really, can't the man look at something else? It's like being confronted by magnets. They're making my insides wobbly.

"You have the most expressive eyes I've ever seen," he says soulfully.

I look incredulously at him. I cross my arms. "Then tell me. What am I thinking now?"

"You're thinking that you'd really like to ask yourself around for a cup of coffee."

My mouth draws into a tight line. "I'm busy trying to solve a murder, if you must know." I start to turn away again.

He reaches out a hand to my arm. His touch gives me an electric shock and I spring away. He looks surprised, then he looks down at his hand. He shakes his head. "Wow, weird."

"*Wow, weird*? What are you, twelve?"

He grins. "I do write books for twelve-year-olds, so maybe you're right."

Ah, it all makes sense now. I stop trying to get away and look fully at him.

He raises his eyebrows. "What did I say? You're suddenly interested in me."

I look at him in mild surprise. People don't read me that easily. "I'm not interested in you," I find myself saying primly, while trying not to watch the way his arm muscles ripple as he stuffs his hands in his trouser pockets. "Four evenings ago, you were taking a walk when you bumped into Mrs. Sharma. I'm wondering if you bumped into anyone else."

"Mrs. Sharma? The short, thin one that always wants to stop and chat with you and feed you digestively-themed jelly?"

I can't help a grin. "Yes, that one."

"I passed by a couple of other people."

I look speculatively at him. "You're new to the area." I eye him. "Any particular reason you moved here?"

He smiles. "I didn't murder Tobias Yards if that's what you're asking."

I make a non-committal noise. "That's what you would say if you *had* murdered him."

"As to that—"

But then he doesn't finish what he was going to say. I feel a gust of a sudden breeze and then a pair of squishy cushions collides into me. I nearly fall over, then straighten myself. It's Tarina, my ex Craig's new girlfriend.

I've only met her once – if you don't count the times I've seen her at the other end of my nifty binoculars, that is – and that was at the Easter fair, when she had stopped me and said, "So sorry. I hope you not mind?" It had been a sunny, breezy kind of day and I had shaded my eyes to look at her with mild curiosity. She was really quite pretty.

"I hope you not mind. I am fiancé to your late-boyfriend."

I'd raised my brows. "One of my exes is dead?"

She trilled loudly. "No, no, Craig. How you say, *ex*-boyfriend?"

I frowned. "No, I don't mind, as it happens. He's freakishly boring."

"Me, I prefer boring," she had responded.

She's smiling anxiously at me now. "Arya?" she says, as if she's not sure it's me. She's leaning close to me, her face centimetres from mine.

"Tarina."

She turns her headlights on to the writer – Branwell.

"Who is this?" she asks, her nipples positively quivering. I don't blame her. There's something about the man's arms. And the eyes.

In fact, it's hard to know which to look at. It's making me twitchy trying to decide between the two.

"Branwell Beam," he says.

I snort, and don't bother trying to turn it into a cough.

He looks cheerfully at me. "It's a perfectly good name."

"If you say so." I turn back to Tarina. "Were you looking for me?"

She looks anxious. She's wearing a pastel yellow matching cardigan and skirt set and sparkly trainers. Her hair is a blonde meringue, and her face all soft and pink, sort of whipped cream and rhubarb, but today there's a hint of a frown. "I am nervous. The police think Craig, he murdered his uncle."

I look at her in surprise. "Why do they think that?"

She shrugs. "He gets the money, no?"

I lift a shoulder. "So? Did Tobias have that much money? And also, Craig doesn't need money." I don't know if you've noticed this, but boring men always seem to have a lot of money.

She does look nervous now. "Well, as to that, you'll have to ask Craig. But the main problem being that Craig was all by himself at home with no lullaby for when Tobias was murdered."

"Lullaby?" I hear the writer ask.

"She means alibi," I say, not turning to look at him. I can feel him though, standing there next to me, looking all clean and relaxed, like he showers three times a day and has all the time in the world to do what he pleases. "What time was that?" I ask Tarina.

"Sometime between nine and ten on Wednesday evening."

I start. I stare at Tarina. Between nine and ten on Wednesday evening! Craig had been alone in his house in that time frame, it's true. But he does have an alibi because I had seen him sitting there in front of his television set, watching football. He hadn't stirred a muscle in that hour after Tarina left him. He'd been there the whole time and in fact from the back of his head I could tell that he had fallen asleep and was possibly snoring. You could say that from his garden, with my natty pair of binoculars, I'd had a birds' eye view of the situation.

I chew on my thumb now. "Right," I say slowly.

"You tell me," Tarina says, jabbing a soft finger in my direction, "how to make him feel better. He's nervous about the police."

I look incredulously at her. "Craig? *I* have no idea."

Tarina nods vigorously. "Yes, yes, you do. Craig says you and he make sex, no? He says you like making lots of sex."

I shift from foot to foot, my eyes veering involuntarily toward the writer. He's smiling. I look severely at him.

"That's neither here nor there," I say sternly to Tarina.

"No, do say more," Branwell says. "It's fascinating stuff."

"No, it isn't," I say firmly. "And I don't see how that's important."

"I would like you to show me some tits, yes?" Tarina says.

I hear a chuckle from the writer.

"*Tips*," I say crossly to Tarina. "And no, I can't show you any tips. And anyway, he doesn't like a woman who likes sex too much."

"Astonishing," I hear Branwell say.

I ignore the man. "Mother him," I say to Tarina. "That should relax him."

In the end, Tarina is not easily convinced, and I basically have to turn her in the direction of Craig's house and pat her on the bottom (a bit like Craig would) to get her on her way. Since we're on top of a hilly bit, I can't help thinking it would work better if she had roller skates on. I can't help noticing that her bottom is as beautifully offset by her tight clothes as her cleavage was. I can't help it, I feel the tightness in my belly, and I know I'm going to do it a second before I do it. I yell, "Yellow marshmallow!" I clamp my hand on my mouth. Shit, I had no idea that was going to pop out.

I turn apprehensively to Branwell. I should get away from the man before I blurt anything else out. People don't like it when you state the truth, I've often noticed it. I grip my hands so I won't say anything about the man's magnetic eyes.

"So," he says, "how do you know what Craig was doing in that hour in which his uncle was killed?" He looks mildly curious. He doesn't comment on my yelling at Tarina.

I try to look as innocent as possible. "I don't know what you mean."

"You know that Craig didn't kill his uncle, but for some reason, you can't tell his girlfriend. When she mentioned the time frame, you knew something."

I scowl. Really, the man is too much. People generally don't read me so easily. "Can you read minds now?"

"Only yours. And only because I want to."

I click my tongue. And then I find I do it again. I lift a hand to my cheek. Damn. Why now! I grind my teeth. I need to go now before I do something worse. I start to turn away.

"Are you having an affair with him, behind his girlfriend's back?"

I turn to look at the man in disgust. I can't repress a shudder at the thought of having an affair with Craig. "It's none of your business."

He looks visibly more cheerful though. "Well, that's good news."

I don't dignify this with an answer. The man can read me like a book. It's most definitely better to avoid him in the future. Who knows the kinds of things that'll pop out of me if I stick around? Much better to make myself scarce and never see the man – or his eyes, or his arms – again. I turn to walk away, run, if possible.

"Pop around if you want a cup of coffee. I make killer coffee," I hear him say behind me.

I guess I could retort that I make a killer tiramisu, but it's probably better that I don't.

Chapter Five

Temporarily ditching the idea of paying Tobias's house a visit, I spend the rest of the day baking and squirting cream. The jelly eyes for the cupcakes take ages to do. The white jelly mound is easy and the black eyeball in the centre isn't too difficult either. But getting red veins in the eyeballs is harder because they have to be thin and not ooze everywhere. I use a hypodermic filled with red paste. It's tricky because if the mixture is runny, it spreads everywhere, and if it's too creamy it doesn't look realistic. I leave a village of discarded eyeballs in my bin.

Baking usually relaxes me, but by the time I'm done with the cupcakes my shoulder is twitching madly and my face is hurting from trying to hold it still. I'm flipping and flapping and yelling out every two seconds and stabbing myself with things – mostly not deliberately. I decide to head out for a run. That's the only thing that'll help. I have to work this out or it'll get worse. Something is niggling at the back of my mind, I can feel it, like a burning in my shoulders. But I don't want to stop and think about it or try to figure it out. Something, something about Tobias's murder that I'm meant to see. Something about his death. But I can't figure out what it is.

Running gear on, I head out toward the woods. I take a long circuit. The evening is balmy, the weather starting its turn from spring firmly onwards into summer. My neighbours' gardens are showing signs of summer bloomers, bursts of stonecrop and Californian lilac, and out here in the woods, I make myself recite the names of the yellow toadflax that springs from the feet of the oaks and the corncockle I spy sprouting around the old building of the boarding school, that nestles in the dip about a half-hour run from my place.

I didn't lie when I said that I don't know a thing about gardening. (In fact, I rarely lie. I try to avoid it if I can. Plus, I'm rubbish at it.) But like I said, Auntie Meera was a practicing witch (herbalist, she would correct me, firmly), and she rarely walked by a plant, herb or tree without murmuring the name, almost as an incantation. She was tall and willowy, her curls (not that different from my mum's, and mine, though mine are darker) were dark brown and greying and down to the small of her back, and she usually wore short-sleeved tops and dungarees and had plants and flowers and often paintbrushes sticking out of her hair. She hardly ever wore makeup, but sometimes she wore a red dot in the centre of her forehead, and now and again, a filmy and sparkly chunni as a scarf around her neck. The only jewelry she had on was a tinkly ankle bracelet that she'd been wearing the very first time I'd seen her when I was little, and that I never saw her take off.

My chest tightens at the thought of Auntie Meera.

I can't help wondering if she would have died if I had visited her more, seen more of her in the last few years. I did visit her, it wasn't that I didn't. But only every few weeks, sometimes every few months. And I guess it had been less than that in the last couple of years. First, I'd gone off to Paris to do another baking course, and got busy with my life, and then, more recently, we'd had that fight. It had been a blazing row and for weeks after it, we hadn't spoken, not even once. And when she had tried to reach out to me, I hadn't responded. When we did start speaking to each other again, we skirted around the fight, choosing not to talk about it or try to sort it out. And an odd formality had come between us, the kind that had never been there before. Since she died, I've thought of little other than our fight, and I can't help thinking that if I had made more of an effort to try to get past it, try to talk about it, or even openly say that I didn't want to talk about it, she might still be alive.

My shoulders burn at the thought.

The day before she died, she had called me and asked me if I'd come around for breakfast the next day. I hadn't thought about it at that time – I'd been in the middle of squirting wilting roses onto a wedding cake, which is always a tricky one because you have to make them look funereal but not too funereal – but later, I had thought she'd sounded different, sort of excited and anxious at the same time, not her usual quiet self. I said I couldn't head over in the morning, because I had a job I had to finish, but that I would try to pop around later on. It turned out that she was killed that morning, the morning I would have been happily sitting with her in her kitchen eating brambleberry pancakes (actually, being a baker, I should know this, but I can't at the moment remember if brambleberries are seasonal in January. Google it, if you must. I would have been eating some form of fruity pancake). As it was, I hadn't been there, and her cleaner who had knocked on her door at noon had found her lying on the floor. There had been nothing, no signs of a forced entry, no struggle, and in fact the first conclusion would have been that Auntie Meera had died of a heart attack. That is, if she hadn't been artistically splayed naked on her floor, her legs wide open, and her hands crossed over her chest. In fact, she had been hit on the head with a blunt instrument. A couple of times, until it was clear that the job was done.

It's the last thing I want to do, to imagine Auntie Meera's last hours or minutes, but now, after hearing about Tobias's death, it's not Tobias whose body is haunting me. It's Auntie Meera's.

I'm twitching by the time I get to Tobias's house, and trying hard to control the movements of my right shoulder. I stop in the driveway and try to breathe deeply. The run doesn't seem to have helped like it normally does. Of course, I hadn't seen Auntie Meera's body lying there on her kitchen floor. She had been moved by the time I got there. But I can picture it, as clearly as if I had seen it. I can see every little detail in my mind. It's hardly bearable when it springs up, fully formed, in my mind when I'm awake. When I'm asleep and I see her, left like that on her kitchen floor, I wake up, heart pounding, sure that she'll still be there, just like that, in her kitchen, if I make my way down the stairs in the dead of night. And the picture of it, the way she died, like a sacrificial offering, all alone and her polite dignity lost forever, I can't get that image out of my mind.

Why, why hadn't I gone that morning to Auntie Meera's? She had asked me. If I had, she might not have died. There is no way I can talk myself out of that one. She had been the most important person in my life, and I'd let her down in the worst possible way. In my dreams, over and over again, I show up on her doorstep for breakfast, for fruity pancakes, and I tell her I survived my childhood because she was in it, because she held my hand and decided never to let go. Again and again, I wake up crying from my dreams.

I cluck a few times to try to release the anxiety. But trying to suppress myself is making me feel sick.

Tobias's house is dark. I stand in front of it, hands on hips, rattled at the thoughts of Auntie Meera. Suddenly, I don't want to go in. Suddenly, I can see Tobias's body. I don't even know how he was found. In what state. In what position. But it's like I can see it, and like it's still there, in the dark house. I grind my teeth. I have to stop being an idiot.

The area is cordoned off by yellow tape. I duck under it. I shake my head. Have the police considered cordoning off areas with electric fencing, or maybe sensors that shoot darts at people if they cross the threshold? Has it occurred to them that a long string of flimsy yellow tape isn't the most effective way of keeping people out of places?

Trying to rid myself of thoughts of Auntie Meera and Tobias, I walk about the front garden, then course around to the back, and do a couple of rounds, not exactly sure what I'm looking for. The police will have done a search, so it's unlikely I'll find any clues, even if there are any to find. And anyway, if I did find something – the butt of a cigarette or a piece of string or something – who could say that they would have anything to do with Tobias's murder? Detectives (well, okay, the ones on TV) look so serious and portentous when they find something on the ground and place it carefully with tweezers into a plastic bag. It always turns out to be significant, but how does one ever know what could be connected to the murderer and not to some random passerby or guest?

Anyway, I find nothing in the garden. Unlike the usual manicured Trucklewood garden, or Auntie Meera's herbal one, Tobias's garden is enticingly wild, wisteria climbing on just about everything, smothering the pear tree, clinging to the fence, curling around the arch. Flowers straggling over each other and trailing on the grass. Bushes untrimmed. Trees jostling for space. I think with a spark of annoyance that Craig will inherit all this wilderness, and he'll have no idea how to appreciate it or what to do with it. He'll probably have it hacked off and concrete put down. And gone will be a part of Tobias's soul.

Rounds of the garden done, I end up outside the front door again, and stoop to feel inside the urn that stands on the right side of the door for the key that Tobias always kept there. I feel a pang of guilt as I do it. Tobias was an intensely private man. As private as Auntie Meera, though in a different way. Tobias would keep people at bay with his frowning face and his growl, Auntie Meera with her polite smile and soft ways. I'm intruding into his space now. I only know about the key because Craig had known about it. I wouldn't ever have used it while Tobias was alive. I remind myself that he's dead now. But the guilt coils in my belly.

I frown because I can't find the key. I rummage further, then I turn the urn upside down. It's about a foot high and on the heavy side. But in any case, there's no key. I put the urn down and straighten. Isn't that a bit strange? Tobias always left a key there. Could the police have found it? Why would they have, though? They would hardly have gone around the garden turning all the urns and flower pots upside down. I screw up my mouth, the better to think. Craig might have told them about the key, I guess. Not satisfied with this explanation, and feeling even more uneasy now than I had on my run, I stand about metaphorically scratching my head. Spotting the matching urn that stands on the left side of Tobias's door, I bend down and put a hand in it. And instantly find the key.

So, Tobias put it in the wrong urn? It's possible, but something about that explanation leaves me dissatisfied. I use the key to let myself in to Tobias's house. It will, of course, have been thoroughly searched. Still, I scout the kitchen and dining area, all as meticulously clean as they were when Tobias was alive. In the kitchen I see no signs of my tiramisu or the pink polka dot platter on which I'd delivered it. I assume the police took them.

I have it in my head that, knowing Tobias a little better than the police had done, I might spot something they hadn't. I turn to head to the study. On my way out of the kitchen I stoop to pick up a small sharp object that's been pushed to the corner of the room. A hairpin. I sigh. This is the kind of thing that in a television show would look intensely significant. After all, it didn't belong to Tobias. But on the other hand, it could belong to any number of police officers, or to Veronica Chives, Tobias's American neighbor who had found the body—or in fact to any number of other people who had innocently visited Tobias before he had died.

I shake my head a little at the thought. Okay, maybe not. Tobias wasn't known to have been the heart and soul of parties. I doubt that he had had a lot of visitors. Still, any number of police officers could have dropped a hairpin. I'm about to drop it back on the floor, but having read too many crime novels in my spare time, I find that I can't, and instead I slip it into my pocket, feeling like an idiot.

I make my way to Tobias's study. The study is lined with books. Besides these there are paintings on the wall, mostly of an abstract nature, an old Picasso print, and some surrealist stuff with screaming faces and hollow eyes. There is a desk and chair and a quick scan of the drawers shows that the police have not got around to them yet. There is no sign of Tobias's laptop, so I'm guessing the police have that. But there are various papers and letters and things in the drawers. I debate with myself for a minute. If I take them to look through at leisure, the police will know they've disappeared. That won't look so good. Instead, I take out my phone and take a few quick photos of the papers, then stuff them back in their drawers. They mostly look like bills, a few official-looking letters. It occurs to me now that I didn't even know what Tobias had done for a living.

Since I can't think of anything else to do in the study, I head up the stairs to Tobias's bedroom. I stand there at the door, feeling suddenly paralysed. Tobias was intensely private. And this is his bedroom. Definitely not a room I would ever have seen under normal circumstances. I firmly remind myself that he's dead. It still takes me a few minutes to get up the courage to go inside. I push the door softly open, and it opens with a horrible creak that makes my heart pound.

The room is enormous, the size of three normal-sized bedrooms. There's a huge four-poster in the center. The light from the window shows me plush velvet curtains. Besides the four-poster, there is beautifully chosen, hand-picked furniture tastefully placed about the room, all dark, real wood, no Ikea or fake wood or laminate for Tobias. There's a massive wardrobe, a dressing table, vintage mirrors on the walls. The carpet is soft and teal, like the hallway downstairs.

A quick scan of some drawers reveals little of importance. Pants, socks, silk eye masks that smell of lavender, little gold bags of dried flowers. Years of cleaning before and after fulfilling my orders makes me methodical, and I try to search quickly and efficiently, but with a minimum of mess. I can't help thinking that my qualms are pointless, given that Tobias would never use these possessions again. I can't imagine Craig doing anything other than getting someone to bag them up and take them to a charity shop or – knowing Craig – more likely, to the tip.

A little drawer reveals sex toys and erotic literature. I look with interest at Tobias's collection of dildos. There are four, one realistic looking, one made of glass, a plastic one, and another covered in red silk. There is also an eye mask or two, a pair of fur-lined handcuffs, and even a leather whip.

"Who knew?"

I feel squeamish about touching these, but I take a picture on my phone for good measure. The erotic literature is stacked, one slim volume on top of another, and I take a quick picture of the spines. There is a bookmark sticking out of one. I pull it out and look at it with interest. It isn't a postcard, as I think at first, but a photograph. A photograph of a group of people. There are five in the group. All sitting, legs out in front of them, some crossed, some not, in a circle. You can't see their faces. The picture is taken from above and shows the five people waist-down, no chest, face or head. But it's obvious which of the people is male and which female, because each of the five is stark bollocks naked, and there they are, genitals and pubic hair and all, all open to the air, sitting on the grass, happy as a lark in the springtime. Two men and three women.

I let my breath out in a whoosh. "Now, Tobias, what *were* you up to."

Instinctively, I place the picture in my pocket.

After I've looked through all the drawers in the room – including the ones built into the bed – I stand for a few minutes looking around the room for inspiration. But I can't think of anywhere else to search. The medicine cabinet in the ensuite reveals nothing out of the ordinary. His heart medicine, and some of the most expensive papaya and avocado moisturizers, sea kelp conditioners and a saffron-based hand cream that money can buy. There's also a bottle of Crème de la Mer.

I cluck my tongue at Tobias's vanity. His skin did look beautifully moisturized though, I have to admit.

I make my way downstairs after a quick and pointless search of the upstairs bathroom and two spare rooms, and nearly die of a heart attack.

Because suddenly something large rubs against my legs.

Heart in my throat, I look down. The evening has lengthened and the kitchen is getting dark. Mouth dry, I finally realise what I should have instantly understood. It's The Marquis, Tobias's enormous shaggy cat. I should have realised it because I knew that Tobias had a cat. But, in my defense, the cat isn't a sociable one, and shoots out of the cat flap the minute a stranger enters the house, a bit like a carefully aimed bullet, and so I've never actually seen The Marquis. He's enormous, very hairy, white as a spring daisy and his face looks like a snowball that's been squashed flat against someone's back. He's scowling and yowling at me now like I'm a personal affront.

"Well, why are you rubbing against my legs then?" A perfectly reasonable question, but the cat hisses at me.

I roll my eyes. I reach behind me toward the pantry to get some tuna. I've seen Tobias get cat food from the pantry. But then I stop short. I can't give the cat any food or the police will know someone's been in here. And I haven't bothered to hide fingerprints, with the idea that the police have already checked for relevant prints.

"Crapola."

The cat is now nudging me, none too gently. I'm calling it nudging, but he's actually butting me quite heavily, more like a ram than a cat. (Not that I've encountered a ram, but the clue may be in the name.) I wonder if I can give the cat some food out in the garden. But no, the truth is, I can't give him any food anywhere on the property.

"Can't you hunt? You're an outdoor cat."

The cat yowls again, in a plaintive kind of way that makes me shudder. My shoulders sag. "Fine."

There's only one thing to be done. I have to take the damn thing back with me to mine. As soon as this unwelcome thought hits home, I grab him – why put off doing something unpleasant once you've decided to do it? That's always been my motto.

At least I try to grab him.

An ungainly tussle ensues where I'm trying to hold on to the crazy animal and he's clawing the air, my face, my arms and my hair with everything he has. The cat has the strength of a sumo wrestler. His arse is thwacking about side to side, he's yowling his head off, he's spitting and hissing and trying to claw my eyes out. I'm screaming.

Still, despite the battle, every time The Marquis escapes me, I notice that he doesn't actually shoot out of the cat flap. It occurs to me that the cat may be lonely now that Tobias is gone. And he probably misses his £150 a pop cat food. The neighbourhood rats don't compare. He hisses at me again.

"You know if you want a friend, that's not the right approach. Believe me, I have some experience with that kind of thing." I cross my arms over my chest and look sternly at him.

Finally, it occurs to me to look for a cat carrier. It's right there, in the pantry.

Stuffing the cat into it turns out to be a mission though. I chase him up and down the kitchen – having had the presence of mind to close both the door out to the hallway and the cat flap before attempting it. But it still takes a good thirty-odd minutes to chase the damn thing down. Apparently even a cat as big as The Marquis can squeeze himself under the oven, the dresser, the dishwasher, and also, he can climb into the washer *and* the dryer. I find myself grabbing his tail a few times, I get my hands around his tummy once, but each time there's a yowling and hissing and scratching, a mad scrabble, a crazy dash for some other cover.

I don't know why I persist for as long as I do, I really don't. Maybe I like a challenge. That's the only explanation. Finally, I get him inside the box. Actually, I stuff him inside, head first, then body, then his enormous arse. I barely have the time to get my hand out and shut the door before he's turned himself around and is trying to take all the skin off my hand.

I march out the front door, feeling battle weary and full of rage. I put the carrier down for a second so I can re-affix the yellow tape with glue that I'd brought along with me for this express purpose. Maybe the police use special glue, but I tape it exactly the way it was before and hope that it occurs to no one to do a random sniffing check on the yellow tape.

Chapter Six

It's nearly nine by the time I get back home. I feed the cat, let him out the back door, yelling after him that I'm not going to fetch him from Tobias's again, so he can forget about going back there. I leave the kitchen window open so I don't have to let him back in in the middle of the night. I yell at him again to let him know I've done this. Mid-yell, there's a knock at my door. I glance at the wall clock. It's past nine. Who the hell could possibly be at my door?

I march to it and pull it open. It's Shona Klues.

"The tiramisu came from you," she says without preamble.

My heart starts thudding, but I cross my arms. "And?"

She glares at me. "Come out for a drink with me."

"Are you crazy? Are you asking me out?"

She rolls her eyes. "Will you quit the idea that everyone vaguely brown is in love with you? And anyway, even if I were in love with you, I'm on duty. And you're now one of the top two suspects."

The other being Craig.

"What's my motive?" I say, sticking to my ground.

She looks heavenward as if she is going to pull a random motive out of there. "Your ex inherits all the money. You helped him along. Hoping he'll come back to you."

"If I wanted him."

"Rumour has it he broke up with you. Not the other way around."

"Sometimes you have to do stuff so it isn't done to you." I frown. The words had sounded more graceful coming from Tobias. "Or something along those lines," I say with dignity.

A scuffle in the wilderness of Auntie Meera's front garden – well, my front garden – is followed by a young man falling at our feet. I look at the heap in mild surprise. The man straightens and shakes himself.

"Shirley," Shona says in a bored voice. "What *is* the matter with you? Can't you walk without falling all over your long nose?"

"Shirley?" I enquire.

"I'm Sherlock Lighthouse, detective," the young man says. He's really quite good looking, in a dainty kind of way. He's wearing a sharp white buttondown, nicely fitted on his lanky frame, a pair of navy cords, and of all things, a gold silk cravat. His hair is wavy and falls gently around his face. He has soft ruby lips, and a dimple or two. And the man isn't even smiling. "I'm Shona's partner."

"Assistant," Shona says.

"Princess."

Whoops, I didn't mean to say that.

To my surprise, the man – Sherlock, really? – suddenly goes carrot red.

Just because I pointed out that he looks like a princess?

Shona is rolling her eyes. "Clearly not just the brown ones."

I have no way to interpret this cryptic comment. Sherlock is now looking heavenward, in fact, anywhere but at me. I shake my head, unable to interpret this either. I happen to look down, then yelp and quickly zip up my hoodie. The cat has clawed off half my top, I now realise, and one bra cup is blaring through wide and clear. And the bra being lacy and black (with little roses embroidered on the bottom halves of the cups, if anyone's interested), my nipple is clearly visible as well. Cripes. No wonder Sherlock is mopping his brow and having an aneurysm.

"Anyway," I say as loftily as I can and apropos nothing, once I've done what I can to my shredded clothing, "I have things to do."

"Here it is," Sherlock says, handing Shona a piece of paper, and looking apologetically at me at the same time. To my astonishment, he mouths *sorry* to me. In his defence, he actually looks sorry. But what about?

Shona waves the paper in my face. "Search warrant."

I look aghast at the piece of paper. "Search warrant?"

"And we have to take all your baking equipment."

I stare at her, open-mouthed. The woman is a genius, asking me out to the pub, lulling me into a false sense of security before launching the bombshell.

"No way." I cross my arms again, though my heart is galloping now and I'm starting to feel sick. "That's my livelihood. You're not taking my baking equipment. You can't even look at it."

"No can do. Apologies," says Shona, the she-devil, without a hint of apology or contrition in her voice or her face.

Sherlock is still looking sadly at me. "We'll be careful with it. And you'll get it back." He winces. "Almost exactly in the same condition."

I purse my lips. "No way. That's how I earn my living."

I hate this about people. That they think I bake because I feel like it. Like it's what I do as my hobby until I get a real job in a real office, filing tons of shit. They say things like, *Oh, how lovely that you get the time to bake. I wish I had the time to bake, but my high pressure finance job/seven kids/boot camp Pilates/running for dementia doesn't leave me any time for baking.* Some of them say, *Oh doesn't it make you want to eat cake all the time?* Well, all I have to say to that is, first of all, doesn't everyone want to eat cake all the time? And second, do you ask a colonically-trained doctor if they want to take a crap all the time? *No!*

"Sorry," Shona says, twirling her hair, not looking at all sorry. "But orders're orders. Truth is, between you and me, I'd leave your stuff here, because you'd have cleaned it all by now anyways, but people miss things, and it wouldn't stand up in court if I said I let a pretty face get off easier than an ugly one."

I stand there, feeling sick. There are damp spots in my armpits. Even though I know it already—I know it very clearly—I'm not going to be able to talk them out of this one. They'll arrest me for obstructing justice if I don't comply. But the thought of losing my baking gear – basically, the only thing that lets me hang on to a bit of my sanity – is making me sweat. I feel the sweat running down my back. My mouth is dry. And there's a pain in my left shoulder. All my baking equipment that I've collected lovingly over the years. All of it. Everything my life and my sanity depend on.

It takes two hours.

The two of them, with the help of police officers that pull up in a car, clear all my stuff, bag it and put it in their car. It's unbearable. I hop from foot to foot, wishing they'd get on with it, do it faster. I can't bear it, I can't bear to see their hands on my stuff. Already, it doesn't feel like my stuff anymore. It feels filthy, it feels like it can no longer do what it's meant to do. It feels like no amount of scrubbing will ever put it right. They take everything, pans, baking trays, spatulas, squirters, everything goes, and it's like they're cutting off my body parts and taking them with them one by one. I don't even know what feels worse, the thought of them taking all of it, or their hands on them. Even though they have gloves on, I can't bear it. The way they dump everything into their bags, the way they don't even stop to look at it. Everything I always clean twice. All of it.

At the end of the two hours, my chest is hurting, and I'm screwing my eyes shut just so I can carry on breathing. If they had cut off my fingers one by one and bagged them up, I'd hardly feel worse.

"Alright?" Shona asks, eyeing me.

I take two long breaths before I answer. I grip my left shoulder. "Fine," I manage to choke out.

"We'll get it back to you. Hang tight."

And she's gone. And so are the rest of them.

When they're gone, my kitchen emptied out, I feel empty too. I feel drained, yet I have so much excess energy I know I'm going to explode. I sit on the floor in the corner of the kitchen, trembling, the sleeves of my gnarly cardigan pulled up to the tips of my fingers, my hands on my mouth. I can't bear it, I can't bear it. I have to do something about it.

And there's only one thing I can think of to do.

I stand up. I'm still shaking, I can see it in my hands, and feel it in my body. I want to howl, scream, throw things, but it won't help. Not really. There's a chance one thing will help, even though it'll be excruciatingly temporary. Still, it's the only thing I can think of to do. I drag out two chocolate rum balls with bloody teeth embedded in them, pop them in some Tupperware, and head out.

Chapter Seven

I knock at the door, and even though it's past eleven at night, it opens pretty quickly. There he is. He looks just as clean as he did earlier on, though maybe slightly scruffy. He's wearing a grey hoodie now, over his white t-shirt and trousers. His feet are bare and I can't help staring at them. He looks surprised for a moment, then he smiles, and I see the tightness in his shoulders relax.

"I was at a tricky bit," he says, miming typing with his fingers. "So you're saving me from myself."

I mutely hand him the box I'm carrying. He lets me in. We're in a longish kitchen, warm-looking, unopened moving boxes around the room, but pots and pans hanging up on hooks, a rustic dining table, a nice kitchen range. I hop from foot to foot.

He instantly opens the box, pulls out a rum ball and takes a bite. I actually see his face light up. "Jesus, did you bake this?"

I nod tightly.

"I'll put the kettle on, shall I?"

I'm still fiddling with my hands. My shoulder is aching because I'm trying desperately not to twitch. I keep twitching anyway. If I manage to stop my shoulder, it's usually my face. My cheek is already hurting. I can't get the image of the police officers fingering all my stuff out of my head.

"Can we just go to bed?" I manage to choke out.

I see his face. One moment, he's all smiling and crinkly, asking me about the kettle, but then my question seems to drain his face of all expression. In fact, it would be safe to say that his face freezes. Just for a second, I have a thought I've never had before. I don't know why, but looking at his eyes, the way he's looking into mine, with that direct stare of his, interested, curious and warm all at the same time, I hope for a fleeting second that he'll say no. That he'll turn me down.

I see his chest rise and fall. He's not saying anything at all now. And I'm starting to feel fidgety and desperate. I see his eyes fall to my hands where I'm working at the sleeves of my gnarly cardigan. He looks up at my face again.

"How about coffee?" he asks, his voice easy.

"It's a bit late for coffee. I won't get any sleep. How about bed?" I stick to my guns.

"Chamomile tea?"

"I hate chamomile tea." It would be more accurate to say that I'm indifferent to camomile tea, or at least I used to be, but there had been a sharp smell of it in Auntie Meera's kitchen that afternoon when I had finally made my way to her house, that day when she had been killed, and since then I haven't been able to stomach the stuff.

"Earl Grey?"

"Look, you asked me around. I'm here. So." I look desperately at him.

"I asked you around for coffee." He's losing the wariness, or whatever it was that had stopped him in his tracks when I asked him about bed. His voice also doesn't sound carefully neutral anymore. In fact, he's fast recovering his equilibrium and going back to being smiley and crinkly.

"But you meant sex."

"I just meant coffee."

I purse my mouth. "Are you saying you don't want to have sex with me?"

He blinks. "No, I'm not saying that," he says slowly. "But I'd like to get to know you first. If that's allowed."

I growl. "Why do men always do that!"

To my surprise, he grins. "My apologies, on behalf of all men. Rooibos?"

I give in. "Fine," I say bitterly. "Later, when I've gone back home, and you're all alone in your cottage, I hope it makes you feel better that you gave me some *rooibos* tea."

He's still grinning. He's walking about his kitchen now, turning the kettle on, throwing teabags in a teapot, pouring hot water, looking painfully sexy in his bare feet. He has two mugs in his hands now. He smiles at me, inclines his head toward the inside kitchen door and says, "Come on."

Not knowing what else to do with myself, I follow him. We walk through a cold stone hallway and turn right into a living room. Like the kitchen, it has a half-unpacked look, but also like the kitchen, it looks warm.

"Sorry, I've only just managed to unpack my office."

"What do you write again?" I ask, taking my rooibos from him, though it's by far not what I need right now and it's not going to help.

"Mysteries for middle grade-ish. Though I'm hurt that you haven't googled me. You've had nearly twelve hours."

My hands are still shaky, and I'm scared I'm going to spill the tea, so I put it down on the coffee table. I sit down on the edge of a sofa, clutching my hands, my foot tapping unbearably fast. He places his cup of tea somewhere too and walks over to me. He pulls up a chair and sits across from me.

"What's happened?"

I cluck. Twice. Then I wince and look up at him. But he doesn't look put out or disgusted. He also doesn't make a joke or a sympathetic sound. And he doesn't turn his face away.

"They've taken all my baking stuff. And I have so much to do tomorrow!" I place my palms on my burning cheeks.

He's frowning. "The police? Why? You're surely not a suspect?"

"It was my tiramisu that had the poison in it."

He raises his brows. "That is a predicament."

"I didn't do it."

"Oh, I didn't think for a moment that you had."

I frown. "Why? You barely know me."

"No, but I like you. And I have flawless instincts."

This makes me frown some more.

"What do you need?"

"Sex?" He's already said no, and I really should have slunk out by now, tail between my legs. But one can't help trying, after all.

"Besides sex," he says calmly. "Baking-wise."

I sigh long and deep. "I need some basic stuff at least." I recite a list. "Why, do you have professional quality baking gear hidden away somewhere?"

"No," he says absently. He looks at his phone. "It's a bit late though. Don't know. It could be worth a try." He seems to be talking to himself now. Murmuring, really. "You need it for tomorrow?"

"I have jobs due tomorrow. I'll go out in the morning and try and get some things, I guess." I sound as bleak as I feel. The thought of having to go shopping for equipment is depressing. It'll take hours and hours and I'll never get everything I need. And the anxiety of losing all my stuff is still gnawing at my insides.

He's nodding thoughtfully now. "Okay, well, she can always ignore me." He starts dialling. "Felicity?" I hear him say, when someone at the other end picks up. "Sorry, shit, did I wake you?" He makes a face at me. "Look, can I take you up on that offer?" Some words at the other end. "Yeah, you see that's the thing. I'd need a shitload of stuff by tomorrow morning. That's the deal. I'm afraid that's the only way I can do it. What do you think?" Some more words. Some more persuasive gentle talking from Branwell. Then words at the other end again. He hangs up. "Done."

"What's done?" I ask, understandably confused.

"Harrods want me to do some product placement for them. You

know, set a scene in the store, have kids running about the place trying to solve a mystery, that kind of thing. A bit like *Peter Rabbit*."

I look and feel even more confused now. *Peter Rabbit?*

"Not a fan? James Corden? No? *Lip balm, it's lip balm!* No? Okay, it's a funny film. But no matter. The point is, if you'll tell me a list of stuff now, I'll text it to Felicity, who does PR for them, and she'll have it delivered to you tomorrow morning first thing."

I stare at him. I'm too stunned by what I think he's saying to probe all the truly demented lip balm stuff. I mean, what was that about? "Harrods?"

He screws up his nose. "Too pink peppercorn and vanilla?" He grimaces. "Too Harry and Meghan and the gospel choir? Too Miss Marple?"

"*Harrods*!"

"So, yes or no?"

"Are you kidding! *Yes!*"

To my utter horror, when the list is sent off to "Felicity," I burst into tears. The anxiety of the day, the niggling thing at the back of my mind that I can't put my finger on, the thoughts of Auntie Meera and now Tobias, the two hours spent watching the police touch my things and empty my kitchen all come pouring out. The writer is sitting next to me on the sofa now, a warm hand on my back. He's not shushing me, and not making jokes. He's also still there, which surprises me. I don't know how long I cry for. And it's not pretty. There's a lot of sputtering and snorting. But when I finally stop, I shrug off his hand and abruptly stand up.

"I'll leave you to get on with your work now." Even to me, my voice sounds stilted. And I'm still wiping my nose on the back of my hand. After all I've shown him of myself today, I can basically never see him again.

He doesn't stand up. "Or you could tell me what's bothering you about Tobias Yards's murder," he says.

Chapter Eight

"Why are we looking at sex toys?"

I cluck my tongue. "Look at them carefully. You're not paying attention."

I'm sitting down again. And holding out my phone to him, showing him the picture I took of Tobias's bedside drawer. Instead of taking the phone, he's leaning closer, looking at it when it's still in my hand. It's annoying, because he smells good, sort of clean and showery and stupidly male. And his neck is really clean-looking too, and strong like his arms. All too depressing.

He looks up at me and shrugs.

I sigh. I point to the objects in the image on my phone. "Look at this one. It's covered in the finest quality silk, this one is leather, this glass one is very expensive, I googled it. Almost everything there is really expensive, some of it over three hundred pounds."

He raises his eyebrows, a hand on his jaw now, his elbow resting on his leg. "Who knew."

"Yes, except look at this one." I point out the cheap zebra-print plastic vibrator. "That can't be more than a tenner."

He shrugs. "So?"

I make an impatient noise. "Tobias ate caviar almost on a daily basis. He handpicked his Champagne from grower estates in southern France that cut it with honeysuckle and hazelnuts and cherries, and he drank it with Benedictine. His hand lotions were tailor made for him with saffron – do you know how expensive that stuff is? – more than gold. Harrods looks like a corner shop compared to Tobias's bathroom cupboard."

"So, he was rich, after all."

I frown a question at him.

"Your ex-boyfriend does come into a neat little packet," he expands patiently.

"Hmm. Maybe. I have no idea if Tobias was rich or not. It's more that he didn't skimp on things. I just can't see him buying this plastic crap." I point to the picture of the dildo again.

"So, someone put it there. A girlfriend, boyfriend?"

"I'd have guessed boyfriend. Though Tobias was really private about basically everything, so I have no evidence either way. And I think you're right. Someone else put it there, someone he was intimate with. But who was he seeing? No one that Craig knew about. I didn't hear of or see anyone." I stare absently at the picture of the erotic literature. Like before, it niggles at the back of my mind, but I have no idea why. I keep reading the names of the volumes, but nothing springs to mind. What am I missing?

"So, you're bent on proving your ex-boyfriend innocent."

"Hmm?" I say absently.

"Still have feelings for him?"

I look at Branwell. He leans back, hands in his pockets again, back resting on the back of the sofa, his eyes on mine. Does the man not blink? It's hard to look away when people don't blink.

I frown. "I don't do feelings."

"You must love someone," he persists. Still the casual tone, but his eyes aren't casual.

I wince.

Yes, yes, I did. I loved my parents at one time, a long time ago, so long ago that I can't remember what it felt like. The feeling no longer has a shape or a tone, it's turned amorphous over time, it's become a concept called "what parents look like when you still imagine that they love you," it's a place never visited, a place locked away, locked and the key thrown out. A place, I often think, that never existed, except in my dreams.

And I loved Auntie Meera. I loved her since the day she took me in, without a word of complaint, without staring at me like I was strange, without wondering what on earth she was going to do with me, without asking herself how it would cramp her life to have me in it, without wondering what was wrong with me that I was so abrupt and awkward and clumsy and strange. Not one qualm or question swept her face, or even flickered in it, when my parents asked her if she could have me. She took me right away. Yes, I had loved her. With a fierceness that still leaves me shaken sometimes when I smell her herbs in a forgotten corner of her house.

But they all left me.

And with Auntie Meera, I can't convince myself that it wasn't my fault. I had pushed her away in the last weeks and months of her life, ever since our fight. What if I had not left her with any choice but to find a friend, a confidante somewhere else, and that's who had murdered her?

Even with Tobias, though, something is bothering me. Something about the loneliness of his sex toy drawer. No, it's not just lonely people who have sex toys, but there's something about the stark contrast between that drawer and his home, his day-to-day life that seemed empty of other people. And that strange picture of the faceless people with their genitals hanging out.

"So, do you or don't you?" Branwell Beam's voice cuts into my thoughts.

"What, love people? I don't." I stand up again. "Especially not people I sleep with. That would be too complicated."

He stands up too. "Interesting," he says slowly.

I roll my eyes. "Oh, please, don't start. I can see it in your eyes. You're getting that look. The look that says, *this woman is a challenge, ooh*! But I'm not a challenge, and I don't play games. I'm telling you exactly how it is, there's no hidden agenda. So, if you're the kind of guy that likes mysterious women—"

He leans forward and shuts me up quite effectively.

Damn it.

His lips are – I don't know what exactly, because I'm having trouble thinking. Gentle but firm at the same time? Exploring but not pushing? Warm? Fitting like a jigsaw piece with mine? And the damn shoulders! Why are my hands on his shoulders anyway?

Now I'm having trouble breathing, not just thinking. Just for a second, I kiss him back, then I push him away. "I have to go."

He nods slowly, his face still close to mine. "Okay. See you tomorrow?"

I search his eyes for a moment. "Why would I?"

To my annoyance, he grins.

Chapter Nine

The next day, after a Harrods van delivers what seems to be their entire stock of kitchenware— probably thousands of pounds worth of stuff—I sit down on a bar stool and weep. This stuff is so beautiful, it's unbearable. It's so glorious and shiny and clean, I want to write sonnets to it. It's so intensely and beautifully *clean.* It can't replace the things I've lovingly picked, hunted for, found bargains for, discovered like treasure in flea markets in Provence over the years, it never can do that. But the truth is, I don't know if I desperately want my stuff back, or if it's so badly tarnished now that I can't bear to see it again. It would be like trying to wear underwear that some weirdo has been sniffing through. It may just not be doable.

Not that I have the option to use my old stuff again. I have no clue where it is. Stored in dank cupboards where blood spattered weapons have hidden before, handled, smeared, thrown about in the same way as cotton buds soaked with DNA and underwear stiff with semen. There's no sign of Shona Klues, or Shirley or any of their minions this morning, so I have no one I can ask, even if I wanted to. There's not even a text message saying, *Hey, your stuff arrived safely, we'll get it back to you soon xxx.* Callous, I call it, callous.

But looking at the Harrods stuff, I can almost forget about that. I need to thank the writer, I really do, and once I can erase the feel of his lips on mine from my memory, I will thank him. He's annoying and presumptuous. And all that casual self-assurance is...absurd. There's no other word for it. I want to put Nutella on it and eat it, but still, it's just plain silly. I feel a dreadful, truly horrible urge to go to his place and hop about like a starling twittering nonsense or have another good old cry about everything that I can't stand about myself, while somehow trying not to sound needy. I want of all things to crash and crumble against his stupid self-assurance. But once I start baking, I'll be fine. I will.

I spend time lovingly unpacking the glorious goods. The Marquis, instead of ignoring me completely or running back to Tobias's, is warily sniffing around the kitchen. I give him some tuna, and approach a cautious hand to scratch him under his chin – at which he yowls in alarm. I withdraw my hand, stand watching him lap up his meal, then turn toward my equipment again. I spend some hours baking. I do what I do best. I lose myself in pouring and mixing, sifting and piping, measuring, soaking, heating and cooling. I disappear into the colors and textures and smells and lose all sense of time, soaking in the familiarity of something I've done to relax, to escape from the world since I was in my early teens, when Auntie Meera had cleared a space for me in our old kitchen. She never said no, no matter what crazy machines I asked for, what outlandish ingredients I wanted to practice my fledgling skills with, and what kind of mess I made. She knew baking was a lifeline to me. It wasn't a hobby, it wasn't a thing I did now and again for fun. I needed it, like people need water. It was where I felt at home, a quiet corner of my mind where I could run from the expressions on people's faces when they looked at me or laughed at me, how loud their voices were, how every time they sneered, even when it wasn't at me, I felt a fissure running like fire across my heart. And I remembered all of it, the things people said, the way they looked, the way they giggled behind their hands, sometimes when it was at me, and even when it wasn't at me but at someone else. It was like I stored these memories, like they etched themselves on my brain and emerged fully intact and even amplified any time I was at my lowest. But in baking, I could escape all that. I could be quiet and still and myself and no one cared what I did or said, I had to answer to no one and no one could turn away from me.

Finally, finally, after a few hours of working at my orders, I start to feel a little calmer.

What would be ideal – my ideal scenario right now – would be to erase everything that happened the day before and carry on with my life. Tobias's death, everything to do with his death, Shona Klues and her two main suspects, the carting away of my precious stuff, all of it, I just want it erased. As for Branwell and his eyes and kisses, those don't need to be erased, because they're not bothering me. Don't think it for a second. I am so not bothered by that.

So all is good with the world.

But even after all the baking, all the cleaning, all the sweeping, it turns out that I can't seem to get Tobias completely out of my mind.

It's not just that I liked him and the man was brutally murdered by some sort of neat freak cheap-sex-toy maniac who didn't leave a trace – who injected my tiramisu with poison, the bastard, I'm not letting that one go any time soon – it's not only that. It's also that Craig is suspect Number One, and boring as he is, I *know* he couldn't have committed the murder, not if it was committed in the time frame the police think it was committed in. I frown.

Why do they think it was committed in that time frame? I make a mental note to try to find out. After all, how are they so sure? In any case, whatever the time frame, Craig doesn't have the imagination to commit a murder. He really doesn't. He's squeamish about killing spiders and flies, and about hospitals and periods and sanitary pads. I mean, the man blanches if you say the words "PMS acne" and takes off for the pub with nary a backward glance. So, time frame doesn't matter so much. He couldn't have done it, and although I have no special feeling for him, I still don't want him to go to prison for something he didn't do. Plus, the thought of someone as boring and strait-laced as him in prison…he wouldn't survive, not for long. Oh, and there's another thing. I'm his alibi, but I can't admit to it without sounding like a stalker. And so, it *is* kind of my responsibility to get him off (not in the way you're imagining, just to be clear).

After lovingly cleaning my shiny new equipment, I carouse down my street around two in the afternoon. I tiptoe into the writer's driveway and pop a little box of cupcakes and a note on his doorstep. The note says, "Last night was boring, but this morning was divine. I can't thank you enough. Two cupcakes for you. Though, it's only fair to tell you, the last time I left a bloke some dessert on his doorstep, he died. P.S. If the skull-and-bones sticker on the box is broken, don't eat them."

Hearing some stirring inside his house, I beat a hasty retreat. I don't want to see the guy again. I owe him one for Harrods, but no, no, I don't want to see him. In the harsh light of the morning after, I'm only feeling the crushing humiliation of being summarily rejected. He'd batted my advances away like a fly. It's much better if I never see the guy again. It suddenly occurs to me as I exit his driveway, maybe the man has a girlfriend. I stop dead in my tracks. Ugh, no, how could I be so stupid! No, wait no, I steady myself. He did kiss me. My brow knits in a heavy frown. Who does that? I shudder. I dislike the man intensely.

I turn toward Veronica Chives's place. In case you don't like having to work too hard to remember things, she's Tobias's neighbour and the one who found his body. She's Texan, red-haired, and creamy-skinned, and owns the frozen custard place that took Trucklewood by storm a few months ago. Frozen custard, you say, what the hell is frozen custard? Imagine a Mr. Whippy, swirly and soft and cold vanilla icecream, with a beautiful little peak at the top that is just asking to dive into your mouth. Now imagine vanilla custard in its place, frozen and whipped to exactly that consistency. My god, the woman is a genius.

I cruise past Tobias's house – there's a busy buzz of police activity around the place. I keep walking at a smart pace without a second glance at my new best friend, the yellow tape, and knock at Veronica's door.

She opens it with a wide smile, and her arms are wide open too. "Hi y'all!" she cries, beaming at me, placing her hands on her hips. "What a crazy na-ice surprise this is, cherub! I had no idea who was standing there, right at my very doorstep this afternoon, now did I? *Did I!* Come on in. Bring your gorgeous little tush into my little slice of paradise this side of the Mississippi! Would you like some frozen custard? Say you will, hon, because you'll break my little Texan heart if you say no."

She's a Barbie-shaped whirlwind. Who says Barbie wouldn't be able to stand on her feet? Veronica is about seven-foot tall, her legs accounting for most of it, she's wearing the spikiest six-inch heels I've ever seen in my life, a pair of jeans that may as well have been spray-painted on, a red-check rancher's shirt, and yet, she's practically skipping about her enormous kitchen. And I'm sitting at a dainty little dining table, complete with gingham napkins and smiling freesias in vases, and licking frozen custard like there's no tomorrow, before I've had the chance to say *reefer*.

"Now, what can I do for y'all?" Veronica says, sitting across from me, crossing her legs in a way that must be sending several inches of denim up her vagina.

I turn my tongue round and round the frozen custard in orgasmic ecstasy. Veronica eyes me appreciatively, jabbers on the entire time I'm eating, about her beagles (she has five), her shop on the high street, her customers, her creamy custard, and my tongue. She's talking non-stop, a mile-a-minute, not showing any signs of pausing for breath. When I'm done with the frozen custard, I look at her, bemused, my head reeling for some time before I bring my palm crashing on to her dining table.

She stops in her tracks and looks at me wide-eyed.

"Sorry," I say, though I'm not. "I couldn't think of any other way of stopping you."

She throws her head back and laughs. "Oh, honey, my ex used

to say the exact same thing! He used to say a train couldn't stop me when I still had more to say – and I can tell you, I always have more to say. I don't know why he left me, I really don't, I'm a hurricane in bed!"

"That's lovely," I say, frowning heavily at her. "I'd like to know how you came upon Tobias Yards's body the other day."

If she's surprised by the directness of my approach, she doesn't show it. "I like a straight talking girl, I do. I say where're your nipples pointing, girl? Down? No. Dithering like a virgin on her wedding night? No. They're pointing straight ahead and so should you! Folks around here are a bit squeamish about women who say it like it is, but I say, the more direct the better."

My eyebrows rise. I can't help it. No one has this sort of reaction to me, ever. She actually sounds like she likes the things I say. I shake my head to clear it. It's like a vision, like a fog clearing. I mean, people hate me, dislike me, are indifferent to me, some even enviously admire that I don't drop my pants at the first hint of a smile from someone. But Veronica sounds like she genuinely likes it.

It instantly makes me wonder what's wrong with her.

She uses her fingers to comb her red locks, even though they're already glossy and there isn't the hint of a tangle or a scruffle in their fiery depths. "I used to drop by and check on Tobias now and again, you know, Arya. He wasn't the friendliest man, I'd say, but a woman can't help trying." She winks at me.

"Wasn't he gay?"

She smiles brightly, showing perfectly aligned teeth, white as chalk. "I like a challenge, don't you?"

I shrug. "Not really. I like it when you get exactly what you want exactly when you want it."

She laughs like this is the funniest thing she's ever heard, and slaps her thigh so hard I expect to see spontaneous flames burst from the denim. "I like a girl who knows her mind. Maybe us girls can get together one time, do each other's toenails." She winks again, which makes me wonder if she means doing each other's toenails as a euphemism. I look down at my fingernails. Completely plain, and my toenails are the same. I haven't seen the top of a pedicurist's head more than once in my life, and that one time was when my friend Tallulah from school (primary and secondary) had been given a present for her thirteenth birthday to go to a nail parlour with a friend.

"I've been trying to get Tarina to join me, you know? We could make it a gorgeous threesome." She winks again.

Tarina, Veronica and me giggling and doing each other's toenails.

Just for a whisper of a second, I lose myself in the vision. I wonder what it would be like to have that kind of normal friendship. Where I wouldn't twitch at the wrong time and smear the nail polish on someone's hand, or more likely, overturn it on Veronica's leopard-print velvet throws, where I wouldn't blurt out something about the two women that would make them look pityingly at me, or worse, hate me forever. Where I'd pretend that I had crushes to talk about, and gossip to add to the pot. Even that I had friends who could supply that gossip in the first place. Where I could be a completely different person.

I shake my head quickly to dispel the vision. I don't do manicures or girly nights in. The thought fills me with dread and horror. The tiny smidgen of longing in there, along with the dread and horror, leaves me wanting to get out of here as quick as my feet can carry me.

"Come on now, Veronica. Back to Tobias." I try to steer her back to the subject at hand. A car with no gas would be easier to push, I can't help thinking.

She waves a hand, dips a surgically manicured finger into some frozen custard and licks it off thoroughly. "I liked to drop by now and again and look him up. He was a lonely man."

My chest tightens at the words. Not that I'm surprised to hear them. Or at least, the fact that someone as gregarious as Veronica should utter them surprises me, but the words themselves only confirm what I had always sensed about Tobias. What had drawn me to Tobias in the first place.

He was a lonely man. People reject other people when they seem lonely, just in case it's infectious, in case it means that when someone is alone, there must be something wrong with them. As if there's some sort of badge to be won just because you're better at being around other people than you are at being with yourself, and you have to try your damndest to be seen to be fun and friendly, not struggling alone with your worst demons.

Don't we like to say, *I did this with my friend, my friends came over, it was my friend's party, I baked a cake for my friend's birthday,* don't we say things like that just so the person we're talking to will want to be our friend too, so that they'll feel reassured that we're normal, so that they won't see into the worst of us, they won't find a peephole into all those times we sit alone, when no one calls, no one responds when we reach out, when there's no one to do things with, and the only one we're confronted with is the worst, most scared side of ourselves? Isn't that what we do?

I like lonely people, though, people like Tobias, who'd rather spend time in their own company than be with people who don't get them, who would rather be lonely than play the game. I didn't see Tobias's aloneness as a disease. I liked him for it. I liked that he never tried to hide it.

I frown. "He liked being by himself." I don't know why I say it. Veronica seems like she liked him. I don't need to defend him to her, and actually, given that he's dead, I don't need to defend him at all.

"Aw shucks, honey, no one likes to be by themselves all the time. I can't stand my own company for more than ten minutes at a time. Give me an evening by myself and I'm climbing the walls!" She laughs again. "Anyway, if it weren't for his little secret—"

She stops abruptly. Her eyes blink rapidly a couple of times, and she sits there for a second, seemingly frozen, her palms spread on her table. Then she uncrosses and crosses her legs again, casually plunges a finger into the frozen custard and licks it, not looking at me.

"What little secret?" I demand.

She looks innocently at me. "Oh, just that he was gay."

I narrow my eyes. "That's not what you were going to say. It wasn't a secret that he was gay. He just didn't make a big deal out of it, one way or another."

She waves a hand again. "Oh, well then. There you go."

She's quiet now, actually quiet. For the first time since I've walked into her house. In fact, I've literally never seen her quiet. She only stops talking if someone ruthlessly interrupts her flow, and sometimes not even then.

"What little secret?" I repeat.

She turns her wide eyes toward me again, green as a cat's. "Oh sweetie, that's all I meant. I didn't know that other people knew he was gay, now did I? I was brought up a good little puritan, and asked to keep my lips sealed and my legs crossed. What do I know about the world? Anyway, what else would you like to know?"

She might seem scatty and like her head is full of makeover secrets, but Veronica is a successful businesswoman. The woman's sharper than a stainless steel dagger. I admit defeat – for now – because there's no point pushing it. She's not going to tell me Tobias's little secret, as she calls it. Not right now. Not until I can squeeze it out of her. I change tack.

"Can you tell me about when you found Tobias's body?"

She leans forward. "Oh, it was dreadful! Truly dreadful. Like you wouldn't believe. It was such a crazy evening. So, you see, the thing is, I can see his driveway from my window, and I saw his cleaner leave around nine or so? Not that I was looking or anything, but I can't help seeing what goes on in his place when mine is almost on top of his, now can I? I saw his cleaner leave. And around ten it must have been when I thought I'd hop on over to his and see how he was doing." She leans forward again. "Between us girls, I get horny mid-month."

I lean back in my chair. "Veronica," I say warily, holding my hands up. "I don't need to know – and actually, I don't want to know..."

She winks at me. "He didn't answer my knock, and the door opened when I pushed it. So I walked in, just to make sure he was alright. He did have a heart condition, and it's only neighbourly to check on your neighbours, that's what my mama always taught me. As she used to say, what's the point making enchiladas, honey, if you're going to eat them all by your lonesome."

"What did you see when you opened the door?"

"Well, this was the thing. Nothing! There was nothing, and I called a few times, but no one answered, so I got a little worried, I have to tell you. I am a natural worrier, though you can't tell to look at me. And I worried about that poor little man, all by his lonesome in his big old house, wanting company but not able to reach out and get it. I mean, so what if he was gay? Maybe he was bi. And there he was, lying on the floor of his kitchen, not a hair out of place, looking as immaculate as ever – I like a man that cares about his appearance, don't you? – but he was dead. I knew it right away, because he was still as a rock, but his eyes were wide open, you know, like in the movies?" She goes rigid for a second, her eyes wide open and unblinking, her hands crossed, to drive home her point.

"There were no signs of a struggle? Nothing unusual?"

"Not at all. There were some used glasses on the table, there was your platter with the tiramisu – I have to tell you, Arya, you make the most gorgeous cakes – but no, there was nothing. I was so sure he died of natural causes, I didn't think twice about it. I didn't question it, not for a second. I just dialled 911. Or whatever it is over here – 999. You could have pushed me over with a feather when I heard those paramedics talking to each other, saying he was poisoned, and then trying to pump his stomach. It was horrible. I've never seen anything so horrible, Arya. And I've stood behind a horse as it foaled, you know?"

"Uh, that's great." I shake my head to clear the image. "So, the cleaner could have done it?"

I know Tobias's cleaner. Her name is Cath and she's a wonder woman. Tobias had high standards, but he was all praise for her, and never gave anyone her phone number in case she was offered work and then couldn't do for him anymore. I've met her once or twice – neither time did Tobias leave us alone for half a second, that's how much he didn't want her poached. Cath had no reason to kill Tobias, and I can't imagine why she would have gone to all the trouble of lacing my tiramisu with poison. But surely the police suspect her, if she was the last person to see him alive?

Veronica shrugs. "I saw him alive, in his kitchen – I can see his window from mine – after she left."

"She could have injected the poison before she left."

"She has no motive, honey. Nothing they know of anyway. I mean, why would she have done such a thing?"

"Hmm." I tap my fingers on Veronica's dining table. "Did you see anything suspicious after Cath left? Anyone else coming to visit Tobias, anything like that?"

"Oh, well, that's the thing, honey, I went off to take a nice, hot shower after Cath left. And it was a long one too, I had to shave my legs, shampoo my hair. All kinds of boring old girly things."

I shudder at the thought of Veronica readying herself up before she went over to Tobias's. "I really don't want to know," I say firmly. I stand. "Look, do you mind? If you think of anything else, would you call me?"

"Sure, honey, of course I will. Now, don't be a stranger. If you want some frozen custard, you know where to find mama! Now come and give me some sugar!"

I stare at her, thinking that she's still talking about her custard. But she's holding out her arms to me. I think she wants me to give her a hug.

I cross my arms. "I don't do hugs."

A peel of tinkling laughter. She slaps her thigh again. Sparks, I tell you, sparks. "Oh, and I don't do it doggie-style!" she cries.

She's still laughing when I reach the end of her driveway.

Chapter Ten

I spend the rest of the afternoon baking a cake that looks like a stomach puking bile. It's tricky to get the bile the right color without using artificial dyes. Spinach will do it, but spinach in a cake is not an easy sell. I play with kiwis and avocados for a bit. When I head out for my run, on my doorstep is an envelope. It says, "Those are the best goddamn pineapple cupcakes I've ever eaten. P.S. I'm still alive."

I look at the note crossly. I was at home when it was delivered, since it wasn't on my doorstep when I came in earlier. I get why I'm avoiding *him*, but I don't get why *he's* avoiding *me*. And they were my pineapple cupcakes too! They're a special recipe, the way people do them in Indian bakeries, with actual pineapple in them, and lovingly layered lightly sweetened cream. I grind my teeth.

Annoyingly, my treacherous brain goes over everything I might have done to make him go off me. Not that he was on me in the first place, but if he was a little bit, now he's clearly not, since he can only leave notes, and not even bother saying thank you in person. I mean, what does it take to knock?

Of course, I could have done any number of things to make him go off me, I usually do:

Cry too much.

I was probably twitchy and nervy and neurotic.

Did I come across as too eager and needy, and also, if I did, what's wrong with that! Why the hell can't he handle it?

Maybe my boobs are too big?

My hands were dry, maybe he noticed. I need hand lotion.

I'm probably not feminine enough. Too direct, that's the problem.

Maybe he didn't like me in the first place and I just imagined it.

Ugh!

I twist my hands to tear the note into bits. Dither in that position for a few seconds, then stuff it through my letterbox instead. I'll deal with it later.

I take a long circuit on my run, trying to sort out my thoughts, scrupulously avoiding any thoughts entitled Branwell Beam. Luckily, at the moment, there's quite a lot to think about.

From everything Veronica Chives said, on the evening that Tobias died, there was no sign of a struggle in his kitchen, just a dead body, nothing more. Nothing that Veronica could tell was out of place, no obvious signs of a burglary. Doesn't that mean that Tobias was killed by someone he knew, someone he let into the house? Doesn't it mean that someone he knew had to have come into his house to put the poison in the tiramisu? I frown. There is one other possibility. That the poison was injected into it – it would have to be in the cake, surely the cream couldn't hold it? – when it was still on Tobias's doorstep where I had left it that morning.

I have to stop doing that. That's stupid. There are all kinds of things that could happen to dessert left on people's doorsteps. All kinds of contamination. From fast growing mould, animals, bird shit, theft, people messing with the cake, all kinds of things.

But wait. If the poison were injected then, then surely Tobias would have noticed that the box wasn't sealed. Wouldn't he have? My mind wanders back to the way I had re-taped the police tape outside Tobias's just the day before. Couldn't someone who was careful do that to one of my stickers? I'm not sure. I have pretty awesome stickers.

I climb a hill for some time, sticks and pebbles crunching under my feet. The trail that curls away into the woods leads up at first, the trees forming a canopy overhead and I follow it. On my right, beyond a fence that ranges all the way up the trail, a couple of muscled horses snort and shift. On the left the field is speckled with cotton-wool sheep and cows staring at my intrusion. Tufts of silverweed and dog's mercury border the trail.

I close my eyes and inhale the scents around me. The hummus underneath the higher tones of thyme, the sting of ragwort, the cushion of mulched leaves soft on the soles of my trainers. I breathe in their smell mingling with the pine and spruce.

I stop for a moment, feeling my breath, my heartbeat, the familiar release around my shoulders and hips as I get further into my run.

If the poison wasn't injected into the cake at Tobias's doorstep – though I can't be sure about this, the seal could be tampered with, or Tobias may not have made too much of it if it had looked like someone had broken it – but say for a moment it wasn't, then it would mean that the poison was injected *after* Tobias took the box in, and then it would have had to be done by someone who was invited in. Wouldn't it? I guess someone could have broken into the house too.

This is confusing. Cath, Tobias's cleaner, was probably the only one who had been invited in. Would Cath have a motive to kill Tobias? Does she inherit anything? It would be like Tobias to remember his cleaner in his will – he was picky about cleaning, obsessive even. What if she were strapped for cash? What if she needed to pay someone off? A debt, a bill, something, and she needed money?

I shake my head. Tobias would have lent her the money. I'm sure of it. Plus, blaming the cleaner is like blaming the butler. It's a bit obvious, and therefore, lame and unlikely.

So, Craig? Could he have done it, after all? Craig had known about the spare key.

I stop short, panting at my sudden halt, digging my fingers into a sudden stitch. The key. The key had moved from its usual place. When I had gone to Tobias's, his spare key had not been in the urn on the right side of his door. It had been in the one on the left. So, could someone who had known about the key have let themselves into the house to tamper with the tiramisu? Surely, the window of opportunity was from the time I delivered the tiramisu – around eleven in the morning that day – to when Veronica found the body? The window wasn't just the one hour when Craig didn't have an alibi.

Still, if Craig inherits all the money – however much it is, I'll need to try to find out – it still makes him the chief suspect. The murder doesn't feel like a random act committed by a burglar; it feels more intentional and planned than that. So, who more likely than a family member?

The trail flattens out. Coming out of the canopy of trees suddenly, I'm at the edge of the woods. The trees start up again in the distance, but here, there's a clear path, cocooned by grassy hills, winding down gently past an unused brick well, and the old sign that advertises the boarding school that stands not far from the woods. I run past the school building. The building is red-brick, Victorian, rambling, with obvious new additions over the decades, all higgledy-piggledy and haphazard. Next to the main building, some outhouses and sheds. I run past them, the building giving me the spooky feeling that it's deserted, even though it's not. The trail curves around the building, then climbs up again, a hill sloping away on one side, the bramble next to me on the other side mated, embroidered with spider webs glistening with drops of dew.

Just past the school building, I bump into someone. A woman. Soft, medium-height, round, with straight, anonymous brown hair, glasses, a fraying hoodie on top of her plain dress. She's taking a walk. I mutter an apology for crashing into her, and she smiles in return. I start running again.

"Arya?"

The one word, uttered in a soft, breathy voice, stops me in my tracks. Instead of turning around and talking to the woman – whose smile I know now, because I know her voice, her way of saying my name with that question mark at the end, even though I haven't heard her say it in such a long time – I stare straight in front of me. Even now, after all these years, I want to keep running, I don't want to turn around. I don't have to. She knows it's me, but I can pretend that she has the wrong person. Surely, I look different enough at twenty-seven than I did at seventeen that I can just about pull it off?

I slowly turn around. "Tallulah."

She smiles, and it's a smile I know. Hesitant, hopeful, reaching out, yet wanting desperately not to get hurt. The look in her eyes, the hesitating eyes, never sure of her place. It stabs me in the heart, that look. Like it had done when I first met her, when she moved to my primary school at age ten.

"You've put the weight back on," I blurt out before I can stop myself. I could stab myself with a poker for the sharp words, words that jumped out of me. I'd do anything to take them back, but there's nothing I can do. I lift my chin and watch her face.

She winces, but then quickly she smiles. That's a familiar look too, the one that's quick to reassure me that she knows I can't help myself, that she's not hurt by the things I say, not really. "I guess it was always going to happen."

"I'm sorry. I shouldn't have said that." My voice sounds tight, through my clenched jaw, even to me. But I can't help it. And my chin is jutting out too, and I can't seem to help that either. Seeing her like this, all of a sudden, out of the blue, is bringing back everything, it's bringing back too much. I pinch the bridge of my nose quickly, as if to stop a nosebleed, but the pain in the center of my forehead doesn't go away.

"But it's true." She tucks her hair behind an ear. "I don't mind really. It's just who I am. I was never meant to be skinny."

"It's overrated." I stare at her, an almost unbearably painful shard of something sticking in my gut. I growl under my breath. What an idiot. After all these years. I thought I'd made my peace with it a long time ago. "What are you doing here?"

"I teach at the boarding school. I recently moved here, actually. Only a couple of months ago."

I raise my eyebrows. "You're a teacher! What do you teach?"

She shrugs. Smiles at me.

"Geography?"

She nods.

"Right." Of course she would. She'd been obsessed with places, the world, cities, countries, rivers, mountain ranges, gorges. She knew all the names, even at age ten, and thirteen, and seventeen. "You always wanted to travel."

She nods. "I have travelled a little, but I can't always afford to. I'm saving up for a trip to Peru over Christmas."

"That's nice." My words are clipped, tight. I make an effort, and it seems to take every ounce of will. "You always wanted to go there."

"It's nice seeing you, Arya. If you're around, maybe we could..."

"I'm busy," I say abruptly.

I don't want to see it, I want to turn away before I can see it, but I'm not quick enough. I should have been quicker. I do turn away from her, but I still see the almost unnoticeable chin wobble, and yet, and yet the attempt at a smile.

Why, why bother to smile when all you want to do is cry? Why, to spare someone else's feeling? I've never understood it.

"Okay, Arya," I hear her say behind me, in her soft voice, trying not to puncture the air around her. Trying to make everything okay. "It was nice to see you."

I don't turn around. I don't nod. I don't do anything. My shoulders tighten, and that's the only response I can give her. Tallulah Sand, at one point my best friend. Until I had broken her heart. Or was it that she had broken mine? I really don't know.

Chapter Eleven

I head back toward home. I keep myself rigidly still so that thoughts of Tallulah, all the old feelings, don't invade me. I don't want to think about her. I don't want to think about what happened. It's not important now. I'm not the person I was ten years ago. She – maybe she isn't either. And yet, and yet the familiar way she speaks, the way she hesitates, the way she tries to protect me from myself. I shake myself. I don't have to think about this. I've spent years, many hours, carving out a life I like. Tallulah is just an old memory.

When I get back to my place, feeling unbearably low, like a lead weight has settled in my tummy, someone is waiting for me. It's Shirley, or rather, Sherlock. I roll my eyes in a resigned way. He really is exquisitely pretty, if you look carefully at him. Skin the color of clotted cream, lips the tone of summer berries. He should be playing Juliet at the Old Vic instead of running about doing Shona's bidding. He looks apologetic again.

"I just wanted to tell you that your stuff is well taken care of."

I look crossly at him. "I suppose you'll want a cupcake?"

He visibly brightens. Then looks concerned. "Actually, maybe I should ask Shona if it's okay."

"Ask her if she'll wipe your bum for you afterwards, won't you?" I cross my arms and raise an eyebrow.

He smiles conspiratorially. "Alright, if you don't tell her, I won't."

I let him into the house and head to the kitchen. I pop the coffee on and am just getting the milk when I hear Shirley say behind me, "Oh, you have a cat!"

I jump, but keep my face firmly turned away from Shirley. "Um, um hmm," I say. Whoops, could Shirley know that The Marquis—who has just jumped in through the kitchen window like he owns the place—is Tobias's cat? Shit.

Completely contrary to how The Marquis treats me—with suspicion and derision, if I had to take my pick of emotional descriptors—the cat is canoodling happily around Shirley's legs. I resist the urge to glare at him. Shirley looks ecstatic. "It looks just like Tobias Yards's cat," he says, nearly making me pour hot coffee all over myself.

"Fancy that!" I manage to squeak out.

I eye Shirley warily, but he's just grinning at the cat.

After settling him down with a cream-rich cappuccino and a red velvet cupcake, I sit across from him and sip my coffee. The cat luckily jumps out the window again. I let out a breath I didn't know I was holding. "So," I say.

Shirley smiles widely. "This is lovely. I don't get to do it every day." He flicks his hair with a careful hand. "If only I were a man of leisure."

"A man of leisure? Your hair took an hour-and-a-half to do this morning."

"An hour-and-forty-five," he says, looking pleased at how close I got. He's sitting on a bar stool, his legs daintily crossed, one arm casually on his knees. He looks like a duchess this morning, in a loose white shirt and a green velvet waistcoat.

I eye him. "Why do the police think that the window of opportunity is just an hour? I delivered the tiramisu at eleven that morning."

He locks his lips with an imaginary key and then takes a deep sip of his frothy cappuccino.

I watch him with hooded eyes. In complete silence. This usually gets people talking.

He eats his cupcake with visible joy. After two bites – I'd have predicted that he'd have cracked at three, but hey ho, that's the magic of the red velvet – he leans forward. "I can't tell you any important details. But I'll tell you what I can."

"So?"

"They don't know. They're still trying to narrow it down."

"Why do they think I could have done it?"

"They don't. But you have the opportunity. The best one of the lot, for obvious reasons."

"But I don't have a motive."

"No, none that we know of as yet."

I tap my fingers on my kitchen counter. "The lack of an alibi is not enough for them to arrest Craig though, is it?"

He shrugs. "There's motive *and* a lack of an alibi. But no, not yet."

"Anything interesting on Tobias's phone or computer?"

He smiles and waves a hand and bats his eyelids a few times. "I can't tell you. You know that, Arya," he says lusciously, and mildly reprovingly.

I cluck in frustration. The boy isn't stupid. In his own way, he's as clever as Shona Klues. He's seemingly telling me stuff, yet nothing I couldn't work out for myself. So much for the power of the red velvet.

He's looking at me now with his doe-like eyes. "Did Tobias have any partners? Boyfriend, girlfriend?"

"None that I knew of."

"Anyone looking for revenge or anything? Did you ever see anyone lurking about, a visitor that seemed out of place? That you thought was behaving oddly?"

I frown. "Nothing that I can think of."

My mind goes back to about six weeks ago, when I had last bumped into Tobias at the Easter fair. Our conversation was brief, but it had left an impression on me. Something about the lightness around his eyes. Something about a smile lurking there. Tobias had liked me, it was true, and I was probably more likely to get a smile from him – even one that was barely there – than most people, but I had caught sight of him before he had seen me. And though I hadn't thought about it then, at least not consciously, he'd had that lightness about him *before* he spied me. He had been standing there in the churchyard where all the Trucklewood fairs take place, in his check pantaloons and waistcoat, surveying the stalls with such an air of a Victorian gentleman that he may as well have raised an eyeglass to his eye.

I think back to it now. I have a knack for going back to a scene and picturing it clearly in my mind, detail by detail. I don't know if it's because I'm good at withdrawing into myself. I've always been good at that—at finding a comfortable home inside my head if the world outside looks daunting, unfamiliar or plain dangerous. At losing myself in visions, and memories if any good ones happen to be lurking about. Smells and colors can especially help recall details of a memory, I find. And there were many smells and sights that day, brought forth by the efforts of various Trucklewood residents who had set up stalls for the day.

Sausages spitting in one stall, where Astrid Gardener, the potter, and her husband Terry, the landscape architect, were cooking.

Bubbles being blown by Mark Close, with various children, his two boys included, jumping and shrieking around him, while his partner Sheshonne Chigozi was brewing espressos. They'd only moved to the area some time before my auntie, soon after they'd had their second baby. They were both musicians.

Willie Arnott, the accountant, who had moved to Trucklewood not many months before I had, he was managing the garden stall. His sister, Maria Arnott, had died just before he had moved, and the local women tended to keep an eye out for him. Or they had their eye on him, I'm not sure which.

There was Mrs. Sharma with her jellies and preserves, talking to him, and Veronica Chives was handing out free samples of frozen custard.

I can see it all now, a view as if from a kaleidoscope, of that morning some weeks ago, a view of what Tobias may have observed from his vantage point where he stood under an awning, while behind him children tried to hook rubber ducks.

Tobias had been standing there, a hand shielding his eyes from the sunshine, taking it all in. Now I remember, even then, just for a second thinking that he looked good. Even...happy. Something niggles at the back of my mind now at the thought. But again, I can't hook my finger around it. What had he been looking at? What had made him look like that, given him that lightness about the eyes?

"If there had been someone new in Tobias's life," I say now, "I doubt that he'd have been shouting it from the rafters."

"Private man, by all accounts," Shirley says.

Veronica Chives's words come back to me. *His little secret...* what little secret? A new lover? Yet, Veronica Chives had been getting waxed and moisturized before heading over to Tobias's on the evening that he died. She hadn't been talking about a new lover. Is Veronica herself the new lover? The thought is so unlikely that I frown heavily. Tobias may not have been averse to an evening or two with Veronica – I have nothing for nor against such a theory – but I doubt that she would have engendered a lightening about his eyes. Then what had she been talking about? What was Tobias's little secret?

Like his boss Shona, Shirley gives me his phone number before he leaves, in case I think of anything new to tell him. Much to my relief, The Marquis doesn't make another appearance.

I schlep about my kitchen, cleaning and putting things away, making sure I have everything I need for the jobs that are due in for the next day. For some reason, I can't stop glancing out my kitchen windows. In fact, every few seconds, I find my eyes veering toward them.

Really, I have no idea why I'm doing it.

I have no reason to do it.

And anyway, if you say to people things like *See you tomorrow* – I mean, why say it if you're not going to follow up on it? It's like saying *I'm going to put the kettle on* and then going and doing some knitting instead. Or announcing you're going to pop to the loo and then doing a headstand. It doesn't make sense. Why say things you don't mean? Floating, meaningless words, words that don't mean the thing that they're actually saying. What's the point using words then? You could make meaningless gestures with your hands and let people draw their own conclusions. That way, if they get it wrong, it's no one's fault but their own. But if you're going to the trouble of stringing together a sentence, why not make it one that you mean to follow through on?

I growl under my breath, slam some unbreakable things down on counters, sweep the kitchen floor vigorously. So much for being a writer, but not even following through on the things you say. My eyes keep twitching toward the kitchen windows that look out on to my driveway. Annoyingly, I keep looking at my phone too, to see if I have a good signal. I don't know why I bother. It's not like the man even has my phone number. Oh, and even if he did, *who cares!*

I nearly jump out of my skin when there's a knock at my door.

I'd lost concentration for a minute or two. I'd been looking in my pantry to check on the status of my baking power and forgot to look at my driveway. From my kitchen windows, I can't see my front door. I glance in panic at my phone. Eight. Oh *god.* I glance at the mirror, do some ineffectual fluffing up of hair and readjusting of boobs. My mouth is completely dry. My hands still look inexplicably dry too. Why can't I moisturize? It's a simple thing to do. Just unscrew the tube and squeeze. Of course, I could just not open the door. That would serve him right.

And also, I could just open it.

"What do you want, Branwell? I'm busy."

"Can I pop in for a coffee?"

"Nope, didn't you hear? I'm busy."

"Can I pop by tomorrow?"

"I'm busy then too."

"You're the most beautiful woman I've ever met. I think I knew you in another life. In fact, it's possible we may be soulmates. Can I shag you senseless on your kitchen top?"

"Oh, *fuck off*! Fine, come in."

This conversation plays in my head now on my slow and wary shuffle toward my front door. It plays so sharply and vividly in my mind, in fact, that within seconds, I've convinced myself it's probably true, that it's just about to happen. The knock is repeated, a little more urgently now. That's good. Clearly, the waiting about is making him impatient. That's good. He's annoying.

I open my door finally, trying to look as nonchalant as possible.

It's my courier service, here to pick up a delivery.

I nearly clobber the man with my antique hat stand. I look at him murderously. "You're late," I point out.

"It's four minutes past eight," the youth – dressed in a baseball hat, t-shirt and baggy jeans – says. "And I've been waiting outside your front door for about eight."

"Whatever," I say, as I hand him the boxes I've made ready for him, all lined up near the front door. "You're very spotty."

He looks bored. "It's sebum."

"I don't need to know your name."

I close the door smartly in his bepimpled face.

I head back to my kitchen, feeling full of rage at the injustices in this world. I clean, sweep, and clean and sweep again. After another hour or two, I finally give up. The man isn't going to show up now. Fine. Whatever. Who cares if he pops around or not? No one cares. I don't. I don't even like him. And he has a stupid name. It's just as well I didn't go to the bother of shaving my legs this afternoon after my run. I'm going to bed.

It's only once I lie down, it's only then, once my back is firmly touching my mattress, once my head is cushioned on my memory foam pillow (£26 from John Lewis, and it will take care of your neck pain once and for all, and you know I'm telling the truth because this is just not the kind of story that John Lewis will do product placement in)—it's only when I'm finally under my summery duvet, it's only then I think of Tallulah.

If at that point, I still imagine that there's any chance of sleep, I'm sadly mistaken.

Tallulah, Tallulah Sands, why is she here? We'd grown up, her and me, in North London, so both of us moving down here seems like a bit of a leap. Had she known I was here and hadn't made a move to seek me out? Or had she not known I lived here? I mean, I run a business, all she had to do was google me and she would have found me. I do google her, now and again, every few months or so. Not all the time. Just every once in a while. I hadn't in the last couple of months, the length of time she's been living here, so I had had no idea she was here now.

I turn onto my tummy and bury my face into my pillow. No, that's another thing I can't think about. In fact, anything would be better than thinking about Tallulah Sand.

Chapter Twelve

I hated school. Of all things I've done in my life, I've never hated anything so much as primary school. Secondary school was bad too, but primary school was a trial. On my first day I was so nervous of being in a classroom full of people – a sea of faces and noises, shrieks, giggles, cries, excruciating smells of socks and apple shampoo and stale milk, gravy wafting from the lunch hall, dusty carpet and plimsoles—that I threw up all over myself. Then I started screaming because now, added to everything else, was the smell and feel of puke, running down my front. In any case, they cleaned me up and sent me home with my dad who picked me up, his mouth pursed and hands shaking, asking if I couldn't hold it together even for one day. *The other kids – do you think they'll want to be friends with someone like you? Don't you want to make friends? Can't you even try?* The anger in his voice, and underneath it, the helplessness, the knowledge that I'd never change, I could hear it all so clearly. He made it sound like I didn't want to change, like I was willfully making it hard for myself. My hands started shaking and my chin trembled at his words. I wished Mum had picked me up instead. She would have noticed the tears streaking down my face in a constant stream, even though I was clasping my hands rigid to try to stop them. She wouldn't have known what to say, maybe, and she would have looked helpless too, but she wouldn't have been angry.

My fate was sealed on that first day. I was Pukey Arya from then on. And in any case, what kind of a name was Arya? Was I half brown? Is that why I was twitchy? Is that why I clicked and clacked through my classes? Is that why I couldn't speak in front of the class without shaking? Is that why I went beet red whenever anyone so much as said a word to me? Is that why I hid in toilets and broom cupboards until a teacher found me and brought me back to class?

I didn't look that different from the others in my class. I looked, in fact, basically white with a hint of honey, with pitch dark hair and dark eyes. The half-brown thing may have been okay, especially in an area like Primrose Hill where there was a rapidly growing population of wealthy Indian people, and increasingly, mixed children too. But the twitching, the anxiety that was visible to all, the shaking, the hiding – I was a marked girl before I uttered my first word.

My early years in school were marked not by a gang of kids waiting for me and beating me up after school or anything—nothing as drastic as that. It was just people laughing behind their hands in class, shoving erasers down my jumper, creeping under the table and placing pencils between my legs on my chair and saying I'd grown a penis, asking me questions about Mum and had she grown up in India with snakes and lions, and did I eat chicken tikka at home. Kids asking me questions and watching as I stuttered and shook. Kids pulling my shorts down as I was climbing a rope in PE. Kids locking me in if they found me hiding in some dank cupboard.

I want to say that I learned to deal with it. And I guess, in a purely superficial way, I did. I was good at sport. I won races, and people, even the ones that teased me, always picked me for net ball. I got really good at playing the cello and did solos in school concerts. I was good at my work too. So, it was harder to pick on me. Or maybe people just got bored. I also learned to school my face. Stare at people. Blink. Hold a silence indefinitely. Answer people in cold monosyllables. And never, ever, seem like I wanted or needed friends. Because I knew it, I had known it for years, maybe always, that as soon as people sensed that you wanted or needed them, it made them draw back, change their mind about you. The more you seemed to need them, the more they backed off.

When I was ten, Tallulah came to my primary school. She was, by age ten, already quite overweight. There are a lot of women who're overweight, and people say about them, *but she's really pretty*. It's condescending, and it always means she's pretty *even though she's fat*. That's what people mean. They think they're saying it because they're kind and unprejudiced. But it isn't. They're saying it to make themselves feel okay about judging someone for being overweight. Anyway, kids had lost interest in teasing me by the time Tallulah appeared on the scene, but there she was. Overweight, not pretty, she wore thick glasses and went painfully red in uneven blotches when anyone asked her anything. I could have let her be teased, to take the heat off me. But having learned the hard way how to deal with the bullies, I stood up for her (and had the revelation that it was far easier to stand up for other people than it was for yourself) and we instantly became friends.

I didn't mean to steal her boyfriend when I was sixteen. It wasn't something I set out to do, or even imagined I would ever do. But when you've had a crush on someone for months, and they're going out with your friend – who's pathetically grateful for their attention – and then they suddenly tell you that they're crazy about you and always have been, and you're pathetically grateful to them because that's the kind of thing that only happens in your daydreams where you're not a fucking stuttering twitching horrific mess, then you end up saying yes to whatever they're asking you to do. In Colin's case, it was a hand job in the grounds behind the school under dripping magnolia sap, which you then end up wiping on your skirt, and the stain never goes away (the cum, I mean, not the magnolia sap). And you think this hand job means that he loves you, and worse, that *you* love him. And then, well, then it turns out someone saw you and told Tallulah.

Tallulah wasn't the kind to go into a deep depression or slash her thighs to show you just what you did to her, to teach you a lesson. Actually, come to think of it, she was exactly that kind of person. That's what I would have predicted if I had stopped to think about it before turning my hand into a loose – but not too loose – fist. After all, she ate herself senseless after every party she went to, during every party she wasn't invited to, before every presentation. She was desperate for friends. For me, she was enough, she was a friend. I hadn't had a friend before. It was a hundred percent improvement in my situation. But it was patently clear from the start that I wasn't enough for her. She needed validation like people need air to breathe. I did too, who am I kidding, but I'd got into the habit of not showing other people that. So, yes, I'd have predicted that she would go potty with depression over what I had done. But she didn't.

She went on some kind of bootcamp regime, lost a few stone over the course of a year, totally broke it off with me, and became friends with the girl-clique from hell who had giggled behind their hands when she was bigger, but now adopted her like she was prom queen.

And they made my life hell.

They laughed at me, got into my locker and cut a hole in my shorts before a netball match – which only became apparent halfway through the match. They wrote letters to Colin – supposedly from me – begging him to let me give him a hand job again. *Please, Colin, please, a blowjob this time!* Oh, the list was endless, it went on for a whole year. And it was all coming out of Tallulah's brain, because the girl gang from Hades was all hair and no braincells. The worst was that one of them for a month or so acted like she'd ditched the gang and become my friend, and desperate case that I was, I'd fallen for it and after a stolen beer or two, I had bawled for an hour about how awful it was to lose Tallulah. Except they then played a recording of it before my netball final and made it sound like I was talking about Colin. That I was crying myself senseless because Colin didn't want me anymore. Everyone heard it. And of course, I was in no state to play the match. Or ever go back to that school.

That was the last I'd seen of Tallulah until this afternoon.

Chapter Thirteen

Now, in the days after I see Tallulah, nothing works for me. Every morning, I spin on my stationary bike, I clean, I bake, I walk around the house banging things. But nothing works. There is nothing I can do to make me hate myself less for what happened with Tallulah. I don't even know if I hate myself more for what I did to her, or what was done to me in retaliation. Is guilt harder to bear or shame?

The thought that inevitably I'll bump into her again sooner or later—that she lives right around the corner, in what feels like a terrifyingly permanent job in which someone like Tallulah would undoubtedly grow old—makes me sick to the stomach. All of a sudden safe old Trucklewood feels like a stinking pit full of unexploded landmines.

Some days after bumping into her, I'm standing in my kitchen. It takes me a shockingly long time to construct a haunted gingerbread house. The zombies take forever – their limbs and heads keep falling off – and the ghosts keep disintegrating and disappearing into thin air. I keep trying to kowtow them into submission, but they have minds of their own.

It doesn't matter that Tallulah lives here now. I lop a zombie head back on. It doesn't matter. So what if for the first time in my life I feel like I have some control over my life? For the first time, I feel like I can deal with the world. I can look it in the eye and not run to the nearest cover and hide. So what if I feel like I have my own space in which to live and hide and breathe? I can deal with this too. I probably won't see her that much. It's not a big deal. I try to poke more substance into a feathery ghost.

Although…here's the thing. What does she have to be out and about for? She lives in a boarding school where she gets fed, where she has all her needs met. She doesn't have to come out. So, I probably won't see her that much. In fact, once I bump into her once or twice, after that, things will go back to how they've always been. I can go back to forgetting that she's there. All I have to do is get past the first accidental meeting or two. In fact, I might even seek her out, just to speed things up.

Yes, that's a good idea. A stonker of an idea. Getting unpleasant things out of the way is what I do, it's my middle name. I could take a walk early afternoon, up to the top of the hill, to the shops, see if I can bump into her, get it out of the way. In fact, why put it off until tomorrow?

Baking done for the day, boxes packed up for my spotty courier, I drag on my jacket. I rummage in the pockets for my house keys and come up with Exhibit A: a hairpin, and Exhibit B: a picture of crotches sitting in a circle.

I sit down right there in the middle of the hallway on the floor and stare at the picture. I haven't worn this hoodie for the last few days. And for the last week, I've been obsessing so much about Tallulah that I'd forgotten all about this picture I'd taken from Tobias's place.

The picture and the hairpin.

What is it about the picture? I scan it for details. It has that retro sixties flower power feel to it, everyone sitting around naked with their saggy tits and their long hair half covering their faces. Yet, not. Because these people don't have faces. And given Tobias's size, it's obvious he isn't one of them. Did he take the picture? Why did he cut off the faces? What is this circle? Was he a part of it? Why is there something a little forlorn about faceless crotches? Like people playacting at the power of the naked body, but not really feeling it, not disclosing who they are. I frown. I'm reading too much into it. I look again at the pictures I took of Tobias's sex toy drawer. The volume that the photograph came from is on the top. I can't see the cover, but the spine tells you the name. *The Power in My Hands*. No author.

I google it on my phone but can't find a book by that name. The book niggles at the back of my mind. There's something I'm missing. Some question I should be asking, some connection I should be making. But I have no idea what it is. There's something about what's happened to Tobias, something I should be seeing. But I can't figure out what it is.

I get up, stuff the picture in a drawer and head toward the front door again.

There's a piece of A4 on my doormat that's been shoved through the letterbox. At first, I think it's blank. But on one side there are a few words: *You're not alone. I see you. You need never be alone again.* Just that and nothing more. Crude black letters.

I frown down at it. People have too much time on their hands. What is this meant to be? A religious invitation? A flyer for reiki? A cult? No contact information. No dates for classes or products to buy. Nothing. I shake my head and put the piece of paper in the recycling.

I walk all the way down to the bottom of my lane, and stand looking up the hill toward the main street. For a moment, I pause there and send Sherlock a quick text message. "What was Tobias wearing when he died?" I ask him.

The answer couldn't come back quicker if the beautiful boy had been waiting up all night just waiting for me to call. "Tracky bottoms. T-shirt. It's in the papers. Xxxxxx"

I frown. Tracky bottoms and t-shirt – that doesn't sound like Tobias, even at that hour of the night. I mean, he could conceivably have owned such clothing. I guess, he could now and again have worn it. I frown. Why does it not feel right?

I'm about to start my climb up to the main street, but then a hundred-year-old woman named Olga Viotchlik, headscarf, long dress, coat and all, walks up to the base and comes to a stop next to me. "It is a mountain!" she says, looking up the hill, shaking her head.

I vaguely know her. She lives about a twenty-minute walk from mine. Her face is a creased walnut. She has one of those comfortable bodies where it's hard to see where the breasts stop and the stomach starts. It's all one thing. Her eyes smile.

I hold out the crook of my arm and she slips her hand in. I don't know Olga well, but I've seen her about. We start our slow climb up the mountain.

"Your name is Arya?" she says. "I haif' see you, around veelage, yes?"

"Olga, I don't like talking to people. Let's just walk."

She grins. "Me, I like to make talk. I like other people to leesen."

She proceeds to make talk the rest of the way up the hill. Mountain or not, the crazy old codger is hardly out of breath by the time we're up on the high street. And she hasn't stopped talking for one second either. She's true to her word though. She doesn't give a hoot if I talk or not, in fact, she actively seems to prefer me to be quiet as she jabbers on. I take her withery old hand out of the crook of my arm when we get to the top.

"Let's do this again, yes? And you – you come for Olga's coffee, best in town. Yes? You make me happy when you come."

I can think of many retorts to this, but I bite the inside of my cheek to stop my natural tendencies. "I wouldn't count on it, Olga."

She's still holding on to my arm though. "Your auntie nice lady. Nice to everyone. Even silly old Olga. But here—" she thumps her chest "she all alone, yes?"

I stare at her, feeling like I've been punched in the gut.

I know that around me, people are walking by, cars driving on the street, the odd terrier stopping to sniff at my trainers. But now, I can only see Olga's grey eyes and the one thousand and one lines on her face. Because the world may as well not be there.

"I should have visited her more." The words come out, all abrupt and stiff. I have no idea I'm going to say them, but then they're out there, hanging in the air. I could curse, bite my tongue, slap my face – in fact, I have a strong urge to do all three. Why would I go and say something stupid like that to a virtual stranger? I clamp my mouth shut.

Olga is shaking her head. "No, no. Not that kind of alone. Sometimes, you need something else to make you feel – how you say, not alone? And sometimes, you can never find anything to fill the hole, yes?"

My throat is burning. So many thoughts crowd my mind. The top one is the one I can't speak out loud. The top one is the one that wants to ask Olga: do you mean Auntie Meera, or *me*? Instead, I settle for something more mundane. Even petty. "You mean I wasn't enough for her? That it wasn't me she needed?"

She pats my hand. "Sometimes you can never find anything to fill the hole," she repeats. "Sometimes, you look in the wrong places."

"What do you mean?"

I can't help it. My mind goes back to that place. That day when Auntie Meera had called me and asked me if I could pop over for breakfast. There had been nothing ominous in her voice, nothing of the *I'm ill and about to die* kind of foreboding in her voice. Her voice had been light, happy even, excited. Not like her. Why hadn't I thought about that then? Why had she sounded excited?

My throat is so tight now, I can barely croak. "Where – where was Auntie Meera looking – for something to fill the hole?"

She shakes her head side to side, her prune-mouth widening, showing a mouth of some pretty good teeth. "Now, if I knew that, it would be too easy. But you, you find out. Yes?"

She toddles off, bent over, her footsteps slow, nodding and holding her hand up to wave at people like she's the long-lost great-grandmother of Tsar Nicholas the Whatever Number He Was and has at least two Fabergé eggs hiding down her bra. I look after her and shake my head. I'd barely ever exchanged two words with her before, and yet here she was, walking up the mountain with me, spouting startling insight both into me and into Auntie Meera. What did she mean? What did she mean when she said Auntie Meera was lonely, looking to fill a hole, and that she had been looking in the wrong places? What was she talking about?

But I have no time to figure this out.

Because the next person I spy is Veronica Chives. She's standing a few feet away from the entrance to her frozen custard shop. She's wearing a short denim skirt and cowboy boots, with another checkered shirt today, blue this time, her red hair plaited loosely on both sides of her head and left there without any rubber bands to slowly unravel over time. The woman has a certain sex appeal all her own.

"Hello, pumpkin!" she calls out to me. "Where're your nipples pointing this morning, I ask you, where are they pointing? *Where* are they pointing?"

Until she speaks, that is. She's using the same sort of tone with me as most people use with especially fluffy and vacant-faced poodles. *Where's* your chew toy? *There's* your chew toy! *Who's* a fluffy poodle? You are! *You are!*

I glare at her, trying to shake off the feeling of doom leftover from the conversation with Olga. I walk up to her. Things percolating in my head over the last few days are starting to click into place. The thing niggling at me is clarifying. But I need confirmation. "What was Tobias wearing when you found him?"

Instantly, Veronica's eyes turn shifty. The expression is not so far off what Barbie's would be if she were telling everyone she's an astrophysicist. "Sweatpants. T-shirt," she says quickly. "The t-shirt was back-to-front. It's in the papers."

"Veronica, what are you hiding?" I cross my arms over my chest. "Tobias would not be wearing *tracky bottoms and a t-shirt*, and back-to-front? I mean, come on!"

She bites her lip, looks left and right. She's wavering. But then I see her eyes lose their shiftiness. She straightens and squares her shoulders. "Well, he was, hon and that's how it is."

Damn it. I thought I had her there for a second.

She turns away and starts walking back toward her frozen custard shop. A perky teen is handing out samples outside the shop, looking like a cheerleader. Veronica turns around and glances at me for a second before disappearing inside the shop. I walk up to the perky teenager, take a frozen custard sample and devour it.

Then I follow Veronica in. She's dealing with customers, so I lean against one wall and stare at her. I told you I'm good at the unblinking eyes thing. So, I turn their full power on Veronica. She does a pretty good job of ignoring me, but I can tell she's rattled, because she can't help throwing glances my way every few seconds, and she keeps dropping change and giggling and speaking in a voice that's even louder than her usual. And she's usually pretty loud.

There's a temporary lull as the last of the customers leave. I saunter up to the counter. "What was Tobias wearing?"

"I told you."

"What was Tobias wearing?"

"I told you, Arya, now I'm a busy lady this morning, so—"

"What was Tobias wearing?"

"Arya, now you just take your tush off—"

"What was he wearing, Veronica?"

She stops trying to count pound coins and turns to me in exasperation.

"You know, you're the unfriendliest person this side of the Empire State Building, and now all of a sudden, you're everyone's best friend. I don't get it."

I roll my eyes. "I don't care. What was Tobias wearing?"

She purses her mouth. "Serena!" she calls.

The cheerleader with the tight shorts and blonde pigtails bounces in, looking perky. She's actually skipping.

"Would you mind the till, pumpkin?" Veronica asks Serena.

Then she jerks her head to me. I follow her to an office at the back. It's small, fluffy and pink. The file folders are neon colors, the notebooks floral, the computer is a flashy orange and looks dressed for the Notting Hill Carnival in feathery headgear. Even the pens have flamingo tails. There's a mirror on the wall. Veronica looks into it for a second, makes a half-hearted attempt at replaiting her runaway plaits and then lets them hang there rubber band-free again, unravelling in the general area of her boobs.

She turns to me, a finger in my face. "Now, you listen to me, young lady, I'll tell you about it, but if the police get wind of what I tell you, I'll know who told them. Capiche?"

"And what will you do about it?"

"You think I've got to my position as queen of the custard without breaking a few bones?"

I look blandly at her. "Veronica, seriously, just tell me."

She dithers some more. Then does that firm-face thing again. "Fine. He was naked, if you must know."

Her words are like a punch in the gut. She's only confirmed what I already suspected, but still, hearing it spelled out like that, my stomach feels all hollow all at once, that sicky feeling you get in the car on a hilly road early in the morning when someone else has bright plans for the day and has managed to rope you into them. He was naked. Tobias was naked.

"Why does the police think it was tracky bottoms and a t-shirt?"

"I pulled some clothes on him, okay? Whatever I could find in his hamper."

I stare at her. "That's tampering with the crime scene!"

"You know, you'd be happier in life if you watched fewer crime dramas and got out more."

I don't argue with this assessment of my life. She probably has a point.

"I couldn't leave him like that, now could I? It wouldn't be very neighborly, now would it? My mama always said what's the point if you look like a goddess if your neighbors have fallen face down in pig crap? He was my friend."

Suddenly, in a flash, I remember what she had done when she told me about Tobias's body last time I had spoken to her in her kitchen. And the thing I've been missing all along, that's been niggling and niggling at me, that I should have cottoned on to days ago, comes flooding into my brain like a tidal wave. Now it's sitting there, a fully formed idea, like it's always been there, just waiting for me to see it. The very thing I had come into this shop to confirm and yet it shocks me.

As I said before, I can go back to a scene and see it pictured clearly in my mind, every detail, often more details than I was originally conscious of. I can see them like they're playing in chrome color in front of me now. When I'd stopped by at Veronica's some days ago and asked her about finding Tobias's body in his kitchen, she had described the body, and she had crossed her hands on her chest. I describe it to her now. I follow it up with a demonstration. I cross my hands over my chest. "Is that how you found him?"

She purses her lips but gives me no answer.

I rub my forehead. "The police don't know that little detail either, do they?"

"I might have shifted the body a bit. He was...on the heavy side. It was the lord's own business trying to get clothes on him, I won't lie to you, Arya. I guess I forgot all about the crossed hands."

"What was the big deal about putting clothes on him? They were going to strip him naked later on anyway. For the post-mortem."

Her eyes shift about again.

"Argh, Veronica, what?"

She lifts a shoulder. "Nothing! I told you, I'm a bit of a puritan, that's all. The thought of him lying there like that, his special parts for the world and their sister to see. A man's special parts are his jewels, Arya, it's what my mama used to say. I couldn't leave him like that, I just couldn't. And it's not like I'm a pro at tampering with crime scenes, now, am I? I forgot about putting his hands back on his chest, that's all. It could have happened to anyone. And just remember, I was still thinking he died of a heart attack!"

I cluck my tongue. The noise is violent in the sudden silence. My head is buzzing. First Auntie Meera, then Tobias.

I glare at Veronica. Something tells me that this isn't the real reason Veronica covered Tobias up. It's not because she's a self-confessed puritan. And not the heart attack thing either. Did she even think it was a heart attack, given the state the body was in, naked, arms crossed, all of it? What is she hiding?

The thought occurs to me. Was she the one who had killed Tobias in the first place? Because he wasn't responding to her advances? Or even inadvertently? A sexual game gone wrong? She's admitting to tampering with the evidence. I frown heavily. What on earth am I going to do with this information? If she didn't murder Tobias, the police aren't going to take kindly to her messing with the evidence.

Damn, I wish I didn't know! I glare at her some more, she blinks a few times, but says nothing more.

I make my way out of the shop and stand outside, wondering what the hell I'm going to do.

Chapter Fourteen

This is the problem with me. In a nutshell.

Okay, there are lots of problems with me, but this is one of them. I think I want something, I go after it, I do everything I can to get it, and then I get it, handed to me on a platter, and I realize I don't want it after all. That I'd do anything not to have it.

Bollocks to everything.

I'd practically forced Veronica to cough up what she knew – some of what she knew anyway. But now that she has, it turns out I don't want the information. The weight of it sits heavy on my shoulders. I have broad shoulders, but they're too small for this kind of crap. Tampering with the evidence! What am I going to do with this little piece of information?

I stand outside the shop, scowling into the distance. There are people around me, walking up and down the street. I've noticed that Trucklewood residents have a tendency to waft. They don't pop into a shop, quickly pop out again with the things they need and make tracks to get home so they don't have to talk to anyone. They spend ages walking up and down the street, actively looking for people to talk to. This boggles my mind.

As I stand there, outside Veronica's shop, I'm conscious of this floating around me. But I can't focus on it. It's like I'm in a bubble, like the air around me has gone numb and time has come to a standstill.

I stare into the distance, at the hilly woods, as if the answers lie there. The trees sway in the early-summer breeze, shafted by the slanting sunshine. They're close-knit, huddling close together. Silver birches, fat oaks, feathery beeches, rippled ash. Nestled on this side of the woods are houses. The ones closer to the high street nudge close together. They're semi-detached and terraced. But the ones further away, closer to the woods are detached, with enormous gardens and sprawling driveways.

Two murders in this community. In the last few months. Surely, I'm making all this up. It doesn't make sense. Surely, it couldn't be the same person. Surely, it's a horrible coincidence and my overactive brain is making up a connection that isn't there.

A sick, hollow feeling in my stomach. I try to rub at it, but it only gets worse. Because this is the thing I have to focus on. Not what Veronica did or didn't do. Not what she's told me. Not the fact that I know her bombshell of a secret now and I have no idea what to do with it.

What I have to focus on is plain and simple and impossible. That Tobias was murdered by the same person who killed Auntie Meera.

I stare numbly in front of me. Veronica's only confirmed what was already simmering at the back of my mind. Auntie Meera and Tobias. Tobias and Auntie Meera. Why, why haven't I seen this clearly this whole time? I've had over a week. Auntie Meera was killed. Killed by someone who walked into her home, not forced their way in, but been invited in, no signs of forced entry. She was killed and then stripped and left on the floor, naked, her hands on her chest, like a sacrificial offering. Like a ritual. A paean, almost. And Tobias was left in exactly the same way. Even before I knew about how his body had been placed, I had known something else. Both Auntie Meera and Tobias had been happier just before they died. There had been something about them, something different. The tone of Auntie Meera's voice when she had called to ask me to breakfast, and that strange lightening around Tobias's eyes at the

Easter fair. There had been something about them and I hadn't seen it clearly until now. Not to mention that Trucklewood was a tiny community. The idea of two murderers running about the place was even more outlandish than just one. How could I not have made this connection as soon as I heard about Tobias?

I try to rub at the knot in my chest. What if I was just making this up? Were they killed by the same person? If they were, it must have been someone who wanted it known that it was the same person, the same reason. They'd left a clear MO. The crossed hands, the naked, splayed bodies. Veronica had messed it up because of something or the other she wanted to hide. And I still don't know what that is. But she'd messed things up because the killer had left their trademark for all to see. And the police don't know about it.

My eyes flicker. There's Shona Klues and Sherlock, walking about, chatting with Trucklewood residents. Not questioning people or interrogating them, oh no, I know Shona's tactics. They're just chewing the fat, the bastards. I square my shoulders and walk up to them.

"Arya," Shona says.

"Shona."

"What's occurring?"

"Not much. How's things?"

"Not bad, not bad, Arya. The hills are alive with the sound of music and all that."

"Why aren't you connecting Tobias's murder with my auntie Meera Patel's?"

Shona's eyes flicker appreciatively. "We're exploring all avenues. All avenues are open," she recites.

"So, you *are* looking at them as connected?"

"We can't rule it out, this being a small community and all. But the MO is totally different. Different weapons, for one."

I chew on this. "What else could link the MO of the two murders? If the weapons are different."

"How the bodies are placed, for example. Or forced entry, done in the same way. Or even similar motives."

Entry wasn't forced in either case, as far as anyone's been able to make out. And there's no clue yet about possible motive. *How the bodies are placed.*

There is no way I can tell Shona what I know about the placement of the bodies, about the splayed, naked bodies and the crossed hands, without giving Veronica Chives away. Honesty is one thing, but I can hardly throw her to the dogs. The police will not be happy about someone tampering with the evidence, whatever their motive and Veronica will be in hot water if I let the cat out the bag. I can see her peering out of her shop, nervously chewing a thumbnail, watching me talking to Shona Klues. I growl under my breath. The she-devil, how could she do this to me! And the reflection that I'd practically forced her to tell me what she'd done doesn't make me feel any better. I turn back to Shona.

"I think that we're looking at one murderer," I say, with as much nonchalant conviction as I can muster. My shoulder blades are still prickling – I imagine Veronica is superglued to her shop window right now.

Shona eyes me casually but closely. "You do, do you now. Well, as to that, I can't say what the police are thinking. Or what we're not thinking." She taps the side of her nose. "Will I see you at the pub later on?"

I roll my eyes at her. "Someone will report you one day soon, you know, for harassing the locals."

She winks at me. "But it won't be you, Arya, it won't be you."

When she walks off, I stand about, hands in my pocket, with no idea what to do next. I have no idea what Shona will make of what I've just said to her. Nothing at all, is probably the right answer. She paid little attention to it. It was hardly the big revelation that it should have been. I grit my teeth.

There's no sign of Tallulah on the high street. So much for my grand plan to get my first meeting or two with her over with. I look around. Tallulah might not be here, but everyone else and their sister seems to be.

Mrs. Sharma is seemingly window shopping, walking up and down the street, but I expect really looking for company. She's eyeing me. The bun on top of her head quivers a little, then she seems to make up her mind to it.

"Fancy seeing you here," she says, strolling up to me with her large slouchy bag tucked under her arm.

"Maybe," I respond. Though I know what she means. I'm not one to lurk on the high street. In fact, I avoid it at all costs. I get everything I need delivered. Even that is too much human contact for me on most days. I'm all for drones making deliveries. I'd invest money in the enterprise if I ever thought about things like investments and shares and dividends, whatever they are. Craig had tried to talk to me about such things once and I'd fallen into a coma, a self-induced one. I look speculatively at Mrs. Sharma. "You know everything that goes on in this town."

She straightens and pats her dress down. "Maybe."

She looks pleased at what I've said, even though I didn't mean it as a compliment. She doesn't even like me. Yet, she looks pleased at what I've said. Like I say, I'll never understand people.

"Do you know if Uncle – I mean, Tobias – had a new boyfriend – or girlfriend – in his life?" I expect her to know nothing about this, to tell you the truth, even if there had been something to know, which I'm not at all sure about, but, to my surprise, her eyelids flicker. I look closely at her. "Mrs. Sharma?" I'm half convinced she's only pretending to know something just to seem important.

She pats her hair. "Well, as to that, I'm not one to kiss and tell tales."

I look incredulously at her. "Are you trying to tell me that *you* and Tobias—"

She widens her eyes. "What? Of course not!" Then she loses the aghast look, and a little smile plays about her lips. "Although, he did ask me out once."

"No, he didn't," I blurt out.

There is no way Tobias would have done that. I mean, *Mrs. Sharma?*

She frowns. “I didn’t take you to be someone racially prejudiced.”

“Uh – what is the *matter* with you!” I say, now truly disgusted. “It’s not because of your ethnicity that Tobias wouldn’t have asked you out. It’s because you’re way too needy!”

Her chin quivers. She turns her eyes away slightly, but then looks back at me.

Heat fills my belly at the sight of her hurt eyes. I shake my head. I want to say I’m sorry. I’d like to be able to say things like that, but as usual, saying one mean thing only makes me desperately want to say another. It’s like people who say they can’t just eat one enormous slice of cake. They have to eat another one right away, just to get rid of the guilt. It’s on the tip of my tongue to ask her if she knows that no one wants her prune jelly either. I grip my hands together. Willing myself to stop talking. I take a deep breath, the words on the tip of my tongue. But she interrupts me.

“It’s better to be needy than to die alone,” she says in a huff before she walks off.

Her words make me catch my breath.

It’s better to be needy than to die alone.

I stare after her.

Hadn’t both Auntie Meera and Uncle Tobias died alone? Neither had been needy. Or, in fact, neither had been able to admit to their need. I know exactly what Olga was talking about when she said about Auntie Meera needing something that she would never be able to find. I’d sensed that in her all the time I’d known her and lived with her. It had killed me. Knowing that I had not been enough for my parents – they’d discarded me like wet tissue – and that even though I could sense that Auntie Meera cared about me, I was never enough for her either. She was always searching and searching, but never finding. I’d known it all my life.

I stand there on the high street, looking at the retreating form of Mrs. Sharma, her shoulders rigid, her head flicking about. First

Olga, now Mrs. Sharma.

I cluck impatiently.

There was always a longing in Auntie Meera that never seemed to go away. A loneliness that was a part of her, a part of who she was. A hole in her heart that nothing seemed to fill. She would spend hours with her herbs and her dried flowers, reading grimoires from around the world, history books about herbology, Ayurveda, plant-based cures from many different cultures, creating her own recipes that she would write with meticulous floral handwriting in her many notebooks. The notebooks themselves were full with sprigs of lavender and old rose petals and dried bursts of wildflowers. She knew Celtic herbalism, Indian recipes, Romanian lore, African pastes. She knew about pagan plant gathering at the full moon. She read it all with a never-ending hunger.

If she'd cared about degrees, I'm sure someone would have given her an honorary doctorate for her knowledge of herbs and plants. But even with plants and herbs and recipes, she went at it not as a hobby, or even something she loved, but like she was looking for something to fill the hole. Like in all her reading and plant gathering and recipe making, she would finally find an answer to something that plagued her. That had plagued her all her life. And when she found it, it would make life worth living.

I rub my face. I hate this. This standing about, talking to people. Hearing what they have to say. The things they say suddenly, out of the blue, that hurt and pinch and pierce. That I will think about for hours, days, maybe years after. That will come back to me again and again. Already, my head feels too full. And I don't want to be standing here thinking about Auntie Meera. Auntie Meera, or even Tobias, both lonely people who had met lonely ends. First Veronica and her secrets, Shona with her investigations, and now Mrs. Sharma. Not to mention Olga. I don't think I can bear to speak to anyone else.

I'm about to turn around and head home when I bump into Willie Arnott, the accountant. I start. Because one second he's not there, and next second, he's standing right next to me.

"Arya, how lovely to see you."

I sag. Really, more people, I have to talk to yet more people? My head is already starting to throb. I look resignedly at the man. He has to be the most anonymous looking man I've ever seen. His face is soft and fuzzy, his glasses standard issue tortoise shell, his eyes vague and impossible to pin down, they seem to wander so much. It's like he's talking to you, but he's also somewhere else at the same time.

I look closer at him, trying to pinpoint even one feature I'd recognize again if he were wearing different clothes or changed his scant hair, but I can't. As I stand there, thinking about weaving my way around him, he half turns and mouths something to himself. I lean forward to catch what he's saying. But then I realize he's not aware he's doing it. It's a thing I've seen the man do before. Like he has conversations in his head with someone only he can see, and he forgets that there are people around.

Willie Arnott must be lonely too, the thought suddenly occurs to me. Like Tobias and Auntie Meera. He doesn't have anyone either. He'd only moved to this community some months before Auntie Meera did. He can't know that many people. And hadn't he lost his sister Maria just before he moved to Trucklewood? Auntie Meera had mentioned it to me once.

He blots his forehead on the back of his hand now and his shirtsleeve pulls back a little. An old burn scar runs up his wrist. I look curiously at it. He gives me a little smile.

"People don't normally stare at it," he says in a soft voice. Almost a whisper. "They look away quickly."

I bite my lip. I hadn't realized that he'd seen me looking. "It's just a scar. There's nothing wrong with it."

He gives me another smile. "Most people don't think like that about deformities."

"It's hardly a deformity. It's just human variance."

He nods slowly. "Most people are scared of human variability though." He hesitates. I see him mouth something under his breath again. Who does he speak to? His sister Maria? Then he says in his low voice, "It's nice to see you out and about, Arya. We worry about you."

My brow knits in a frown. I was leaning forward slightly to look closer at him, but I jerk back at his words. "I don't need people to worry about me." I scowl for good measure.

And anyway, who is *we*? I know in a small place like Trucklewood, there will always be gossip, but the thought of my neighbors talking about me when I'm not there, my quirks and ticks, the way I talk to people, the way I push people away, the thought makes me feel sick again.

He inclines his head.

I'm about to turn away, but then I stop. "Why did you move here?" I blurt out.

He gives me that tiny smile again. "My sister died. I needed a fresh start."

I look at his wrist again, but he shakes his head. "This is an old scar. She died of disease." He is trying to sound stoic about it. He has that clipped tone people get when they don't want to get too close to the thing they're saying, but I hear the scratch in his throat.

"I'm sorry," I say tightly.

To my shock, he leans out a hand and squeezes my shoulder. The gesture is so unexpected, I flinch. His hand doesn't dislodge. Before I can stop myself – and to my horror – I try to bat it away. Then I do it again. Like he's a gnat.

But he doesn't flinch or snatch his hand away. He looks sympathetically at me – and that's so much worse than if he had snatched his hand away.

"Not everyone hates human variance, you know, Arya," he says. "There are people here that would accept you as you are. If you give them a chance."

I flinch like he's slapped me; I can't help it. "I don't know what you mean." My voice doesn't sound tight now, it sounds strangled.

His hand on my shoulder, it hurts. I want to claw it off. What is he talking about, what does the man mean, how can he possibly be saying something like this to me? What does he even know about me?

He looks at me again, with that sympathy that I don't want. He pats my shoulder twice, and then he turns around and heads up the street. I hold myself rigid. My shoulder hurts and I can still feel the imprint of his hand on my shoulder.

I rub harshly at it.

Why, why am I exposing myself to this, to this *sympathy*, to people that seem like they can see right through me? Because of Tobias's death? Auntie Meera's? Is that why I'm doing it? I rub my shoulder red. I've spent years trying to carve a space, somewhere I can live and not be bothered by what people think or say about me. And yet, how is it that everyone seems to be able to see through me? How have I left myself open to it?

I need to stop pretending that I'm trying to find something out about these murders, or that there's any chance I can do it. I need to stop talking to people like I'm a normal person who does that.

I turn toward home, feeling utterly deflated.

Chapter Fifteen

Next few days, I manage to avoid everyone. I bake every morning, I send my orders off with my courier, I use my sports bike instead of going out for a run, I clean obsessively, I make sure I have everything I need for the next day's orders. I even manage to tickle The Marquis's chin once when he isn't paying attention, and it takes him a whole three seconds to notice and yowl at me.

It was a mistake trying to talk to people. Searching out Tallulah to get our first meeting or two over with, that was a mistake too. Who do I think I am? I'm so overwhelmed by just that one trip to the high street that I hide my head in the sand for days after. I don't need to see Tallulah, I don't need to find out what happened to Tobias, or if Tobias and Auntie Meera's deaths are connected. The police can do that. It's their job, not mine. I never seek out people, I'm not Auntie Meera.

In my obsession to clean, I'm working through a drawer in a cabinet in the living room. I had cleared out all the rooms of Auntie Meera's things after she had died, except for her workshop that remains untouched upstairs. So, I don't usually come across anything of hers, but today, a few days after my excursion to the high street, in my frenzy of obsessive cleaning, I come across an old receipt for one of her clients. It's made out to Janet Long.

I tease out the creases in the rumpled piece of paper. I smooth it out and sit there on the floor, cross-legged, next to the cabinet and look down at the receipt. I trace the words Auntie Meera had written with my thumb. The receipt is either a copy of something she gave the client, or she never managed to hand it over to Janet Long.

I didn't come across many of Auntie Meera's clients, not since I moved out to head to university. But I remember Janet Long. Auntie Meera was always making healing recipes and amulets for people, concocting her own, and not just sticking to ones practiced by other people or written about in books. About a year before she died, she had had a client who had terrible injuries all the way down one side of her body. Terrible scars that caused the woman a great deal of pain. Having apparently exhausted medical interventions and options, the woman had asked Auntie Meera for natural remedies that could help her. I had been there when she came to see Auntie Meera. I'd come around for lunch, and I tried to stay out of the way when the client arrived, but I could hear them upstairs in Auntie Meera's workshop. The woman's voice was high-pitched, and I could hear every word she was saying.

The woman, Janet Long, was rude to Auntie Meera the entire time she was in the house. *I know this won't work*, the woman kept saying. *Fleece people all you want, I'm not really taken in, I wasn't born yesterday.* And Auntie Meera kept on being unfailingly nice. "I'm very sorry," I could hear her saying. "I hope you find some peace. I hope this will help you with the pain." *I know how you people make your money, you take advantage of other people's pain. I know how it works.* This went on for nearly an hour. It was clear that Janet Long had found a willing punching bag to let off her anger and pain. Auntie Meera just let her get on with it. Never once did I hear her being rude or even mildly impatient. I stood in the landing downstairs, my hands clenched into fists, willing her to say something, anything, to tell the woman to fuck off, but she never did. She kept talking to the woman in a low, soothing voice. It made me so mad to hear them that I had to leave the house and stay hidden in the back garden so I wouldn't throttle the woman when she came down the stairs.

When the woman finally left, I marched back into the house. I couldn't hold it in. "I don't know why you'd let someone talk to you like that," I flung at Auntie Meera. I wasn't angry at her, not really. I was angry *for* her. "Why were you so nice to her? She was being a bitch. Why do you have to let people treat you like a doormat?"

Even as I was letting off on her, I couldn't help thinking she looked unusually exhausted. There was more white in her hair, and deep circles under her eyes. I felt a guilty pang at the sight of her. At the tone of my voice. The way I sounded. Why didn't I visit her more often? And why was I haranguing her about how nice she was? It was like something visceral in me couldn't stand it, though, watching her talk like that. It was unbearable to see her being nice to someone who seemed to have not a stitch of kindness for her in return.

When I told her off for it, I expected her to say—like she'd said to me many times before—that it wasn't out of meanness that people spoke like that. That the woman, the client, had been in pain. That you have to look beyond the things people say. I expected she would say something like that and put me in my place. But she put her arms around herself, sitting there on her tatty sofa in her lace-knit green cardigan with the tassels that wound around her.

"I don't know, Arya. I think it's because I can't stand it when people don't like me."

I stared at her, shocked at her words. It wasn't the first time I'd been impatient with her unfailing politeness. She would always say that other people's rudeness didn't justify yours, or something along those lines. But not that day. *I think it's because I can't stand it when people don't like me.*

I had never heard her say something like that before.

I had quickly shaken my head. "No, of course that's not it. It's only because if you say something mean to her, you know you'll hurt her, and then you'll hate yourself for it afterwards. Because you know she's already hurting." I'd leapt quickly to her defense. I'd defended her against myself.

She shrugged, her head lying back on the sofa, eyes closed. "Isn't that the same thing?"

I remember it now, the hint of something in her voice. The tiredness. It was about a year before she died. I can't remember her looking quite so weary before this conversation. Or since, come to think of it.

I try to push the rawness away. It's nearly impossible thinking about Auntie Meera. The loss of her is an open wound and I can't bear to sit with it. If only I'd been there for her, if only I hadn't pushed her away. If only I hadn't let a silly little argument fester and create a gap between us.

I tear up the receipt that's in my hands, turn the remnants into a tight ball, walk to the hallway and chuck them in the bin.

I stand there in the hallway looking down at the tight little ball of paper.

Tobias had been the same as Auntie Meera, not letting people see that he needed them. Pushing people away with his rudeness – or, in fact, his bluntness. I shake my head again, a bit more gently this time. We all have ways we keep people away. We all have our ways of keeping other people out. Auntie Meera with her intense politeness built as much of a barrier around herself as Tobias with his bluntness.

I take a shaky breath. Because here it is, the crux of the matter, the thing that's troubling me the most. Auntie Meera and Uncle Tobias, they were just like me.

It's better to be needy than to die alone.

I can't help it. Mrs. Sharma's words, said to me in a fit of annoyance, ring in my head. Was I just like Auntie Meera and Uncle Tobias? Did I protect myself with an iron shield? Would I end up like them, all alone and unprotected?

The only problem is, what if you do let your guard down and you show your needs – if you know how to, which I don't, I have no idea – but what if you do and what happens if your needs chase people away? Then you're left alone either way. Exactly where you started, except worse because now you know what you've always feared is true. That you will never be accepted for who you are.

Being all alone because you never showed yourself to the world. Isn't that easier to bear than revealing yourself as you are, and being abandoned anyway?

I growl.

I don't want these thoughts.

"I don't want these thoughts!" I yell at no one in particular.

It's been days since I've so much as stepped out of the house. But now, all of a sudden, I can't bear to stay in a minute longer.

Auntie Meera is playing on my mind. Her loneliness, her unrelenting politeness. Tobias's death is hovering there too. What held the two deaths together? Or am I just imagining that?

And Tallulah. I still can't get her out of my mind either.

I stomp up the stairs. If someone knows of a way of escaping your own head, I'd really like to know it. I fling on my running clothes, wedge my trainers on my feet, clamp a rubber band around my unruly hair, clatter all the way down the stairs again, and head out. I stride down my street, not looking left or right, my hands clenched into fists. I veer off into the woods and do several circuits.

The run, under the clear crystal blue late-June sky, should clear my head, but it doesn't. If anything, at the end of a few laps, I'm feeling more edgy and restless than I have been for the last few days. Well, so much for that bright idea.

I dash over to the high street to pick up some strawberries from Waitrose for an order that someone's changed last minute. I get what I need quickly, pop out of the shop, intent on heading home. Maybe it was a bad idea, after all, to try to head out, to try to escape the house. My shoulders are tighter than they were before, and my temples are starting to hurt too. I turn toward home.

But find my way completely blocked. I come to an abrupt stop, outside the shop.

I'd picked lunchtime to be out and about, so most people would be indoors, eating their lunch. But apparently not everyone.

Mark Close, the fiddler (as in, the violinist, not a perv) is standing outside the hair salon next to Waitrose, eating frozen yogurt. His older boy is probably in school this morning, but he's still surrounded by what feels like an army of preschoolers. A baby in a sling (that's probably his younger baby), and three other, slightly older children. I stare at the group, thrown by the fact that the pavement is completely blocked, and also, *what's with all the children?* I look from face to face. The edginess I'm feeling is starting to turn to hysteria. Why did I think it was a good idea to come out here again! Did I learn nothing from my disaster of a trip to the high street the other day?

Mark is mechanically feeding himself frozen custard, like he's not even tasting it. The baby seems to be staring unblinkingly at nothing. An older child in a buggy is violently punching a teddy bear square in the face – a teddy bear that's already lost an eye and has wool poking out of its belly. And two hyperactive toddlers are running in circles around Mark with pointy sticks in their hands, one shouting, "I'll kill you! I'll kill you!" – the other yelling, "You're dead, you're dead!"

I gape at them. Who on earth would voluntarily choose to surround themselves with this…this awfulness? If someone forced it on you, you'd surely emigrate. I stand there frozen.

Then, some latent spirit of self-preservation kicks in through the haze, and I try to skirt around the group, like you would if a family of tarantulas were bearing down on you. It's the only sane thing you can do under the circumstances. Make a quick getaway before you can be sucked in and eaten alive. But I can't pull it off. Any time I so much as move an inch, I bang straight into one of the toddlers, who seem to have the ability to be in six different points in space all at the same time. One runs straight into me, falls over, straightens himself and starts running full tilt again without drawing breath. The other, for some reason, is pulling at my backpack and trying to get it off my back. Then he gives up, cackles long and deep, and starts chasing the other one again.

Oh my god, oh my god, what is this hellhole?

I swallow hard. Maybe Mark makes a sound, because I turn to stare at him. With all the kids surrounding him, he may as well be an alien life form, that's how strange a sight he is to me. He looks exhausted, his sandy hair sticking on end, something that looks like ketchup on his shirt, a white mark on his trousers that may be sick. By the color and depth of the bags under his eyes, he looks like he hasn't slept since Take That broke up. He's feeding himself frozen custard, not even trying to mop his mouth as he goes. I'm not sure he knows what he's doing. He's fidgety, he keeps staring from one child to another, his head jerking with each shift, like he can't take his eyes off any of them for too long in case they burst into flame.

I want to run for my life, but I'm frozen to the spot. I'm paralyzed. Rigor mortis is setting in pre-mortem. How can anyone do this? I ask myself, frantically looking around for an escape. This isn't a job; this is a scene from hell. How can anyone choose to do this? The edginess of the morning, of the last weeks, sneaks up on me all at once, and I'm completely paralyzed. And worse, I'm back in primary school and just about to throw up all over myself.

When he sees me standing there, Mark's lips move in what is probably meant to be a smile but looks like a death grimace. Even the freckles around his nose look desperate, and his eyes are blinking spasmodically. The running toddlers have included me in their circuit. They're running and yelling and one of them is singing something at the same time. It sounds like, *do you want to build a snowman?* A song that I've not heard before, but given the tone he's singing it in (sort of a banshee growl-yell), it must be the theme tune from a slasher film.

I mean to say something to Mark, but now I can't look at anything but the toddlers. My eyes follow their every move, my entire body follows them, is completely alert to them, and my shoulder starts twitching at the noise they're making. Then the baby, all of a sudden, with no warning, starts bawling. I look at it in shock.

"Why do they do that?" I ask in a strangled voice. I claw my throat with one hand. I hold my hands up to my ears to make the howling stop. The noise, the noise is too much! I'm properly back in primary school now, where the PE hall was always so full of an echoing mob and splinters of high-pitched laughter, that I almost always sat against a wall, trying to hug my knees and rap my ears shut with my hands at the same time. Why are all the children making such a godawful racket? I can't look at them, and I can't look at anything else. I'm completely mesmerized.

Mark starts swinging about up and down and side to side. The baby in the sling bawls louder. It's gone red like a tomato. It's wailing at the top of its lungs, its entire body contorting.

The noise is too much, and the toddlers are still running about, round and round around me, and I'm feeling utterly sick.

The noise, the chaos, the threat of imminent demise (the kids', Mark's or mine, I'm not even sure which) is so overwhelming, I can't move.

This is why it's better to keep my distance from people! *All* people. But especially small people. I can feel splotches starting on my neck. I scratch at them with my elbow, unwilling to let go of my ears, but it only seems to make them hotter.

"*Why?*" I find myself gasping. "Why?" I have no idea why I say it. I have no idea what I'm saying. Mark looks around at all the children. He's still swinging wildly side to side and up and down, and this is doing nothing but making the baby scream louder.

"I want to murder all of them on a daily basis," he says, his eyes glazed.

The baby is still bawling, the toddlers are still running in circles, really close to me, and now the child in the buggy who has so far been content murdering the teddy bear suddenly throws it on the ground, flings her head back and screams her head off. "Teddy!" she's screaming. She's raising her head in the air like a werewolf and really going for it.

I can't breathe, I can't breathe.

Dark spots hover in front of my eyes.

Suddenly, I know I'm going to faint.

My worst nightmare is about to come true. I'm going to faint in a public place, in this village, where everyone already talks about me and no doubt laughs about me. Right there, in front of their eyes, I'm going to fall unconscious. I'm going to – oh shit, oh shit – I'm going to pass out – dark spots – my knees buckle, I'm going down—

Then there's someone at my side. I feel it, an arm around my back.

I turn frantic eyes toward whoever it is. It's Branwell Beam. I look frantically at him. "I just – I just –" I say, not sure where I'm going with this.

And then blissful, blissful relief.

Because he steps closer and puts his arms around me. Just that. His warm arms. His warm chest. All of a sudden, the sounds of the children are cut off. And there's blessed dark and quiet. Complete, soft, warm quiet. The beautiful darkness of his chest. I hold myself rigid for ages, trying desperately not to shake, panting hard, and I can't let go. I'm never going to let go.

But then, as his arms stay around me, finally, finally some of the warmth seeps in. Against it, even I can't hold myself back.

I forget for a moment that I don't do this.

I forget that I never, ever, let anyone see. And I lean against him. I'm shaking, so violently that he must be able to feel it all the way down to his toes, but he doesn't pull away or offer to call 999 since I'm clearly having a seizure. His arms get tighter and warmer.

And this, I think, as I drown my face in his neck, this is the worst of all. This pretense that someone is there just when you need them. That they see you and they still want to be there. This surely is the worst thing to happen this morning.

Chapter Sixteen

I pull away. Maybe after a few minutes, or maybe I've been standing with my face in Branwell Beam's neck for hours. I notice for the first time that Mark Close and his posse of lethal assassins has disappeared. I look about me, but there's no sign of them. I look back at Branwell.

His arms are no long around me, but his hands stay on my waist in a way that makes me feel faint. He's wearing a white t-shirt and cargo shorts today. It takes nothing away from his stupid muscly arms and those piercing eyes.

"I don't know what you're doing," I complain. There's a shake in my voice, but at least I'm not about to pass out or be horribly sick all down my clothes. That's something. "You say you don't want to take me to bed. And here you are, standing about with your hands on my waist."

"I never said I don't want to take you to bed," he says, in a way that makes me have a spontaneous orgasm on the spot.

"Now?" I ask meekly.

"Not now," he says, in an intensely irritating male way that says it's His Timeline, and I must follow it. He interlaces his hand in mine, lifts mine to his mouth and kisses the back of it. "Now, what's bothering you?"

I give him a tiny pointless shrug in response, feeling like a total loser, because the feel of my hand in his is possibly what I've been waiting for all my life, and I didn't even know it. I'm pretty sure if he wanted to pull his hand away right now, I'd cut mine off and give it to him, so I didn't have to unlock mine from his. "There're too many people here. I don't know what I was thinking coming up here this afternoon. I – I thought it would take my mind off things. I already made the same mistake the other day."

He tucks my hand in his arm. "So, tell me about it."

Before I can protest, he starts strolling up the street, like it's 1865 and we're walking in Hyde Park and watching military horses practice their paces and rotund matrons fan themselves in the heat as geese peck at their fat hands.

"You can't hold my hand like that," I protest.

"Why not?"

"Because people are staring at us."

This isn't entirely untrue, though I've only just become conscious of it. First, it's Shona Klues, in the distance, frowning in our general direction. She's standing outside the florists, notebook and pen out, like she's actually doing something productive this afternoon. As I watch, she places her hand on the side of her head and mouths *call me*. Then it's Veronica Chives, pointing her nipples straight ahead like headlights and winking and grinning at me from her shop door. Mark Close and his posse, I notice now, is standing some distance away. He's staring in my direction, though he could have fallen into a coma, it's hard to tell for sure.

"And you care about that?" Branwell enquires. "Anyway, tell me what's on your mind."

I stop complaining about his hand and stop worrying, for a few seconds, about the devastation it'll wreak, when he no longer looks at me the way he's been looking at me ever since we bumped into each other this afternoon, like he's seen the one thing he was looking for all day, or possibly for the last hundred-odd years. Like I'm the answer to a question he didn't even know he had. Like I'm the answer to all his questions. It will inevitably stop, the way he's looking at me now. I jerk my head.

"The murders. Tobias's murder, and it's bringing up my aunt's murder too."

I try to drag my mind away from Branwell's beautiful chest muscles (how do they move like that, like they have a will of their own?) and the stubble on his neck (I can't get the image out of my mind of his shaving his neck and face, standing there in his bathroom, with no t-shirt on...holy Christ), and try instead to put my mind to Auntie Meera and Uncle Tobias. I won't lie, it takes a few minutes. But that thing is back again, the niggling thing at the back of my mind. The thing that buzzes in my mind whenever I think of Auntie Meera and Tobias, buzzing like a persistent and very irritating fly.

"Can you keep a secret?" I ask Branwell.

I look shiftily around me. Shona has disappeared into the florist's. Veronica is no longer standing at her shop window. In fact, I can't see her at all. Even Mark Close isn't looking at me anymore. He's bending down, trying to shovel goop into the little girl's mouth, the one sitting in the buggy. Most of it seems to be making its way down her chin.

I shudder. I turn back to Branwell. I take a deep breath and tell him about the placement of the two bodies, with their hands crossed over their chests, and the fact that neither was wearing anything when they were found.

When I stop, I expect him to soundly tell me off, I expect him to say that I have to tell the police what I've discovered and at once. That he will if I won't, and so forth. But he just keeps on walking, my hand sedately tucked into his arm.

"Aren't you going to tell me I need to stop perverting the course of justice and tell Shona over there about the MO?" I demand.

"Well, no. If you believe that you can't tell her, then I firmly back you up."

"And why is that? Because you have impeccable instincts?"

He looks back at me. "Because I like your cupcakes."

One might say that I've heard those words a lot in my professional life, but still, the way he looks at me when he says them, makes me wet myself a little bit.

"You have to stop doing that, you know," I say crossly.

"Eating your cupcakes?"

"Looking at me like that."

"Like I want to eat your cupcakes?"

"Oh, fuck off! I've been asking you to eat my cupcakes ever since—"

He half turns, lets go of my hand, grabs hold of my waist and kisses me.

Damn it! Why does the man always catch me by surprise when he does that? I moan into his mouth. "You can forget about eating my cupcakes," I say breathlessly. "You've lost your chance, sir!" I grab his shirt and kiss him again, hard. My arms go around him, and I press myself to him. This time, he groans, and he holds me so tight I'm afraid I'm going to start popping ribs.

When we're promenading again, when I finally catch my breath, and when I'm squirming a little less at the wetness of my knickers, I turn to him again.

I tell him about Auntie Meera. About her murder. About how she was found. "There was something about her. Something different in her voice when she called me the day before she died. I can't put my finger on it. But it was there. She was excited about something – or someone. I mean, Auntie Meera wasn't the type to hop about squealing when she was excited, but there was something in her voice. A new something." And I can't help remembering that lightness I'd seen in Tobias's eyes at the Easter fair. What does it mean? I shake my head, frowning hard.

"You think she'd met someone?"

"Well, *if* they were killed by the same person—" I shake my head. "The MO is similar. But I could have imagined the tone of her voice."

As we come to the top of the hill and turn around to start

walking down the street again, we bang straight into Tallulah, when she pops out of Waitrose, much like a bemused rabbit out of a top hat. I start. I snatch my hand out of Branwell's arm before I know what I'm doing.

Tallulah gives me a tremulous smile. She looks nervously at Branwell, then back at me. "That's nice," she says firmly, squaring her shoulders.

The words sound like they're apropos of nothing. Yet I know exactly what she means. She's saying it's nice that I have someone, even though she doesn't. That's what she's saying. That the past is in the past. That she doesn't hold it against me, what happened with Colin. That she's happy for me.

Is that what she means?

I feel a horrible moment of doubt. The truth is, I have no idea what Tallulah might mean, all these years later. I barely know her now. I remind myself we haven't been friends for ten years. That I don't know what's happened to her in that time. The uncertainty in the eyes is familiar, yes, but the little smile that's playing around her mouth now, that isn't one I know. Who is she now?

"This is my friend Branwell," I find myself saying, as I introduce them.

The three of us make some meaningless conversation about the neighborhood, the weather, Waitrose stocks of burgers (full fat vs. reduced, original vs. caramelized onion, beef vs. beef and lamb combined), and her job at the boarding school. We do it for what feels like hours, just standing there on the high street, talking in an endless stream about nothing. Branwell does it effortlessly, the idiot. Tallulah like she's determined to be normal and do social chitchat. And me like I'm being trampled repeatedly by a heat-crazed mad buffalo. But still, we do it. It's with sheer relief that I turn away from her when we're done. The words we exchanged have meant nothing, yet each one felt like a dagger in my chest.

I can't help it. I can't help thinking and wondering – would she look like this – even bigger than she used to be, that uncertainty in her eyes all these years later worse than it used to be – if I hadn't stolen her boyfriend from her? Would she still be alone if I hadn't done that? She wouldn't have ended up with Colin maybe – who, when all is said and done was a right loser – but maybe she would have had the courage to be with someone else. What if I'd destroyed that? What if I'd caused that? What if she would have been a completely different person now if I hadn't given her first – maybe even her only! – boyfriend a handjob behind the school wall under the magnolia sap?

"Tell me," Branwell says, as we start walking again, "about Tallulah."

Chapter Seventeen

I spend the next week or two focusing on my baking. I have a flurry of orders for garden parties that keep me busy day and night. Hysterical customers who want *everything to be perfect, just perfect, that's all, you know what I mean, you know?* And who keep calling me and amending orders till my hair is turning grey in my sleep. Some want lengthy conversations, they ask for my advice about whether cupcakes or a large three-tier cake – or in fact, five completely different cakes – would be more appropriate for their particular garden party, which is, apparently, different from all other garden parties. They explain to me in detail exactly *how* their party is different from all others. *And the weather,* they keep saying, *what if it rains, what if it's breezy, what if its cast-over, what if it's thundery, it's so humid, I bet there'll be a storm, do you think there'll be a storm, Arya, do you think there'll be a storm?*

I bake endlessly. A large batch of spider granola, with silvery sugar spiderweb threaded through it and chocolate spiders. A Bellatrix Lestrange cake with crazy hair and murderous eyes. (Just to be clear, I've tried to make ones that don't look like Helena Bonham Carter – not because I don't love the woman, I do, you can't not, but because, let's face it, the Harry Potter books are the real deal, the films aren't, but people look gut-wrenchingly disappointed when I do that, so I stick to the film version of the character now.)

Poopyseed muffins with – well, the clue is in the name. Let's leave it at the words: gooey, thick icing pouring down one side of each muffin, of the color brown. I do cakes, and layer cakes, tier cakes and mountains of creamy pie, a shedload of chocolate brownies and cups and cups full of chocolate mousse with blood pouring down the side.

Using my new equipment gives me the shivers, it's so beautiful. It's not familiar like my old stuff. It doesn't have the usual quirks – like the heart shaped cake tins whose bases didn't fit properly, or the knives that went blunt in a particular place, or the cake-decorating turntable that snagged. I don't look lovingly at the new stuff *and* curse the day it arrived in my house all at the same time, all in the same breath. No, it isn't my old stuff. But it fills me with a deep sense of wellbeing, nonetheless.

I can't exactly say why, but most days, when I'm done with the morning's baking, I end up in the region of the high street. Most afternoons, I bump into Branwell. Often, we promenade up and down the street eating frozen custard, sometimes chatting about the murders if I can manage it, other times discussing space tourism, free university education, WhatsApp groups that add you on without asking for permission, at what point *The Walking Dead* should have come to a graceful end, the merits of classic vs. chunky peanut butter KitKat, whether YouTube videos of animals riding on other animals are funnier or kids going nutty on their helpless parents, if bitcoin is a real thing, would we give up sushi or chocolate, is woke *really* woke or just pretend, are people rude if they don't acknowledge that you've held the door open for them, are evenings lonelier or mornings, Blu Tack or White Tack, or, in fact, thumbtacks, is your creativity really trying to kill you, rocky road ice cream vs. plain vanilla. Sometimes we don't talk at all and the silence is the best thing of all. Other times I point out that we're not Victorian, we don't need to amble up and down the high street, and would he just kiss me already. He usually obliges.

I can't help it. Despite my reluctance to like things and people,

I kind of half-like the walks with Branwell. I kind of half-look forward to them, and I generally don't look forward to anything. I'd struggled with myself and then finally asked him why exactly I hadn't had sight nor sound of him from when I'd first met him to the day he bumped into me on the high street. Why had there been nothing from him all the way from when Harrods turned up with half their shop's goods up to the time I was nearly murdered by Mark Close's posse?

"Book tour, of course," he told me. "I was away and I didn't have your phone number. I thought about you every single day, I promise."

I stop now in the middle of squirting butter cream and look out my kitchen window. The last couple of times we had gone for a walk though, something had shifted, or Branwell had tried to shift it. Two days ago, we'd been parading up and down the street, and we'd been silent for a few minutes, when he asked me about where I had grown up.

"North London," I said shortly.

And then, inevitably, he wanted to know more about it. What were my parents like? Where were they now? Did they like to pop over for coffee on my free days? Casual questions that people ask other people when they're getting to know them. I answered shortly that they lived in Barcelona at the moment, and then I quickly changed the subject, started talking about whether or not I liked the new fudge-flavored frozen custard that Veronica was handing samples out for. I chattered on. And Branwell obliged, jumping enthusiastically into the conversation. But I'd seen him, I had seen his eyes. The way they searched my face. There was no point saying it – that I don't do that. I don't go there. I don't talk about my childhood, and more importantly, I don't get close to people in that way. I don't get close to people, period, in fact. And that if he wanted to go there, go deeper, than it wouldn't be with me. There was no point saying that. Because the conversation had moved on. I rub the back of my neck now at the memory. The searching eyes. The queasy, unsteady feeling in the pit of my stomach. The way Branwell had of making me want to do nothing but sit at his feet and stare up at his face all day and all night and yet the desperate urge I had to run and hide any time his eyes probed me, when they seemed to want to know more, go deeper, see everything about me, leave nothing out.

When I'm done with my baking, I try to turn my thoughts from Branwell and spend a few minutes calling out to Tobias's cat. He generally only drops by when he's hungry. And sometimes I don't see him for a whole day or two. A lovely mid-July afternoon like today, he'll likely be stretched out in the hottest corner of the garden he can find.

On days that he doesn't show up, I leave him food outside the kitchen door. When I do that, it disappears promptly, but I have no idea who's eating it – Tobias's cat or other cats, or even foxes. I've also got into the habit of leaving my kitchen window open, and muddy paw marks all over my kitchen (not my work kitchen, my own kitchen – I thought I'd clarify that for the health and sanitation conscious) inform me that he's been in. Occasionally, very occasionally, he lets me stroke him if I catch him when he's eating, and he doesn't take all the skin off my hands.

I call out another couple of times now, but there's no response. I've often had the opportunity since I got the damn animal from Tobias's to think that it sounds demented standing at my garden door and shouting, The Marquis! The Marquis! That's a stupid name for a cat. I pop out the back door, but he's not there. I wind around to the front, shouting The Marquis! when someone calls back from the street. It's Willie Arnott, the accountant.

"Nice of you to look after Tobias Yards's cat," he calls with a wave.

"It's not nice. He doesn't appreciate it even one bit."

He smiles and walks on.

I spend some more time trying to call the cat, but no luck. He doesn't appear.

"Go hungry, then!" I call loud as I can.

I enter the house again. I stand in the landing and look up the stairs. Branwell had told me that he was away today for a book reading. So there's no point going up to the high street. (Not that he's the reason to go up to the high street. That would be crazy.)

But now, as I stand there at the foot of the steps, I acknowledge to myself something I've been pushing to the back of my mind for days. Or is it weeks and months? How long has the thought been lurking in my brain?

I dither at the foot of the stairs. Maybe I should clean my work kitchen again. But I've already done it three times. Even I can't convince myself that it needs a fourth clean.

I look up the stairs again, and toward Auntie Meera's workshop.

I had cleared out most of the old furniture from the house after Auntie Meera's death. I'd completely turned the kitchen around, of course, making the larger part of it my workspace, and a tiny, partitioned corner for my own, much more mundane use, and I'd made the bedrooms my own. I kept the largest, airiest bedroom for myself, and done the other rooms with enormous bookshelves for my baking and decorating and macabre inspirations books, storage for my equipment, and the little room for exercise. A lot of Auntie Meera's stuff had been around for years, and needed to be chucked out, but more to the point, I wanted to feel like this was my space, and not haunted by Auntie Meera. But I had left her workshop untouched.

I make my way up the stairs, all the way up to the loft, slowly, one step at a time, my hand tracing the banister, my heart plopping loudly in my chest.

I haven't been up here much since she died. I stand outside the door, my heart racing now. I could simply turn back and head down the stairs. I mostly forget about the room; I forget that it's there. I don't have to go in there.

I reach out a hand and push the door open.

The smell of the room hits me like a punch in the gut.

It's stronger than ever, now. The musk of police feet, the disarray of drawers searched and left open, fingerprints dusted, surfaces sprayed have all departed and left behind only Auntie Meera's smell. I take shuddering breaths. Mustard seeds and rosemary, musk mallow and night-scented catchfly, ark seed balls and crushed jasmine. Undertones of cacao beans, chicory, and sandalwood.

I slowly enter and try to acclimatize to the smell, the familiar sight of her things, the awful anger than still burns me when I think of her being snatched away like that. I take deep breaths. I try to get used to the smell, so I don't have to feel it like an ache anymore.

I run my hand on her gnarled wood apothecary's table. I look at the little wood apartments she'd set in the walls that hold all kinds of essential oils and potions. Carrot seed, rose, jojoba, manuka honey – her skin oils. Lavender, chamomile, ylang ylang – her calming serums. Cacao, peppermint, wild orange, basil – for energizing potions. I make myself look at each and every one, reading the label, looking to see how full the bottle is, if it's dusty or has finger marks. Some have skull and crossbones drawn on them and the word *Poison* written on them.

I make a mental note to try to find out what poison was used to kill Tobias. Would Veronica know? No, maybe not. Her source of information had been the paramedics, who wouldn't have known right away what poison was used. It makes me scowl to imagine someone injecting my tiramisu – *my* tiramisu – with poison. I make it the Portuguese way, with extra thick clotted cream and dollops of good Barbados rum, so it's extra special. I'm not sure I'll ever be able to make one again.

I open my eyes and look around me. I walk slowly through the room, making myself look at everything in turn. I turn to her table and open all the drawers. Tools, knives, sharpeners, notebooks, pencils, amulet bags, threads, ribbons, pestle and mortars, it's all there.

I look at the stack of journals. I open one at random. It's full of pages of recipes and notes about why she's using one kind of oil and not another, what effect a particular herb will have, where she might be able to find some unusual ingredient. I flick through the pages. There's an Ayurvedic recipe that uses tulsi, turmeric, fennel seeds, sage and honey. The notes flow over to the next page. I turn to it. The entire page isn't a recipe though. After a sentence or two about her recipe, the rest of it is a journal entry.

"I can't protect her forever, I know I can't," I read. "She's off to university tomorrow. I wish she weren't going off to Durham, it's so far. I wanted her to be closer, but she wants to go. She keeps saying she's fine. She keeps telling me it'll be fine, stop nagging, Auntie. I'm trying not to stand on her head. I'm really trying not to. But I can't help it. I keep walking about, fretting. I keep imagining her alone, by herself, with no one to turn to. For some reason, I can't stop thinking about Brendan right now. I don't think about him much. I try to avoid it. The man is not worth my time and my blood boils when I think about him. All he ever wanted was to change her, turn her into the child he wanted. He kept telling her off for not being brave, for being scared of everything. But he never saw how brave she really is. How everything hurts her and how she keeps fighting back."

I fling the notebook away from me like it's a venomous snake. It lands with a thunk on the apothecary table. I stand there staring at it, at its rough blue cover.

How everything hurts her.

The words are a punch in the stomach. The breath is literally knocked out of me. My hand goes to my sternum. I try to breathe.

I stand there, staring numbly at nothing. The breath enters my body, and leaves it in a harsh, sharp exhale. From not being able to breathe at all, I'm panting. From being able to smell, to feel everything, now I'm frozen solid. Or maybe I'm dying. Maybe this, this much pain, this is what it feels like. How everything hurts her and how she keeps fighting back.

How everything hurts her and how she keeps fighting back.

After many minutes, when the dark spots recede from in front of my eyes, I reach out a shaking hand, I pick up the journal and find the entry again. "I hate him. He's my sister's husband, but my god, I've lost count of the times I've imagined him having a paralyzing car accident. I hate the man. When he and Surya dropped her off at my old house to live with me (they said it was only for a short while, it's affecting their marriage, they said, and they need time off), I thought to myself *I'll do better, I'll do better than either of you ever could.* I watched them for years. The impatience and anger that was always there when Brendan so much as looked at his daughter. God, the disgust on his face, that was the hardest to bear. I stopped myself from slapping him in the face so many times. And Surya, like a frightened sparrow, hopping between the two, trying to mediate, trying to soothe Brendan. *She's different, Brendan, I know it's hard. She's not like other children.* What's the point getting an education—both of them qualified, successful corporate journalists—if you don't have a clue how to love your child? I couldn't bear seeing Arya's rage. And I thought I'd do better if she was mine, if they left her with me and never came back. *A few more months, Meera, can you have her a few more months?* That went on until they got jobs out in Berlin. *We could take her with us, Meera, but you know, the language, a new place. It'll be hard for her.* I wanted them never to come back for her – I always worried that they might. I should have known better. But she's off to uni tomorrow, and I don't know if I've done any better. Should I have been stricter, should I have pushed her more, and not let her have her anxieties? What if she goes off by herself and it's all too much for her? How will the other students look at her when she clicks and twitches? Will she cope?"

I can't read on. The tears are choking me.

I push the journal away again. I want to burn it. I wish I'd never seen it. I can't ever see it again. I will never be able to stop hearing the words.

"No," I keep saying, "no."

I don't even know what I mean. What do I mean by *no*? No, I don't want to read this? No, you did do a good job, you don't need to question it? No, you were all I had, how could you not know it? No, I wish people didn't see right into me like that, talk about me like that, think about me like that, worry about me like that, see everything I want to hide and erase?

Or do I mean, no, I can't believe you thought of me like that too. I can't believe that even you saw me as broken and damaged. I thought everyone else did. I didn't know that you did too, Auntie Meera.

All of it, none of it.

There are a handful of journals, rough textured covers, thick lined paper. "If they're anything like this entry, I may as well fling myself out the window now," I mutter, trying to stem the tide of tears that won't stop. I keep rubbing my face on my sleeve. I stack the journals to carry them downstairs and hope I won't have to drink myself into oblivion trying to get through them.

Chapter Eighteen

Still sniffling uncontrollably, I turn away from the journals and carry on my scan of the room. There are just the books now. The plant books – history, biology, world religions, goddesses, recipe books, various pop books on drawing down the moon, and reading charts and palms, and all kinds of other stuff. I shake my head when I look at the titles. Really, Auntie Meera, you were a little bit gone with the fairies, I can't help thinking. But also paperbacks, most of them bought from Oxfam and British Heart, stacked next to each other, with no thought to alphabetical order or genre or even size.

My heart nearly stops when I see the thing that I now realize I've been looking for all along.

The Power in My Hands, says the title.

I reach out for it. There's no bookmark this time. I don't know why I expect there to be, as if every copy of the book comes with the same flower power picture, the naked circle, taken from a low aerial view, as if by someone standing over the group, their faces cut off.

It isn't so odd that Tobias and Auntie Meera should have a copy of the same book. In fact, if I look at their range of literature, there's no doubt that I would find more similarities. Auntie Meera has a copy of *Middlemarch*. I'm pretty sure I've seen that on one of Tobias's downstairs bookshelves. Auntie Meera has basically every book ever written by A.S. Byatt and most Margaret Atwoods. Tobias had both of these authors on his shelves. I rub my chest again, where my heart is still galloping. Why is this book significant? The fact that I found a copy of it next to Tobias's bed—in effect, in his 'naughty' drawer—or that it had that weird headless picture in it means nothing.

I gingerly place Auntie Meera's copy on my stack of journals, ready to take downstairs with me. The book has a completely plain white cover, like those blank canvases that you see in exhibitions, with just one black dot in the center, or in fact, nothing at all, just a plain white canvas. Concept art that no one gets, that is probably saying something deeply meaningful and not just expressing, as is my opinion, the plain fact that the artist has the mother of all artist's blocks and can't come up with squat. The cover of this book is plain white, with the title written in black. It looks like a self-published chapbook. If anything – and for no precise reason that I can identify – I'm more scared to read it even than Auntie Meera's journals.

I don't know if it's the journal entry I read, or the finding of the book, or the smell of this room, but now, I can't bear to be in it for even a few more seconds. I speed up. I walk around closing drawers and putting things I've shifted back into their place. A strange dread takes over, and I can't slow myself down, no matter what I do.

I quickly pick up my stack of books. Drop some in my rush, pick them up quickly, haphazardly, turn off the light, close the door shut behind me.

And really, I'm surprised I don't fall head over feet all the way down the stairs, given how I can't get away from the room fast enough.

After taking care of my baking the next morning, I don hoodie and leggings and head out for a run. Trucklewood has a crisp edge to it. The sky is razor-sharp, the air a mouthful of truffle, the woodland in the distance fogged with breezy summer sunrays. It's a relief to get out of the house. There's nothing there really to remind me of Auntie Meera, but for some reason, since last night, her specter hangs over me more than it has since she died, more even than the last month or so since Tobias died. The very *aloneness* of her room, the feeling not that it's been left behind, but that it was inhabited by someone searching for answers that she couldn't find, searching for something, anything, has left me restless and uneasy. I try to shake off the feeling as I head out. But the unease lingers.

I speed up outside Branwell's house, and my neck starts aching from how hard it is not to turn my head and look over his hedge. I could go and see him, I could go! But the idea is foreign. The idea that I can simply go and find someone when I need them. It's not something I do. The casual sauntering up and down the street when I'm feeling more level, that's one thing. But this. No, I can't do it, I won't!

I'm twitching within minutes of leaving the house. Damn the man! Damn everything and everyone, in fact!

I march on, full power ahead, my body intent on not turning around, taking his hedge in one neat bound, banging on his door and demanding to be let in. The contradicting needs to run away and to go straight to him are so acute I feel like a thief tied to the rack, ankles and wrists being pulled in opposite directions to instill maximum pain.

I dash straight into Craig and his girlfriend Tarina.

I come to a complete standstill.

"Shitty biscuits," are the first words to come out of my mouth. "What do you want?" I frown at them, even though it's hardly like the pair is knocking at my door or even standing outside my house. They're just out for a stroll, it seems, Tarina in matching bright-pink velour sweatpants and hoodie and a leopard-print headband, apparently for all the sweat she's working up, and Craig with his hair neatly slicked back, and wearing excruciatingly boring tailored trousers, white shirt and shiny work shoes, even though he's patently not at work. I look Craig up and down and shake my head. "You're such a wanker."

"Banker," Tarina corrects me.

"How's that any different?"

Craig is looking at me with the exact same expression on his face that he's had in every one of our handful of meetings ever since the time he broke up with me. Sad, accusing eyes, a tad on the resentful side, like it was me that broke up with him and he's determined to hold a grudge in case I weasel my way back into his broken heart. Really, it makes me want to punch him. I stuff my hands inside my hoodie pockets in case this thought turns swiftly into action – which my thoughts can often do, without any warning whatsoever. If I let myself imagine this punch in any detail, I know I won't be able to stop myself from carrying it out.

Before I can say something rude—well, more than I've already done—someone joins us. It's Branwell, of course. How else would this impromptu meeting go? How could I stand out here outside Branwell's house and hobnob with my ex and his current, and our local resident children's author (middle-grade) not turn up with his (top-grade, really stand-out) arms to add to the car crash?

"What do you want?" I ask him, trying to ignore how good he looks in those casual trousers of his, his trainers, and an olive-green t-shirt.

"Hello, darling," the man says cheerfully and gives me an open-mouthed, full-tongue-action snog right there and then, in front of Craig and Tarina.

I flail about for a few seconds, trying not to drown. I'm pretty sure my feet aren't touching the ground. When I emerge, breathless and in need of CPR, Tarina giggles. "You make lots of sex then?"

I pat my hair. "Yes," I say demurely, after I've stopped panting.

"Yes," says Branwell.

The fucking idiot! *What* sex?

Craig looks sadly and accusingly, and a shade resentfully at me. "I don't see how there's any need to be quite this blatant about it."

"Makes you squeamish, does it?" I ask.

"I think it is sexy," Tarina says, turning kissy lips toward Craig. Craig, the great big bozo that he is, ignores her and keeps on looking at me like a bristling Chihuahua just before it does an anxiety-provoked wee right where it stands.

Tarina stops doing her kissy lips and starts looking at her manicured fingernails, like this was where she was headed all along.

"He was always a bit of an old prissy," I say in her direction.

"A pussy?" she asks.

"That too."

"Just because I asked for a bit of decorum in bed, Arya – a bit less noise, a bit less, you know, like a racehorse on amphetamines—" Craig goes a bit red, hot and bothered at his own words.

"Me, I like a good racehorse," Branwell murmurs, soulfully kissing my hand.

I snatch my hand away. "Not that this isn't the best conversation I've ever had, but I've things to do and places to be." I turn, but then I stop in my tracks and whirl around. "Why do the police think it's you anyway? Just because of your inheritance?" I demand, looking at Craig. "What kind of money are we talking about?"

I've been trying not to think about the murders, I have, but now, maybe after the evening spent looking through Auntie Meera's things, I can't help asking this question that I didn't even know I had in my head.

Craig mentions a figure that makes me nearly fall over.

"Get out of here!" I scream. "You're joking," I say, even though Craig never jokes.

He shakes his head.

Tarina is looking down at her fingernails still. "Craig never makes jokes. He never makes sex *or* jokes."

I ignore her statement of the obvious and gawp at him. "Tobias had that much?" I shake myself to recover my equilibrium. "I'll be damned, what an old codger! That's a tidy little packet. Still—" I frown, "Aren't you loaded? It's not like you needed his money."

Craig swallows drily and his eyes waver. "As to that, a bloke makes mistakes."

"Curiouser and curiouser," Branwell says next to me.

"I lost most of my savings in bad investments," Craig elaborates. He inserts a finger in his tight collar and wriggles uneasily.

"Betting," Tarina helpfully adds. "Not shares. Yes?"

Craig purses his lips. "The difference between the two is academic."

"Racehorses?" I goggle at him.

He refuses to answer. I turn to look at Tarina.

"He bet half of his money on it that Trump will never become president. And then the other half that Brexit will not happen." Tarina shrugs and studies her shiny silver fingernails again.

"Tough luck, mate," Branwell says.

I shake my head. I have a smidgen of respect for Craig's politics—or at least for his misplaced belief in other people's politics—but none at all for his business acumen.

"So, you did have a motive." I chew on my thumb nail. "Why do they think that the murder was committed in that one hour when you were watching foot—" I stop dead in my tracks, but quickly recover, "uh, after Tarina left yours and before Tobias was found dead by Veronica?"

I keep my eyes firmly away from Branwell. The man will never miss my little slip. But he doesn't say anything.

Craig shakes his head. "They don't. It's just that the cleaner left Uncle Tobias's, and then an hour later Veronica Chives turned up at his."

"The cleaner has a name." I poke a finger in Craig's chest. This physical violence gives me a brief—though still intense—sense of well-being. I do it again, just for good measure.

"Ow! I remember that about you," he says, wriggling inside his shirt collar again. "You don't have to turn every little thing a man says into an opportunity for a social revolution. A man can't eat his toast in peace when that happens. You don't need to take a radical position on everything."

"What other positions did you like to take?" Branwell murmurs.

I ignore him. "Did Cath eat any of the tiramisu?"

Craig shrugs.

"Then how do they know when it was laced with poison? It could have been any time after I delivered it, not just in the hour that you don't have an alibi."

Craig shrugs again. "I'm still the one with the best motive."

I nod slowly. "That's true."

"They also think I could have done it," Tarina says.

I turn interested eyes toward her. "Why?"

"Tarina leaves Craig's, is unaccounted for, for the next hour, then Tobias turns up dead," Branwell says. "Adds up."

I make an impatient sound. "But what's the motive?"

"Same as Craig's," Branwell answers.

"I didn't want you to find out like this, but we've set a wedding date," Craig says, his mouth pulled down, looking at me with his resentful-hyena eyes. "I know you still have a thing for me, and—"

"Oh, stuff it, Craig," I say crossly. "And congratulations," I say grudgingly. "Marriage sounds like exactly the kind of daft thing you'd do." I don't know if I'm talking to Craig or Tarina. "Now, if you'll excuse me." For the second time, I start to leave and then stop in my tracks. "Do you know if Uncle Tobias had anyone new in his life? A new love interest?"

Craig is in the middle of shaking his head, but then he stops and his eyes flicker.

I turn the full glare of my interest on him. "What?"

He shrugs. "I don't know. I can't put my finger on it. He wasn't the type, in one way, you know? But there was something about him the last time I saw him."

He has my full attention now, possibly for the first time since I've known him.

"Something about him," he repeats. "He looked...at peace or something."

My brow clears. A quick vision of Tobias at the Easter fair, the look I'd caught on his face. The utterly uncharacteristic serenity of it. The feeling, for a few seconds, that he was at peace. Craig has hit it on the head.

"Had you never seen him look like that before?" I ask him curiously.

He shakes his head. "I don't think I ever did. I mean, he liked you. So, he looked happier, you know, when you were around—" He touches the skin around his eyes.

I nod.

"But nothing to this scale. Uncle Tobias had a very hard life when he was young. He was bullied in boarding school."

"Really? I didn't know that," I say softly. A hard lump in my throat. I try to rub it away.

Craig shakes his head. "I don't know the details, but I get the impression it was grim."

"Right." I grimace.

I whirl around a third time. Then, before Branwell can stop me with his eyes or words or arms or whatever, I make tracks to get away from his headlights.

"Come by later," he calls after me.

"Maybe!" I call over my shoulder, without turning around. I'm really not sure I should be around the man in the fragile state I've been in since my excursion to Auntie Meera's workshop the night before.

I'm frowning, not thinking about where I'm going, trying to digest everything I've heard. So, Tobias was loaded and Craig inherits a fair amount from him. And Craig actually did have a motive. If Craig needed money and Tobias was leaving him bucketloads (and if I have the measure of the man, I imagine Tobias, though generous, would have told Craig no can do about paying off his debts), then Craig has a fairly solid motive. And no alibi – unless I confess to stationing myself outside his house and snooping on him with my binoculars. Because that's the rub of it. Motive or no motive, in debt or not, if the hour before the murder is the problem time, then

Craig couldn't have killed Tobias. He was in his house, watching television the entire time. I saw him. Damn it, damn all of it. No matter how you look at Tobias's murder, there are too many red herrings and secrets racing about, and I'm privy to way too many of them, if you ask me. It would be much better for me in general to not know anything about anything or anyone. I'm not cut out for it. I march up the road.

Nearer Tobias's house, I bump into Shona Klues and Shirley.

Shona's eyes sparkle at the sight of me. Shirley, dapper in his orange silk cravat, his Edwardian white shirt and his pantaloons glances down at my breast area, most likely to see if I have anything hanging out again today.

I give him a severe look. "Stop looking at my tits. Don't you have any work to do?"

Shirley has the grace to go pink, in a Victorian-debutante kind of way.

"As to that, we are working," Shona says. Her eyes are now hovering in my chest region. "We're looking for clues in the bushes, of any comings and goings. But I'd like to be the one to tell you, that your equipment is clean." Her eyes twinkle.

I wave a hand. "I know that. What would have been my motive, in any case?"

Shona glimmers. "You might have something coming your way in the will. A little something. Though my lips are sealed, and it's neither here nor there for me to say. I'm the soul of discretion, me. An Egyptian catacomb, rife with misleading clues. A Tudor maze. A Bletchley Park code to break all codes." She frowns. "Though he was just about to change his will."

I raise my brows. I'm touched that Tobias thought of me in his will. But now I'm more interested in the other intel. And trying to ignore the thought that Shona is not just quirky, but actually mad. What's she going on about Egyptian catacombs for? I shake my head. "He was about to change his will?"

Shona nods. "We don't know in whose favor either."

This goes with my working-theory of a new love interest. If Tobias were in love with someone, someone he was serious about, he might have thought about changing his will. He did have an innate sense of fairness. Plus, he came across as the sentimental sort, in some ways. Though, now the beam of suspicion falls squarely on Craig again. If Tobias's will was imminently going to be changed, and Craig knew about it, then his motive gets even stronger. I scratch my chin.

"A penny for your beautiful thoughts?" Shona enquires.

"You," I say severely, "won't find the bushes in my chest."

I turn smartly around after this cutting rejoinder. But then spoil it by turning around again. "What was the poison in the tiramisu?"

Shona mentions the name.

I recognize it as a plant-based poison but can't remember if Auntie Meera had any in her stores.

I turn around again and attempt to carry on with my run.

Next, I bump into Mrs. Sharma. This is the most interrupted run in the history of runs. It's less like a run and more like a teenager learning to drive for the first time and trying to come to grips with a clutch. Of course, I could keep on running past Mrs. Sharma, but I want to ask her something.

"Cuppa?" she asks hopefully, but also like she couldn't care less if I said yes or not.

"Stop asking, just stop, Mrs. Sharma. It isn't pretty," I tell her, purely in the nature of a social service. "Now. You seemed to imply that Uncle Tobias was seeing someone new. Who was it?"

She pats her hair, even though not one tendril escapes the egg on top of her head. "Like I said—"

I cluck impatiently. "That you don't like to kiss and tell. Yes, I know. This is a murder investigation, though," I add, at my most self-righteous.

"And who might you be, Poirot or Miss Marple?"

"I was always partial to her spy novels, to tell you the truth. But in any case. Do you or don't you know who he was seeing?"

She shrugs. "I don't know, as it happens. But every couple of weeks, he used to dress up to go out somewhere. I don't remember what day of the week it was, so don't ask me. And he always looked happy on those days, not like his usual grumpy self. He was even civil, or at least not as rude. Which some people would do good to emulate." She purses her lips at me.

I choose not to take her words personally.

I head off again, my feet turning in the direction of the woods. A nice long run would help clear my head. I don't know how detectives do it. But now clues and total non-sequiturs are rolling around in my head like clanking dice. I keep twitching, trying to escape the over-crowding of my brain. But words keep colliding in there. Journal, tiramisu, poison, naked, splayed, hand, power, will, outsider, murder, bullying, love, loneliness, rude. I have no idea which are important words and which not, which to do with the murders, and which mere red herrings.

Damn it!

I think about the poison used to kill Tobias, but whatever I do, I can't remember if I've seen it in Auntie Meera's stores. I think about Craig's revelation that he needed money, and Shona's revelation that Tobias may have been about to change his will. I frown. Craig has an alibi, though I can't admit to it. Unless, of course, the poison was injected not in that time frame, but earlier on. Does he have the imagination to murder someone, though? I shake my head. He really doesn't. And on top of that, try to make it look like it was the same person that had killed Auntie Meera… No, Craig's brain wouldn't work like that, or even that much.

I'm deep in thought but I still have the sense to skirt around the boarding school. I've bumped into Tallulah now, had a nice chat or two. Surely, I've done my bit. That's all I wanted to do. I don't have to do any more.

But, as luck would have it, and keeping with the genre of the day, I bang straight into Tallulah as I come around a clump of trees full tilt.

"Tallulah," I say, resigned now to the fact that I can't seem to step out of my house without bumping into everyone who lives in Trucklewood.

I know it all of a sudden. This newfound interest in talking to people—even if it's just to find out what happened to Tobias and Auntie Meera—this will be the death of me.

Chapter Nineteen

"Come in for a cup of tea, won't you?" she asks in that soft, breathy voice of hers. "I've been hoping I'd bump into you, but I haven't seen you in a couple of weeks."

"I don't want to," I blurt out, before I can stop myself.

The words are out in a flash, they're a crack in the air, the sharp retort of a bullet being fired. She gives me a quick smile. It makes me suck in my breath, hard and cold. Something sharp pricks me bang in the middle of my chest when I see that quick smile on her face, the familiar *it's okay, I understand* smile. That wretched smile. The one she used to give me every time I called her fat, or broke something of hers, or every time I wasn't there when she needed me. I could never explain to her that I wasn't the right person to turn to when you needed someone. That that was not me. Find someone else, I wanted to say, please, just find someone else. But she would only give me that smile. The *I know you don't really mean it* smile. I can't bear to see that smile now. I swallow hard and convulsively.

"Tea is fine." I clear my throat. The words are hard, they hurt.

"It's a Saturday. No classes." She hesitates. "Are you sure? I mean, about the tea? You can say no if you'd rather not."

I take a shaky breath. I remember this too. The hesitation, the not wanting to take up space. *Don't be pathetic*, I want to say. I want to shake her. *Don't be so pathetic, people will only walk all over you.*

I nod quickly before I say something awful, before I say something quite so Arya. I follow reluctantly behind her, wishing desperately that I had said no, that I hadn't agreed to tea out of guilt.

The teachers' rooms are in the outbuildings round the back. Tallulah has a little one-bed cottage, anonymous on the outside, just a solid square, really, like every other solid square that surrounds it, but her living room is floral and chintzy, with soft rugs and throws and cushions and fluffy stuffed animals everywhere. I goggle at the army of cottony bunny rabbits of all shapes and sizes that inhabit every available surface, with their floppy ears and endlessly gape-eyed faces.

It turns out Tallulah owns an enormous grey cat, named Creampuff, that's sitting on a rug bang in the center of the floor. His head is roughly the shape and size of a bull's, his eyes red and unbiasedly homicidal – in fact, he bears an uncanny resemblance to Hannibal Lecter. I've never seen anything so misnamed in my life. He doesn't bother to acknowledge me, not with the flick of a tail or even a blink, other than maybe his nostrils flare at the sight of this unwanted intrusion. I want to give the cat a high five, he's clearly a kindred spirit. I bend and give his chin a tickle. He looks utterly disgusted, like now he'll have to take a shower, but he doesn't chew my hand off, which makes him better behaved than I am.

"He hates me," I say cheerfully.

"Oh, no!" Tallulah says. "He bites if you disturb him. He doesn't like to move. This is really friendly for him. Sorry, I should have warned you. What can I get you? You'll make yourself comfortable, won't you?"

"He doesn't like to move?"

"Oh, no, no. Nothing will move him. He can barely make it out the door when he needs to—you know—go. He won't move for love nor money. He's the laziest thing in the world. No, no," she says hastily, eyeing the cat, who's eyeing her back like he's Mrs. Danvers and she's a slug. "He's not really lazy. Just, you know, he likes his rug, that's all."

She's fluttering about, patting cushions, looking red and breathless.

I turn to look at her. "You don't need to put yourself out, Tallulah."

She's straightening rugs and picking up a stray mug, some old tissue, a pair of wellies. "No, no, I'm not. It's just nice of you to come. I want you to be comfortable. What can I get you? I don't have much in. I don't even have any biccies, Arya." She places her hands on her cheeks. She genuinely looks put out by this.

"Stop it, Tallulah," I say sharply.

She blinks, then gives me that tremulous smile of hers.

I rub my mouth. "Sorry," I mutter.

"I know, don't worry, don't worry a bit."

I look away, not wanting her to see how she makes me feel. And now I remember that even though I used to think of her as my best friend, I always felt like this with her. The hasty smile, the way she flinched at things I said or did, the way she tried to hide it, the way she was quick to reassure me that she wasn't hurt by the things I said, the way all of it made me feel jittery, like she knew I was cracked inside and she knew I could at any minute say something that would hurt her and she had to put up a barrier in case I did. How she tiptoed around me, and how that made me want to jump out of my skin.

I remember now how being around her made me desperate to be somewhere else, someone else. I'd forgotten that over the years. Though of course, even back then, there had been no one else to turn to.

She's tidying still, putting books away. I catch a few of the titles. Mostly books on gardening and geography. One with the cover torn off. Called *Lustful Desires*. There are one or two more like that, skinny, cheap erotic books, with no covers. She's trying to hide the titles, so I try not to say something about them. I have to bite my tongue not to blurt something out, even something friendly or frivolous.

She's finally satisfied with the state of her living room and gets us mugs of coffee. I realize that I've gone from trying not to say something that might hurt her feelings to not being able to think of a single thing to say. I sip my coffee. My hand is shaking a little, so I put the mug down. I clamp my hands together. I get up and pace up and down the room. Tallulah has that look on her face that says it's fine if I want to do that. I'm thinking now that this was a mistake, to come here. I'm about to say it, when she stops me.

"I just want you to know, Arya, that I've not spent a day in the last ten years and more when I haven't regretted what I did to you."

I stop in my tracks, bang in the middle of the room. Creampuff softly growls under his breath to point out that I'm too close.

Tallulah places her mug carefully on a little side table. Her face looks the same as always—podgy, bland, soft, kind, all the things she normally looks—but her chest is moving up and down, faster than usual. I swallow hard. If I was already feeling restless, now I want to crawl out of my skin.

"It's fine," I say. "It was my fault."

She shakes her head quickly. "As if I don't know, Arya. Colin would have let anything that moved give him a hand job."

I can't suppress a snort. I nod quickly. "Let's not worry about it, it's in the past. I want to move on. I just—" I clasp my hands to try to stop them shaking. "I just wanted you to be happy. Not so lonely. I wanted not to have made things harder for you," I blurt out.

She shakes her head, more serenely now. "No, you don't need to worry. I told you, I'm happy you have someone. And as it happens, I have someone too."

She says it softly. I look up at her face. It's changed as soon as she mentioned that she had someone. I can't help noticing the softness around her mouth, the inwardness of her eyes.

I take a deep breath. "That's nice."

"It's okay. I know you think it's odd – that someone would like me, I'm a house…"

My brow stitches in a frown. "That's not true," I say, and it sounds harsher than I mean it to.

"I don't mind, Arya, it surprises me too."

I want to explain to her, I want to say that when I mention her weight, to me, I'm stating a fact as I see it, I'm not judging her, but she's never believed me when I've said that, so I don't say it now.

"I'm happy you have someone," I say.

She nods. "Then that's fine. We both do."

I shake my head. "Oh no, not me. You know I don't do relationships. Branwell – he's just, you know." I shrug.

She hesitates, then she says, "You have to let people in, you know," she says softly.

I jerk my head. "No."

"Arya, not all of them will…you have to let people see you."

"No," I say again. "No, I don't."

She looks at me with her pity written large on her face, and that horrible quick smile of understanding that I wish I knew how to be grateful for, but I don't. I just don't. I can't explain to her that I don't want understanding and definitely not pity. I want to be around someone who doesn't mind the things I say and do, who doesn't have to make an effort to understand and be kind. Who doesn't see me as damaged. But I don't bother saying any of this, because what difference can it possibly make? She's quiet for a really long time. I finish my coffee and get ready to leave. I've been staring senselessly at her collection of pebbles and stones. She tells me to take one. I look at the collection that lies in a large ceramic plate, pick one—grey-black on the outside, cracked in the middle, pomegranate on the inside—and absently put it in my pocket.

At the door, she says, "Come around. Maybe we can make cookies."

Something twists in my stomach. We used to do that. We used to bake. The smell of the cookies we used to bake—orange peel, Oreo, chocolate, Ribena once, raspberries, oatmeal and raisin—hits me and I feel faint from it. The longing. The longing for what, though? I don't even know what. The longing maybe not to have any longing in the first place.

I shake my head. "Thanks, Tallulah, but…"

She bites her lips. Then she smiles and nods.

Chapter Twenty

I'm so restless after my truly awful joke of a run that when I get home, I can't sit still. I shower, I wipe down the kitchen, even though it's completely clean, I move things around, I look at receipts and orders. Something is niggling at me again. Something chipping away at the back of my mind. But the more I chase it, the more it wriggles away. I go over what I know of Tobias's death and Auntie Meera's. I even go over the meeting with Tallulah. But it only gives me a throbbing headache. My head tells me there's something, something about the chat with Tallulah that I need to focus on. Something she said that I need to see. But I can't imagine what. When I'm done in the kitchen, I walk out to the hallway and see a piece of A4 on my doorstep. A flyer for something or the other. *Betrayal does not need to be your only companion*, it reads. *People have hurt you, but you can heal. Feel the power within.* Crude black letters. A flyer. Like the one I'd found before that I had completely forgotten about until I saw this one. I frown down at it. It's strange and anonymous, with no actual information. Just...words. I reread the words. *People have hurt you.* I shake my head. Just someone with too much time on their hands, nothing more. Everyone in the neighborhood has probably got exactly this piece of paper on their doorstep, it's not personal, not just for me. I'm rattled by the meeting with Tallulah. That's all. I scratch my neck. I'm still staring down at it when my phone rings.

"What?" I bark into it. "Don't you have books to write? Is that why you're not that successful?"

"You *have* googled me. I'm very pleased. Want to pop over? We can talk through all the clues. I missed you when I was away."

The relief at his words is so great that I whimper. All dignity forgotten, I'm at his door in about three minutes.

He gives me that crinkly smile of his that instantly makes me wet my knickers. He has a grey t-shirt on and he looks shamelessly clean. God, I hate him.

He makes me a cup of rooibos again. I pad about his living room, looking at books and things in packing boxes that he hasn't got around to unpacking yet – record collection, an old gramophone of all things, artwork no doubt collected in charity shops, old books about jazz, proofs of his books, various rusting knickknacks collected from car boots. The man is like a magpie, if magpies collected old tatty stuff that no one else wants. I have the odd thought that I'd happily just do this, be in his house, looking at his things, with him pottering about, doing whatever he's doing. I remind myself I don't do that.

I hear him moving something behind me. I crane my neck around to look. An enormous blackboard.

I nearly swoon at the sight. It's not just how his arms look, lugging the thing around. It's also that I really like blackboards. And stationery in general. The colors, the textures, the neatness of it all! I shudder.

"I use it when I'm trying to work out my stories. Thought it might be handy tonight."

I beam at him.

It makes him stop in his tracks.

"What?"

"I've never seen you look at me like that before."

"Don't be boring. In any case, it's nothing. I just happen to love blackboards, they're sexy. Come on now. Help me with this." I walk over to the blackboard.

He brings out colorful chalk. I nearly fall over when I see the colors. "I love them," I say breathlessly.

He grins. He writes Craig's name on the blackboard. Under the word *Suspects.*

I frown and chew on my thumbnail.

He's looking consideringly at me. "So, what were you doing outside Craig's house on the night of the murder?"

I don't even bother to act surprised. I knew he would pick up on this nifty little detail the other day when I was talking to Craig and Tarina. I roll my eyes. I don't answer.

"Do you still have feelings for him?"

"What do you care?"

He doesn't say anything for so long that I finally have to look away from the blackboard and look at the man.

"Do you?" he asks, without the crinkly smile that I've got used to from our walks. His eyes don't waver, they stay firmly on my face.

Here I was thinking the crinkly smile is the thing that leaves me feeling funny in the tummy. But turns out it's worse when he isn't smiling.

"I don't." I keep my eyes firmly on his face when I say it.

He's still looking directly at me. "So why do you mind if the police suspect him?"

"An innate sense of justice?"

He's still looking unblinkingly at me.

I cluck loudly. He doesn't flinch or look away, just keeps looking at me. I cluck again. I rub my cheek to stop the clicking. "I don't know if he did it or not. He does like looking out for Number One. Though I don't know why he'd have killed Auntie Meera – and I still think it was the same person for both." Then my brow knits. I remember something that hadn't occurred to me until now. When Auntie Meera's will had been read out, a few weeks after her death, it had turned out that Auntie Meera had left Craig something. It wasn't much, just an old rusty motorbike that had been in her shed for centuries seemingly. When I'd asked Craig about it, he'd said it was because he'd sorted out some investments for her. I frown now, trying to work it out. I look up at Branwell, who's still looking at me. I flick my head. I turn my eyes to the blackboard again. "Put Tarina down as well."

He doesn't say anything for a second, but then he does what I've said. He writes Tarina's name on the board. "Poison being a woman's weapon, and all that."

"It was a blunt object with Auntie Meera, though."

"So, who else?"

I raise my hands. "Basically, anyone in Trucklewood could have had the opportunity. I haven't been able to step out of the house for the last few weeks without bumping into just about everyone." I'm usually better at only stepping out at unsociable hours or avoiding busy streets. The two murders are wreaking havoc on my social life. Or rather, my preferred lack of it. "The problem is there's a chance Tobias would have left some of his artwork to various people too. He wasn't sociable, but he was kind. Cath, his cleaner. I bet he would have left her something."

Branwell puts Cath on the board.

"I need to speak to her. She might be able to help narrow the timing down. Maybe he left expensive artwork for other people too. He might have for me. And then, there's the mysterious love interest. I wish I knew who that was. Problem is, it might not be someone from Trucklewood. The other thing is," I say slowly, "Veronica Chives messed with the body. I mean, what if she killed him and then changed things around?" I shake my head. It doesn't make sense.

"That doesn't make sense," Branwell says, echoing my thoughts. "You wouldn't hide your own MO."

"Unless it's a double bluff."

"Why did she put clothes on him?"

"Puritan?"

Branwell inclines his head. "What if there *is* a secret there? You said you thought she was hiding something, something she knew about Tobias."

"What could it be though?"

"A physical thing, something she knew Tobias was private about? His size? Body hair? A scar?"

"Hmm. I wonder if Craig knows. I'll check."

We talk through some of the other residents. Other than the fact that Tobias didn't give people the time of day most of the time, or that he might have left someone something in his will, it's hard to come up with any real motives. And even harder to reconcile the two murders. Could I be wrong? What if the second murderer only put Tobias's body naked, splayed and with his hands crossed over his chest to act like it was the same killer as Auntie Meera's to send the police off on a wild goose chase? If the police started thinking that it was a serial killer on the loose, then they might not look for more personal motives for Tobias's murder. What if the two murders weren't connected, after all? What if Veronica Chives's inadvertent messing up of the body had put the police right back on the correct track?

My throbbing headache comes back with a vengeance. Does Tobias's love interest have anything to do with his murder? If the will were going to be changed in his or her favor, then why would the man or woman murder Tobias before the will was changed? I blow air out of my mouth.

Maybe I'm barking up the wrong tree, yet…yet there's something about them, something nebulous that I can't quite put my finger on. I cluck again. "I can't help it. There was something lonely about Uncle Tobias, and also about Auntie Meera. I know that sounds like a tenuous connection. Lots of people are lonely. But – I can't explain it. They were lonely in the same way." I make an impatient sound. Something niggles at the back of my mind again. I rub my forehead, where the blood is pounding.

Branwell is half perched on his desk near the blackboard. "Expand."

I shake my head. "I don't know. Some people are circumstantially lonely. Other people existentially."

"And these two were the latter?"

I nod slowly.

"You think someone specifically sought them out? Preyed on them?"

The words make me uneasy. I've been connecting the two murders in my mind, but I've never put it into those words.

"I know that sounds crazy. And unlikely."

"Trust your instincts."

I look up at him. I almost laugh. I make an impatient sound. "My instinct is to hate everyone."

He crosses his arms casually. "Not everyone."

I look at him for a long time. The casual way he's leaning against the desk. The crossed arms, with the soft springy hair on his forearms. The t-shirt. The directness of his eyes. I like the directness of his eyes. But there's something else there too. The way he looks at my face. I've noticed that on our walks, just a hint now and again. The way his eyes search my face sometimes when I've rambled off on a tangent, or when I'm deliberately turning away from him. There's a need there. A need to know more about me, to be closer. And I don't want to know about that. I don't want to see it. And I don't want to hear its echo in my body.

I impatiently flick my head. "You don't know anything about me, Bran. You think the things I do and say are cute, or that I don't mean half the things I say. But I do mean them." I walk about the room. I throw up my hands. "At some point, I'll say or do something that'll hurt you and put you off. It could be tomorrow or in a few weeks. But it'll happen." I can't help it. As often happens, words I've said in the past to any number of people—strangers, neighbors, people I don't know that well, but especially people close to me, my dad, Tallulah, my fight with Auntie Meera not long before she died—all of it runs through my mind.

My dad, the way he used to flinch when I would tick or click.

The way he'd look intensely uneasy at the things I'd say, the way my body would convulse suddenly, the way I'd make a sudden loud noise or run out of the room in the middle of a conversation. The way he'd look like I was twisted and broken. The way I'd try my best not to be like that when I was with him, and how that pressure to behave would make it so much worse, so that the anxiety would build and build in my stomach and erupt suddenly. The way my stomach would hurt to the point that I would get sick.

I stop my pacing and come to a halt near the blackboard. Even Craig, I think, even Craig, the things I could blurt out, even when we were in bed, even then, there was nothing to stop my mind from wandering. It couldn't have been fun for Craig to be with someone who was like a cricket commentator, pointing out just about everything – smelly feet, a glazed, stupid look in his eyes, a lost erection. It can't be fun to be with someone like me.

I look up at Branwell, who's looking seriously at me. It's that look again, that look he gives me sometimes when we're walking on the high street. I make an impatient sound. "I don't have feelings for Craig. I don't have feelings for anyone. Nothing except annoyance and hate. That's all there in inside. I can't put it plainer than that." I don't want his sympathy or his understanding. I need him to know. "Can't you see?"

He stands there for a few moments, his hands stuffed in his trouser pockets now. His face is completely still, his eyes intent on my face. A piercing in my chest now, that I can't name. I don't know what it is, because I've never felt it before.

He walks up to me and lifts me gently on to the desk behind me. He twines his fingers in my hair. I find my arms and legs—almost involuntarily—twining around him. When he kisses me, I can feel it deep in my belly. He pulls me closer. His hand moves up my ribs, a thumb feels the underside of my breast. I sigh into his mouth.

"It's only a matter of time before I fuck you off and you hate me." The effort to keep my voice neutral is so huge that I have to squeeze my eyes shut so I don't start twitching. I can't start twitching. I *can't*.

But I can feel the pressure building inside me. The more I try to clamp it down, the more it builds.

"Arya," Branwell says.

"Yes?" I squint up to his face, one eye still closed.

"Stop talking."

"What?"

"Stop talking and lie back on this desk."

"Okay," I sigh.

I want to say we have mind blowing sex. But it wouldn't be true. The man's scruples are more extravagant and flamboyant than a Victorian virgin's. But the things the man does with his tongue on my neck, well, that almost makes up for it. I'm only saying *almost*.

Chapter Twenty-One

The next couple of weeks, I'm overrun by garden parties again. Some days, I'm baking most of the day and cleaning for the rest of it. I try to tell myself that the murders are not my problem. That the police can deal with them. Yet, the questions and details play on my mind day and night.

One morning, I get a call from a lawyer, informing me that Tobias Yards has left me a couple of paintings in his will. "It might take some time to get them to you," the man says in a bored voice. "Or it might not. It's hard to say anything at this point, to be honest."

I'm touched, even though Shona had as good as told me that I might have something coming my way. When I put down the phone, I swallow hard to dissolve the rock in my throat. I'd admired one of Tobias's canvases once. Most of his art was classical. But this one had been a painting of St. Ives by a woman called Emma Jeffries. I'd exclaimed at the vast vista of turquoise, the houses that speckled the beach in the distance, and the vantage point of a circle of red and pink flowers through which you saw the rest.

I know it, suddenly, as I stand there staring at my phone, that he'd have left me that one. Tobias was that kind of person.

The next day, the last Sunday of July—for some reason a busy day for birthday parties and garden parties—I spend most of the day touching up decorations, some baking of last-minute orders or changes in orders, packing, and sending things off with Sebum, my courier.

He keeps telling me his name isn't Sebum but rather Josiah. I tell him not to be so stupid, Sebum. The first time I called him that, he giggled, and I realized he thought I'd called him Semen. I told him off for flirting with an older lady – him being no more than twelve, clearly – and explained – kindly – to him that I didn't go for boys that still had wet dreams. He went red and said he hadn't had one of those in months. Weeks, he admitted. It was last night, wasn't it, Sebum? I asked him kindly.

The day is hectic, and I can't wait till it's dusk, and everything is done, so I can try to head out for a walk in the woods. But then a cake goes wrong at the last minute, and it's eleven at night by the time I'm done with cleaning and putting things away and checking orders for the next day. By the time I've managed to take a shower it's creeping closer to midnight.

On my way out, I see something white on my doorstep. Another sheet of A4. I'd forgotten all about the first two. I frown down at it. Crude black letters like the first two, typed, with hardly any writing on it. *If people you loved betrayed your trust, taught you that you could not be loved, then you can help yourself. You have the power. Look no further.*

I frown down at it. Crumple it up. It must be some local crackpot with loads of time on their hands. I don't know why the simple piece of paper with the strange anonymous words makes me feel uneasy. Something about the words, about the anonymity of them. I throw it in the recycling, this time with a flash of irritation, hoping that whoever it is gets bored and stops sending these around. There's something creepy about it.

I head out toward the woods, thinking that this, really, is the only way to step out of the house. At nearly midnight when everyone else is in bed and there's no danger of bumping into loads of stray walkers who want to talk to me.

Auntie Meera's death hadn't had this effect. I'd been quick to ward off sympathy and invitations. Trucklewood residents had reached out to me since I was new in the area, and since they had no idea what I was like, but they'd quickly got over it. I'd made my feelings about making small talk—and let's face it, generally about Other People—clear pretty quickly, and they'd moved on. But now, now, I can't help thinking that it's all my fault for talking to people about Tobias's death and for making them think I'm turning into someone normal and sociable when I'm not.

This, this is the way to do it. This is clearly the only way to step out of the house. I don't pass any stray Trucklewood residents. In fact, the world seems to be sleeping. There isn't even anyone putting out last minute bins or pulling the blinds down or having a sleepless stroll.

The night is silvery. There's a shard of a moon, hardly there. A black cloud plays with it, drifting past it and hiding its tentative light, and then unveiling and revealing the shadows in the woods.

When I was working, I'd managed for some hours to suspend my thoughts, and got caught up in mixing and squirting and timing and packing. But now, it's like those hours come crowding in on me, and my head is full, not in dribs and drabs, but all at once. It's a jumble, thoughts cramming together, colliding for space.

Branwell, I can't think about him and the way his mouth feels on my neck and his thumb on my nipples. There is no need to dwell on that. I shiver a little but turn my head resolutely away.

Auntie Meera—the journals I can't bring myself to read. That's where my head goes next. Surely, the police will have already done that? They will have read the journals. Surely, that would be the place to look, to see if anyone suspicious had entered her life recently, or if she had been scared of someone.

No, I shake my head. She hadn't been scared of anyone. I'm sure she hadn't been scared. She'd called me the day before she died. She'd invited me to breakfast. Whoever it was she had met—either someone she'd known for a while or someone new—she hadn't been scared of them. Like Tobias, she had seemed at peace, perhaps for the first time in a long time.

I frown. I crunch the leaves underfoot. I weave through the trees. Not running, just walking at pace now. The shadows are deep, the smell of pine high and fresh. I have the impulse to stop, to just lie down and look up at the sky and not think about any of it. I keep on walking. Not venturing out to the clear, open hills, but staying in the woods. I turn once to see Trucklewood lights in the distance, the sprinkling of houses, the clean, manicured lawns.

Was it someone from this little community who was responsible for the murders? If, instead, it was a stranger, then why would they target two people from the same community? The strange book that both Auntie Meera and Uncle Tobias had – I looked it up, and it had no publishing record. I know I need to read it, but like Auntie Meera's journals, something about it repulses me. I don't even want to touch it. I've successfully managed to avoid the journals and the book since I found them in Auntie Meera's workshop.

I weave through the knotted trees, in and out, trying to rub out the clump of something that seems to be lodged in my chest. The clump I don't want to feel. I don't know what's bringing it on. If it's the murders, the clues and questions that keep running through my head, even when I'm sleeping. Or if it's the new sociability, which is fast getting old. It's already crowding in on me. Or if it's Branwell. The horrible longing that I hate in myself. It feels like a longing that's always been there, always been a part of me, that I've tried so many times to cut off me, that he seems to call up at the blink of an eye. I don't want to feel it.

I come to an abrupt standstill near a nub of trees. They're gathered in a circle, the trees, smaller than some of the beeches and oaks around them. In the intermittent moonlight, the huddle of trees seems to shift. I frown and look at the trees. But it isn't the tight cluster that's stopped me, nor the way the moonlight makes it bump and shift, like they're from another time. It's something else. Something about the trees, the way they seem suspended and breathless. There's something behind them.

I know it suddenly and clearly, even though there's no sound.

My heart starts thwacking in my chest.

I'm utterly still in the dark. I turn, without making a sound, to look behind me, because suddenly I can't help feeling like I'm surrounded. Being watched from all sides.

The clump of trees is dense and surrounded by the larger trees. Just behind me are the lights of Trucklewood. I remember suddenly and clearly. There's a clump of trees around here that people call Witch's Tuft. I've never noticed it before, though I must have passed here many times, but this must be it. It's the slant of the full moon, landing squarely on the huddle that's made me notice it. That, or a sixth sense.

I can hardly breathe; all my senses are attuned to the slight shift in the leaves in front of me. I walk, as if involuntarily, forward, slowly, being utterly careful where I put my feet. I realize I'm good at moving soundlessly, I'm good at hiding.

At the little henge now, I stop.

My breath, already shallow, clots in my throat all at once as I try desperately not to make a sound.

The sight is so strange and yet so fitting that I almost whimper. A knot of people stands inside the clump of trees. In dark robes, hoods covering their heads. They're utterly still when I spot them. And I'm sure, I'm certain, that they're not of this world, not of this time, that I'm seeing something from another time that I was never meant to see. This is private.

Then the knot moves, and my heart nearly stops beating at the suddenness of it. They were standing utterly still when I saw them, just a circle of people, as if made of stone, but now they move away from the center. In the center of the circle, I see objects. They're shadowy, and I can't make them out. A gown maybe? Some sort of cloth, at least. Some objects, maybe a photo frame, a few books, I can't tell for sure. There are sticks and twigs piled around the little collection.

One person now lights a match and sets alight a torch. He or she bends forward and lights the little pyre that they've built, made up of the objects and some little logs of wood and twigs and sticks. The fire, when it lights, isn't big, but it's energetic and blue. It sings and springs and consumes the objects. The huddle of people is tight, and it's unlikely that the light from the bonfire can be seen at any great distance. I watch breathlessly. What are they burning and why are they burning it?

The circle falls further back. It's still a circle, made up of seven people, but it's a little looser. They were almost touching before, but now there's some space between them. As I watch, they all lift their robes. The vision of naked limbs, some skinny, some not, is pale and shocking in the light of the embers, so hairy and veiny and vulnerable, it makes me put my hand to my mouth. I'm not supposed to be here. But I'm afraid now, if I move, I'll give myself away, I'll break the spell, and this spell wouldn't be safe to break. I don't know why I think that.

And then it gets worse. Because the robes keep on lifting, higher, until it's not just limbs I'm seeing but more than limbs. My fingers clutch my mouth. I don't want to see this. The robes don't go all the way. They stop at the belly, some small, some large. The circle of people sits down. I can't stifle a gasp. It's the circle in the photograph I found in Tobias's book. The exposed lower body. That photo was in daylight, on grass. This is on grass, earth and twigs, and it's in the dark, and it's wider, the circle, but it's the same. Hands reach down now to find flesh. A humming begins, coming from the circle.

It's not until I feel a hand clamp on my mouth that I realize I'd been on the brink of giving myself away. I'd been about to scream.

Chapter Twenty-Two

I don't struggle. I'm dragged backwards, softly and quietly, by someone built along the same lines as an ox. I don't make a noise. Whatever sound I do make is drowned out by the curious humming, the keening sound coming from the clump of trees, and the crackling of the bonfire that is eating away at the little mound of objects I'd seen in the center of the circle. Whoever is pulling me is freakishly strong, but I don't make a noise. I'm more afraid of disturbing the circle than whatever it is this person can do to me. Plus, this is one person, and I think they're fully clothed. I'd rather deal with them than the seven half-naked people in the clump of trees.

Finally, at the edge of the woods, and on the crest of the hill that leads down to Trucklewood, the person stops pulling and dragging.

"What 'ees matter with you?" the person hisses.

It's Olga. I gape at her. Then I jerk my hands in the air. "What are you, a weightlifter or something?" I whisper-shriek.

The relief of being away from that clearing is so acute, I can't think straight.

"I vos almost in Olympics at young age," she says.

"I can bloody well believe it! What are you doing up here in the dead of night?" I hiss. It must be past one in the morning. Does no one look after this hundred-year-old lady?

"I veel ask you same question, young lady." She waggles a finger in my chest. "'Eet is not safe. As you see."

"Who are they? Have you seen them before?"

"I haif seen people go up to the woods, that is all. I see no one, no one sees me, that is the number vaan rule of Olga Viotchlik. It is how Olga Viotchlick escape bad men who want to do bad things to her in the war. Olga is inveesible."

She looks so nonchalant about it, she freaks me out. And which war is she talking about? I suddenly feel like I've stepped back in time by a hundred-odd years. She may well be a vampire, for all I know. All things are possible.

"Who are they?" I jerk a thumb. I'm still hissing, unwilling to make a louder sound.

She shakes her head. "Like I say, Olga keep herself to herself. You do same, yes?" She pokes a finger in my face.

My brain moves at a rapid pace now that I'm away from that eerie clump of trees. "Is this what you meant?" I demand. "Is this who Auntie Meera was involved with? When you said she was looking for love in the wrong places?"

"I never use the word love, that is your word." She shrugs. "People look for something. People always look for something. But the hole in here," she thumps her chest, "nothing can fill hole. Yes? Can anything fill *your* hole?"

I wisely decide not to try to answer this question. "You're a philosopher and you don't even know it. And a weight-lifter."

She nods sagely. "I do know it. Come now, let us leave, before they finish."

I swallow. Finish. Oh god, my eyes. I will never get that sight out of my mind. Naked flesh, old flesh, weathered flesh, and those hands moving down and down. Oh god. I shudder.

I drop Olga off at her cottage, though she patently does not need me to babysit her.

"You take care, Arya Winters," she chides. "Not be wandering about in dark woods at night."

I turn toward my house.

I stand on the doorstep. I move aside the recycling box, with that crumpled flyer still on top of the pile of paper and cardboard. I move the box inside and enter the house.

The next morning, I feed The Marquis. He seems to keep out of the way most of the time, but then when I'm not expecting him, he frightens the life out of me by suddenly brushing up against my leg in the dark kitchen or letting out an ominous purring when I think I'm alone in the house. I'd started by feeding him every day and then trying to tickle him, but that strategy failed miserably. So now I've taken to tickling him under the chin before I give him any food or sometimes during. He grudgingly puts up with this. I look at my kitchen door and wonder how long before I give in to getting a cat flap put in. I can't leave the kitchen window open indefinitely.

After I'm done being glared and spitted at by The Marquis, I take a deep breath. I know I can't put it off any longer. *The Power in My Hands.* I walk to my living room and I finally pick up the book. It's Monday and the day is my slowest one in terms of orders. I don't have much to do.

I don't want to touch the book, but I know I have to look through it. After what I've seen last night, the image of which is forever burnt into my brain, I have no choice.

At the end of the hour it takes to read the whole thing, I want to wash my eyes out with chlorine. The main message is nothing much to write home about. The book is advocating group sex and masturbation, which hardly comes as a surprise after what I saw the night before. It's the tone and the language that makes me curse loud and hard throughout. The book goes on and on. *Take the power of your soul in your hands*, it says, *elevate your spirit, use the power of your ecstasy, align your energetic field with the universe's rhythm.* It keeps on telling you to *breathe*, with 'breathe' always in italics. *Connect with your breath, connect with your core, breathe, heal yourself from trauma, release*. The book, instead of being repulsive, is just plain boring. There really don't need to be this many words written on this subject. The words *healing energy fields, releasing trauma,* and *sacred whore* appear way more times than they need to.

The words remind me of something, I'm not sure what, though. I frown at the book. It leaves me no more enlightened than before. What has this book got to do with Auntie Meera and Tobias's murders? I wonder if I'm barking up the wrong tree entirely. The book seems to be some sort of cheap manual distributed at a local fair, from someone who wanted to write it, and for people to read it. It's not titillating, it's not sinister, just a bit boring.

But then I think about the circle I saw last night.

I sit there for a long time and frown. I keep thinking about what I'd seen the night before. The bonfire. Never mind the people, the naked limbs. The bonfire.

I don my running gear and look to see if The Marquis is around. I can't see any sign of him. I head out toward the woods again. I climb up the hill that Olga and I had come down mere hours before. I circuit through the trees. It doesn't take me long to find the copse.

I enter it cautiously, even though it's just a huddle of trees now, there's no one here. The bonfire has been cleared away. Just a blackened gash remains in the grass. A crisscrossing series of gashes. There is not much left of the little conical bonfire, or the objects that had been burnt in it. Cold hard charcoal. I finger the bits, trying to make some sense of what they may have been before they were burnt. But there are no clues. There is a wisp of material. Charred beyond recognition. I put it in a little plastic bag that I've brought with me for this express purpose. Then I draw back from the remnants of the fire. I start circling it in ever widening circles, staring hard at the ground.

At first, I find nothing. There's matted grass, but also some dry patches.

Then I see something that makes me clutch my throat. It's a dull glint in the grass, half covered by a leaf. I bend down to it. I lift the leaf up, but I don't touch the object that's hiding underneath it. It's a large signet ring with a stag on its face. I stare at it for a long time, willing it not to be there. Finally, I use the sleeve of my hoodie to gingerly pick it up and put it in my bag of meager evidence. My heart is pounding, and I can't help looking around me again. I think it may well be time to talk to Shona and Shirley.

Chapter Twenty-Three

I walk up the high street. Reluctant as I am to see people unless I absolutely have to, I find that the normality of the street is a relief after the night before and after seeing the remains of the bonfire. Predictably, Shona and Shirley are walking about, talking to people. Mark and his partner Sheshonne are walking with their coterie of children. Astrid Gardener, the potter, and her husband Terry, the architect, are around today too, trying to chat with Mark and Sheshonne over the shrieks of the children. Veronica Chives is standing outside her shop, hands on her waist, an uncharacteristic frown on her brow, glowering at nothing that I can see. As soon as she sees me, she frowns harder, then disappears inside. Luckily, I have no qualms about talking to people who don't want to speak to me. It's the ones who want to speak to me that I'm scared of. I charge right in. Veronica's nowhere to be found. I speak to her pigtailed assistant Serena and demand to see her.

"I'll just stand here until she comes out!" I serenade. "I'll keep eating frozen custard until there's nothing left in the shop! I'll start dropping things on the floor! I'll start—"

Veronica emerges from her office, arms crossed over her chest. Her loose red plaits frame her freckled face, her checkered shirt and sprayed-on jeans are dapper as usual.

"You know, I never would have guessed you were an emotional

blackmailer, Arya. So many people are. My ex-husband, now he was a real pro at it. But you? Never." She actually looks hurt, like I've been deceiving her about my true nature all along.

"It's where my nipples are pointing this morning, Veronica." I walk up to the counter. I glance at her assistant. "Now, I can do this here or I can do it in your office."

We glare at each other for some minutes. I can't help noticing that Veronica has the creamiest skin, with soft blonde down on her cheeks and very pink lips. She has a permanent Barbie smile with perfect white teeth, so aligned that they seem to be all one unit instead of individual teeth. She's got the smile on now, even though she's glaring at me.

"Do you ever stop smiling?" I'm genuinely curious.

"I've forgotten how to stop."

"Why do you do it?" Seriously, I just want to know.

"I don't know how else to get people to like me."

"Why do you want people to like you?"

"Everyone does. So do you. You just want it on your terms. Like the rest of us, honey. You're not that different."

"I don't want to be liked. In any case, enough chat."

She holds a quick hand up, her eyes on her assistant. She impatiently waves me into her tiny neon office. I sit across from her.

"What's Tobias's secret? The thing you don't want to tell me. Tell me, or I'll tell Shona and Shirley you messed with his body."

"I'll deny it."

"I recorded it when we spoke about it."

"Show me."

We stare at each other for an extended period of time. I roll my eyes. "Veronica, I think someone murdered both Auntie Meera and Uncle Tobias. Someone was preying on them, their insecurities or loneliness. I'm not exactly sure. But this person could keep on going. What if you're next?"

"I'm not lonely," she says defensively. She moves sheaves of paper around on the desk between us, moves a pen with a koala bear climbing up it to the right, a radiation-green feather—a *feather?*—to the left.

I cluck my tongue. "You so are. You said you were." Still, I don't know why, but I know it. Veronica wouldn't fit the type. She's not lonely in the way Auntie Meera and Uncle Tobias were. She's looking for company, she's looking for sex and friendship and she'll do what she can to find those things. But she doesn't have a deep well of loneliness that nothing can fill. I tap my fingers on the table between us. "Come on, Veronica. What was it Tobias was hiding?"

"He had a tail."

I abruptly stop tapping my fingers. The answer is so not what I was expecting. "A *tail*?"

Her arms are crossed over her chest. "He didn't want anyone to know. Alright? He was bullied for it when he was young. Bullied somethin' bad. Maybe worse than bullied. That's it. There it is. Done. Bye bye."

"How did you know?"

"I told you. Now and again—him and me, you know—we liked to get jiggy with it. I told you about it."

I exhale. "Right. Why didn't he mind you knowing?"

She shrugs. "You might not think it, hon, but some people think I'm the sympathetic sort. I don't judge."

I look clinically at her. "Oh, I don't know. I think you have something there."

She beams in surprise. "Well now, I wasn't expecting you to say that. You don't like anyone! I'm so touched. You've touched my heart today, Arya, you really have."

She looks hugely relieved now that she's told me the thing about the tail. Which just goes to prove my point. Other people's secrets are a great burden and it's better never to know anything about anyone.

I come to my feet. "I'm just stating a fact. You *are* sympathetic. I'm not saying it's a good or a bad thing. Anyway, thanks."

"Anytime, hon. And remember what I said, everyone needs a

friend sometimes."

"Not me." I turn to leave, then stop and look at her. "Do you know if Tobias was seeing someone new?"

She screws up her button nose. "Well, now, what made you think that?"

"I don't know. Was he? Would you know?"

She thinks about it. "I don't know. But you know, he was amenable to me popping over now and again, once a month or so. I told you, when it's *that* time of the month…"

"Yes, you said. So?"

"So, he wasn't as amenable to it in the last couple of months. I mean, I kept trying. You know, he wasn't bad in bed. But he wasn't so up for it recently."

I look curiously at her. "Didn't you mind?"

"It's nice to have company. But a girl can look after herself when there isn't any. I'm not saying a glass member does the job as good as a real, flesh and blood, silky, hot—"

"Yes, yes," I say hastily, "I really do get the picture."

I walk out of her office, grab some frozen custard off the assistant, and drown my face in it until I've licked it all up. Sympathetic *and* a frozen custard goddess. There's something to be said about that. I stand outside Veronica's shop, staring into the distance.

A tail. Tobias had a tail. It's an unsatisfying answer, in some ways. Was he really so self-conscious about it? What does it have to do with the circle I saw last night? Though at least it explains why Veronica was so quick to cover up his body and protect it from prying eyes. At least, it would have come out sooner or later, once there was an autopsy. Had Veronica felt squeamish about them standing about, staring at Tobias, perhaps giggling at him?

As I stand there, dithering about my next steps, Shona Klues wanders by. "How's tricks?" she says.

"Alright, Shona, alright. How're things with you?"

"Life goes on, Arya, life goes on. Que sera sera and all that." She's eyeing me, then looking behind me to peer into the frozen custard shop. "You and Ms. Chives are bffs then?" She sniggers at her own joke.

"You think Veronica Chives can't make friends?"

"Oh, I'm not surprised about *her* having friends."

I shrug and look down at my hands. The heat is rising from my feet and is up to my pelvis now. My legs are tense, my thighs starting to hurt. I need to get away from her. I haven't decided yet what to tell her. I need to think about it, but the pressure to blurt something out is so sharp and so loud that I'm sure I'm going to do it. I try to walk away. She doesn't stop me. But my feet refuse to move. I slice my mouth shut so I won't say something.

She's looking at me with interest. "It's a sexy thing, a woman fighting with herself."

I splutter. "You know you can't say things like that! It's sexual harassment, that's what it is!"

"Come, Arya, tell Auntie Shona what's on your mind. You know you want to."

I fight with myself for some minutes. Maybe I can do it. Maybe I can keep myself from blurting something out. Maybe if I just hold it together. Sometimes thinking about something else helps. Maybe I can think about Branwell. Now, there's an idea. Maybe that'll help me.

"Sex circle!" I say, high and loud and in a squeak.

Shona's eyes glimmer. "Now, there we go. Doesn't that feel better?" she says, much in the same tone as someone would kiss your finger and ask if your boo-boo was all better.

I clamp my mouth shut with my hand, though it's by far too late for that. I lift my hands up in the air and make an impatient sound. "Fine. If you want to be sent on a wild goose chase, my theory is that someone is leading some kind of sex circle in the area."

She looks speculatively at me. "And what's wrong with a sex circle?"

"Nothing at all. Except that I think this one might have something to do with Auntie Meera's death and also Tobias's. That's all I know. So there." I stop. Surely, I should hand over Tobias's signet ring. The one I've found at the outskirts of the remains of the bonfire from last night. But then, I can't do it. I have no idea why. I'm pretty sure whatever I have or haven't withheld from the police up to this point, *this* is definitely withholding evidence. Even if the circle has nothing to do with Tobias's death, even so, it's still Tobias's ring.

I turn slowly away. Maybe if I just put one foot in front of another, I can make my escape.

To my surprise, Shona doesn't stop me when I try to leave. I make tracks, making the most of her distraction. As I turn away from her, I bang straight into the accountant Willie Arnott, who, as usual, seems to have emerged out of thin air. He gives me a thin smile, and again, I try to focus on his features to try to recall later what they look like, but they're so vague—almost like a faded picture—that I can't grasp them. Are his eyes blue or grey, small or medium size? Is his brow large or his hair receding? Is the hair brown or reddish? The lips thin or medium?

"It's very worthy of you to try to find out more about Tobias Yard's death," he says softly.

I purse my mouth. "I see that the Truckleworth grapevine is working."

"It's just…" He hesitates.

"What?" I say, half-bored. If he's going to go on about people who are different and how we just have to accept it, or whatever trite nonsense he'd uttered last time, I might scream.

"Many of us care about you." His voice is so soft, it has no tone, no substance.

Argh! We, us, Trucklewood! I wish the man would stop making me feel like everyone is talking about me behind my back. I narrow my eyes at him. "What were you doing on the night Tobias died, may I ask?"

He smiles again. Clearly, nothing anyone says offends him. "I was in my house, all by myself, with no alibi."

"Yes," I murmur. "As was all of Trucklewood, it seems. Apparently, none of us are very sociable."

"People are getting more and more distant from one another. What with social media and technology. It leads us to feel alienated. It leads us to cut away from one another. It results in more depression—"

Yeesh. "What is it about me that's giving people the impression that I want to stand around talking about self-evident crap like that?"

Surely the man will be offended now. But he just smiles. "Attacking other people is one of the first signs that people need love."

I walk away from the man before I throw up all over him. I'm not looking where I'm going because I get surrounded by a posse of little creatures who are all of a sudden clinging to my legs.

"God almighty," I say, looking at the curious things. It's Mark and Sheshonne and their ninja army.

Sheshonne smiles at me. She's wearing a bright headscarf today over her braids and Hollywood-red lipstick. There are little hands clinging to my legs. I look down in dismay.

"They're weird, right?" Sheshonne says.

I look up at the woman. "Uh, why do you have so many of them if you think that?"

"They're alright," she says. "Just weird. Kids are. Plus, Mark and I nanny. So, it's the job. I ate one of your green goblin cupcakes the other day, I wanted to tell you. Loved it."

"Thanks."

"People bothering you?"

I raise my eyebrows.

She smiles again. "I wouldn't get sucked into Trucklewood too much. I always admire how you keep yourself to yourself. I can't in my line of work. I don't mean music; I mean the part-time nannying. But you can."

I can't help goggling at her. I realize I've hardly ever exchanged two words with this woman. But it also occurs to me, though fleetingly, that that may be my loss. It's an unusual thought and I shake myself. The lack of sleep coupled with the unprecedented socializing is pickling my brain, clearly. It occurs to me that a young couple like Mark and Sheshonne is likely to have an alibi for the deaths, so I can write them off.

Mark looks up now, looking like he hasn't slept for weeks. "Shi – sugar---" he says, passing his hand through his sandy hair. "They're especially a handful this morning. That bit of chocolate was a mistake." There are toddlers running all around him, all shouting at the same time. Even the baby in the sling, presumably not high on chocolate is wriggling and fussing. "Teething," Mark says. "Though I would say that, wouldn't I? It's what everyone says about a fussy baby." He rubs his face. He really does look tired. There are circles under his eyes.

"Where were you last night?" I blurt out. Then I bite my lip. "Sorry, this whole detective stuff is getting to my head."

"I was watching reruns of *Line of Duty*, if you must know. We both were."

Sheshonne makes some sort of movement. A flinch or a glance at her partner. I'm not sure exactly what she does. I look at her. Is Mark lying about where he was last night? Why would he? It isn't even a night he or anyone else needs an alibi for. I look curiously at him, then at Sheshonne. She isn't looking at me anymore.

I walk abstractedly down the high street. I shake my head. I'm seeing ghouls everywhere. This is what happens when you start interacting with people. Everything they say becomes a piece of highly suspicious and possibly dangerous evidence for something. I just don't know for what. Was Mark lying about being in? If so, why? Had he been part of that circle I'd seen? I frown. I turn my mind back and wonder if I can tell if Mark had been one of the seven people in the circle. I don't know if you've noticed this before, though. It's nearly impossible to match someone's naked genitals that you've seen by the light of the full moon with their fully clothed body in the sunlight. If asked to play one of those matching games you're asked to do in kids' magazines, I just wouldn't be able to do it.

As I'm walking down the street again, pondering if I was imagining that Mark was lying about where he had been last night, I spy Tallulah coming out of the frozen custard shop.

"Divine, isn't it?"

She goes pink, even though I don't think I've said anything so odd. "I know I shouldn't be eating it."

I take a breath to brace myself, so I don't say something impatient. "You can eat what you want, Tallulah. No one has the right to say anything about it."

"Yes, yes. I'm just stupid. I wish I was more like you and I had the confidence to do and say whatever I wanted."

This irritates me even more. I'm wriggling about like that baby in the sling now. Why do people say things like that? I'll never understand. If you want to be more forthright, then do it. What's the point saying you want to do it – and then never doing it? I cluck impatiently, though I don't mean to.

She winces. "I know I irritate you. I'm sorry."

A growl escapes me. "Tallulah, why do you keep apologizing for yourself?"

I'm about to walk away when she stops me. She takes a deep breath. "I have met someone. I told you. And maybe it'll give me more confidence. Sorry," she can't help adding.

Something niggles at me at her words. Or maybe it's just that *sorry* again. But before I can probe, she gives me a little nod and turns around to walk away. I rub the back of my neck. Something is still bothering me. Something I should be paying attention to. Something about the circle last night? Or what Tallulah said? I shake my head. I'm too sleep deprived to make sense of anything.

I turn to head down the hill and in the direction of my house. I approach it slowly. I stand outside it, abstractedly, trying to make some sense of my thoughts.

Something happens as I step forward to unlock the front

door. I don't know exactly what. It's like time itself slows down. Or everything goes silent. Or maybe it's that the skin at the back of my neck prickles. I slowly enter the house. I can't help thinking that it's the same feeling I had when I entered the house the first time after Auntie Meera's death.

For some reason, my footsteps are slow as I step inside. And all my senses are heightened. Yet there's no sign of a disturbance. Things are where they normally are. Things look just the same. I shake myself. I'm being stupid. I'm seeing murder everywhere. What's wrong with me?

My heart is pounding as I walk across to the kitchen. It occurs to me suddenly—and I wonder why it hasn't occurred to me before—that the tiramisu I left for Tobias could have been tampered with in this very house. The poison could have been injected into it while it was in this house, before I took it to Tobias's. I make a mental note to check if Auntie Meera had any of the poison that was used to kill Tobias in her stocks.

The police were focusing on the hour in the evening when Tobias died – the hour between when Veronica Chives saw him alive in his kitchen and then found him dead. They've also been asking questions about people who could have had the opportunity to mess with the tiramisu from the time I delivered it in the morning at eleven. But, in fact, the tiramisu had been set and ready to go for a full hour or so *before* I delivered it to Tobias's doorstep.

I walk into the kitchen. The feeling of everything suspended, of things waiting, is even stronger in here. I stand there in the dark. The blinds are down, the lights are out in the house, and it's gone a bit dark outside as well because of a sudden rain cloud. And then I see it. The huddle. My backpack crashes to the ground at my feet. And then I scream.

Because lying in a nasty puddle of something dark under the large rustic dining table, is a white furry clump.

Chapter Twenty-Four

I want to say that after the first scream, I find my head, walk about my kitchen, survey the situation from all angles, and call the police. In actual fact, I completely lose it. I run out of the house screaming, hands flapping above my head, all the way across the gravel driveway and to the road.

I bang straight into Willie Arnott, the accountant, again.

He looks shocked and slightly embarrassed. I don't know if this is general embarrassment at the hysteria of women or if it's the fact that after banging into him, I ricochet off his body, fall on to my bum, recover quickly and come to a kneeling position, my mouth firmly at his crotch level. It's hard to say for sure which of these things is causing him more embarrassment. I'm still panting. He clears his throat as I come to standing.

"The Marquis," I whisper.

"Have you had a shock, my dear?" he says kindly. His face and tone suggest that he thinks I've probably seen a spider in my kitchen. I wouldn't be surprised if he said *did you see an enormous wee beastie, lass?*

"The fucking cat is fucking dead!"

He winces at my language or my banshee screech. Again, I'm not sure which. "Yes, yes. I'm sure it is." He gingerly reaches out a hand and pats my shoulder. "Do you maybe need a cup of tea?"

I growl in his face.

He visibly blanches and takes a tentative step back. He holds his hands up. "Now, now—"

"My god, stopping now-nowing! Call Shona, call Shirley, call anyone and fast!"

I don't know why I think it needs to be fast. It's not like the cat is mysteriously disappearing bit by bit and thereby wiping out all evidence. It's going to sodding lie there (in its sodden mess, oh god), until someone does something about it.

He holds up his hands again and nods. "Yes, yes, yes."

He then does a fruitless search for his phone. In all his pockets. Each and every one. He finds it at last, in the very pocket he had first searched for it. After a lot of scrolling, he looks up at me like he doesn't want to admit whatever he's discovered. He clears his throat. "Who are Shona and Shirley?"

"Christ almighty!"

He springs back again. I grab his phone off him. Mine is in the backpack I'd dropped inside the kitchen a few minutes ago. Irrationally, the thought of my bag—with my phone, water bottle, various completely pointless old receipts and tissues and half-eaten cereal bars—in there, with The Marquis, makes me feel worse. It makes me feel a little lost. First my lost equipment, now this. This invasion of my space feels even worse than the deaths I've tried to look into. It occurs to me now that I have no idea what I'm doing about the deaths, anyway. I have no idea about any of it. Who do I think I am, Poirot?

I scroll pointlessly on Willie Arnott's phone. There's a remarkably small number of contacts. Those that are in his contacts list are often listed just by first name. Ambiguous names too, like Mary, Jane, Charles, George. Anyway, I don't know why I'm looking. Of course, Shona and Shirley aren't there. I have Shona in my contacts because she gave me her number. I could dial 999 but I can't imagine that the police will take kindly to people who call emergency lines in order to report a cat murder.

I jump. A cat *murder*. That's what I have to remind myself. It isn't just a cat death. It's most definitely a murder. I spring into action. "I need to go back inside and find my phone. I need to call the police." I look sideways at the man who's standing patiently waiting for me to say anything that's vaguely enlightening. I remember though where I dropped my backpack. It's inches from that dark puddle. I swallow. "Any chance you could come with me?"

He looks a little surprised. I'm not surprised by his surprise. I've literally never—not once—invited a Trucklewood resident to mine. This is unprecedented stuff. Still, needs must. I can't stomach the thought of going into that dark house by myself.

We walk toward the house. I let us in. I turn the light on in the hallway. This should make things better. After all, I'd seen The Marquis in the near-dark before, what with the blinds and curtains all done up, and it frightened the life out of me. Now, in the light, I should feel better. We walk gingerly toward the kitchen. I ask him to stay at the threshold, murmuring that this is a crime scene, so not to move. I flip on the light in the kitchen. I look at every step I'm taking, so I don't step on something, any bit of evidence. I don't look at that dark furry shape. My phone has fallen out of the side pocket of my backpack and onto the floor. I pick it up and beat a hasty retreat, like the ghost of the cat might come to life and jump at my back. It turns out that Willie Arnott has completely ignored my instructions to stay on the threshold and is standing in the kitchen, staring down at my dining table with a blank face. I whip him out of the kitchen and rush us outside. After I've called Shona and asked her to make tracks, Willie Arnott and I wait for her to arrive, sitting on my doorstep.

Even though she gave me a stern speech on the phone about not messing with the crime scene until she gets there, it takes Shona a good hour to arrive. Her hair is a little scatty today, but the sharp maroon shirt, trench coat and beige slacks are firmly in place, along with her little notebook. When Willie Arnott sees her, he gives my shoulder a sympathetic squeeze, tells me he'll be going now that I don't need him anymore, waves goodbye to Shona and is off.

"What's occurring, Arya?" Shona says. "So, you can't live without calling me then?"

I'm hopping from foot to foot by this point, mad with impatience. "You need to stop flirting with your suspects!"

"I never thought you were a suspect," she says, brushing a speck of dust off her arm. She's showing no signs of urgency about going indoors to check on The Marquis, whereas I'm twitching like a maniac.

"Why did you take all my stuff, then?" I demand.

She nods slowly. "Yes, I know that drove a wedge in the early days of our relationship. But I had no choice. Procedures must be followed. But, to tell you the truth, it's instinct that solves a crime, not procedure. I've been saying it for years, and you can't make me say it any different. Unless my boss asks, of course, in which case, I never said it was anything other than procedure." She looks around her, apparently to make sure her boss isn't lurking and listening in. "You're not the murdering kind. The overtly rude aren't usually. Read all the crime novels. It's always the nice ones. Like your new boyfriend. Did you know he earns not a lot from his writing?"

"He isn't very successful," I say, sounding as uninterested in this line of conversation as I actually am. "What of it?"

"I see you don't deny the boyfriend part," Shona says accusingly.

I have to say I'm quite surprised at this myself, now that Shona's pointed it out. I frown. This needs to stop. Leave people before they leave you, and so on. That's always been my philosophy, and it was only with Craig that I let my guard down, mostly because he didn't seem to have the gumption—I've always thought gumption a singularly underused words in modern times—to break up with anyone. Normally, it doesn't creep up on me like that. I can't let this whole Branwell business get to me.

"I don't need to deny the obvious," I say stoutly to Shona. "And anyway," I glance in the direction of the front door, feeling my shoulders burning, "aren't we going inside—"

"Glad to hear he's not your boyfriend," Shona interrupts, smoothing her top down. "What I'm saying is, I bet you didn't know that Tobias Yards left your non-boyfriend Branwell a largish painting, likely worth thousands."

I start. I've been twitching every two seconds, glancing at the front door of the house, expecting I don't know what, but I now focus on Shona.

I didn't know that, as it happens. Why would Tobias leave Branwell anything at all? How had they even had the time to meet? Branwell had only just moved into the area, right around the time that poor Tobias was getting murdered, in fact. I frown. More importantly, why had Branwell not mentioned this little detail to me, given my interest in Tobias's murder?

"Thrown you a bit, has it?" Shona asks casually.

I look severely at her. "Are you just going to stand here chatting with me or are you going to go inside and look at the cat?"

"As it happens, I'm waiting for Shirley. You don't go into a crime scene without your partner. The perp might still be lurking about. It isn't safe."

"It's a cat!" I say in exasperation.

Just then, on cue, Shirley shows up. His raven hair is dapper as ever, with a neat flick to it, his lips becomingly pink, his silk waistcoat gold in hue, his skin white as silk. I can't help noticing the man bears more than a passing resemblance to Snow White. He saunters up to where we're standing outside my front door.

"Did it take you this long just to get dressed?" I demand. What is wrong with everyone?

He smiles, his bow mouth curls prettily. He touches his hair. "Thanks so much for noticing. Shona never appreciates my style. Where's the vic?"

The two disappear inside.

I don't dare venture into the kitchen, but I follow them into the house and hover in the hallway. They spend a maddeningly long time looking in there.

Finally, and by this time I'm burning with impatience, they emerge from the kitchen. They look serious, the pair of them. I feel sick at the sight of their face.

"There is blood spatter everywhere. But I'm not sure it's from the cat. Though we'll have it analyzed," Shona remarks.

I frown. "Why do you think it's not from the cat?"

"Come and see."

I hold my hands up. "I'd rather not."

"Come, you might want to see it."

I know I wouldn't, but I reluctantly follow. The lights are on in the kitchen. We don't go too far in. She's right, there *is* blood spatter on the floor.

Shona directs my eyes toward the white clump under the table. I can see it clearly now. It's horribly rigid. I shudder, swallow thickly and look away. Shona is looking sympathetically at me. "Not seen that many dead cats then?"

"I haven't, as it happens."

"If you can bear looking closer, you'll see the rigid way the cat's legs are all standing to attention, pointing into the air. It's not real, Arya. It's a stuffed toy."

I nearly collapse at the words. I look at the clump again. And see what I should have seen all along. The damn thing is a toy. A toy! *A toy!*

I splutter. "Someone went out and bought a stuffed cat that looks exactly like The Marquis and placed it under *my* dining room table in my kitchen!"

I almost feel more affronted than if it had been The Marquis. Who in their right mind would do such a thing? And where is The Marquis? "What's the blood from?"

"It's real blood. Not the puddle near the cat. That's just colored water. But the mild spatter. But, like I said, we'll have it looked at."

I rub my face. "My god."

"Look, Arya, real cat or not, this is not an innocent trick. And the perp seems like he—or she—may have come via the kitchen window, said kitchen window being open as we speak."

I wince.

Shona, not missing a beat, looks interestedly at me.

"I leave it open for The Marquis to go in and out at night. That way, when he wants something, he can just come in. He likes to pop up to my bed sometimes."

Her eyes widen. "Another boyfriend? I must say, Arya, you're breaking my heart with every word that comes out of your beautiful mouth. Do you have lipstick on or is it your natural color?"

I throw my hands in the air. "I don't have makeup on, though I don't see that that's your business. The Marquis is the name of the blasted cat!"

"Oh, that's alright then. I was imagining a man dressed as a seventeenth-century Frenchman, mask and silk gloves and flowing curls and all. Not that I'm averse to a bit of role play."

"Hair powder," Shirley adds. "A beauty mark. A stick that's actually hiding the murder weapon. Leather boots. A dainty walk."

"Heaven help us," I screech. "Are you two quite done? Are you telling me someone actually climbed through my kitchen window just to – just to – leave that stuffed toy in here?"

Shona shakes her head. "Hard words to hear, Arya. But, yes, the kitchen window looks like the most likely entry point. The kitchen door is locked from the inside. Anyway, the kitchen is very clean. Did you clean recently, or did the perp do that?"

"I clean the kitchen several times a day. That's my work kitchen. The one off to the side behind the door—that would have been the pantry in Victorian times—is for my personal use."

Shona's eyes twinkle. "Beautifully thorough with the cleaning. It's always the ones with the explosive sexuality that are like that. In any case, I found only two things on the floor. Backpack – yours, I presume?"

I nod, ignoring the comment about my cleaning prowess.

"And this nub of a pencil."

I stare at it. "It's not mine. Oh, wait, it must be Willie Arnott's.

He was in here when I came in to retrieve my phone."

She looks sternly at me. "Messing with the crime scene, Arya, is not something I take lightly, not even from someone as buxom—I mean, as intelligent—as you. Especially not someone as intelligent as you. You shouldn't have let someone else in. You should really have stayed out too. But that's neither here nor there. What's done is done, I say. Let's not dwell on what can't be changed. Let's look at opportunity and motive now, shall we? Can I trouble you for a cup of tea? And also, maybe one of those bonbon things I saw sitting in your kitchen just now? Maybe just don't mention it to anyone because, technically, they're part of the crime scene."

Chapter Twenty-Five

It takes the nasty incident with the stuffed cat to get me to finally turn to Auntie Meera's journals. If for no other reason than I can't sleep the night after the stuffed cat turns up in my kitchen. There's no question of doing any baking, my kitchen is out of bounds for now. I'm exercised out. And even helping myself to a chocolate-chunk muffin doesn't work. There's not going to be any sleep. I can't dwell on the stuffed cat, either. Not to mention that I haven't seen The Marquis all day. Did I see him yesterday? I can't remember. Would someone leave a stuffed animal in my kitchen, *and* kill the real one and hide the body somewhere else?

I don't want to think what it means. The thought of someone climbing into the house through the kitchen window with the express purpose of planting a stuffed cat in my kitchen seems unbearably ominous.

I pick up the journals and sit reading them through the night, lights on all over the house. I keep my ears pricked for any sound of The Marquis returning. I twitch at every sound. But the cat doesn't appear around the corner. I try to focus on the journals. As the hours wear on, I start to notice that something changed in Auntie Meera's journals in the weeks before she died. She was quite practical in her entries most of the time, it seemed, which was better for me because it made them easier to read. As it was, the occasional reference she made to me or my parents are too much for me. "I wish Arya would let herself see who she is and what she's made of. She's plagued by demons, she thinks of herself as weak, or broken, somehow, when instead I wish she'd see how plucky and resourceful she is. But how can she, when her parents left her with me without a backward glance? When her dad flinched every time she spoke, when he got angry with her for things she couldn't help? When her mum left too? I have nothing against my sister, I really don't. But my god, I'd happily murder the woman for what she's done to her own daughter."

It's because of entries like that that I scan Auntie Meera's journals with one eye closed. And it isn't as if she labelled my entries 'Arya'. Or references to my parents 'Surya and Brendan'. Or more aptly: *sad musings about my pathetic niece Arya and the parents that abandoned her when she was just a child.*

Nothing so easy.

The musings about me spring out of nowhere. Like what she wrote was a stream of consciousness and not planned or structured. Like if she was writing a new tincture, she'd write that and then her head would drift to something someone had said that was nothing to do with the tincture at all. References to me or my parents are often mixed up in recipes, things she'd discovered about local plants and herbs, historical references to witches and their ways that she liked to collect, scraps of material or dried herbs that she would stick on the pages, and occasional references to her neighbors.

I keep looking for some clue to her state of mind in the days and weeks before she died.

"Mrs. Sharma wanted me to try some of her gooseberry jelly today. I can't say I'm one for jelly, but she looked so lonely, I couldn't say no. But after two hours of listening to her telling me about her ulcers and stomach aches and how some days she woke up and didn't have any inspiration to do her ceramics, I was wishing I hadn't gone. I did suggest she try some basil or lime in her recipes. She liked the idea and said I'd be the first to get some when she did a batch."

"Veronica Chives dropped by with some of her frozen

custard this morning. It was nice of her. Though I find her a little overwhelming. She's one of those people who doesn't pause for breath. She seems happy enough to keep talking until you push her out of the house. She keeps talking about a girlie night out. I don't have the heart to say that I've never done girlie night outs, even when I was a little girl. I never had that many friends."

"I've never had anyone do my accounts before, but there's nothing I hate so much as the annual nausea at the thought of doing them. I asked Willie Arnott to help this year, and it made the whole thing so much simpler. I'm never doing them alone again. He was very nice about them. He didn't heckle me about my record keeping or receipts. He never said, *why do people pay you for packets of potpourri or tinctures that don't really work* like I thought he might. He was quite surprising."

"I bumped into Tobias Yards again on my walk. I don't know why people think he's rude. He's blunt. He asked me how I was. Though I didn't think he meant to. We literally bumped into each other around a corner, and he happened to say *Are you okay?* And I was feeling a bit low, and I happened to blurt out *I don't know why I feel so lonely at the moment.* And he said, "But is that any different from usual?" How the man can know something like that about me is hard to understand. We've only met once or twice. He said *I want to tell you something, if you want to hear it.*"

"It's hard to explain to people sometimes. Arya was here yesterday, and we got into the worst fight we've ever had. It doesn't happen a lot. We both like to keep ourselves to ourselves, we've always been solitary. So, we don't often get in each other's way. But Surya has told me about Brendan being ill. (It seems it's terminal, though he might have a year or two.) And I urged Arya to make peace with her dad. I said she'll regret it if she doesn't. I've never asked her to try and connect with her parents. I've always thought they made their bed. She stormed out and told me to mind my own bloody business. She said she had nothing to say to her father and never had. I should have stayed out of it, I know that. Arya and

I only have each other. Why drive a wedge, and for someone like Brendan? The trouble is I suppose I've always regretted not telling my stepfather how I felt about him, how small he made me feel, how I would rather die than think about the things he did to me when I was too young to fight back."

I slap the journal away like it's trying to bite me.

But it's too late because it's bitten me already. This is the thing with Auntie Meera's journals. They seem full of everyday things like rose hips and marigold seeds, gooseberry jelly and frozen custard and haphazard accounts. But then, just as you're lulled into a false sense of security, she slings something at you that you didn't want to see. That you can't bear having seen.

My mind is whirling. And I don't even know how to begin to unpick the things I'm learning. I slowly go over them, not wanting to think about that last entry. Not daring to look at it.

She and Tobias knew each other. Enough so that Tobias already had an inkling what she was like, how solitary she was, how fiercely protective of her solitude and yet how the need for people ran deep too. Deeper than she wanted to admit. Maybe even to herself. And what was it he had wanted to tell her? Why hadn't she written that bit down? What did it have to do with her loneliness?

And, of course, our fight. It must have hurt her as much as it did me. I'd felt betrayed by it, by her insistence that I talk to my dad. I couldn't understand how she didn't know how I felt about it. She was right, we were both private and solitary, but she knew more than anyone how I felt about my parents, about how there was no going back. About how I'd survived their leaving me by hacking off the side of me that needed them or needed anyone really. There was no healing some amputations. I hadn't been able to understand how the one person in the world that knew how I felt about my parents could be asking me to reach out to them.

Mum hadn't even bothered to tell me that Dad was ill. She had told Auntie Meera and asked her to tell me. My parents hadn't even been able to face telling me themselves. Yet, Auntie Meera had asked me to reach out to them. It had maddened me that she could have misunderstood something so basic and fundamental about me. If I forgave my parents, what would be left of me? Of the person I'd built brick by brick over the years since they'd gone from my life? Of the person I'd vowed to be?

Now, though, now, all I want is to have the chance to make amends. Not with my parents but with Auntie Meera. She was as lonely as I was, more maybe, and I had cut her off in the last months before she died. If I hadn't done that, if I hadn't cut her off, I can't help thinking that there was a chance that she might have lived. I can't help remembering that she felt low and lonely that time when she bumped into Tobias. I wasn't there for her. And over something so little. It's not like she could have forced me—or even tried to force me—to talk to my parents. All I had to say was no. Instead, as usual, I'd driven a wedge between me and the one person who had always been there for me.

But these things in Auntie Meera's journal, these are not the worst.

It's the last thing I read. The thing I wish I had never seen. What did she mean by the reference to her stepdad? The things he did to her? Nausea ripens in my throat. It seems Auntie Meera knew exactly what it was like when the people who were supposed to look after you betrayed your trust. In fact, it seems she knew so much better than me. Whatever my parents had done to me, it was nothing compared to what it seems her stepdad might have done to her. Why had it never occurred to me to ask her about her life, her childhood?

I look down at the journal. Not reading the words now.

No wonder she could never reach out to people, no wonder for all the years I knew her she never seemed to have a significant relationship. Or close friends. Whatever her history was with her stepdad—and her words, though hardly detailed, left little doubt what that history was—she'd been too scarred to reach out and connect with other people because of it.

And then it occurs to me. The connection I need to see. Both Auntie Meera and Tobias had secrets. Secrets that they were deeply ashamed of. Auntie Meera with her history with her stepdad and Tobias with his shame about his tail and the bullying—or worse, Veronica had said—that he had experienced as a child.

What does it mean? Does it mean anything? Is it significant?

I have too many questions and no answers. I have a question. I don't know why I care, but I suddenly want to know if my mum experienced the same thing that Auntie Meera did with their stepdad. I glance down at the journal, one eye closed. But there's nothing more there. And I doubt that I'll ever know now. It's not like I'll ever ask my mum.

I push the journal away. It's too late for that though, because I'll never be able to unsee what I've seen. I sit there for a long time, staring blankly in front of me, feeling the unbearable weight of knowing things about Auntie Meera that she hadn't been willing to tell me herself. I think about it now, me reading her journals. Her private journals. What a terrible betrayal. I put my hands to my face. Shouldn't I have done it? But her murder, it was to find out about her murder, and not for anything else. I sit there feeling wracked by grief, guilt, anger and who knows what else.

I don't know how long it is, but I finally come out of the grieving haze I've fallen into and give a minute or two to my current problem. The Marquis.

Shona and Shirley had spent ages searching the kitchen the day before, taking copious pictures, discussing the thing from all angles. It had taken so long that I'd gotten completely exasperated with them. By the time they were done, I'd been hopping, pacing up and down my hallway and cursing. The sensible thing would have been to escape into my living room and read something. Or go for a run. But the thought of the cat, the thought of Shona and Shirley in my kitchen again, looking for clues in my new, clean, shiny things, I couldn't bear it.

They had finally cleared out the stuffed cat and helped me find someone who could do a deep clean of the kitchen. I didn't want to think about the stuffed cat. I didn't want to think about where on earth I was going to bake for my orders now that my kitchen couldn't be used.

But it was the thing Shona had said to me before she left, that was the thing preying on my mind. Before she left, she had said, "Think about it, Arya. Think about if someone is trying to give you a warning. There's something not right about this. It's one thing if they had killed the cat – then I'd put it down to the local cat murderer, if there is indeed such a thing. But this, this deliberate planting of a stuffed cat, and that blood, there's something unhinged about that kind of planning. You take care of yourself. Close your windows. Call me," she added before she left.

I push the journals away from me, and even though it's after three in the morning, I go out to the garden at the back, torch in one hand, a cast iron frying pan in the other, and I do a thorough search. I stop and whistle, half under my breath, I call out a few times. But the cat doesn't appear. I search under the overhang of every tree, in every bush, behind every clump of plants, in the little shed at the back. But he's not here.

Surely, he's just gone off on a hunt? The blood can't be his. Surely, he'll turn up in a day or two. I could even head over to Tobias's and look to see if he's gone back there. I tell myself, there's an innocent explanation for his disappearance.

But I can't get Shona's words out of my head.

I can't help wondering who is trying to give me a warning. And if I didn't heed it, what they would do next. And there, standing there in the pitch-dark garden on an overcast night, suddenly the two flyers—or whatever they had been—that had been pushed through my letterbox come to mind. A warning, Shona had said. Think if someone is trying to give you a warning. I shake my head. No, I'm imagining things. The flyers weren't a warning. They weren't – anything. I'm seeing warnings everywhere I turn.

I head back into the house. Feeling more uneasy than ever.

Chapter Twenty-Six

I sit in Branwell's kitchen the next morning, sipping his infernal rooibos. He sits across the kitchen island on another bar stool.

"I need your kitchen," I tell him. "For a day or two. I'll have to clean it out, and you won't be able to cook in it. And also, you can't tell anyone that I'm fulfilling orders in here, because I'm not supposed to do that when you don't have all the certificates for hygiene and cleanliness and so forth."

He sips at his tea, looking unperturbed at the idea of his premises being used illegally. "Will I get a steady supply of baked goods in return?"

"You can have a steady supply of sex in return."

"Soon."

I look fiercely at him. "Are you going to tell me you have a problem with sex too, like Craig? I don't know what I've done to deserve this!"

He smiles his slow smile. He picks up my fist and kisses it. "I want more, that's all."

I open my eyes. It's like I can still feel the imprint of his lips on my wrist. Damn it. "What kind of more?"

"You, all of you."

"Well, for crying out loud. I'm here, aren't I? It's not like I've left half my limbs behind at mine. I'm here all the time!"

"I was with someone for three years."

"That's a great story, but—"

"Sometimes I think we never got beyond sex."

I want to say something clever back but something in his face stops me.

"I kept telling myself that's how she was. That's how she showed her feelings. I told myself what I felt for her was enough too, that it was as good as it gets, and the rest is just fairytales. I mean, I didn't know a heck of a lot about relationships. My dad was never in the picture and my mum died when I was thirteen. She had a string of short-lived relationships with some truly awful men."

I look silently at his face. "I didn't know that."

"It's not a big deal. But it does leave you knowing very little about intimacy. Or about yourself. You get good at hiding what you need. Even from yourself."

I can't help it. His tone is matter of fact but what he says makes me catch my breath. *You get good at hiding what you need. Even from yourself.*

I have a sudden burning need, the kind I've never had before, to hold his face and kiss him hard, so he won't hide anymore, so that I won't need to hide anymore either, so we can see each other like no one else has ever seen us. I shake my head at myself. I'm losing it. Maybe this is what having a stroke feels like. I shake myself more thoroughly, like a dog. I squirm. It's bad enough having my chaotic thoughts in my head all the time. It would be infinitely worse to start feeling like I can read Branwell's, even the things he isn't saying.

"In any case, by the end of it, it wasn't just me she was having sex with. To tell you the truth, maybe it was like that throughout the three years, and I was just too much of an idiot to see it. For a long time afterwards, I told myself she was the only kind of person I deserved, and she was the only kind of person I would get. I hadn't liked her enough, I'd been happy enough to turn a blind eye to the fact that there was nothing there, that our relationship was hollow. I told myself that maybe that's why she turned to someone else."

I can't think what to say. The need to make the moment stop, that's my first and only instinct. An instinct of self-preservation, of not getting sucked in, of not wanting or needing, that's stood me in good stead for many years. I don't want to hear or know the things he's saying. It makes me feel incomplete and inadequate, but more than anything, I want him not to feel like that, I want him not to be sad or lonely or upset. I want that more than anything else. And that's unbearable.

He gives me his sideways smile. "Anyway, enough about me. I just want to take it a bit slower, that's all. I knew it the second I saw you. Well, the second you collided into my chest."

I can't help myself. "What did you know?"

"That you're…kind of important."

It's not the words. It's not *just* the words. It's the way he looks at me, from under his eyelashes that makes me catch my breath. I don't know what to say. *Stop being boring* would be my response of choice. It's on the tip of my tongue to say it or something like it. I can almost imagine the hurt in his eyes. I almost want to see it. Anything but what I actually see in his eyes. Anything but the heat I feel in my stomach at his words, the horrible need. But then he looks away, he takes me off the hook.

He smiles slowly, not looking at me. "Don't know what to say to that, do you?"

I narrow my eyes at him, but he's still not looking at me. "Please, give me a break. I'm never at a loss for words."

"You can't help it. You like me too. You don't want to, but you do." He links his index fingers together. "We're like that, we are. Some people fit together, from the second they meet."

I purse my mouth. I clutch the edges of the kitchen island. His words are making my tummy feel all churny and tight. Then I remember something. I stop squirming. "Here's what I was thinking, if you really want to know. Why didn't you tell me that Tobias Yards left you a painting? How did you even know him?" Ah ha! Take that, Branwell Beam with the direct eyes and all the words and the churning he makes me feel in the depths of my stomach.

He looks at me. I think he's going to tell me not to change the subject. But he's getting to know me. He knows I've already done this—this conversation with him about his past, the words about us, the way he's looking at me—more than I can bear. He looks steadily at me. I stare right back. He nods slowly. "Yes, I thought you'd have a problem with that when you found out. We didn't know each other that well. I bumped into him when I came over to look at this house. We got chatting. He seemed to like me, and he didn't like many people."

"Why?" I ask suspiciously.

He wraps his hands around his mug and sips his tea. "Oh, you don't like that, I see? That Tobias liked other people, not just you?" He grins.

I pick an invisible bit of lint off my hoodie arm. "I have no problem with people liking each other. I just like to know why. It's purely philosophical interest. Aesthetic interest, even, like why do people go on about Monet's waterlilies when *The Artist's Garden* is the thing they should be looking at. It's the same kind of question."

"Don't know. My beautiful eyes?"

I look clinically at him. "They're quite direct, I suppose."

He looks pleased. "You've noticed. I really only thought it was my—how do I put it delicately? —my manhood you wanted."

"Your special man parts? Yes, it is only that that I'm interested in. Or do I mean that in which I am interested? It's just you can tell how a man will kiss and fuck—though given your preference for Victorian forms of reference, let's call it *congress*—by the quality of his eye contact. Craig, as an example, only makes vague eye contact at best, and in bed he barely moved at all and let you get on with it until you were done. Whereas you probably have a much more forthright approach."

"You like my approach?"

"Not that you're letting me find out, but I'm hoping it's suitably vigorous," I say primly. I stop talking, feeling a little breathless for some reason. I shake myself. "Regardless! What did Tobias like about you?"

He's smiling. He sips his tea. "My lack of bullshit? My innate inability to prevaricate? My infinite charm?"

I shrug. "It's unlikely. But he was generous. And impulsive. So maybe it was just that he knew that your books only achieve mediocre sales—"

He smiles coyly. "You've been looking at my Amazon profile."

I slap my forehead. "Why do I keep forgetting to talk to Cath? I'm going to do it right now."

Branwell doesn't argue. I like that about the man. He gives you space when you need it. Sometimes even before you know you need it. He gets up and starts clearing things away in the kitchen.

I sit staring down at my teacup. I keep forgetting I need to find out what might have happened to my tiramisu between the time I delivered it to Tobias and the time that Veronica found his body. I should have spoken to Cath ages ago, but what with one thing and another, I keep forgetting to do it. After all, Cath and Veronica are the last two people to have seen Tobias alive.

Then another thing floats through my head. A thought I've had a few times before. I frown at my tea.

Couldn't Veronica have killed Tobias first and then called the police about finding his body?

I tap the kitchen island. I try to think this through. *Could* Veronica have done it? I should really settle this once and for all.

It's hard to see a motive. Poisoning my tiramisu would hardly equate to a sex game gone wrong. I stare into the distance trying to work it out and thinking that those boards they use on BBC crime dramas that they're always scribbling portentous things on would be quite handy right about now. I'm wondering if I should ask Branwell to bring his out again when there's a buzz on my phone.

It's a message from Tallulah, tentatively asking if I'm free for a cup of tea the next evening. I drop the phone with a bang. Branwell jumps slightly. I look guiltily at him. He's drying dishes with a floral kitchen towel.

"You should see how many times I drop mine," he says casually.

"Yes, but you don't do it on purpose."

"Did you?"

"Yes, I did. I had to do it so I could stop thinking about doing it." I glare at him. "See?" I stab the air with my hand. "*See*?"

He smiles. "You can't put me off, you know."

I don't say it. I don't tell him that I will, I will put him off. And maybe I will do it just so I can stop worrying about when I inevitably will. Disappoint someone now so that it's not a ticking bomb in your head, waiting for you to fuck up. I want to tell him that I desperately, desperately don't want to disappoint him. But luckily, before I say something stupid, he goes back to drying the dishes. He flips the kettle on again.

I look down at Tallulah's message. Tea tomorrow.

I flick my head a few times. I slide off the barstool and pace about the kitchen.

I don't want to do it. I don't want to go over to Tallulah's for tea. I've done my bit, tried to make it so we can bump into each other on the high street, and not be too uncomfortable. In fact, it's much more than I'd ever do for anyone else. I have little trouble handling awkward, even uncomfortable, social encounters. I rarely have any other kind, in fact. But I know she doesn't like them. And I've done my bit to try and sort it out. But this, this prolongation of our contact, I don't want to do it, I can't do it. Yet, yet old familiar guilt niggles at me.

"Sure," I type quickly back, before I can think better of it. I can't focus on Tallulah right now. I'll deal with the problem tomorrow when the time comes, and not a second sooner.

I call Cath.

Chapter Twenty-Seven

I watch as Branwell walks about the kitchen, cleaning. I admire the thorough way he cleans, and also his bum. More so his bum. I mean it's unlikely his cleaning will match up to my standards—no one's can, really (maybe Hannibal Lecter's?)—but his bum certainly meets my standards. In his grey trackies. He's barefoot again today. There's something unbearably sexy about his bare feet. Clean and bony and broad at the toes. He's turned away from me, doing the dishes, then he suddenly wiggles his bottom. The stupid man. I don't know how he knows that I'm looking at it.

The phone rings a few times before Cath comes on the line.

"Cath, it's me. Arya. Arya Winters. Craig's ex."

She snorts. "I know who you are, Arya. You don't have to give me Craig's reference. Tobias had good things to say about you. And he did let us meet once or twice. He normally doesn't trust anyone to meet me. I'd say he liked you, in his own strange way."

Something twists in my chest. I clear my throat. "Thanks, Cath. I guess he hadn't had the time to get to know me properly." I mean it to be a joke, so I don't know why it comes out sounding so forlorn.

"He liked wounded things. But especially ones that had no time to feel sorry for themselves."

Now I wish I hadn't pushed it. *Wounded things*. I rub my eyes with the back of my hand. Bloody hell. "Well, like I said, he hardly knew me. We didn't see much of each other. Anyway, I've been meaning to call you for ages, actually. I was wondering about your last day with him. I mean, the police will have asked you all about it. But—"

"Don't worry. I want to talk about it to someone who cared about him. There were so few who did."

I close my eyes and sit down on the edge of a bar stool. Then I get back on my feet again and pace about. Then I sit again. Then I get up again and clatter about. Basically, I can't be still.

I glance at the back of Branwell's neck. I expect to see impatience, I expect to see him fidget as people do when I can't sit still. I expect him to glance at me to see what the hell I'm doing. I expect him to try to hide his growing restlessness. Or get a scared look on his face, like Craig used to. But there's nothing. He's getting on with cleaning. He's padding about. He's refilling our mugs of tea. He's even whistling.

I go back to Cath. "Will you tell me what happened on the last day?"

I picture her. Her brown hair has blonde highlights. She's sharp and energetic in her trainers and leggings and hoodie. She has a brisk, no-nonsense way in which she moves the Hoover about, the way she puts it down in the corner of the room and moves the furniture, the way she bends and straightens in a spare and efficient manner to clean under things. She's not one of those cleaners who'll do the bare minimum. Only what you can see on the surface. She's fierce about her work and her standards.

"Nothing much happened, to tell you the truth. But I did taste your tiramisu."

I hold the phone closer. "What time?"

"Hard to say. I mean your tiramisu is really good, Arya, but not so good that I noted the time when I ate a slice." She laughs at her own joke. "Anyway, it might have been around five, but don't hold me to it."

"So that's why the police think whoever put the poison in it put it there *after* you left." I frown. I know Veronica Chives has no apparent motive, but she certainly has the best opportunity. What if they were in the middle of some sex game, and that's why he was naked and had to be dressed haphazardly, but she also wanted to do away with him? Buy why? "Was there anything about him that was different?" I think back to the Easter fair a few weeks before he died. The unusual relaxed look about him, almost as if he'd—I try to articulate what he had looked like—like he had found his place in the world at last. Like he had been searching to belong all his life and now, after all this time, he did. I frown. Surely, I'm overreading things. Find his place? What makes me think that it was that profound, whatever he was involved in?

Cath makes some thinking noises for a few seconds. "See, that's the kind of question the police should ask, but they don't. They ask about timings and any lurkers and that sort of thing. But they didn't ask me if there was anything different about Tobias. They asked if I thought he was afraid of anyone. But he wasn't. But there *was* something different."

I press the phone to my ear.

"Tobias was always nice to me. I have to say that. The local idea that he was rude, well, he wasn't rude to me. He didn't mince his words, but I never minded that. I don't mince mine. But he was more – relaxed maybe. Recently. There was something."

"A kind of lightness about his eyes," I say slowly.

"Yes, maybe that's it. A lightness about him."

"Like he'd met someone?"

"Maybe. It's possible. In anyone else, I would have said maybe they'd met someone. In Tobias…I don't know. I've never known him to be like that about anyone. I mean, his neighbor—" She stops.

"It's okay. I know he had an on-and-off thing with Veronica Chives."

"Yes, I see you do. But see that never changed how he was. A night with her, a night without her, he was never any different. You see what I mean?"

"Do you know of anyone who might have had a motive?"

"There's me with opportunity. I could have put the poison in the tiramisu before I left. And he was kind enough to leave me a tidy sum. And don't let anyone tell you that's not important. Money is important. It gives you independence."

"What about Veronica Chives?"

"Jealousy?" she asks. "If he were seeing someone new?"

"Hmm. Then she should try to kill the new lover. Why kill Tobias?"

"Anger? Woman scorned and all that?"

I tap my fingers on Branwell's countertop. "Do you know if he was planning to change his will, Cath?"

She's thinking again. "I wouldn't know anything like that, nothing concrete." She stops like she's trying to concentrate. "I don't know. I got the impression that he was thinking about things, that there were things on his mind. I found him in his study doing paperwork more often in the last few weeks. But I guess that's neither here nor there."

"Okay, thanks, Cath. Will you let me know if you think of anything else?" Then something else occurs to me. "Cath, how many people knew about Tobias's key – the one in the urn?"

"Well, I did. And Craig and you. You because of Craig using it. Other than that, I mean I don't think even Veronica Chives would have known."

"How much of the tiramisu was left after you'd eaten some?"

She thinks about this. "Well, we each had a slice." She goes quiet again. "I think I cut it into eight slices. But I don't know how much there was left when they found him later."

"Thanks, Cath."

I sit thinking through this, then I quickly call Shona.

"Can't live without me, can you?" she asks, sounding pleased.

"Shona, how much of the tiramisu was left when you saw Tobias's body?"

She goes quiet for a minute. "I think there was half."

"So, four slices?"

I hear chattering in the background like she's in a busy office. There's the sound of rustling.

"Here," she says, "here's the picture. It's exactly half of the foil tray in which you gave it to him. Cut into four slices."

"Thanks, Shona."

"Don't be a stranger," she says, before she clicks off.

I sit frowning into the distance, looking out of Branwell's kitchen window.

So, Tobias ate a slice with Cath. And after Cath left, two more slices were eaten, presumably one by Tobias and one by someone else. Yet, no one else had turned up dead. So, the murderer ate a slice but managed to poison the remainder of the tiramisu? Then he or she waited until Tobias was dead and then stripped him naked and arranged his hands over his chest? Did he or she watch Tobias die?

Now I can't sit still at all. I pace again.

The picture is too grim to contemplate. Whoever did it was able to clinically watch Tobias eat a slice of cake. They themselves were able to sit there and eat a slice of cake with him. Then they watched him die. They waited for him to be dead before they stripped and arranged the body. This presents a picture of someone cold and clinical. Hardly someone who killed someone else in a fit of anger. I rub my forehead.

My phone buzzes again. I wonder if it's Cath. Maybe she's remembered something.

But it's Tallulah again, sending a message. "Sorry, Arya, something's come up. Any chance we can postpone tea tomorrow?"

I glare at the phone. "The cheek!"

Branwell has disappeared in the direction of his living room, and I can hear him typing. I look down again at the message from Tallulah. It's one thing that I was fully planning on crying off last minute tomorrow, sending her a text to say that I couldn't make it, after all. But this is a bit much. I hadn't even wanted to go! You can't invite someone over and then less than an hour later take the invitation back, and with as measly an explanation as *something's come up*! I cluck impatiently and dial Tallulah's number.

"Sorry, Arya," she says breathlessly, when she comes on the line.

"What's so important that you've cancelled?" I demand.

"Sorry. It's just, I told you, remember?" Her voice peters out. She sounds distracted.

I screw up my brow. I can hear vibrating. "What are you doing?" I ask suspiciously.

"Oh, sorry, just checking if my shaver works. It's just—"

"You're chucking me over because you have a *date*?" How old is the woman, *sixteen*? Who does that? Throwing off a friend because a lover can give you five minutes of their time? I'm outraged on behalf of all women whose friends have done that to them. I can't believe what I'm hearing. "I can't believe this, Tallulah."

I somehow expect her to say that she'll cancel on her date. That's what the old Tallulah would have done. Not out of a sense of ethics, but because she didn't like conflict. Because she didn't like to feel guilty or responsible for hurting other people.

"Sorry, Arya. It's just…it's important."

I hear it, I hear the new something in her voice. I can't define it. She's not even thinking of cancelling on the date. She's definitely going to cancel on me instead. I don't stop to think that I was planning on cancelling on her anyway. I don't stop to wonder who this date is, and what that new thing is that I can hear in her voice that I've never heard before, not even back in school when she liked Colin. A sense of calm purpose, maybe. I should pay attention to it, but I don't. As usual, I'm only interested in how I feel.

"Well, let's just see if I'm available next time you want to have a cup of tea!" I say, sounding as incensed as I feel.

"Arya—"

"Nope. Goodbye, Tallulah, it sure was nice to reconnect. Have a good life."

I click of the call and throw the phone on the floor, where it disintegrates.

Chapter Twenty-Eight

I spend the next morning baking in Branwell's kitchen after banishing him into his living room with strict instructions not to come anywhere near me. I can hear him typing. I take a peek into the living room after I finish my eyeball granola and before I start on my bloody red velvet cake. He's typing industriously, looking intense and sexy. I can't help it. It's the absolute focus. I walk in and give him a quick kiss on the back of his neck. He turns on his swivel chair. He looks surprised and pleased.

"Don't get excited. It was a spur of the moment thing. I was taking a one-minute break."

He holds my hands. I try not to look surprised and pleased too. He entwines his fingers with mine.

"You've never done anything like that before, that's all," he says.

"Kissed you?"

"Not like that. Not affectionately."

"That's ridiculous."

"Hey, I have a book reading coming up next week, at the weekend. It's in the Lakes. I was going to drive up, do the reading on Saturday night. It's a bunch of snotty middle-graders."

My fingers are still laced with his. His hands are warm. "That's a lovely story, but—"

"I was wondering if you'd like to come along. We could spend

Sunday there. It's beautiful up there."

I take a deep breath. "Bran, I told you I don't do that."

"Walk?"

"This whole couple thing you're imagining. I don't, okay?"

He's quiet but I can see he's thinking. "We don't have to call it that. A couple thing. Walking usually involves putting one foot in front of another, left and right, left and right, or just to mix things up you can do it right and left." He looks at my face. "It might be nice."

I don't want to see the hesitation in his face, the feeling that he might be walking on eggshells around me. I pull my hands away.

"We could try it." That hesitation again. He's still looking at my face, with those hopeful eyes that I don't want to see.

I flick my head. "Do it with someone else, Bran."

I head off into the kitchen, feeling irritated for some reason and not waiting to see how he might respond to my words. I half want him to march into the kitchen behind me and convince me—in a bold and physical way—that I'm the only one he wants, but (half) disappointingly, he doesn't.

I zone him out, even though he's not making any noises. I turn my mind to more important things. Bran can do his lovely couple walk up in the Lakes with someone else. I flick my head a few more times. It doesn't have to be me. It can be someone else, someone more…normal.

This thought makes me feel even more irritated. I never said I was going to be normal, did I?

"I never said it," I mutter under my breath. For some reason, I can't get the feel of his warm fingers entwined with mine out of my mind.

I measure out the buttermilk for the red velvet. I lay out the cider vinegar for the cake and the block of cream cheese for the cream. I add a good wallop of red color (beetroot, always beetroot), then add a dash more, to get the blood right. I'm not happy with the texture of the batter, so I add buttermilk. I flap about the kitchen a bit, banging things. Half hoping that Branwell will come in and complain about the noise. With the blood red cake in the oven, the icing done and chilling, the kitchen given a good sweep or five, I look toward the living room again. I fight with myself. I could just head home for a bit, come back to check on the cake. But then I walk into the living room. He's still working away. I don't like to disturb him, plus, I like seeing him frowning at his computer. He's cute when he does that.

I walk around his living room. He's unpacked some more now. There are prints on the walls, crowded, jostling for space. There are contemporary abstract ones and some jazz posters and a few charcoal studies, one old copy of a Renoir with a pastoral scene amidst it all. They're not arranged by theme or period or color, but there's something pleasing about the patterns that the frames, the sizes, the textures make on the walls. I like looking at the frames. There's one that's burnished gold, another that is otter fur, and a Greek mottled-wall blue. A silver one, fluted and ribbed, and an Art Nouveau, feathered at the crown like a woman's headband. I walk about, giving each my attention.

I thumb through the records next. And some more photo frames that he hasn't put up yet. I glance at them, and then look at his back and shoulders when he's typing. I've seen him at work before. He starts with a good, straight posture, but when he's concentrating, the frown deepens, and his head bends forward, putting his neck out of whack. There's something delicious about the set of his shoulders, and his broad back, even as his shoulders hunch. I have the painful urge to rub the chinks out of his shoulders, but I stop myself, not wanting to give him the impression that this is something I do. I wander about the room again, looking at his things, so that I can keep on resisting the increasingly painful urge to put my arms around him.

And then I see it. In the bookcase.

My eyes skim past it at first because I'm distracted by his back. But then I look again. It's only a skinny, tatty volume. Nothing special. And anyway, anyone could have it. It doesn't have to be what I think it is. My heart is thudding. I look closer, making sure to read the name clearly in my head. I straighten, still willing the book not to be there. I don't know what it means, I remind myself, I have no idea what it can mean.

But I can't stop staring at it.

It's one thing for Branwell to have met Tobias – it's one thing that he didn't think to mention the meeting to me. But this. This is something else. I turn slowly and look at his back again. He's still typing, stopping every few seconds and frowning at his screen.

There's a reason I don't trust anyone. A good reason. The simple truth is no one ever lives up to someone else's trust. And in fact, as soon as you start to let your guard down, this kind of thing happens. Something twists hard and fast in my chest.

"Why didn't you tell me you knew Auntie Meera?" I ask calmly.

I see it. I see the ever so slight, the almost not there, freezing of his shoulders.

I wouldn't see it maybe if I didn't already know the backs of his shoulders so well. If I didn't spend many minutes—or is it hours? —gazing at them. He turns slowly around. His eyes have gone all distant. The warmth that he has in them when he looks at me, even that's not there now. I wonder why I didn't see it before. The way his eyes look when he's not putting on the charm, the *I want to look after you* act that he does with me that I'd started to fall for. The *I need you* act that I've been trying so hard to resist. When he stops with that act, there's distance and coldness. Suddenly, he's a different Branwell.

"What gave me away?"

I reach over to the bookcase, I take out *A Woman's Book of Herbs*. My heart lurches now that I look at it closely. If someone had asked me to recall the titles of Auntie Meera's books, I wouldn't have been able to bring up the names. If someone had mentioned this one, I would have remembered seeing it when I was growing up, but I wouldn't have been able to recall the wear in the spine, the bend in the front cover in the top right corner, the way some of the pages are lined or marked, with notes in the margins in her tight, floral handwriting. Yet, now, when I glance down at it, the merest glance, the book is as familiar to me as the back of my hand. I've seen it countless times growing up, at Auntie Meera's bedside, on the kitchen counter, lying horizontal on the bookcase that used to stand in her living room before I moved in and transformed the place, on the grass next to her garden chair.

"She lent it to me. I meant to give it back."

I look at him with hooded eyes.

I don't have to remember it, the many, many times I've looked at my dad like that, when he had me standing in front of him, with these exact same hooded eyes. *Why do you do it, Arya, just to show me up, why do you embarrass me like that? Can't you try to be normal?* He would wait, wait for me to respond. *Arya, we'll have to keep you home if you can't control yourself. You think people will want you around?* I swear it, my dad used to wait for me, keep saying more and more cutting things, waiting for me to give in, cry, shout, wail. But, over time, I got good at not doing that. I got good at giving nothing away. I stood as still as possible, looking at him, my lids half closed, my eyes cold, holding my body painfully rigid so it wouldn't betray me, give away how small he made me feel, how helpless and unlovable. I wouldn't give in and I wouldn't give myself away. The pressure would build and build, but I wouldn't give in.

Sometimes people don't fight back. Not because they're scared, but because they don't want you to see how you make them feel. They'll do anything to stop you from seeing the pain. I look at Branwell with those exact same eyes now.

"I don't care if you meant to give it back or not. I'm not so very worried that you have it, that you might have stolen it. What I want to know is, how did you happen to even meet her?" My voice is as hooded as my eyes, giving nothing away. Calm as a lake in the moonlight. A silver penny could drop in it, slice through it, without a whisper or a flick of water.

"I meant to tell you."

His voice is calm.

I wave an equally casual hand. "Oh, I'm not asking why you didn't tell me. I barely know you. You barely know me. You owe me nothing."

He flinches. "Arya—"

"I'm only surprised that you even came across each other. That's all."

He looks at me steadily for a minute. "The deal on this house fell through. I was here, looking at this house months before I actually got it. At that time, the deal fell through. But then it came back on the market a few weeks later. When I was first here, I was out walking, looking at the area and I met her in the woods."

"Yes, you told me you like to walk. And she happened to lend you her book, that she just happened to be carrying with her in the woods? Under her arm, maybe?" My voice is sweet now, sugary sweet and not hooded.

He's still looking at me. He's holding himself still too, I can see it. Maybe he doesn't want to give himself away either. "She asked me back to hers for a cup of tea. I told her I was looking for local herbs for a book I was writing. Something that could cause a stomachache, something that didn't look poisonous. She asked me back to tea, and she lent me this book. She said I should be able to find some interesting tidbits in there. She said she was planning on getting a new copy anyway and I could take as much time as I needed. I meant to mail it back to her when the deal on the house fell through, but it slipped my mind. When I moved here finally, she was already dead."

Why didn't you tell me? I want to ask him. Because, of course, that's the real question. Their meeting sounds innocent enough. It could have happened. I'm surprised that Auntie Meera asked a stranger to tea like that, it wasn't what she was like. But it could have happened. What I want to know is why he hadn't bothered telling me. But I can't bear to ask him. I can't bear for him to know that I care. I can't bear it that I care. I put my tea down, surprised to see how steady my hand is. I wipe my hands on my leggings.

"Well, I'd better be off. I'll clear out the things in your kitchen later on. We can't have my things cluttering your kitchen now, can we."

He doesn't move from the chair. He doesn't stand up. His hands are resting on his thighs. He's still looking at me. But there's something in his face. Maybe he does know me better than I realize. Because there's an awareness on his face about what this means to me. This betrayal. There's a roundness to his eyes. That tells me that he knows that I won't get over this.

"I didn't tell you. I should have told you."

I don't meet his eyes. I don't turn to look at him. I'm looking at the bookcase again. "Like I said, why would you?"

"I meant to. I didn't the first time because I didn't know you were Arya."

I turn around at that. "That I was Arya." My heart plops a few times, hollowly in my chest. "She spoke to you about me."

"She mentioned you. You'd had some kind of fight. She mentioned it."

Tears spring to my eyes. Despite myself, despite how desperately I don't want him to see how I feel. They sting. I blink them furiously away. "She told *you*—someone she'd only just met—that we'd fought." My voice sounds choked now. "Why would she do that?"

"Because when I'd come upon her—"

"What?"

He hesitates. But he's still looking steadily at my face. "She was crying. She said she'd tried to reach out a day or two before – and you hadn't responded."

It's my turn to flinch. I wipe my eyes with the back of my hand, hard and vicious.

He's holding himself very still. "She didn't mean to tell me. I didn't pry."

I laugh. It sounds harsh and broken. "No, of course you didn't.

No, you're good at not prying. You're good at being hands off. And yet, people trust you anyway. That's the funny thing, isn't it, Branwell. People trust your direct eyes and your smile, and they tell you things they wouldn't tell other people."

His face is different now. Pulled in. Yet, he knows, he knows there's no point reaching out to me. He knows. He doesn't move.

"So, she told you. You already knew about me when me met. That's the funny thing, isn't it, Branwell? You already knew about me. You knew I was heartless enough not to reach out to my dying father." I say it as casually as I can. Yet, the words are full of hatred. For my dad, for Branwell, for Auntie Meera for giving me away. Or just for myself.

"She didn't think that. She told me how he was—" He stops abruptly. Now I can see his chest rising and falling. Harder now, faster, a pulse beating in his neck.

My face twists. "She told you how he was." My voice is completely neutral again. Auntie Meera. The one person I had trusted. What did she tell Branwell? My dad's anger? His disgust? Did she tell him how he used to tie my hands together to stop me from ticking or dropping things? That I'd stay like that for hours sometimes?

His eyes, I can see his eyes. I can see it. Pity, maybe. Yes, of course, pity.

"I don't think she meant to tell me anything. But she was sad. And she was worried about you."

"You already knew about all of this the first time you met me." The way he'd looked at me even then. Those wide-open eyes, the way his beautiful eyes had looked at my face. He had already known. "That I was too much of a bitch to reach out to my dad. That I was too much of a bitch to listen to Auntie Meera pleading with me." My voice is twisted now. "You already knew when you met me."

He shakes his head. "I didn't know who you were then. I hadn't made the connection. I did by the time I saw you again."

"Why didn't you tell me?"

He hesitates. Then he says, "She was sorry she'd told me. She hadn't meant to. She was just worried. She said if I ever met you, maybe I could keep it to myself. She said you didn't like people knowing."

This hurts more than any of the rest. They had been talking behind my back the whole time. Poor Arya, poor stupid Arya. And I had thought—just for a smidgen of a second when we met—that he liked me for me.

"What else?" My voice is hard. And there's a crack in it.

He shakes his head. "She said she wished you had someone looking out for you. That's all."

I nod slowly. I manage to get some more words out. Through my clenched voice. "So, that's what you were doing. The cups of tea. The Harrods stuff. Lending me your blackboard and your kitchen. Well, thanks." I turn to head out. I stop at the door to the kitchen. "You've paid her back in full now for the loan of the book. Thanks – for looking out for me. You're off the hook now."

He comes to his feet. "That's not what—"

Something in my face stops him.

"It really doesn't matter. It was fun while it lasted. I'll be by for my kitchen stuff later."

Chapter Twenty-Nine

I end up at my place first. But then I see it, the yellow tape around the kitchen that's waiting for Shona to give the all clear, for the deep-cleaners to come, the quiet, brooding stairs that go up to Auntie Meera's room—the house itself feels dark and unclean. I can't bear to be in it. Not for a second. And I can't wait around for it, the thing in my chest that's choking me.

I head out for a run. I can't be still. I don't know why though. What have I really lost? I barely knew the man. Most people turn out to be disappointing. What did I know about him? He didn't tell me about knowing Tobias and he didn't tell me about knowing Auntie Meera. For all I know, he's the one who preyed on them. He's good at putting people at ease. He managed to do that to Auntie Meera the first time they met. She had not only lent him a favorite book, but she had told him about me. Not just who I was, not even just about our fight, but about me, how *I* was, how she was worried about me, how I needed someone to look out for me because I couldn't do things on my own. And she had told him about my childhood.

However upset she was, I couldn't see how he had got her to do that. She knew, she knew how I felt about people knowing. She knew I didn't even explain to friends—the handful I had—how I was. I made her swear she wouldn't tell my teachers, even to excuse my bad behavior at school. I was always causing disruptions. Paper flying everywhere –airplanes with rude sketches on them, pens thrown at people, chalk stamped on, work rarely done. I was always shouting at people. And when I wasn't shouting, I was falling out with them, finding bones to pick, getting defensive and putting people off, picking fights, even where there were no fights to pick. There wasn't a slight small enough that I couldn't scratch and gnaw at it. The teachers wanted to know my history, they wanted to help, they asked Auntie Meera about me. But I wouldn't let her explain things to them. Wouldn't let her explain how much I obsessed over other people's words. Not just their words but their tone and expression. Every word and look picked over and stared at, until I couldn't bear it anymore. I didn't want her to explain that the thing I found the most terrifying in the world was other people, letting other people see me as I was. It was easier to be angry than scared.

She knew that. She knew how I was about it. Yet, she'd told a complete stranger.

And Tobias had trusted him too. Enough to leave him something in his will.

I run up the hill, not looking where I'm going, blindly running. I wipe my nose on the back of my hand, anger making me alternately hot and cold. I had started to like him. No, I had liked him. A lot, if I'm completely honest with myself. I had begun to turn to him, to call him, to go to his house when I needed something. That's the worst thing of all. Worse than Auntie Meera's betrayal, worse than the rest of it. I had liked Branwell, and he had known about me all along. He hadn't wanted me—why had I ever imagined that he would?—he had pitied me.

Well, isn't that nice, Auntie Meera. Thanks so much for letting him know what a pathetic loser your niece is, how she can't manage on her own. Thanks for that. And me, I'm so careful about letting people in, yet even I had started to fall for it. I rub the knot in my tummy. The knot of longing and grief, for everything I wanted to be, and everything I was not.

I run up the hill, never minding that my chest hurt, that my legs were burning. I run ten laps, fast and hard, and finally feeling a little calmer, I head up to the shops to pick up a few supplies. Supplies for me, not for my customers. Supplies that I often tended to forget until I was actually starving. I get a few things I need and stuff them into my skinny backpack. On my way out of Waitrose, I bump into Shirley.

I whirl on him, grab his beautiful velvet jacket lapels and look him straight in his black opal eyes.

"When can I have my kitchen back, you he-devil with the stupendously improbable dimples?" I growl.

He doesn't struggle. He just closes his eyes and shakes his head.

"Tell me *now*."

He opens his eyes. "In a few days," he squeaks.

I hold him tighter. I grab his throat with one hand and squeeze hard. "That'll be your balls next."

"Tomorrow," he says. "Tomorrow."

I let go of him.

He straightens. "You do realize this is vintage." His voice is mild, but his eyes are hurt. "I thought you'd appreciate things like that. I really thought that, Arya." He genuinely sounds hurt about his purple lapels.

I snarl. "Tell Shona I want my kitchen back tomorrow. Or I'll complain to – to – to someone – a lawyer! – about how you're harassing a working woman and stealing her livelihood! Twice, now, Sherlock, twice!"

"Well, as to that, we're only trying to protect you. The cat thing – the *toy* cat thing. We're sure it's a warning, you know. You really should watch your step."

"Are you threatening me?" My face is centimeters from his. "Through your astoundingly fleshy bow-shaped lips and your impossibly white teeth?"

He backs off. "Try not to breathe on this waistcoat. That's vintage too. It gets water spots."

I propel a finger in his face. "I'll show you water spots! I'll spit on your waistcoat!"

He goes ashen. "You wouldn't!"

Shona cruises over. "Try not to assault my assistant, Arya."

I whirl around. "I'd better have my kitchen back tomorrow, Shona, or else."

"Tiff with the boyfriend?" she asks, looking down at her notepad, her voice suggesting that she's known it all along, that it wouldn't last, my little thing with Branwell.

This makes me crosser than I was. "He's not my boyfriend."

"Makes my heart glad to hear it, Arya, it really does."

"Do you have any idea who put that stuffed cat in my kitchen? Do you?"

She taps the side of her head. "We have theories."

I narrow my eyes.

She shrugs. "It's not just the stuffed cat, is it? The real cat is still missing. The two things are obviously linked. The blood – we think it's cat blood."

I feel a little sick. "Cat blood?"

"There's not a lot of it, so your cat—Mr. Yards's cat—what did you call him? The Duke?—might well be alive. But we've had words with Tobias's cleaner, Cathleen Clark. It turns out the cat hated your ex Craig. Isn't that interesting? Even more interesting that Cathleen thinks—" she leans closer, "that it was mu-tu-elle."

"Craig hates all animals!" I say in his defense.

Shona taps her head again. "The law is closing in, Arya, the law is closing in. You be careful now. All I can say to you is this: it's almost always an ex when a beauty such as yourself turns up naked and splayed on her kitchen floor."

They walk off, Shona looking at me over her shoulder and tapping her head again. I shake my head to clear it of the vision of me, naked and splayed and very dead, on my kitchen floor.

I spot Willie Arnott, who I realize I haven't thanked properly for his support when I had found the stuffed cat in my kitchen. I walk over to him. He's got a basket on his arm. I notice the things in it. A box of calming herbal tea, bags of vegetables and sausages. Everything seems to have a *buy one get one off* label, or a *grab it before it's gone* sticker. There's the cheapest, most anonymous pair of new socks too that look like they'll disintegrate at first wear.

He looks sheepishly at me. "I don't have a lot of money."

I start, having the grace to feel ashamed at the way I was staring at the contents of his basket and judging him for his cheap tastes. I wonder why he lives here of all places, where people buy painfully expensive stuff that's designed to look not expensive, but that's what tells you how expensive it is. He wriggles under my gaze, and I notice the paper clip holding his green-check shirt together at the top where the button seems to have fallen off.

"That's not a crime," I say.

He smiles and nods. "Yes, you're right. One can't help judging oneself though. Seeing oneself through others' eyes. You're right to chide me on my vanity."

I stare at the scars on his wrist again, the ones I had seen before when I bumped into him on this street.

"They're all down my back too."

"I'm so sorry," I say stiffly. "I don't mean to stare. I don't know why I was."

"It's really nothing. My sister bore the brunt of our father's wrath."

I wince. "I'm sorry. I didn't know." I can't help it. Just for a second, the uncharacteristic, unheard of thought, that this man and I have something in common, after all. And I don't have bruises to show for my childhood, like he does. But these thoughts make me uneasy. I don't want to have anything in common with this man. To be fair, I don't want to have anything in common with anyone. At danger of repeating myself: I don't do that.

"It marks you out as a child," he says.

I snap my eyes up to his face.

Does he mean me? Had Auntie Meera told *everyone* about me? Had I just imagined that she knew me, that she cared, that my secrets were hers to keep safe? But then I realize he means himself, and maybe his sister, that his voice and face are neutral. That he isn't talking about me. That he can't be.

And I remind myself to breathe.

Secrets, it occurs to me. Auntie Meera with hers, Tobias with his tail. This man. I study his face, the anonymous, almost hazy features that seem to fade in front of your eyes, the nervous eyebrows. Is he the kind of person who might be preyed upon too? I almost say something. I almost lean over and tell him to be careful. That there's someone about who preys on people with weaknesses. But then he nods and is off. I see him stop and exchange a word with…with Tallulah.

My face hardens. Tallulah. She's talking shyly to the man. Like she does to everyone. Her eyes hesitating at his. He's talking kindly to her. No doubt some wise words about human variance. She nods at what he says. Then he's gone.

To avoid Tallulah, I make a sudden sideways move—a sort of jeté, followed by an arabesque—which means I end up in the frozen custard shop. To tell the truth, this could be because I want frozen custard. Just to make it clear, I always want frozen custard, this isn't just a one-off. I stand inside the shop for a few seconds, disoriented by my sudden move.

"You've turned me into an addict." I look crossly at Veronica. I peer out of her window for a second. I can see Tallulah, looking a little confused about where I might have disappeared. So, she had been looking for me. I turn back to Veronica, relieved to have so narrowly escaped.

She smiles. "Aww, shucks, hon. Come to Mama and get some sugar."

"Uh, no thanks. At least, not if you mean a hug. If you mean frozen custard, on the other hand…"

"I mean you can have whatever you want from Auntie Veronica."

I glare at her. "Are you flirting with me too?" What's the matter with everyone?

She goes off into a peal of laughter. I notice she's not in a working-man's shirt today. She's wearing a denim shirt, the top three buttons undone to show a fluorescent pink bra underneath, encasing a pair of truly giant Texan-bred knockers. And a pair of black jeans and her cowboy boots. "Do you have a dick?" she says, wiping her tears. "Because if not…" she shrugs.

"I'm with you on that one. Though having a dick doesn't always mean someone will use it," I say bitterly, not knowing exactly where I'm going with this.

"Oh, I don't know, darling. Men whip it out quicker sometimes when they don't care."

"And sometimes they don't whip it out because they don't care." I get tangled in my syntax. (It doesn't happen often. Enjoy it while you can.)

"Don't tell me you and that dishy young man have had a falling out, hon! Come to Mama!"

"A falling out? No. We're done. That's all. Don't worry about it. My relationships don't last. Not that this one was even that. And stop trying to hug me. I don't do hugs."

She smiles and seems to shimmer in the sunlight coming through the shop window. "What can I do for you?" she asks, handing me an enormous frozen custard.

I dive into it and emerge a few seconds later.

"I imagine that tongue could do a great deal of damage," she murmurs.

"Oh, you bet it can." I poke a finger in her face. "That secret of Tobias's."

Her face closes up at once. She crosses her arms over her chest. "It's not nice of you to bring that up again, Arya. I'm a discreet gal, and I can tell you I'm ashamed of myself for having told you about his secret."

"Did no one know but you? I mean, any lover could have." I

try to lick the last of the custard out of the recyclable cup in mildly orgasmic desperation.

She shrugs and looks down at her bright orange fingernails. "I suppose so, yes. But as far as I knew, he didn't have many of those. He was always grateful for our...you know."

It's hard to imagine Tobias being grateful to anyone.

Maybe she reads my mind. "Oh, I don't mean gratitude like someone would be for someone else's company. I mean physical gratitude. When you need a release, and someone gives you one, and generously. Of course, he was always generous in turn. He had an incredibly long tongue, like you wouldn't believe—"

"Jesus, woman, do you not have an off-switch?"

"Well, you English are so squeamish about details. What's the biggie? Anyway, I did think he'd met someone recently."

"Hmm. Yes, you and everyone else. An open secret. Is nothing secret around here?"

She shrugs. The door tinkles behind me. Veronica's eyes flicker. I turn to look. It's Mark Close, minus the entourage. I almost don't recognize him when there are no children hanging off of all his limbs. He looks less harassed without his ninja army. Veronica seems to warn him with her eyes, she seems to say *not now*, but he comes in anyway. He may look less harassed, I note, but he does look generally worn out, the lines around his eyes making him look older than his mid-thirties. I raise my eyebrows as Veronica goes to him and they whisper in a corner. He shakes his head, rubs his face. She puts a hand on his arm. The hand could be a friendly hand. There's nothing much in it. He glances at me and nods, but then gives himself and Veronica away by the way his hand brushes her waist before he leaves the shop again.

I place my hands on my hips. "Mark Close? He has a *wife*. Really, I thought better of you, Veronica Chives."

She has the grace to blush. "He thinks his wife is having an affair."

I glare at her. "My god. I thought you said you were discreet.

You can't keep a secret to save your life."

Her eyes flicker nervously, and her fingers work together. "Sorry, Arya, it's just you have a very non-judgmental face."

"I do not. I judge everyone. And hate everyone, come to it. I'm leaving now. Don't forget to close your legs afterwards."

I mean this to be a pointed comment, but she looks unabashed as ever. As I exit the shop, Mark Close goes back in. I can't help glaring at him malevolently as we cross each other. What the bloody bejesus is wrong with everyone in this town? Can no one keep their dicks in their pants?

It occurs to me – was this what Mark Close had looked so guilty about last time I'd seen him? I had wondered if he was hiding that he wasn't at home that night when I had seen the circle in the clearing. I had wondered why he was hiding it. Maybe it was just this? This was his secret, his affair with Veronica. Maybe it hadn't been anything to do with the murders, or the circle, after all.

I rub my forehead. There are more secrets flying about this village than balls in Wimbledon.

As I step out of the shop, I can see at once that my foray into frozen custard—I'm not kidding about that, I still have some on my nose, I'm saving it for later—has been of no avail, because no sooner do I step out of Veronica's shop than I bang straight into Tallulah. Dang it.

"I'm so sorry about tonight," she says without preamble. "How about next week? Saturday?"

I start. Because that's the night Branwell had said for us to go up to the Lake District. I had said no to him, and there was no way I would have gone with him anyway, but now that the possibility has been snatched away from me after our fight – no, our breakup, I feel used and abused.

"Please, Arya. I'm sorry about cancelling tonight. And it's school nights—busy mornings—for the next few. They're doing some sort of summer club thing. But I'd love to do next week Saturday. Can you do it? Do you have plans? Please?"

"Fine," I find myself saying, mostly, I expect so I can get away from her sad, guilty eyes, but also because I, all of a sudden, can't stomach the thought of spending that particular Saturday night alone in my living room reading Regency romances, conversing heavily with D'Artagnan, and spasmodically checking my phone.

I walk away from Tallulah and turn my thoughts from my trusty vibrator and bang straight into Branwell Beam, local middlegrade author.

I grit my teeth. The gods of coincidental meetings are having their merry way with me this morning, even more so than usual.

I stand there, glaring at him.

"Can we talk?" His voice is rigid, but his eyes have that searching look. That look that says *I need you, but I don't know how to show it.*

I square my shoulders. "There is nothing whatsoever to talk about. I never do awkward exes. That's for other people. I get over things pretty quickly. Especially when it's not that important in the first place."

"You get over things pretty quickly," he repeats in a neutral voice.

"I always told you. You didn't want to see it."

He grits his teeth.

"Toodle-oo." I make tracks, not wanting to look at his sad eyes for a moment longer.

This is fine. *Fine*. I may have to do that a few more times, but then we'll get over the awkwardness. I never make things awkward. Like I said, it was fun while it lasted. There's no more to it. The dead feeling in my stomach – that, that's nothing, nothing at all. That will go away. With time—a few days, no more—I'll stop seeing the man's sad eyes floating in front of my face. And I'll stop waiting desperately for the sound of his voice at the other end of the phone. All in all, I'll stop feeling like I've lost something I didn't even know I had.

Chapter Thirty

I spend the next few days ignoring everyone. As I say, I generally don't find this too difficult to do. And there's certainly a lot to think about, what with the murders my brain is still working away at. In fact, there's so much that it's hard to pick the skeins apart. I sit down with Post-its one morning and try to organize my mind.

The facts are these: Cath and Tobias ate some of my tiramisu. At that point in time, around five in the afternoon on the day he died, the tiramisu had not been poisoned (unless Cath is lying and killed Tobias herself.) Veronica saw Tobias in his kitchen after Cath left. Then she went off to have a shower (unless she's lying and killed Tobias herself). An hour later, she found him dead. By that time, two more slices of the tiramisu had been consumed.

And Craig inherits Tobias's riches.

Could Tobias have been about to change his will? I shake my head. Craig didn't kill Tobias, though, motive or not, so the potential change of will hardly matters. Craig has an alibi (me) for that one hour that the tiramisu could have been poisoned, and even if he didn't, I can't overlook the one solid fact that Craig doesn't have the imagination to kill anyone.

Tobias and Auntie Meera knew each other. A search of Auntie Meera's room upstairs confirms that Auntie Meera had had the plant poison used to kill Tobias in her stores. There isn't much left in the bottle. Does this matter? Even if the murderer had got it from Auntie Meera, all this proves is that the murderer knew Auntie Meera and also knew Tobias. And I already know this, don't I?

What had Tobias wanted to tell Auntie Meera when he bumped into her in the woods? And in fact, he had told her, but she hadn't written it down in her diary. Why hadn't she? Because it wasn't that important, or, in fact, because it was very important to her?

It's a jumble.

In between the baking and the trying to work things out, I spend hours calling out to The Marquis. As the days pass, I start to get a horribly sick feeling in my stomach. What if the same person that left the stuffed cat in my kitchen also actually killed The Marquis? I shake my head. Surely not. If he had killed The Marquis, then why not leave the dead cat in my kitchen? Why just a stuffed cat?

This nasty thought somehow leaves me with a sliver of a hope. That maybe The Marquis isn't actually dead. Theoretically, The Marquis could have got a horrible fright when the person with the stuffed cat came around and that's why he's gone missing. Maybe The Marquis doesn't want to come back. Or maybe he's tired of me and has found someone else to feed him. I rub my face.

A few days into the solitary week I'm desperately trying to have, I bump into Craig and Tarina on one of my runs. I stop abruptly, then glare at the man.

"You." I poke him in his chest. "Do you know Tobias's cat has gone missing?"

He rubs his nose with the back of his hand. He looks agonizingly average today, in his tailored trousers and his shirt and his tie, and next to him Tarina looks like a coral macaroon filled with quince cream.

"I hated that cat."

I glower at him. "You know, this is the kind of thing that I don't understand. Do you have to say things like that? This is exactly why Shona and Shirley think you're the friendly neighborhood murderer, and not just of cats."

He shrugs. "It wasn't a secret. The Marquis hated me. He hissed every time I so much as got near him."

"He did that to everyone."

"That doesn't make it any better," Craig admonishes. "What has it to do with me that he hated everyone?"

"Lord save us. And stop reading Joseph Heller, it'll mess with your mind. They'll arrest you, you know, if you don't stop going on about how much you needed Tobias's money and how much you hated his cat. Why did my aunt leave you a rusty motorbike?"

His face saddens. "She was kind. She knew I like machines. Plus, she had no idea what to do with it."

"Craig make nice words with your auntie," Tarina adds helpfully. "Craig makes nice words with women, in general."

I turn the force of my glare on her. "Just so you remember this, Tarina, nice words won't scratch that itch."

I leave with these satisfying parting words. It only occurs to me when I'm halfway down the hill to wonder why Auntie Meera didn't just hand over the motorbike to Craig then and there. Why did she put it in her will? Why make a new will in the first place, after she moved to Trucklewood? What was the rush?

I spend the next few days doing what I do best. Continuing with my mission of ignoring everyone. It occurs to me that I've let myself get over-involved, a sin I'm not usually guilty of. I don't know what it is. Tobias's death, bumping into Tallulah after all these years, the shock of finding out about my tiramisu, or meeting Branwell and his direct eyes. But I'm so over it now. I'm so over all of it. A temporary phase, that's all it was. I bake, take orders, clean, I run when no one is about so I get the streets and woods to myself. And I keep calling for The Marquis, knowing that I'm spending each minute in the house on edge, waiting for him to slink his way around a corner and bang into me, scowl at me, jump up to my bed in the middle of the night, any of these things, all of these things. But the house is terrifyingly empty.

But it's worse than that. Conversations held over the last days and weeks filter through my head at all hours and I still can't make any sense of them. Even when I'm sleeping. Disjointed, chaotic thoughts, about all the Trucklewood residents and their secrets.

Mark Close's wife Sheshonne might be having an affair too? Veronica had said as much. Veronica and Tobias, and now Veronica and Mark. Mrs. Sharma's prune jelly. Tobias's eyes as they swept over people at the Easter fair. Auntie Meera's journals. Secrets, secrets everywhere. Tallulah.

I don't want to think about Tallulah.

I wish she had stayed away from Trucklewood. I wish I hadn't seen her. I don't want to feel responsible for her. I don't want to have to make her feel better. There's something especially vile about trying to make someone feel better about *you*, about the things you do and say to someone. And I don't want to do it.

A clean start, maybe. Maybe I need to move on, live somewhere else. I don't want to live here and bump into all these people as soon as I so much as step out of the house. Tallulah. Branwell. Reminders of Auntie Meera. Maybe it had been a mistake to move here in the first place. After Auntie Meera died, why on earth would I have moved to the place in which she died? I could have sold her house and moved somewhere else. Is this what I want? To see reminders of her everywhere? Isn't that what this has been about? Obsessing about Tobias's death just because I can't get over Auntie Meera's? Maybe it's time to move on now. It's what I do best.

The universe colludes with my wanting to forget everyone and everything because I have a flurry of orders. I bake away. Several batches of granola, a few lots of cupcakes (a party of a hundred and fifty wants slime cupcakes), several birthday cakes. It takes all my attention to sort out the baking, the couriering, the logging of orders, the incessant cleaning.

On one of my runs through the woods, I bump straight into Sheshonne.

I've been so good at keeping everyone at arm's length for the last few days that I stare at her like she's stepped out of nothing and nowhere, materialized in front of me like a ghost. Her long braids are as impeccable as ever, all shiny black like a raven, sleek across her prettily shaped scalp and down her back, she's wearing a brown wraparound skirt and an ankle bracelet, but I can't help noticing that she looks skinny, and her eyes look pinched. This is what happens when you cheat on your husband, I almost say, but I stop myself just in time. I'm about to carry on with my run, when she grabs my arm.

"Why do you think the murders of Tobias Yards and your auntie—Meera—are connected?" she asks abruptly, in a brittle voice.

I stare at her, my heart hammering and not just because of my interrupted run now.

I look pointedly down at my arm, which is still clasped in a vice-like grip in her long fingers. She withdraws her hand.

"There were some similarities. But I suppose," I add grudgingly, "anyone could have copied the MO of the first murder to make it look like it was done by the same person. To tell you the truth, I don't really know what I've been doing or why. I've been wasting my time."

She looks uncertainly at me. "So, you don't think they were done by the same person?" She looks nervous, even agitated. I peer closer. But this is a mistake. She instantly closes up. "I'm making too much of it." She takes a step back.

"Wait. What do you know about the murders?"

She shakes her head. "Nothing. Nothing at all. Tobias, I mean, even if I could connect him – but not your auntie, she wasn't even—" She stops talking. "It was uh – good to see you. Just—" she bites her lip. "Just be careful, Arya."

She's gone.

I shake my head and stare after the woman. Moving away from Trucklewood is clearly the only thing left to me now. My instincts are correct. I've made the mistake I don't usually make. I've let myself get involved. And I can't help, like the other time I'd spoken to her, I can't completely help liking the woman, I don't even know why. Two sentences exchanged do not a friendship make.

I can't shake off an uneasy feeling. I can't tell if it's from Sheshonne and her pinched face, or if it's something else.

I automatically take out my phone to call Branwell.

I growl at myself when I realize what I'm doing. I've even got as far as finding his name in my contacts. Just because of a twinge of unease. How much have I borne that in my life? The restlessness that starts in me when people speak to me, when I'm afraid I've built up expectations that I can never live up to? When I watch their face closely, minutely to see if they hate me, are disappointed by me, are losing interest in me? Only all my sodding life! And yet, in a matter of weeks I've let a complete stranger into my life, and I can't even bear a flicker of unease without needing to hear his voice. What is the matter with me?

It occurs to me suddenly.

Tallulah.

I don't need to call Branwell. I don't need to miss Auntie Meera. I can call Tallulah. No, I don't need to call her. I can see her tomorrow, Saturday. I don't have to talk to her about Sheshonne or Branwell, or Auntie Meera, or any of it. But she'll be there, familiar Tallulah, loyal in her own way. Maybe we can bake cookies! She's known me forever, and you can't put a price on that.

For the first time since I bumped into her in the woods all those weeks ago, I feel a tiny iota of gratitude that she's back in my life.

My phone buzzes as I carry on with my run.

It's a message from Tallulah.

"I'm so, so sorry, Arya. Can we postpone tomorrow night again? Please don't hate me. Could we do tea the next day instead? Maybe Sunday?"

I stare at my phone in disbelief.

I can't fathom what I'm seeing. The cheek of the woman to invite me to something— to pressure me with her guilty face—into agreeing to do something that I don't want to do and then to *blow me off again!* I can't believe what I'm hearing. Instead of turning around and heading homewards, or even continuing with my run, I find my feet banging away on the dirt track toward the boarding school. In ten minutes flat, I'm knocking on the door to Tallulah's cottage. It's nine in the evening. She's bound to be in and not in school.

She opens the door. "Oh, thank goodness," she says, nervously looking at my face. "Please forgive me—"

"No. This is too much, Tallulah."

She flinches.

I ignore the face, the guilty eyes, the fear in her eyes.

"No, I will not forgive you! This is what you always do. I feel sorry for you, you know that? I feel sorry for your guilty face and your eyes and your stupid way of thinking you're trying to protect me when all you're doing is making me feel like shit for who I am. That's all you've ever done. With your nervous smiles and your quick reassurances that I've not hurt you. That's all you've ever done, and I keep on trying to make up for it, make up for how I am."

"Arya—"

"No, Tallulah. Don't text me again, don't call me to tea. Don't talk to me. I don't want you here. No one wants you here. Even this – this man you're seeing, he'll soon enough realize that he doesn't want you here. I have to say, it's hard for me to see what he sees in you in the first place."

Her face crumples.

The words have come out like my words often do. Like I have no control over them. And yet, yet, don't I mean them? I almost say it right there and then: *Sorry, Tallulah, sorry, I didn't mean it. I hate myself. You know that.* But I don't say them. I don't want to see her face. I'm not going to see it. I can't bear to see it.

I turn around and head home, wondering if it's possible to hate myself more.

Still, it's better than hating everyone else.

Chapter Thirty-One

I spend the next morning baking and cleaning, two things sure to bring some equilibrium back. At least, normally they are. At the moment though I can't get Tallulah's face out of my mind. The things I said to her ring in my head. I can't stand myself; I can't stand the things I said to her. I meant them, I tell myself, I meant them, she hurt me. I scrub and scrub.

I bang things about for good measure. Banging pots and pans, swiping spatulas in the air, thrusting trays in the oven, burning my hands because I forget to put on my mitts properly.

"Damn and blasted fucking hell!" Instead of putting ice on my burning hand, I let the burn sizzle, half enjoying the sheer pain of it. "Ow, ow, ow," I keep saying, "that stings." Tears sting my eyes.

What I want is to get people out of my head. Everyone. I want everyone's sad eyes out of my head. Is that too much to ask? Why, why do people expect any better of me, why do they expect anything at all? They know me, I make sure they know me, so why do we keep coming back to this, where they get hurt by the things I do and say? And Tallulah. I know so well. I won't go back to her. But if I did do that, if I did that, she would forgive me. Her face would be all hurt and sad and even afraid in case I lash out at her again, but she would assure me that it was fine, that she knew I couldn't help myself.

I close my eyes as I hold my burnt hand. My god, the thing hurts like the underside of hell.

That's the problem. Tallulah would forgive me, but she shouldn't, because I would only hurt her again. Inevitably, sooner rather than later.

I keep picking up my phone. I keep half typing *I'm so sorry, I didn't mean any of it, any man would be lucky to have you,* but I can't do it. I can't type it. If I type it, she'll forgive me. And then I'll do it again. Maybe worse next time.

There's only one thing to do. Only one solution. With her living in Trucklewood, and Branwell living here too, my plan to move away, that's the right thing to do. Escape all this. Not have to be here knowing all these people, trying to avoid them all the time. Wherever I go, I won't make the same mistake again. I won't get involved.

The doorbell rings.

It's my courier. I bang the door open so that it slams on the wall in the hallway, leaving a dent in the paint.

"It's Saturday morning," Sebum says, in a bored voice. "Do you wake up raging?"

"Shut up and wait there. I'm not done packing."

"They don't pay me to wait," he says, scratching his head under his baseball hat, with a pencil.

I hiss at him. "Wait. Or I'll tell them your fly was undone when you rang my bell!"

He rolls his eyes. "Hurry up."

I bang more pots and pans for good measure as I'm packing things up for Sebum to take. I load my little trolley up with boxes. Make sure all the seals and stickers are on. I wheel the trolley out to the hallway. Sebum carefully takes the trolley over the step. I follow him out. I supervise as he loads his car. He's always careful with this part, so I don't need to watch him like a hawk. But I never allow the boxes to be loaded unsupervised. When he's done stacking and making sure there isn't enough room in his boot for the precious cargo to wobble, I hold out my hand for the trolley.

"I'll wheel it back to the house for you," he offers.

I lead the way. He again steps the trolley carefully over the threshold, through the narrow hallway, and into my kitchen for me.

"Good you have your kitchen back?" he says.

I frown. "I didn't use unauthorized premises for cooking, if that's what you're banging on about."

"All the same to me," he says in a bored voice.

I follow him back out to the hallway again, and he crosses over the threshold once more. Something in the hallway catches my eye.

"Take this table away to the tip!" I say, pointing at the narrow but solid hardwood table in my hallway that I've been meaning to get rid of for months but that keeps getting covered in things—magazines, mail, jackets, umbrellas, shoes—and I keep forgetting about it.

"I'm not a binman," Sebum informs me. "Now, could you sign here?"

"I'll give you two cupcakes." I sign the form he's holding out, stabbing the pen hard in the paper. All the stabbing and banging and bashing and burning my hand (that still bites like hell) hasn't taken my restlessness out of me yet.

His eyes don't waver. "Done. I'll be back with the van. Give me ten."

"I'll leave the door open. Don't disturb me. I have more baking to do."

He looks hurt, making his spots look oilier than usual. "Don't use me like that, Arya."

I roll my eyes. "I'll add another two cupcakes. That's four altogether, for your slow brain."

He nods, not at all offended by my scathing opinion of his functional skills. "Done."

I'm in my kitchen, baking monster muesli ten minutes later when I hear my front door creak open. I frown, not stopping. I have to get the amount and drizzle of honey just right or it won't crisp up properly. I concentrate, get the last drizzle on the jumbo oats, give it a careful mix and place it on the lower shelf of the oven on a low heat to crisp up evenly. I can hear footsteps in my hallway. I've forgotten to leave cupcakes for my diehard courier, so I walk out to the hallway to hand him the box I've prepared for him. But it's not Sebum in my hallway, it's Branwell.

I place the cupcakes on the side table and cross my arms over my chest. "Do you break into people's houses now?"

He stands there, in his grey casual trousers and his black t-shirt, a slight scruff of beard on his cheeks. "Is this how quickly you get over people?" he demands, as way of answer. His eyes are fierce this morning, not cold, not distant, not even hurt, just blazing. "This is how quick it is, just so I know?"

I stare malevolently at him. "That suggests I had feelings for you in the first place. When I didn't. I told you I didn't, I distinctly remember it."

He rakes a hand through his hair. I can't help noticing that it has a shake in it. He looks like he hasn't slept properly for several nights. My eyes flicker at the tiredness I see in his face. My hand almost reaches out to try to trace it away. But I clench my fists.

"You're right, Arya. You're so right. You told me you don't feel anything. You told me you're dead inside. I just didn't want to see it."

This hurts. This cracks me in two. I grit my teeth. "Yep, I did. I told you."

He nods. "Well, isn't that brilliant, because I see it now, I bloody well see it. You don't have to tell me again. I see what you're like inside." His face looks torn, the eyes are exhausted.

I grit my teeth. "Well. Good."

His face is tight. He's grinding his teeth. We stare at each other.

Suddenly someone appears at my door. A bit like a Jack-in-the-Box. One second there's no one there. And then – there is. I turn to look at him.

"The table," Sebum says.

"I don't care about the table," I growl.

He looks offended. "Well, why did you make me come all the

way over here with my van then?" he complains. His eyes flicker to the pink polka dot box that's lying on the table. "Can I at least have the cupcakes?"

I move the cupcakes away into an alcove in the wall well out of reach. I glance at Branwell. And then turn back to Sebum. "No, but if you come upstairs, you can shag me senseless in my bed."

A twitch from Branwell. Or a jerk. Or something. Still, an admirable amount of self-control. It's all quite nicely held in really. A bit too nicely.

Sebum goes pink as a grapefruit. "Go on then," he says.

He starts to step inside. Branwell pushes the door shut in his face and turns the force of his wrath on me. "No, he bloody won't!" The self-control is slipping.

"Yes, he will," I say, as sweetly as I possibly can. "He positively, absolutely will." I march forth and open the door, where Sebum is still standing patiently. "Come on now, dear, chop chop, drop the pants. I don't have all day."

Sebum looks willing. Branwell slams the door in his face again. His shoulders are bristling at this point. His eyes are practically bulging. His hands as he throws them in the air are shaking. The self-control is not so easy anymore, I'm pleased to see. "I told you, he won't!"

"He bloody will!"

I lunge for the door. So does Branwell.

There's an unseemly tug of war. With me trying to pull the door open and Branwell shoving it closed. I'm trying so hard to open the door I'm skidding about the hallway.

"You know what your problem is," Branwell growls, while still putting all his weight against the door, while I'm still trying to pull it open, "you know what it is? Stop scratching me! You want me and you need me, but you can't admit it. Not even to yourself. That's your problem – one of your many, many problems. Your long list of problems!"

I put all my weight to pull the door open. "Well, I don't need you, so there!"

"Yes, you do!"

The door opens an inch, having been pushed open from the other side. We both slam it in Sebum's face this time. I think he calls, "I'll be going now then." He doesn't say anything for a few seconds. "Unless you still want that shag!"

We both open the door and yell in Sebum's face, "Go away!"

The door slams again. I vaguely hear retreating footsteps on the gravel.

We're glaring at each other.

"Well, isn't that great that you know all about my long list of problems," I spit out.

"Yup," he says, practically snarling now, "yup, lucky escape, if you ask me."

"Why are you still here then? No one asked you."

"Well, I'll just go then!"

"You bloody do that." I poke him in the chest with a sharp finger. "The sooner the better!"

We're standing there, staring at each other, centimeters from each other's face.

He grabs my arms. "Well, I do bloody need you. And I want you so much it's painful staying away from you. You think I pity you. You think I know about your childhood and I pity you. When all I feel is how much I want you. Everything you say, every little thing you do that makes you think I won't want you, only makes me want you more."

We stand there, chests heaving. For once in my life, I'm speechless.

And then somehow, I'm undoing his trousers and he's pulling my t-shirt, none too gently, off me. I give up on his trousers, he can do the damn things himself, I strip my knickers off and hoist my skirt over my hips. He grabs me, and we fall against one wall of the hallway. I clutch his hair and moan into his mouth. We crash against the opposite wall, my body pressing into his. He holds my face and kisses me, hard and hot, his mouth opening mine, his tongue pushing into my mouth. I claw at his back; I fight his tongue with mine. I can hear a wild panting – it's coming from my mouth, open on his.

I'm back against the wall again, splayed against it. His hands clutch my bottom. He lifts me up and plants me on something – it's the hardwood table. I lift my legs and wrap them around him. And then he's inside me. All the way inside me with one motion. I gasp. He stays utterly still for a moment, his face in my neck, his breathing ragged, and in that hard, hot stillness I can already feel myself convulsing around him. I moan. I can already feel the waves building. I can hear him breathing into my neck. Short, hot breaths. If he moves, I might shatter and I might never recover.

He moves, withdraws a little and then thrusts again. I moan and thrust back at him. His hands are on my breasts, his mouth on my neck. I stretch my legs wider so I can get more of him. I want all of him. He bends, takes a big mouthful of nipple as he pushes into me again. I grab his face and bring it up, I lean forward and bite him hard on his neck. He's pushing into me now, and I'm thrusting back, hard as I can, feeling him long and hard in the depths of me.

His hands are everywhere, his mouth at my breasts, his mouth back at my mouth. I'm panting, clutching at him, arching to get him deeper.

"Hard," I keep gasping, "harder!"

He thrusts in a rhythm that makes my soul ache.

It builds and builds in waves, the heat flooding my body. It builds forever, endlessly. And then finally when it can't build any more, it crashes all about me, as I feel him, the endless movement inside me that I never, never want to stop. And I feel him, waves and waves, the deep endless throbbing that starts me off again, the way his mouth feels on mine when he comes. The way he moans, harshly.

We clutch each other afterwards. Me, still perched on the table. Him still inside me, for endless moments, before he withdraws.

We stay there, forehead to forehead, breathing into each other.

"Fuck," he gasps.

He holds me close, face in my neck. It takes many minutes for our breathing to steady. I'm still feeling endless aftershocks building and subsiding inside me.

The ding-dong of the bell nearly gives us both a collective heart attack.

With shaking hands, he smooths my sports bra, grabs my t-shirt from the floor and pulls it over my head. I help him with his trousers. He pulls my skirt down over my hips. I slide off the table. He opens the door a couple of inches.

"Can I at least have my cupcakes?" asks Sebum reproachfully.

Chapter Thirty-Two

"Have you been standing there the whole time?" I demand. My voice is torn to shreds.

"The whole time what?" Sebum asks.

"What?" I ask in a daze. My brain has completely stopped working.

"I left. But I'm back for the cupcakes."

I grab the box from the alcove, walk over to the door, wobbly on my legs, and hand the pink polka dot box to Sebum. Branwell is leaning against the doorjamb for support. He's not saying anything. I can't tell if he'll ever be able to say anything again. There's still a shake in his breath.

"I can take the table if you want."

"I'm never getting rid of it," I croak.

Sebum leaves, plus four cupcakes, minus hardwood table. I've no idea how much he heard. I don't want to know. I swing the door shut.

Branwell pulls me into his arms and kisses me. Not so ferocious anymore, not so hungry, but slower, gentler. No, it is still hungry, the kiss, but in a different way.

"Arya," he says, a crack in his voice.

And the urge is there, I want to say it, that I don't do this. I can't do this. This, afterwards, the painful tenderness that breaks me in two, that terrifies me more than anything else. That I want more than anything else in the world not to ruin, not to shatter. But I don't have the words. I lean my head on his chest.

"Can we do that again?" I ask.

"Give me six or seven minutes."

All I can say is, reader, I do.

By the time Branwell leaves to head up to the Lakes for his book reading, I'm pleasantly sore. The hardwood table has had another rumble. We never did make it upstairs, not today. Most of the baking is done for the day and the house seems unnaturally quiet. I give the kitchen another clean. And then, feeling like I've been neglecting the rest of the house, in favor of my workspace, I give that a tidy too. I wonder if the ache in my muscles – upper back, hip flexors, thighs, the burn in my arm, all of the pains, if I can have them all the time. I realize that I quite like them. I call out to The Marquis. It's become so automatic now that I don't even stop to think that I hardly dare expect a response now. Still, I keep listening, sometimes thinking I can hear a faint meowing in the breeze.

"Wish you were here." Branwell writes me a message.

"Maudlin," I write back.

Feeling restless and trying hard to resist the urge to call the man just to hear the sound of his voice (for crying out loud!), I plonk myself on the sofa in the living room and flick casually through Auntie Meera's journals. I have in mind to see if she wrote anything about changing her will. I look back to the entries in the early days after she moved to Trucklewood. Many of the entries are about the local flora. The herbs and wildflowers she's collected, the terrible (in her eyes) way in which Trucklewood residents massacre wild plants and favor severely manicured lawns, the stifling way her neighbors encroach on her space, that she says politely is very nice of them, but she's not used to it and she half wishes they'd mind their own business.

Her entries reveal her opinions about the many Trucklewood residents.

Mrs. Sharma asked too many questions about her being an herbalist (except Mrs. Sharma kept saying *witch.*) Auntie Meera apparently tried to explain to her that she wasn't a *witch*, she was someone who specialized in medicinal uses of herbs and plants and flowers. Mrs. Sharma remained resolutely unconvinced.

Apparently Sheshonne had come around, asking if there were natural remedies to help her conceive, since they weren't having any luck with a third baby. Auntie Meera had recommended meditation and a healthy diet, and had made her a tea of black cohosh, chaste berry and cinnamon. Auntie Meera wrote that it had seemed like Sheshonne had just needed someone to talk to. That she had seemed troubled, like she wasn't sleeping.

Willie Arnott had been around to look over her receipts and sympathized that the village was bourgeois and provincial at the same time, that people were only too prone to pry.

Even Craig was mentioned. "A boring young man, a little full of his own importance. I was tempted to ask him if he wanted anything to boost his libido a bit. He looks the anxious sort. But I didn't want to embarrass him. As it is, he seemed to feel there was something emasculated about his financial difficulties. I suggested that he take the old bike a client left me once, in case he could make any money out of it. But he felt like it was too generous – he explained that the bike could get good money, once refurbished."

So, that was an explanation for why she had left it to him in her will instead of giving it to him outright. There's one mention of a meeting with her lawyer, a few months into moving to Trucklewood.

I frown into the distance for some time.

Then, finding a lawyer's firm in an old phonebook of Auntie Meera's that I fish out from a drawer, I call the number. It's nearly nine and I don't expect anyone to answer but to my surprise, someone does.

"Clive Masterson."

I'm a little taken aback by the sound of a voice. "Sorry, isn't it late for you to be at work?"

"This is nothing," the man says. "I'm here till midnight most days."

He sounds tired. I feel foolish now, but I try and explain why I'm calling. I vaguely remember now, speaking to him soon after Auntie Meera's death, when he had called me to explain the estate and death duties. I had forgotten all about it until now. He explains at tedious length about client privilege and confidentiality. I say to him that Auntie Meera is dead and I'm not asking for any confidential details. I just want to know if he can recall her state of mind when she contacted him about making a will. I realize I'm asking him to remember a client that he saw nearly a year ago.

"Sorry, I can't imagine that you'd even remember her now."

This is apparently the right thing to say because he says, slightly admonishingly, that he remembers clients from twenty years ago.

"Of course, of course," I say quickly.

He goes quiet as he thinks. "Her state of mind, yes, let's see now. I'd have said quite positive."

I don't quite know what to ask now. I don't know what information he can possibly have to give. "Do you feel like she was expecting to die?" A foolish question.

"Not at all. I felt nothing of the sort. And if I may say so, I have above-par instincts about people. She seemed to be taking care of business. I admire people with her forthright attitude. I wish there were more people who had that attitude – it would make my job easier. Most people don't understand the business of death."

"So, there was no real reason why she chose to remake her will at the time that she did?"

There's silence for a few moments as he thinks. Then he comes back. "You know, I don't believe there was anything specific. She had moved to a new area. I got the impression that she had made new connections and wanted a fresh start with her provisions. I didn't get the impression that she expected to die at all. She seemed

– at peace."

I put down the phone.

Yes, that's the thing. That *is* the thing. Both Tobias and Auntie Meera seemed at peace toward the end. But what does it mean? I can't put my finger on it. I can't get over the lurking feeling that I'm missing something. I keep going over details of their deaths—and the things people have said about them—but I can't figure out what I'm missing. I can't figure out what I'm meant to be seeing. I can't even figure out if I'm making things up in my head, because I'm obsessing about the deaths so much, that I'm imagining connections that don't exist.

My brain seems to have stopped working. I keep yawning and stretching and falling over sideways on to the slouchy burnt-orange sofa with the colorful cushions. At around ten, I get a text message. Expecting it to be Branwell—and thinking about telling him about the wonders of the sinky-in bouncy sofa I'm lying down on as I speak—I look at it quickly. But it's not Branwell.

It's from Tallulah.

"Please," it says.

I scowl at it. Please! *Please?* What does *please* mean? There's not even any punctuation, let alone it making any sense. All the years wasted in school being encouraged to complete our sentences! What does the woman want now? There is no way, no way I'm going to answer that text message. What does she want anyway? And why is she writing at all? Does she have no self-respect? I wish people would have some self-respect!

I growl low in my throat. After the terrible things I said to her, she should ignore me. She should cut me any time we bump into each other. Why send me a pathetic plea? I don't want to see it. I don't want to see it so much that I delete the message. There, that's done. Just for good measure, I delete her from my contacts. There's no way I can undo the things I said to her. I can hear them echoing in my head if I so much as think about her. And I can't bear it, I can't bear her trying to explain me out of this.

This is who I am. This is what I do.

Plus, plus there's a part of me that wants to hurt her more. That's the thing. That's the thing that I'm only too painfully aware of her. I want to hurt her; I want to see her hurt face when I do it. I don't want to write back; I don't want to call her. I want to hurt her for that moment I had in the woods when I had thought maybe it wouldn't be so bad if she were in my life and I could turn to her when I needed someone. I want to hurt her for that moment, and I want to hurt her for blowing me off again. By doing that, I want to erase the pain in my chest. I want to erase years of hurt and guilt and rejection and shame, not just from Tallulah but from everyone else in my life.

Just as I'm staring down at my phone, it rings. It rings and rings and even though I've deleted her from my contacts, I know it's her. I let it ring out. Then I delete the record of the call from my phone so that I'm not tempted to save her number again.

I get up and plod to the kitchen for a glass of water. On the way back I stoop and pick up a piece of A4 that's lying on the mat just inside the front door. My heart starts thumping.

The power is in your hands. If you have experienced trauma, if you think you are alone, I can help you. You can help yourself. You don't have to spend your life searching for meaning.

It's nearly three in the morning when I'm startled awake. I lie there, still on the sofa in the living room, heart racing, wondering what woke me. I'm not easily scared, certainly not of the dark. Things that other people are scared of—the dark, snakes, heights, bullies—these generally hold no fear for me. What I fear are not usually things that other people are scared of. Needing people, wanting people, reading their faces to see if they still want me. Those are the things that scare me.

I lie there. And realize what it was that had wakened me. A sound. No, I had imagined a sound. A meow. Damn it. The Marquis is haunting me. My eyes acclimatize to the darkness. And I realize that there are chinks of light coming around the edges of the living room curtains. The room isn't as dark as I had thought. I shake my head in the darkness, trying to feel less weary. Some filigree of the dream that I'd been having comes back to me. Footsteps. People lying on the ground, half naked. Looking at me, beckoning me. You're like us, the whispers said. You're just like us. Come and join us. *If you have experienced trauma, if you think you are alone, I can help you. You can help yourself.*

I think sickly of the words. The piece of A4, still lying on the mat inside my front door where I had dropped it. I don't even know what scares me more. That someone had left it there, dropped it through the letterbox. That that someone – surely, surely, they were the same person who had given the book to Tobias and Auntie Meera, and they could well be the person who had murdered them. Surely, that wasn't a leap too far? Is it that that scares me? Or the other thing? *If you have experienced trauma.* What did they know about me? How did they know anything about me? But it's worse than that. What scares me even more than all this, what makes me sick is the thought that they're right, that I'm just like Auntie Meera and Tobias, except worse. I'm broken, I push people away, anyone that wants to be close, I make sure to cut them from my life with the things I do or say. Isn't it just a matter of time before I do that to Branwell again? Isn't it? Won't he get tired of me sooner or later? Won't I put him off, like I do with everyone?

I sit up abruptly.

"I'm not like you," I whisper into the dark room. I don't even know who I'm speaking to. Not to Tobias or Auntie Meera, but maybe the person who's given me the invitation. *If you have experienced trauma, I can help you.* An invitation. That's exactly what it is.

I deliberately stop myself from turning on the light.

"I'm not scared of being inside my own house on a dark night."

I say it loud and clear. Even though no one is listening. I can't help thinking somehow of the dark room upstairs, Auntie Meera's room. That book. The diaries. The things I've learned about her, about her childhood. Suddenly, I feel like I'm not alone in the house. My breathing quickens.

"Don't be stupid!"

I can't believe I'm letting the murders affect me like this. The cat. The murderer had been inside this house, when they had put the stuffed cat in the kitchen. And The Marquis still isn't back. And the pamphlet. Through my letterbox. I'm panting now. The murderer had been in this house not once, but twice. The first time was when he or she had killed my aunt. I clutch my throat. I close my eyes, then quickly open them again.

Was that something I heard? A whisper? A footfall? My eyes turn to the window. I nearly scream when I see a shadowy form. But then realize that it's the branch of the hawthorn that's just outside the window. That's always there. Not just today, not just right now.

"Fuck's sake!"

I stand up. I make myself walk slowly to the light switch. I nearly lose my head when I click it on, and nothing happens. I walk quickly to the lamp. That doesn't come on either. I'm panting now. Why the hell are the electrics not working? It occurs to me for a wild moment that I'm still asleep, still dreaming. I want to claw myself awake. But I know I'm not asleep. There's a simple explanation. The electrics must have got overloaded and turned off. That's all it is.

There's that sound again.

I nearly scream my head off. Even though at the back of my mind I know it's just—it must be—the branch of the hawthorn again, I can't stay here a moment longer in the dark house.

Before I know what I'm doing, I'm standing outside the front door. I feel so much better out of the house that I stand there for a full minute in the shadowy garden, the sky canopied by light cloud, masking the moonlight. I feel a little stupid now. I can see the hawthorn from here, budging against the living room window. I look up. My heart nearly stops because I see a shadow move in the upstairs window, in Auntie Meera's upstairs window.

"Fucking hell," I whisper.

Then I see it isn't someone inside her room. It's a moving cloud, a reflection in her window.

But my heart is racing. There is nothing that will make me go back inside. Nothing at this moment can make me put even a foot inside the front door, let alone find a chair to stand on, to flick on the mains that are lodged above the front door, on the inside.

"No way," I mutter.

There's a sharp chill in the air. And though I've got my trainers still on and a t-shirt, I'm still cold. It's August, but it's cloudy and breezy. If nothing else, I need my jacket. I stand there, paralyzed for many minutes. My heart booming in my head, I step toward the front door. I climb on to the step; I open the door. It takes me about three seconds to grab my jacket off the coat stand and to come pelting out the door again.

I stand there, panting. I rub my forehead. No, there's nothing that'll make me go back in there. I can't go to Branwell's for the night either. He's up in the Lakes. Why, why didn't I go with him? I shake my head. This is what happens when I'm too much of the person I am. He had asked me again to go with him and I had said no. What a first-class idiot!

He has another reading coming up in a few weeks, at the end of August. He had asked me if I'd go to that with him, spend the weekend in a village in Yorkshire. I quickly text him now and say that I will. The second I send it, I notice that it's nearly four in the morning. I clutch my forehead. I'm losing my mind.

I stand there now, wondering what on earth I'm supposed to do now.

There's nothing that'll make me go back in the house, and there's literally no one on this earth that I can turn to. I feel very hard done by. I've done nothing but speak to people in the last few weeks. There's literally been not one single time that I've stepped out of my house without banging into a phalanx of chattering people and yet I can't think of a single person whose doorstep I could turn up at and be invited in. I growl, feeling like most of my adult life has been a royal crowing waste.

Feeling a little stupid, I half turn toward the house again, but then I jink up the driveway as fast as my legs will carry me as the reflection of the clouds moves again in Auntie Meera's window.

I walk about aimlessly. The night is chilly, but it's also a hundred times nicer being out here than in my own house. Even thinking about the house is bringing up images of Auntie Meera splayed on her kitchen floor (even though I hadn't even seen her body when it was in her kitchen), and The Marquis dripping blood, though I haven't seen that either. I can't even get Tobias out of my mind. Tobias with his tail. No, even though it's chilly out, I'd still much rather be out here than back in there.

I look down at my phone. Branwell hasn't texted back. Yes, I'm aware that it's four in the morning now, but still. I feel very ill used. Who puts their phone on silent after the kind of day we had had? I glare down at the text message I'd sent him. "I'll go with you next weekend." It sounds so needy. I scowl down at it. I nearly write to him again to tell him that I won't. But then I stop myself.

Just to keep warm, I speed up into a slow run. This is quite nice, maybe I'll even get used to this, being out here in the cold early hours of the morning. Maybe this is the ideal time to exercise out of doors, when there's no danger of banging into someone. I run through the residential streets, then find myself entering the woods. I can't help thinking that the woods are beautiful. There's a crunch underfoot, a soft glow from behind the grey clouds. There's something eerily beautiful about the hush.

I run for a long time, wondering if the apocalypse happened when I was sleeping on the couch and I'm the only person left in the entire world. The thought occurs that no one in the world knows where I am right now. I have the wild impulse to text Branwell again, to tell him where I am.

What an idiot.

I nearly scream my head off when something large and furry scrapes my leg and lets out an almighty yowl. I'm pretty sure I'm having a heart attack brought on by this encounter with the local resident midnight banshee. A large furry shape. A cat. Jesus, a blasted cat.

"What is the matter with you, you foolish animal? Don't you have a warm home to go to?"

It looks accusingly at me, as if to say right back atcha, sister. Its eyes are orbs in the darkness. It yowls again. I roll my eyes. "Stop trying to wake the dead. Anyway, these woods don't belong to you." I look around me. I've been running for so long – I'd lost track of how long, but the damp patches on my back and under my armpits tell me that it's been a while. I look down at my phone, it's after four. I notice a few lone cottages that all look symmetrically the same. I'm near the boarding school, the teachers' cottages. I glance down.

It's Tallulah cat. It yowls again and rubs ferociously at my leg. In fact, it won't stop yowling. The woods around me seem to go unnaturally still. I think in that moment I know. I look up slowly and spy Tallulah's cottage about twenty yards away. I look down at the cat that's too lazy to ever leave the cottage, to ever move from its special place that is bang in the middle of Tallulah's living room. My heart starts thudding.

"It's okay, it'll be okay," I say softly.

I don't know if I'm talking to the cat or to myself.

I take my phone out of my coat pocket again. I dial 999. But I don't press the call button. I keep it dialed. I walk slowly toward Tallulah's cottage, my heart yammering. I stand outside her front door. I touch the door. I should knock. I shouldn't knock. This is stupid. She's probably fast asleep, or not even here since she'd had a date. I'm being intensely stupid. But her cat is still with me. It's quiet now, but staring at the front door, its hair standing on end.

I'm panting. I push the front door. It's locked. I can't help it, but I'm relieved that it's locked. I don't want to push my way in. And for what? I walk around the cottage. I approach the kitchen window. I try to peer in. It's silent, no light. The cat—Creampuff—has disappeared. I cup my eyes with my hands and lean toward the glass again, to look in.

The clouds part for a second. But it's enough to show me. Enough to show me a large naked form splayed naked on the kitchen floor. It's enough to show me Tallulah's face, her eyes closed, her hands crossed over her naked chest.

Chapter Thirty-Three

Sometimes there are moments that time stops, moments when the world stops, and you stop living. For a moment, everything you are and everything you're not and never will be, all flash through your mind. Every mistake you've ever made is clear for everyone to see. Every failing, everything you've got so hopelessly wrong in your life, that you can't go back and change, everything rises sharply in your mind.

I kneel on the chair outside the ICU, looking at Tallulah through the glass. If I can keep watching her, maybe she'll wake up. Maybe I can keep breathing for her. Maybe I can keep staring at her and I'll see her move. If I don't blink, maybe it'll be better. All I have to do is keep looking at her, not take my eyes from her face. Not blink.

An induced coma, they call it, her body sucking in juices from apparatus that are attached to her. A feeding tube in her hand, monitors beeping and hissing. Bandages all around her stomach where the knife had plunged again and again, leaving her as good as dead.

Please.

One word. Not *please, can you speak to me again, can we see each other again*. But *please, help me*. That's what she had been trying to say in her text message last night. From the amount of blood she had lost, Shona had estimated a time for the attack. It might have happened around the time that Tallulah sent me that message.

And I had not texted her back.

Then she had gathered up the last remains of her strength and called me, dialed my number. Not the police, *me*.

Why? I think helplessly. If she had dialed 999 instead, she could have got some help. Why did she call *me*? Me, the one person who has no idea how to be there for anyone.

"Why would you call me?" I look through the glass at her sleeping form. "No one in their right mind would do something like that. No one, Tallulah."

I look helplessly at her through the glass. *Please*, I whisper.

An efficient tick-tock approaches. It's Shona. She sits down next to me. She hands me a plastic cup filled with mud-colored piping hot tea. I automatically take a large scalding sip.

"It's hot," Shona says.

I don't pay attention to the burning in my palate.

"I have to ask you, what made you go to Miss Sand's cottage at four in the morning?"

I shake my head. "I wasn't going to her cottage. I couldn't stand being in my house…" My words peter out. I lose my train of thought.

"Why?" Shona asks, her voice gentle.

I look blankly at her. She prods me, repeating the question.

"Oh. I don't know. I woke up, it was dark. The Marquis, I keep hearing him meowing…"

"Enough to make anyone nervous. So, you decided to go for a run."

I shrug.

"To Miss Sand's cottage?"

I shake my head again. "No, not really. I wasn't paying attention to where I was going. I bumped into her cat in the woods. It was acting strange. Meowing really loud, and just the fact that he was even out and about. He doesn't usually – he's very lazy." I take another scorching gulp of the tea. But I don't feel it. My hands are shaking. I hold on to the hot tea for dear life.

Shona looks sympathetically at my shaking hands. I hold them tighter, but it only makes it worse. I take another sip of the burning tea.

"Arya, I must tell you, it's not looking good for your ex."

I look incredulously at her. "Craig? What the bloody hell does Craig have to do with Tallulah?"

"He was seen coming out of the woods near the boarding school last night."

I stare at her. "Why on earth would Craig launch a vicious attack on Tallulah? He doesn't even know her."

"We think it all might link back to you."

My shoulders sag. "You've got it all wrong," I say weakly.

"People do things—unbelievable things—when they've been hurt."

I cluck impatiently. "*Hurt*? Craig wasn't *hurt*."

"Men are good at compartmentalizing. They don't always show their feelings."

I try to imagine Craig with dark, intense feelings burning away under his staid exterior. The mind boggles. "Uh, no. He doesn't have any."

"He might not be showing them."

I cluck impatiently. "With Craig, you get exactly what you've paid for. Staid and boring. Miffed and paranoid."

"Hidden depths…"

"No."

"We can place him at all the murders, more or less. He has no alibi for his uncle's death or for when the stuffed cat appeared in your kitchen and the real cat disappeared. And he was on the scene at about the right time for your auntie's and Miss Sand's attacks. He had the opportunity. And he had some motive. With his uncle, it's the money. And he was trying to get to you, maybe get back at you, so all the others make sense too. And anyway, Arya, murderers aren't the most rational people in the world. If they were, they'd think of easier ways to get out of their difficulties. I can't imagine that murder would seem the easiest solution to most people. I say if he's burning in love for you, and then you take up with someone new, *and* he's already desperate for money because of his debts closing in on him..."

I try to imagine Craig burning in love for anyone other than his Arsenal socks that he wears every time they play and that haven't been washed in years because then they might lose their lucky powers. I shake my head, feeling unbelievably weary.

"He didn't even know me when Auntie Meera was killed. And..." I decide to make a clean breast of it. "As for an alibi for Tobias's death, I was sitting right outside his window in the time Tobias was killed. So...I'm Craig's alibi."

I nearly hold my hands out so she can cuff them.

She looks reprovingly at me. "You have a big heart, Arya." She looks for some silent seconds down at my big heart. "But inventing an alibi for someone – that's not something I'd recommend. Gets you into all kinds of trouble. Next thing you know, you've incriminated yourself, put yourself on the scene of a crime, and you become the primary suspect."

I look heavenward. My god. "It's not a made-up alibi. I *was* sitting right outside Craig's living room window. After Tarina left, he did nothing but sit in his chair and watch football. He didn't budge. Not for a second. That's the window of opportunity for Tobias's murder. And he was there, in his house, the entire time."

"I don't believe you, Arya, though it's kind of you. But even if this were true, his girlfriend Tarina could have done it. For him."

I make an exasperated sound. "Does she have a burning love for me too?"

Shona looks down at her green fingernails. "Well, as to that, I don't know."

A growl escapes me. "I don't have an alibi for Tobias's murder. Or for Auntie Meera's. And I was the best placed to do the thing with the stuffed cat, and with Tallulah! So, why not look at me while you're at it?"

Shona presses my hand. "I'll be going now. I'm just saying, things aren't looking so hot for Mr. Yards. And he won't tell us what he was doing in the woods last night either."

I frown. Given Craig's loathing for nature, it's hard for me to imagine. When Shona leaves, I stand about staring for some time. I drink more of my scalding tea. A nurse comes and checks on Tallulah. I spin around to look through the glass again, suddenly hating myself for forgetting to look at her when I was talking to Shona. I press my hands to the glass, my heart thudding.

I watch through the window, suddenly sure that Tallulah will die as I'm standing here, no, she may already be dead. The nurse is going to raise the alarm any minute now. The alarm, people running past me, the pronouncement of time of death, I can see it all play out, I can feel it in my bones. Any second now. The air is crackling with it. I just know it.

But it doesn't happen.

I stand there, frozen, looking bleakly through the window, willing Tallulah to wake up, to be all right. I keep looking at her chest, I keep taking deep breaths, breathing for her. The nurse checks everything, fiddles a bit with things, fluffs up a pillow, pulls the blanket closer around Tallulah, and comes out again. She gives me a quick smile before she walks away.

I stare at Tallulah for a long time, her chest moving up and down, up and down, slowly, really slowly, but moving at least.

I call Craig. "What were you doing in the woods near the boarding school last night?"

"Well, as to that, I was exercising. Running."

I make an exasperated sound. "Craig, you could at least try to say something plausible."

"I *could* have been exercising."

"You hate nature."

"I wouldn't say hate."

"Tell me the name of a flower. Any flower."

The phone goes silent. After a minute he says, "Give me a

minute. I'm trying to think."

"If you just tell them what you were doing, then you'll be off the hook."

"I have to say, Arya, it warms my heart to think how much this means to you, how you're sticking up for me. I'd almost think you had feelings for me. If you generally had any feelings."

A joke? Is the man making a joke? I stare down at my phone. "You're right. I don't have feelings. I feel a certain sense of responsibility for people that I've rejected though."

"*I* broke up with *you*," he says petulantly.

"Only because you knew I would do it sooner or later."

"Sour grapes, Arya. I always knew I meant a lot to you. All I can say is, it wasn't you, it was me."

"Stop being a dick, Craig."

After a day spent staring through the glass at Tallulah's unmoving form, I'm ready to climb out of my skin by the time I head back home. Remembering the panic in the middle of the night, I turn all the lights on. I bang about the house. Even my trusty friend—baking—doesn't help me, today. I can't even bear to log on to the computer to check on orders placed through my website or Instagram, much less actually bake anything. I have the mother of all twitches in my shoulder. I keep jerking about, and by the end of half an hour, my shoulder is burning. And then I hear it. For a few moments, I think I'm imagining it, just like I have been for days. Then it sinks in.

I can hear meowing. I walk slowly to the kitchen. I stand there staring, not daring to look out the window. I make myself walk to it. I nearly jump out of my skin. Because The Marquis is standing there yowling outside the back door.

I quickly open it and let the cat in. I can't believe my eyes. The Marquis. The Marquis is alive! He's not dead. I crouch down next to him, hardly daring to touch him, hardly daring to breathe. He's hissing at me and rubbing on my legs at the same time. He's covered in dust and cobwebs, he's about half the size he was before, and there are bloody patches on him. I dare not touch him for fear of hurting him.

But suddenly I am angry beyond belief. First Auntie Meera, then Tobias and Tallulah, and now this. I want to scream in rage, but I'll scare the life out of this poor cat that's already been tortured. I can't tell if I'm more relieved or more out of my mind full of rage at whoever did this.

I call Shona. "Shona, The Marquis is back. Tobias's cat, I mean. He's starved and wounded, like he's been shut away somewhere. You'd better come and look at him quick, if you want, because if you don't, I'm going to clean him."

After the phone call, I give the cat food. I still don't dare touch him. I don't want to scare the life out of him. I don't want him to streak out of the house and never come back. The piteous way he eats nearly breaks me in two.

Shona arrives so quickly, I nearly kiss her. She brings a vet. She takes samples, the vet looks after The Marquis. They both look grim, though the vet, at least, tries to look reassuring, leaves me all manner of expensive antibiotics, suggests I get pet insurance, a tag, a proper cat flap, deworming medicine, anti-flea treatments, jabs. I don't have the energy to even glare at her. Finally, when they leave, I try and settle the cat upstairs in my room. He's so thankful to be out of whatever dark hell he's been in for days that he barely does more than scowl at me once or twice.

This, I think to myself, this, The Marquis. He's back and it's a sign that Tallulah will be fine too. I just have to hang in there.

There's a knock at the door around nine. I open it to find Branwell, looking unnecessarily cheerful. But as soon as he sees my face, he says, "What's wrong? What's happened?"

Apparently, the man can still read me like a book. It's all I can do not to leap into his arms. I drag him in, sit him down on the sofa and it all comes spilling out in a mad rush, Tallulah, The Marquis, all of it. He listens patiently, just looking intently at me as I tell him what's happened. He doesn't interrupt, not for questions. Not even sounds of sympathy. He just listens. The relief of telling him is so acute that I forget that I don't do this. I hold on to his hand like it's a lifeline. I can barely stop myself from whining, *please don't leave me, whatever you do, please don't leave me.*

"You're really shaken, you're trembling."

"I'm fine," I say in a small voice. If I'm not careful I'm going to burst into tears.

"And you're holding my hand. You must be feeling really shit."

He gets a weak smile out of me.

He looks seriously at me for a long time, then he says, "Arya, you know this is not your fault."

I stand up, clutching my shoulder to stop it from jerking violently. I pace about the room. "She texted me. She texted and called me, and I didn't answer. I didn't bother to even answer. If she'd got help sooner—" I rub my shoulder hard. It's burning.

"And how exactly would you have known why she was calling? You think everyone else in the world answers their phone every time it rings or beeps a message? You think everyone else does that, just not you?" He's sitting in that pose that he was in the first night I'd gone to his house. Elbows on knees, thinking through things, looking so intensely like Branwell that I want to stop pacing and curl up near his feet and go to sleep. But I can't. I can't do that.

I flick my head painfully twice. "I wanted to hurt her. That's why I didn't answer. I wanted to hurt her. That's the difference."

He stands up and puts his hands on my arms. "Arya, this didn't happen because of you."

I shrug away from him. "There's a pattern," I mutter. "There's a pattern. I saw it with Tobias and Auntie Meera. I didn't connect it with Tallulah. They'd all met someone just before they died. Why didn't I see it? I should have seen it. I've been thinking of little but the murders. Who else could have seen the pattern? I should have seen it. I should have seen it and I should have prevented Tallulah from dy – from being attacked. Why didn't I see it?" I think of the flyers left for me. I'm part of the pattern too. Is that it? The attacker sees me, sees that I'm broken too.

I'm properly shaking now. When he tries to come near me though, I shake him off. No, I don't want him to comfort me. I don't deserve to feel better about this. I don't deserve to be loved.

He backs off and looks patiently at me. "No one would have made that connection. How on earth would anyone imagine that people as different as Tobias, your aunt and your friend could all have met the same person, could all have been happy or at peace or whatever you think they were because of the same person? It's too far-fetched. I'm not sure it even adds up. This person—whoever's behind the murders—sounds like a psychopath. A serial killer."

I shake my head. "No. I mean, yes, he or she might be. But there's more to it." The image of the circle I'd seen in the woods flashes through my mind. But Tallulah hadn't been in that circle. I hadn't seen the faces under the hoods, but I would have recognized her. She's a distinctive size. I wouldn't have missed something like that. None of the people in the woods had been her size. There had been people smaller and bigger, more or less wrinkled, more or less saggy. Various shades of pale.

Except for two. Only two people had not been pale.

I abruptly stop my pacing. Two people had not been white. I think of Sheshonne Chigozi. I think of her nervous conversation with me in the woods. I think of the way Mark had been cagey about where he—or maybe she—had been that night, the night I'd seen the circle in the woods. I had thought he was cagey because he wasn't at home that night, that he was with Veronica Chives. But what if he was cagey because he knew that *Sheshonne* hadn't been home? That she had been elsewhere? Veronica had said that Mark thought his wife was having an affair. But what if she wasn't? What if she had been in the circle?

"There's someone I need to speak to."

I flip through my phone. Even though I don't have her number. Why would I? I ask Branwell if he has it, but he shakes his head.

Mrs. Sharma. Mrs. Sharma is the kind of person who would have everyone's phone number. Everyone in a five-mile radius. I don't have Mrs. Sharma's number either.

"Let yourself out when you're done," I say abruptly, horribly, to Branwell.

He doesn't say anything. He knows me so well, he lets me get on with it. He doesn't try to stop me. I grab my coat. At the front door, I turn to him. I don't meet his eyes. "She called me, and I let her down. I'll never forgive myself for that. I keep trying to tell you what kind of person I am. This is what I do. I think you need to see it."

He's silent for a second. "I won't hang around now," he says finally. "But I'll see you tomorrow. Don't be out too late." He walks up to me and kisses me on my forehead. "And stop trying to push me away. Because it won't work."

Chapter Thirty-Four

I knock on Mrs. Sharma's front door.

She looks surprised to see me. She pats her hair nervously. "Tea?" she asks reluctantly.

"Uh, no thanks. I just want Sheshonne Chigozi's phone number."

She looks miffed. "I'm busy."

I look past her. "Watching Corrie?"

"What of it?"

"It'll only take you a second to give me her phone number."

"What's it to you anyway? You never want to talk to anyone."

I look heavenward. "Mrs. Sharma, can I please have her phone number? I don't want tea, I don't want to be anyone's friend. I'm a heartless shit. But I need her phone number. And you're everyone's friend, so you're likely to have it. I can't go barging in on her at this time of the night. I'd rather call her."

She looks both pleased and annoyed at the same time. Maybe my description of her, or maybe my description of me, I'm not sure which. She elaborates. "As to that, I am a sympathetic sort. I can't help it if people take to me." She frowns. "You don't mind knocking at *my* door in the middle of the night."

"It's half past nine," I point out. I make an impatient sound. "She lives at the other end of town. And I've barely ever spoken to her." I clutch my head, which is now pounding. "Come on, Mrs. Sharma."

She dithers. "Well, I've never seen you looking distressed." She fights with herself. "Are you sure you don't want tea?"

"I just want the phone number."

She makes a big thing of looking through her phone, taking her time, looking as bored as she can. She finally reads out the number to me.

I key it into my phone and then walk off. I hear her slam the door behind me. Then it occurs to me. I walk back. I knock again. It takes her ages to come to the door this time. She finally opens, widens her eyes expressively. "Yes?" she asks, with exaggerated politeness.

"Is there a sex circle around these parts?"

She stares at me. "You're very strange, you know that?"

"Yes, I do, as a matter of fact. Anyway, is there or isn't there?"

"Well, if there were, I would hardly know about it." I can't help thinking she sounds a little miffed about that. "If you ask me, that Veronica Chives would be exactly the kind of person who'd know."

I shake my head. "No, no, it isn't her kind of thing," I say half to myself. If I'm right about the circle, there's someone in it that preys on people who're lonely. Bone crushingly lonely. Not Mrs. Sharma's kind of loneliness, or even Veronica's. Something else. Something more profound than that. I shake my head. "Never mind," I say to Mrs. Sharma. "I'm probably making too much of it."

"Don't be a stranger," she can't help saying behind me.

I call Sheshonne Chigozi.

She sounds surprised and not too pleased to hear from me. I explain to her how I got her phone number. "Have you joined a circle of some kind?" I say at once.

There's silence at the other end. Then I hear shuffling, then the opening and closing of a door. She comes back, her voice lower this time. "I don't know how you heard about that. I don't know what your game is. Whatever it is, I'm not going to fall for it. You can threaten to tell my husband if you like—" She sounds breathless.

"Sheshonne, I'm not interested in doing anything like that. I'm not even interested in talking to your husband, much less about you and your secret." I sound as annoyed as I am. What is wrong with people? I'm not the nicest person in the world. But my god, I hardly go around telling people about their partner's affairs. "I'm just worried that the circle is…" I stop. I'm walking in the dark, cold street outside my house now. Branwell has left one light on for me in the house. I feel a little crumpling in my stomach at the thought that he's gone back to his. I imagine—just for a second—going back to mine and climbing into bed with him and finding him there next to me when I wake up in the middle of the night. I shake myself. I don't know what to say to Sheshonne. The circle is – what exactly? "Sheshonnc, it might be dangerous. I mean, who runs it?"

She makes an impatient sound. Her voice is still low. "I don't know. Now, if that's all—"

"Oh, come on." I almost spill it out. I saw you, I almost say. I realize at once that that's not something to say to someone. That I can't say that I saw her. For a second, I'm quite pleased with myself. It isn't often that I'm accused of minding someone's feelings. "You're part of the circle. Someone must have recruited you," I say instead. I think of the piece of A4 that had been shoved through my door. Yes, these people were being recruited.

"I have nothing more to say about this. I don't know who runs it, or even the members. You just get letters. And—well, all I can say is that they—the letters seem to get you, it's like they know you and understand you." She makes an impatient sound. "I can't explain. Sounds a bit stupid said like that. But in any case. You never see faces. I have to go now."

"Sheshonne, wait, do you have any of the letters? Are they…" I hesitate. "Are they more like flyers?"

"Flyers, letters, yes. They get more and more personal, like they're from someone who really knows you. But then they give you a phone number. Not at first, not right away. But later on. You're supposed to burn them." She hesitates. "I think some of the members might know each other. Some have...private sessions. I never knew anyone. And I'm not doing it anymore anyway. It was a one off. And it was a mistake."

She's gone.

I frown at the ground. I believe her. I believe everything she's said. She didn't know any of the people. The members, or the person that recruited her. I remember the entry about her in Auntie Meera's journal. The entry about Sheshonne seeming lonely. Well, she would be if her partner is having an affair with Veronica Chives. Or did that come after Sheshonne joined the circle? I shake my head violently. This is so not any of my business.

Yet. Isn't it? Auntie Meera, Tobias, Tallulah. And I've had the flyers too. Whoever it is, they think I'm the same as these people, these intensely vulnerable people.

Before I've had a coherent thought about it, my footsteps start heading in the direction of the woods and the boarding school. Half an hour later, I'm outside Tallulah's door. I've had success with this before. I take the yellow tape off, carefully noting exactly where it's tacked up.

I avoid the outlined shape of Tallulah's body in the kitchen. In fact, I avoid the kitchen entirely. What I want is the bookshelf. I look carefully through the entire contents, frowning harder with every passing minute. The book—the skinny authorless volume—is not there. I look at each and every one of the books again. I read the name of every thin book – but they all turn out to be Graham Greenes and Muriel Sparks.

I frown into the dark. I'd been so sure. I had been sure that the skinny volume—*The Power in My Hands*—would be here. Just the way it had been in Tobias and Auntie Meera's homes. There's something about the two of them and Tallulah that attracted a murderer. And unlike what Shona thinks, that thing they have in common isn't me. Someone is preying on them, their weaknesses and vulnerabilities.

Tobias who was ashamed of what he must have thought of as his deformity, Tobias who had been bullied as a child and who kept people at arm's length, and yet, who needed people too.

Auntie Meera who had been abused by her stepfather when she was a child, who craved intimacy as an adult but found it near impossible to find it. So much so that she'd taken me on, taken on a child, a full-time job, that would keep her at a safe distance from adult relationships.

And then there was Tallulah. I close my eyes at the piercing pain in my chest. Tallulah, Tallulah who is going to be alright. She survived the attack. I rub the painful rock lodged in my chest.

I can't join all the dots yet, but I know it now, someone out there is preying on weakness, on loneliness. Getting close to these people. Someone with some empathy, surely. Or else, how would they be successful? All of these three people wanted, craved empathy, real empathy. Whoever it is, is obviously good at seeming to be empathetic. They're good at pretending. Isn't that the profile of a psychopath?

But the book isn't here.

I look beyond the living room. The little cottage is all on one floor. Its single chaste bedroom lies beyond the living room. I feel a strange reluctance to go to it, to look through Tallulah's intimate things. I remind myself that I saw her naked body not so long ago. That looking through the things in her bedroom was hardly worse. I had seen her more exposed than anyone had ever seen her. Me, and a phalanx of crime scene investigators, I remind myself.

I walk slowly toward the bedroom, the pain in my chest sharp and booming.

Similar to the living room, it's furnished with pretty things, cushions, throws, teddy bears. There's a queen size bed, one side of it is presumably Tallulah's and the other side belongs to her cat because there's a furry oval-shaped mat there that is liberally made fatter with cat hair from Tallulah's cat Creampuff. I groan a little bit. First The Marquis, and now Creampuff. There's no sign or sight of him at the moment, but a sinking feeling in my tummy tells me that, yet again, I'm going to have to take a cat home with me and feed it.

He bites, Tallulah had told me, and doesn't like to move. And will probably hate me *and* The Marquis.

"Great," I mutter.

The book is there, in the bedside table, along with two cheap vibrators.

A bitter taste in my mouth at the sight. I knew it, I think, as I look at her drawer. I knew it, I knew there was a connection. A connection between the three victims and the weird outdoor circle I had seen. I shudder. I don't touch anything except the book. I only touch that because I want to check if there's anything in it like there had been in Tobias's, but there's nothing. No picture, no bookmark. I place it neatly back.

I walk back to the living room, and from there to the kitchen. I avoid looking at the outline in the middle of the floor. I look around though, at the floor. I don't know why I bother. It's not like I'm going to find any incriminating evidence. The police have already combed this place up and down. I don't know what I'm looking for. Subconsciously I put my hand in my hoodie pocket. And there I find it, the hairpin I'd found in Tobias's kitchen when I had searched his house after his murder.

My heart starts clanging so hard and loud in my chest that I'm afraid I'm going to alert the police somehow to my presence in this crime scene. I stare down at the hairpin.

No, what I'm thinking, what I'm imagining is completely far-fetched. It can't be. My brain is jumping to unlikely conclusions. I'm making connections that aren't there because I'm desperate to find answers.

I stare at the hairpin. Unlike the more common black or brown, this one is made for blonde hair, or at least lighter hair. This one is a beige-gold color. My heart is still doing its horrible plong-plong in my chest and making me feel sick. Surely, I'm wrong. I can hardly use my instincts to figure out a murder. I don't like most people. So, it's hardly like my prejudices are any real inkling.

And yet, yet, I can't get it out of my mind.

I close my eyes and think back to the circle I'd seen in the copse in the woods. Yes, if I close my eyes, I can picture the people there. Sheshonne had been there that night, I know it now. The color of her skin and her long limbs had given her away. Tallulah hadn't been there that night. She hadn't known Tobias, so she wouldn't be there when they were burning his things.

But I think now that I recognize one of the other people who had been there that night. I think I finally, maybe, see a picture.

Chamomile tea. The smell of chamomile tea in Auntie Meera's kitchen the day she had died. The hairpin found in Tobias's kitchen. That cheap book.

I can hardly breathe. I step carefully out of Tallulah's cottage, still fingering the hairpin. I tack the tape back on. I haven't tried too hard to wipe my fingerprints. I've recently been in this cottage. Presumably they already have my fingerprints. I had been careful in the bedroom and with the tape, but that was all.

I stare into the fathomless woods around me. I call Shona.

"What's occurring, Arya?"

"I think I know who's behind the murders."

"Well, I always knew you were more than a pretty face."

"I think the sex circle I told you about—well, not the circle itself—it's just I think that that's how someone got in touch with all the…the victims."

She makes a non-committal sound.

"What?"

"Well, nothing, Arya, but a sex circle might seem a little dodgy but isn't automatically a vicious thing."

I make an impatient sound. "I have no problems with what people do in private, or even in public, for that matter. I'm telling you though, this isn't an ordinary sex circle. I think someone's preying on people…"

"Yes, um hmm, well…"

I can see she doesn't believe me. I cluck. I change tack. "I found a hairpin on Tobias's kitchen floor."

"Now, Arya," she says sternly, "don't tell me you've been tampering with a crime scene."

Whoops. I glance around me. I'm nearly at the border of the woods, but I look around guiltily in case someone's seen me tampering with my second crime scene.

"It was after you'd taken the tape off," I say. I have no real way of knowing if the tape around Tobias's front door has even been taken off yet, but I cross my fingers, hoping I'm not wrong.

"That's fine then," she says. "Though it still counts as breaking and entering a dead man's property. Or at least, his nephew's property, technically."

"I didn't. I found a key." I cluck again. "Shona, stop distracting me! Why was there a hairpin on Tobias's floor? He didn't use them. I don't. You and Shirley don't. Veronica doesn't. Neither does Cath. The only person it could have come from is the murderer."

She sighs. "Look, Arya, we already think we know who the perp is."

Oh, here we go. "Shona, it isn't Craig."

"Look, loyal of you and all that. And no one likes to think that someone out there is killing people off, all out of love for them—"

"Oh, for the love of god, Shona! Craig doesn't love me!" I growl. This isn't going to work.

Shona is saying something, but I don't bother to stay on the line. She's convinced Craig is the murderer. There's no point wasting time with her. I think I know who it is, but I could also be making up some far-fetched thing because I'm sleep-deprived and losing my mind and desperate—desperate to find answers so maybe now and again in the middle of the night I can stop feeling sick about what I've done to Tallulah. And the thing is, even if I'm right, how on earth would I go about proving such a thing?

I shake my head. I tell Tallulah's cat that I'll have to come back for him. He looks hatefully at me.

My footsteps point me toward Olga's door.

Chapter Thirty-Five

A few nights later, Olga and I are watching a group of shadowy forms in the copse in the woods. She had predicted that the group was likely to meet on a new or full moon, and so here we are, watching the group from the periphery of the copse of trees. At the moment, they're walking around in a circle, silently. I don't want to watch the next bit. I just want confirmation that the person I think is responsible for the murders belongs to this group. That they're here now.

I watch in disappointment and then pull Olga away.

"Not there," I mutter when we're at a safe distance.

"And you veel not tell me who it is?" she asks chidingly.

I shake my head. "I can't. They've moved recently to the area. If I'm wrong, then I'm saying something about them that's not true. Innocent until proven guilty and all that."

"Not so, my policy. When I vas hiding from the Russians, I learned to think of every man, vooman and child as guilty, until you prove that they are innocent, which most of the time, you could not. So."

I look severely at her. "That's a lovely philosophy."

"Always feed the birds your bread before you eat it."

"What, so they won't go hungry?"

"So that if they die, you know it's poisoned."

I look down at her diminutive form and her scarfed head. Oh lordy. "Right, thanks, Olga, I'll remember that next time I'm running from the Russians."

She scoffs. "They do not use poison *now*. They use nerve agents, like the Breets."

"The Brits use…" I chide her with a finger. "Stop distracting me. You'd better not have a nerve agent lying about your house, Olga."

To my slight dismay, she doesn't say anything about this, but smiles enigmatically. If Trucklewood residents all fall down dead in the near future of unknown causes, at least we won't need to look far for the perp then.

"The *person*," I say, to get the woman back on track, "that I thought should be in the circle wasn't in the circle. This makes my whole theory go kaput." I rub my face. Damn it. I was so sure I was right. Over the last few days, since that moment in Tallulah's cottage, I'd convinced myself that I was right.

"Unless," Olga says, wagging a finger in my face, "you are as—vat you say—gullible as you look."

"Hey, that's a low blow. And really unnecessary. What do you mean?"

"Maybe the person you are looking for is using this chance for further assassinations."

"Well, it's a bit soon after Tallulah's, isn't it? I mean, she isn't even—"

My blood runs cold. Olga is now looking shrewdly at me.

"I have to get to the hospital." My voice is choked, and I can hardly get the words out.

I turn around and start running. Olga doesn't try to stop me but calls after me to stay underground and try not to be seen, because I might be next.

I whip out my mobile and start dialing. "Shona, can you get to the hospital?" I pant. "I'm worried that someone will try to finish Tallulah off."

I leave the message on her voicemail. I only belatedly realize that it's nearly midnight. Hospital visiting hours are long over, and this should reassure me, but it doesn't. It's a small local hospital, and I remember only too well that they'd let me stay outside Tallulah's ICU room long after visiting hours were over, the night after she'd been admitted. If someone wanted to get into the hospital late, they probably could.

My fears are realized when the security man at the hospital recognizes me from my visits to Tallulah, listens with a beatific face to my pleas that I hadn't been able to see Tallulah all day and could he let me in now, and shoos me in.

By the time I'm at Tallulah's ICU floor, I'm starting to feel foolish. I'm acting crazy. I have no proof that the person I think is guilty is actually guilty. I have even less proof for the idea that he could be here tonight, that he's going to try and finish Tallulah off on the night that he's supposedly taking part in the circle, potentially using the circle as an alibi, since the people in the circle might not know that he's not there with them. I shake my head as I tread cautiously toward Tallulah's room. I'm exhausted and I've made up an unlikely story. It's just as well Shona was asleep and didn't take my call.

My tiredness evaporates as I come to a halt outside Tallulah's door. Because he's in there, wearing a doctor's coat. My heart nearly stops, then starts thudding so loud and hard that I think for a second that I'm going to pass out. Except every one of my nerve endings is awake. Completely and utterly and entirely awake.

In his hand is a syringe. It'll take a second for him to plunge it into Tallulah's arm. I look toward the distant nurse's room. There's no one there. Neither is the policeman or policewoman who's supposed to be guarding Tallulah's door. In the distance, outside the main door to this ward, I see the nurse and the security guy chatting, drinking tea. I grit my teeth.

I slip in through Tallulah's door. "Just stop," I say.

The man doesn't even flinch. His hand with the full hypodermic doesn't budge. It's an inch from Tallulah's arm.

"I know it's you. What will you do, kill me too?" Every cell in my body is on high alert, in sharp contrast to the man's demeanor. He seems just as calm as he always does. I wonder if I've ever seen him not calm. I can't remember such a time. He's always calm.

"Of course not, Arya," he says, half reproachfully. "You want to live. Despite your childhood, despite your loneliness, you want to live. I would never help anyone who wanted to live. Surely you understand that."

"Help?" I can't help the disdain in my voice, even though it's probably a mistake to let him see how I feel about him now. "You're helping these people, are you? You helped Tobias and Auntie Meera and Tallulah?"

He looks almost hurt at my question. "You of all people. You knew all of them. You cared about all of them. You know I'm helping them."

I shake my head. "No, this isn't for you to decide. You can't decide who lives and who dies."

The sadness pinches the flesh around his eyes. "You should see the relief, Arya. When I do it. The calm, the peace."

"No." My voice is hollow in the intense quiet. The only sound is the beep-beep-beep of Tallulah's heart. It sounds slow. I hope that's a good thing. I look at the hypodermic in the man's hand.

"They were at peace in their last days. This is what they wanted. This is what people want – they want peace, they want to feel like they finally belong. You know that, Arya. You know it, you'll do anything to belong. So would they. I gave them that. I finally brought them peace. That was all they wanted. To belong."

I can't help it, I shudder. He knows me, he knows people. He understands people instinctively. The man has empathy. That's the thing I was wrong about. I had assumed the murderer must be someone who had no empathy, someone who could show empathy when they didn't feel it, like a psychopath. But I was wrong. This man has maybe too much. I'd seen that in him again and again. Why had it taken me so long to understand who he was? Now that I see him standing there, calmly, his eyes looking sad, it seems inevitable that it was him all along.

I have to keep him talking. He knows now that he has nothing to lose. I know who he is. I'm nearer the door. Even if I can't stop him from plunging the syringe in Tallulah's arm, he knows there's no way out now. I have to tread carefully; I have to stop him from plunging the hypodermic in Tallulah's arm. There's a remote with buttons that would alert the nurses, but he's nearer to it than I am.

"I'm not afraid, Arya," he says gently. "I know I did the right thing. I helped them find peace, in life and in death."

I look beseechingly at him. "Just because they were lonely didn't mean they wanted to die. Tallulah doesn't want to die."

He looks sympathetically at me. "Someone like you, you're strong."

"I'm not strong," I whisper.

"You are, Arya. You might not know where you belong, but you don't mind it, not like they did. They've always been haunted. I helped them."

"Through that…that circle?"

"Anyone is welcome to join the circle. But with some of them, I work one-on-one."

I feel the sudden bitter taste in my mouth. "One-on-one."

He nods. "Yes. I bring them peace. They learn that no one else needs to love them. That their own love for themselves, that's all they need."

I shudder violently. The thought of Tallulah, Tobias, and worst of all, Auntie Meera, with this man. To forget their past, to forgive the people who hurt them. Tobias, his bullies, Auntie Meera, her stepdad. And Tallulah? Colin and me? The world?

Getting the key from the urn, putting it back in the wrong one, letting himself in for his appointment with Tobias. I was wrong, I've been wrong all along. He isn't a love interest, and no one saw him as such. But maybe as a tribe, as a coming home, as a therapist who never judged.

"I help them find peace, Arya."

I can't help it. I can see it. The peace that his three victims had found. "How did you do that?"

He shrugs. "It isn't anything sinister. It's just a gradual awakening that we don't have to wait to be loved. We can love ourselves, and that's the biggest gift we can give ourselves. It was my sister first."

I groan a little at the thought. "What did you do with your sister?" I think of the sex circle.

He shakes his head quickly. "No, no, that came later. Of course, I wouldn't. But she wanted to die. She wanted above everything for the pain to stop and I helped her. You have no idea what it's like to grow up with someone violent. The pain of the burns. It's something you can't imagine." His eyes cloud with tears at his own words. I can see it. I can see his love for his sister. I see the burn marks on his wrists. Whatever had happened to him and his sister had been horrific. I don't have to see the burn marks to see it. I can see it in his eyes. And I remember the way he still talks to her, when he doesn't know that other people are looking, the silent mouthed words. He still talks to his sister. And maybe she did want to die. Maybe she asked him, and he helped her.

The others didn't though, the others didn't.

"If those that are supposed to love you when you're a child teach you to loathe yourself," he says. He shrugs.

I squeeze my eyes shut for a second. He's persuasive. He believes what he's saying. And I can feel it too. The anonymous face. The strange, light eyes. The burn marks. The soothing voice. And above all, the empathy. *If those that are supposed to love you when you're a child teach you to loathe yourself.* Even I know that he's right about that. And so did Auntie Meera, Tobias and Tallulah.

"You knew about the key in Tobias's urn?"

"He told me about it. We used to meet."

I wince. "As lovers?"

He smiles, like I should know better. "Of course not, Arya. More as a mentor, a teacher, a guide, if you like. A friend."

Yes, yes, that makes more sense. Branwell was right. It was hard to imagine the same lover, for Auntie Meera, Tobias and Tallulah. That hadn't made sense. But they hadn't met a lover. It hadn't been a boyfriend. They had found a sense of belonging with this man. In themselves. In a strange way.

"You visited Tobias that evening, the evening he died?"

He smiles again. He's talking to me. But the hypodermic is still in place, steady and unmoving, near Tallulah's arm.

"Yes. You make excellent dessert. I had not had the chance to eat any before. I can't afford it normally."

"How did you poison just his slice?"

"I didn't. He said he had already had a slice and didn't want another one. I took a slice for myself. And I injected all of the rest with the poison." He pauses. "It was something I had bought from your Auntie Meera, in fact. In any case, then Tobias changed his mind. He was never one for self-control, that was one thing I had tried to work on with him, but I wasn't entirely successful. He ate it there in front of me."

I squeeze my eyes shut for a second. But I can't focus on that now. I want to keep him talking. I want his hand to move away from Tallulah a little. It hasn't so far. It hasn't budged an inch.

"Why was Tobias about to change his will?" He may not know, but I want to ask.

He smiles gently. "I suppose because when people find me—find the group—some people think they want to reevaluate everything. I didn't want the money. It means nothing to me."

I think of the cheap groceries, the cheap socks. But I have to keep him talking.

"You tortured Tobias's cat."

He looks regretfully at me. "As a warning to you, Arya. I'm sorry for that one. I don't like to hurt creatures needlessly. And I didn't hurt him, not exactly. He used to come into my basement sometimes, and I simply shut him in." He looks regretful. "How did you know it was me?"

I shrug. "I didn't, really. I just remembered that you hold your shirts closed with paperclips and hairpins. I've seen it before. I remembered it. I found a hairpin in Tobias's kitchen soon after he was murdered. And I saw you with come chamomile tea in your shopping basket. Little things like that, but they got me thinking of some of the things you said to me. It wasn't much."

"I don't mind. I still did the right thing."

I look fiercely at him. "It was up to them to decide if they wanted to live or die. You couldn't decide that for them."

For the first time, something flashes in his eyes. And I realize that the empathy isn't a simple one. It burns away inside him. He's a fanatic. His voice is harsh now when he speaks, for the first time.

"This is what they wanted. Each of them. My sister told me it's all she wanted. She asked for my help. The others didn't put it in words. But they all wanted it too. They wanted peace. Peace from the memories and the constant, crippling self-doubt. And you have no idea. I helped my sister, but that was the first time in my life that I found peace too. I knew it's what I was supposed to do. To help people."

I glance down at Tallulah. "They were living their lives. They might have been lonely, but they were living their lives."

His eyes flash again. "They wanted to die." The hypodermic draws closer to Tallulah's arm. It's touching her now. "None of them had anyone in their lives that they loved. You need that, in order to want to live."

"Auntie Meera had me."

He shakes his head. "But you weren't speaking to her. She told me."

My breath catches in my throat. "Please, Willie. Tallulah's really young. You don't have to do this. Leave her alone. Please."

He shakes his head. "I don't mind what happens to me, Arya. But I have to do what I can to help people who can't help themselves. Who were betrayed when they were too young to do anything about it. The things our father did to my sister." The bitterness in his face.

"Please, Willie. I understand why you did it," I say desperately.

"You can't bear to see their pain. I get it. I really do. But let Tallulah be. She's only young. Not even thirty. She has her whole life in front of her. And she didn't tell you she wanted to die."

"She told me about you. She told me about you and her when you were teenagers. They all told me things like that. They wanted to unburden. She told me too. She told me she'd never forgiven herself."

"But I've forgiven her." I say it now, knowing that it's too late, knowing that these are words I should have spoken sooner, and to Tallulah. I should have told her in no uncertain terms that I didn't blame her for what she did to me, for siding with the other girls, for turning secondary school into a living hell. I should have told her I only blamed myself, for what I had done to her. I knew what it meant to her to have a boyfriend, something she had never thought was possible. I knew it and I ruined it for her, like I always did. I should have told her.

The hypodermic plunges into Tallulah's arm. I lunge at the man. My hand on his makes his arm flail wildly. I have no idea what this will do to Tallulah. The heart monitor is beeping wildly. The door bursts open. I don't—I can't—turn around to see who it is. It's taking all my strength to make sure the liquid in the syringe doesn't go into Tallulah's arm.

"Stand aside, Arya."

I can't though. I can't let his arm go.

"It's too late, Mr. Arnott," Shona's voice says. "Please step back. I swear I'll have to shoot you if you drive that syringe any further."

Chapter Thirty-Six

Some nights later, I'm jerked awake, again, and I know before I even look at my phone that it's three in the morning, as it's been every night for the last several nights. Branwell's arm is around me. I'm in his bed.

I have to be able to do this, to spend the night at Branwell's. To pop in at his and have lunch. To go out for walks. To watch things on Netflix. To spend the night. It's not such a big deal, it's not strange. It's perfectly normal and I should be able to do it. I know I just have to get past the strangeness of it, the newness of it. Not the acts themselves, but something else. Underneath the newness is the fear, the constant fear that I might hurt him, that he would stop looking at me the way he looks at me now. Underneath is the burning fear that is so much a part of me that it's almost my friend. Almost.

I tell myself I can do this. I can be in this relationship. It's a matter of practice, of putting one foot in front of the other. Needing someone needn't automatically spell the loss of them.

Yet, I wake up every night at three. I wake up and I lie awake for hours. I make it to half-past-five this morning and then I jump out of his bed. I plod downstairs. I make breakfast. Toast, eggs, porridge, the works. He makes his way down the stairs.

He puts his arms around me. "Not that I'm complaining, but do we have to eat breakfast at the crack of dawn?"

"You maybe don't have any work to do, but I have a shitload on."

He nibbles at my ear. I resist the urge to push him away. But I can't help going rigid. He backs away. "Arya."

I shake my head. "It'll take some getting used to, okay? I'm not used to it."

I don't turn to look at him. I hate seeing the look in his eyes, like he's waiting, waiting for me to back away. To run away from this. I'm trying not to, I want to say. I'm trying my best, and I've never tried for anyone else. I've never even thought about it before. But I'm trying. I should tell him, I should say something. Something simple. Like he's important to me. That should be easy to say. Or that I'm afraid of hurting him. Yet the words stick in my throat and I can't get them out. I keep thinking of Auntie Meera. Why did I push her away? Why didn't I come back to her when she asked me again and again? And Tallulah. Who's still in the ICU, fighting for her life. If I'd listened to her plea....

As if he can sense my thoughts, as he often seems to, he says, "She isn't dead. She would have been if you hadn't saved her."

I wriggle away from him. I shake my head. No, no, I didn't save her. I nearly let her die. "She wanted to go to Peru. She told me when I first bumped into her. She was saving up to do the one thing she'd always wanted to do. To travel. To go to Peru. At Christmas."

"She's not dead."

I nod. I take shuddering breaths. "Yes. She's not. You're right."

He's looking at me now, with that direct gaze of his. I look up to his face finally.

"Will it ever be okay?" he asks. "Will you ever – want me the way I want you?"

"Please." I look beseechingly at him. "I'm trying, Bran. I really am. I can't do any more than that."

He looks at me for a long time. Then he nods. "Sure."

He gives me a quick kiss on my forehead. He walks away to the living room with his coffee. I see him through the doorway. He sits himself down at his computer. I stare at the bent of his shoulders.

The way the muscles in his back ripple as he moves things around on his desk – notebooks in which he writes his research, the desktop mouse, many pens, a chart he seems to have impaled with colorful Post-its, one chart for every book he's working on. I stare at the familiar way his neck bends forwards as he starts looking through the files on his computer.

I take a deep breath. I walk into the living room. I kiss the back of his neck. "I'm going with you to that book reading soon. I'm looking forward to it." I can do that much.

He doesn't turn around. But I can sense the easing of his shoulders and the smile. "Not as much as I am, Winters."

He says no more. He asks for no more.

I head out to my own place. I spend the rest of the day baking. There's a load of orders to get through for the weekend. Since I'll be away with Branwell, I need to get everything done early. I'll miss out on two whole days of baking. Other bakers have assistants, or they take days off. Mondays are lighter for me, but I tend to work through the week, spreading the week out into seven days. I shake my head. I wonder with Branwell in my life if I'll suddenly start having to spread it over five. He's already changing the way I do things.

I've checked with the hospital about Tallulah, about me being away for the weekend, and they've said she seems stable. Critical, but stable, they say.

At the end of the day, it's all ready. Monster cupcakes (but not too scary, they're for a three-year-old's party, the instructions had said). My dagger chocolate fudge. Vampire granola, with sugar canines littered all through it. I check through all the orders, and I make sure I'm happy with everything, the way it looks. I clean the kitchen twice. I help Sebum load the car. He lingers like he always does now, for a few seconds, probably wondering if there's a chance I'll invite him up to my bedroom again. I shake my head at him. "Off you go," I say, as I always do.

On an impulse, I call Craig. I do need one thing cleared up. He had sent me a message soon after I had got Willie Arnott arrested for the murders and thanked me for getting the 'coppers' off his back, but I hadn't texted him back.

"What were you doing in the woods all those nights ago?" I ask when he picks up.

He mutters something. I don't catch it. I ask him to repeat what he's saying. He says something about losing weight for the wedding. And something that sounds suspiciously like *exercise is recommended for the male libido*. I ask him what he's gabbing on about, but he tells me in a rush that he has to go.

I click off the call. Well, that's that cleared up. Next time I see Tarina, I must remember to give her a high five. I look down at my phone. Sheshonne had texted me a few days ago and asked me if I wanted to go out for a drink. I haven't responded. I put the phone back in my pocket. Maybe. Maybe I'll text Sheshonne back.

I walk inside the house, now that my orders have been sent off. I briefly touch Auntie Meera's journals that are sitting in the bookshelf. I'll never forgive myself for her death. If I had made things up with her, there was a chance she would still be alive. I wish I had seen how things were with her. I had been so self-obsessed that I hadn't wanted to see her as anything other than my guardian. A voice inside me insists that she wasn't as badly off as Willie Arnott had made out. That none of his victims had been as badly off as he wanted to believe. They had been lonely, but they had also been coping. He was the one who had been so lonely he hadn't been able to cope.

But this argument doesn't work. It never works. I sigh. In a few days, I'll take the time to put the journals away. Maybe I'll see if any neighbors want any of Auntie Meera's books and herbs and oils. Mrs. Sharma might want some. I'll deal with Auntie Meera's room at some point and sort everything out.

The last of the cleaning done for the day, I lock up and head to Bran's. We eat dinner together. He's made spaghetti – again. "I need to expand my repertoire," he says.

"Don't worry. You make up for it with your other repertoire."

He looks pleased. "Yes," he says simply. "I like showing you my other repertoire."

"Show me now."

We spend a couple of hours in bed. We're supposed to head to Yorkshire for his book reading tomorrow.

When I wake up at three in the morning again, I take a few deep breaths.

It'll be good to get away. It'll be good. I can do this. This is normal. And if I can't feel normal, I can pass. I can fake it until it gets easier. Unlike the other nights, I swing myself out of bed. I try to be quiet. Though I needn't bother. Bran, always a deep sleeper, just turns on to his side, flaps his hand a few times to try to find me, but then falls back to sleep.

I try to breathe through my clenched chest. He's right. I need to get over myself. I can't forgive myself for Auntie Meera's death maybe. But I had nothing to do with Tobias's. And Tallulah is alive. Gradually, maybe, I'll start to move on.

But I can't get back into bed. A glass of water. Yes, maybe water will help. I never sleep well if I'm thirsty, and the one next to the bed is empty. I wrap a bedsheet around myself, tiptoe out of the bedroom and pad down the stairs.

I stand at the kitchen window. I drink some water. I notice Creampuff out in Bran's garden. He lives at mine for the time being, so long as Tallulah's still in the ICU, but sometimes Bran sees him in his garden too. I'll take him back to Tallulah's soon, when Tallulah's ready to come back. When she's conscious, I'll ask her what she wants me to do with him. He's just as bullish as ever, his shoulders hunched, his eyes suspicious, but he doesn't sit still at mine like he used to at Tallulah's. He prowls. He's yowling now. I peer out the window. That's not like him. Why is he yowling? He may be restless without Tallulah around. So, he prowls. But I rarely hear him make any noises. What's he yowling for? It's almost the cry of a werewolf. It's loud and keening. It makes me uneasy. I wonder if he's found a dead animal or something.

My phone rings and I nearly drop it. I catch it just in time. My heart is banging in my chest at the sudden buzzing noise. The buzzing has stopped. But then before I have time to see who was calling, it rings again, in my hand. It's Shona.

"Shona?"

"Sorry, Arya, I didn't want to leave a message. I maybe shouldn't be calling you at four in the morning. But I thought you'd want to know."

I'm confused. Something about Willie Arnott? Why couldn't it wait, though? Do they not have enough evidence or something? Shona had heard his confession outside Tallulah's that night, after all. She had headed over to the hospital when she got my voicemail. And he hasn't even been denying what he did. "Willie Arnott?" I ask in confusion.

"No, Arya. He's fine. We have him. You don't need to worry." She hesitates. My heart sounds loud in the dark kitchen, with the moonlight streaming through. I hear Creampuff's keening cry again. "It's Tallulah, Arya. I'm really sorry. She died about an hour ago."

I don't clutch the phone. I don't sit down. I don't do anything. I look numbly out of the window.

"It wasn't because of anything Willie Arnott managed to inject. We don't think he got anything in her. It was her original injuries. She succumbed to them. There was always that chance, Arya, I'm sorry. She's been in the ICU for such a long time."

I should do something about Creampuff. He's still keening. I should probably try to get him back to mine.

"Thanks, Shona."

I put the phone down and stare blankly out the window for ages. I feel nothing. I feel nothing at all. I stand there for a long time. For a long time, like things are finally falling back into place. Like they've been all over the place for some days, some weeks, but now they're finally falling back into place. And I realize that I feel calm. Calmer than I have been in days and weeks. Because I know now. I know I've just been playacting. Pretending to be normal. Acting like I can have a normal life like everyone else. It was never going to last. And it's a relief to get it over with.

I walk over to Bran's living room. Luckily, my clothes are all down here, having been taken off in a hurry downstairs the night before. I drop the bedsheet. I pull my clothes on. Calmly, I put everything back on. I turn to Bran's desk. The desk I'm so familiar with. The notebooks, the pens, the charts, the printed sheaves that he marks with corrections, one of his published books in which he's checking an old detail. The color of a character's hair, what someone said, the age of someone, the description of a setting he's used before. I touch them all for a brief second. I peel off a post-it. A neon pink one. I bend down and write on it. With one of his fine liner pens.

"I'm sorry. I can't do it. It was never me."

I put it on his desk, next to his computer, where he'll see it when he wakes up. When he comes downstairs, expecting me to be restlessly up and about. Maybe he'll be relieved. Maybe he's been waiting for me to crack. And now he'll no longer need to wait. I touch the post-it again, before I head out.

I walk out of the door, closing it softly behind me. Out into the crisp September air, fingering the pebble in my hoodie, the one that is smooth and black on the outside, with a cracked heart the color of a pomegranate seed.

I walk over to Creampuff. He walks with me. Another shadow joins us. It's The Marquis. He falls into step with Creampuff and I. "Come on," I say gently to my companions. "Let's go home."

THE END

Acknowledgments

Thanks goes to a lot of people.

To my partner and kids for always being enthusiastic about my writing and for understanding the need for writing time, for making me laugh and making it okay for me to be me.

To Chantelle Aimée Osman, for sparkly enthusiasm about Arya, for taking a risk, and more importantly, for helping me take a risk. (Thanks also for the apostrophes – you know what I'm talking about.) To the team at Polis/Agora, and especially editor Jason Pinter, cover designer Mimi Bark – I love, love, love your work – and the copy-editor – apologies for all the British-isms and the made-up words. Thanks also to Linda Biagi.

Michelle Danaczko, for your heart and immense generosity, your human approach and general clear-sighted guidance. To fantastic colleagues. Superstars Danielle Tran, Siobhan Clay and the team – I admire and value your thoughtful and compassionate take on the world. Very cool people near the sea, Arun Sood and Ben Smith. Sabine Sorgel, Shantel Ehrenberg, Catherine Brown and Jaya Savige for inspiring commitment to your work and writing. Creative folk like Maria Thomas and Farhana Shaikh. Sophie Page, Nazneen Ahmad, Michelle Phillips for doing fabulous things in your work and for the opportunities you bring my way. The team at Harper Collins, and especially Charlotte Brabbin. The SI Leeds superwomen, Jamilah Ahmed, Stella Oni, Harkiran Dhindsa, Fran Clark and Winnie Li. Matt Jones, Hannah Marriott, Claudia Tonietto, Isobel Bloomfield, Francis Angol and Dympna Oliver – I admire your dedication to your creative process. And all my unbelievably brilliant students everywhere.

To friends, for all the chats. Charlotte Hennessy, Ananda Breed, Ciara Flood, Helen Holmes, Grainne Butler, Andreas Otte, Doro Shoene, Karen Wilson, Arpita Lal, Damini Malhotra, Monica Germana and Julie Pinsonneault.

Thanks to my sister, Anisha, for bringing home to me that Arya isn't going away, that she's kind of important, and for helping me see what's working, what needs works and what there is just no point working on. And for generally keeping me sane – or at least not minding my craziness.

Thanks family and friends!

About the Author

Amita is a writer, based in London, who previously lived in Delhi and California. Her first novel, THE TROUBLE WITH ROSE, came out from Harper Collins in 2019, and her short fiction has won the SI Leeds Literary Prize, and has appeared in *Wasafiri*, *SAND Berlin*, the *Berkeley Fiction Review* and others. She's held writerly residencies with Leverhulme/University College London and Plymouth University/Literature Works, and has taught advanced fiction at the University of East Anglia and CityLit London.

Find her online @AmitaMurray and www.amitamurray.com

Continue Reading for a sneak peek at the next Arya Winters novel

Arya Winters and the Deadly Cupcakes

When loneliness has been your one reliable companion, you tend to hold on to it for dear life. You become reluctant to let someone breach it. You have an inkling that deep down you don't know how to do without it. You know that letting someone in, someone who can crack that last defence, carries the risk that you'll become somebody else.

Problem is that once you turn that corner, once you open yourself, there's no going back. The person you were is gone and you have nothing left, not even yourself. People have called me all sorts of names over the years. Prickly, narky, confrontational, solitary, difficult to love, just plain difficult. I'm used to it, I even use it to my advantage, because people tend to leave you alone if they think you're cold. I don't know why – I have no idea why – then it's so much harder to bear that Branwell doesn't call me any names at all.

Chapter One

"We would require your services for a fortnight," says the voice on the other end of the line. "We would not have a problem with you fulfilling other obligations simultaneously – one does not like to monopolise – as long as you understand that your commitments to us come first. I can have my secretary draw up a mutually suitable contract. I am certain that you will find that we will be more than generous."

Crikey. You'd think I was joining the royal family as a nanny to their Corgi's new puppy's chew toy.

To my horror, I find my voice mimicking Fiona Wooten-Tottle's. "Splendid." I pause. "Positively splendiferous. Rather."

There's silence at the other end. I'm wondering if I've mangled my chances of getting this cushy job living in a posh estate for two weeks – a paid holiday, really – within seconds of getting it, and if she's going to demand if I'm making fun of her, and then have me arrested. But she speaks again.

"I see," she says, sounding perplexed. "I can't tell if you're joking. I have never been much good at understanding other people, I'm afraid."

Something unexpected twists in my heart at her words. A stranger's words, someone I've never met, someone I've only spoken to for a few minutes on the phone. I can't help thinking *you and me both, sister, I'm actually pretty crap at it myself*, but luckily for me, for once, I manage to keep the words down. Well, I manage to keep *almost* all the words down.

"Crap." I bite my lip, but of course it's too late to take it back.

"Pardon?"

"Hmm?"

A pause. "I see. Well, you will hear from my secretary soon-ish."

Just for a second, a fraction of a second, as I click off the call, I have an inkling. A breath of an inkling, so quick that it's gone before I'm completely conscious of it. A floater in the air, a sense that it may have been better if I had managed to piss Fiona Wooten-Tottle off. An instinct that I'm walking headlong into disaster and I should turn around and run in the other direction as fast as my feet will carry me. But it's gone in a flash. And seconds later, I'm not even sure it was there at all.

I spend the month before I need to head to the Wooten-Tottle estate – charmingly called Monk Hole, I mean where do I even start with that name? – in my usual way. Baking every day, sending my day's orders off with Sebum, my trusty courier, and taking off for my usual run in the evening, but only once I'm sure that I'll be able to avoid absolutely everyone that lives in my neighbourhood.

Normally, I wouldn't consider doing just one job for a fortnight. But I've taken on the two-week stint with Fiona Wooten-Tottle for several reasons. One, because she's asked me to head over to her for the first two weeks of January, and my business is a bit slower at that time of the year, what with people being in a deep funk about their Christmas pounds and dragging themselves doggedly to use their new gym memberships (and quickly losing the will to live, but that's another story). And so only taking on one residential job isn't as much of a problem as it might be at other times. No one else will want cake in the first half of January.

Two, a country estate, in the heart of Sussex, in the middle of nowhere. I mean, that sounds kind of nice. I haven't taken a holiday in years. In fact, I'm finding it hard to remember if I've ever taken anything resembling a holiday. The thought of so much obligatory fun and the possibility of mingling with People leaves me twitching and on the verge of a panic attack, so I tend not to take holidays. But a working holiday sounds right up my street.

The third reason I want to take the job is because I'm tired of trying to avoid everyone in Trucklewood. I made a mistake over the summer,

I admit it. Against everything I've worked hard to do all my life, against every instinct of self-preservation, I started to get involved. And getting involved with people, I lay myself open to the thing I decided a long time ago I'd never expose myself to. A long time ago, I made up my mind that I would never put myself in situations where I cared, where I scanned every expression on someone's face so I'd know what they thought of me, where it mattered if I hurt them with the things I said and did, where it mattered if they saw me as I really was, and then didn't want me anymore. If you ask me, there's a reason we live behind our self-protective bubbles. We take a lifetime to carefully build our walls and defences brick by solitary brick. I say we hold on to them with everything we've got. Not so much of this psychobabble of letting people in, thanks very much. Living with all your freaky barriers up is grossly underestimated. Our barriers are all we've got.

This summer I let myself forget all that. I let myself get involved. I let myself care about whether or not people stuck around, or if they – as so many people have done in my life – turned away instead, and found me hard to understand and difficult to love. I did that and quickly learned to regret it. And so here I am, trying to avoid everyone.

So, yes, I spend the month after that phone call half looking forward to January. Which is quite a lot for me. I tend not to look forward to anything, expecting most things to turn out worse than I imagine.

I look up Fiona Wooten-Tottle. It turns out that she's quite a well-known acrylic painter, a painter of nudes mainly, but nudes going about the normal business of living, sitting outside a café reading the newspaper, driving a car, getting on a bus, gardening, that kind of thing. Twice or thrice a year, she hosts painting retreats at her countryside estate. She charges a hefty fee, but, apparently, her retreats fill up pretty quickly, and, her website informs me, that there is a 'thriving waiting list'.

She has catering and cleaners already lined up for the retreat, but she wants me to do dessert, dessert to be made available to her students at all times of the day and night. (I realise that she and I have this at least in common, our firm belief in the power of cream and sugar. People who say they don't like those things are plain lying, or there's all kinds of things wrong with them.) She had informed me when she called me that given the emotional nature of the painting retreat – "it triggers all manner of demons," she had told me – the students crave sugar, and I need to be able to hit that spot with my baking.

"In past retreats," she said, "if there's one thing that was less than perfect – and I believe in self-reflection as a way into self-learning – if there's one thing that was less than ideal, it was that there was not enough pudding."

Her secretary gets in touch soon after her phone call and sorts out all the details. The salary is more than generous – she was right about that. They want various forms filled, which basically ask me to say that if I'm injured or killed on the premises, it'll be entirely my fault. I give them so many details about my life (bank, passport, National Insurance, Unique Tax Number, bra size) that someone carrying out an elaborate identity theft could hardly ask for more.

"We will be pleased to offer you our hospitality," says the bored voice of the secretary. "You will find the stay most felicitous."

I can't help thinking that the man is reciting the words, like he's said them way more times than he cares to remember. I should probably pay more attention to this, the little edge of something in his voice, but I don't.

"Will I?" I enquire, mildly curious.

A pause. "People generally do."

"But that doesn't automatically mean that I will," I point out.

A longer pause this time. "Well, luckily, unlike all the other jobs around here, it won't be my job to entertain the staff. I'm afraid you'll just have to make do."

I only snort *after* I put the phone down. Really, the growing maturity is shocking.

CPSIA information can be obtained
at www.ICGtesting.com
Printed in the USA
LVHW020206280921
698818LV00003B/3